THE DOOR CRASHED INWARD.

In it stood Sergeant Evola, a small submachine gun in his hands. He brought down the heavy boot with which he had forced entrance and for a moment stood there, legs spread, alert for reaction. Behind him crowded more Security men. His gun was centered on Pete Kaptiz, but he took them all in one at a time and seemingly found no immediate cause for calling upon his firepower, or the support of his men.

He said dourly, "You cloddies are like in a revolving door. It's getting monotonous rounding you up. Don't any of you ever get smart?"

Then he shook his head, as though it didn't make any difference. He walked a few steps into the room and swung the gun again. Four of his men entered behind him, all Gyrojet armed. They were typical heavies, burly of build, expressionless. There were still more of them out in the hall.

"Jesus, Joe," Tony Black blurted, hustling to his feet. "You came just in time."

TROJAN ORBIT

MACK REYNOLDS WITH DEAN ING

science fiction

A Baen Book

Baen Enterprises
8-10 W. 36th Street
New York, N.Y. 10018

First printing, March 1985

ISBN: 0-671-55942-7

Cover art by Tom Kidd

Printed in the United States of America

Distributed by
SIMON & SCHUSTER
MASS MERCHANDISE SALES COMPANY
1230 Avenue of the Americas
New York, N.Y. 10020

A MESSAGE TO THE READER

Before his death in 1983 after a long illness, Mack Reynolds had taken several novels to first-draft stage and then, perhaps driven by a sense of mortal urgency, gone on to the next. When it became clear that Mack would be unable to bring them to completion, I, with Mack's and later his estate's approval, commissioned Dean Ing to take the entire group to a fully polished state. Dean's purpose has not been to collaborate posthumously, but to finish them exactly as Mack Reynolds writing at the utter top of his form would have done.

We believe that Dean has succeeded to an almost uncanny degree. For any writer, and particularly one of Ing's stature, to so subordinate his own authorial personality is a remarkable achievement.

Requiescat in pacem, Mack.

—Jim Baen

I liked Mack; I liked the way he lived; and I liked his tequila. That's why . . .

—Dean Ing

"There are three kinds of people who go to work in Alaska: those who like adventurous life; those who have a romantic but unrealistic notion of adventurous life . . . and return as soon as the first contract is over; and those who go there for money, even though they hate the life. The percentage of the second and third categories is very large. The same three types might be attracted to space communities."
—Magoroh Maruyama, Professor of Systems Science, Portland State University

Chapter One

Rick Venner got off the second-class bus at San Miguel de Allende, in the north-central State of Guanajuato, Mexico. He first secured his sole piece of luggage, then went on into the small bus station and checked it.

He looked like an easygoing type and it extended to his clothing. He was fresh and friendly of face, and at first meeting, at least, could project himself as much as ten years younger than his thirty-four years. Only his eyes detracted from his cheerful good looks; they were a rather colorless blue-green. He moved easily, almost lazily, but one got the impression that he'd stand his own on a tennis court or even perhaps at amateur boxing.

He looked up and down the street, decided the center of town was below, put his hands in his pockets, and strolled in that direction. At the first corner, he noted that the street was Calle San Francisco. There was a small, neat plaza there, flanked on two sides by Spanish colonial churches. On the corner opposite him, on a pedestal, stood a weathered bronze statue of a medieval gentleman, telescope in one hand, a roll of papers in the other. Rick looked up at it.

A voice beside him said, "Columbus. There are only three statues of him in all Latin America. The Indians wish the hell that he'd stayed home."

Rick looked over at the other, an obvious local inhabitant, about Rick's own age, and even more lackadaisical in his dress.

Rick grinned and said, "I don't blame them. Look, is there any place in town where I can buy a guidebook?"

The other pointed. "Yeah, go on down to the Zócalo—that's the central square—and cross it diagonally. There's an English-language bookstore called *El Colibri* under the arcade."

Rick told him thanks and went on.

The town was unique—an art colony. He'd already read a little about it in tourist folders. A Spanish colonial national monument. There were no signs allowed in the city limits, neon or otherwise; no supermarkets, no service stations, no advertising. You weren't allowed to build in San Miguel other than in accord with the 17th and 18th century local architecture. Except for some electric wires and a few TV and Tri-Di antennae, you could have been in a two- or three-centuries-old Spanish town of about 25,000 people, if it hadn't been for the vehicles on the streets. Most of these were recent-model hovercars, and possibly a third of them had American license plates.

He arrived at the square and crossed it as instructed. It was the typical Mexican plaza. He had witnessed many in his crossing of the country by train and bus, after entering through Merida, the capital of Yucatan. This one seemed more pleasant, cleaner, better kept than most. There was a bandstand in its center, trees with steel benches in their shade, nice stretches of flowers and grass. The Zócalo, as his informant had named it, was flanked on three sides by old Spanish colonial buildings with shaded arches and, on the fourth side, a cathedral-sized church at least as old as any of the other architectural specimens.

El Colibri was largely devoted to paperbacks and art supplies, and was presided over by an elderly American woman. Yes, she had a guide, complete with town map. He bought one with pesos, not too sure about the money as yet.

She obviously typed him immediately—though quite inaccurately. She said, "In town for long? An artist?"

"In a way," he agreed, smiling. "There wouldn't be a telephone or some other kind of directory, would there?"

She brought forth a paperback booklet, obviously locally printed. "The *Juarde*," she said. "Sort of a joke; the Mexican equivalent of 'Who Are They?' It lists all the permanent gringos in town, addresses and phones. It's fifty pesos."

He paid up, took the two books, and returned to the square. He found an empty bench facing the looming church, stuck the directory in his pocket, and turned to the map in the guide.

Rick Venner felt uneasy in a town he didn't know. He liked to have the layout. He liked to know where the streets went, particularly the roads leading out. He studied the map for a while, then brought forth from a side pocket of his jacket a Mexican road map. He located the State of Guanajuato, found San Miguel de Allende, and traced the routes leading respectively south to Querétaro, northwest to Celaya, and northeast to Dolores Hidalgo, and hence to Texas.

He came to his feet then, the city map in hand, and for the next couple of hours walked around the art colony, up one street, down another. He decided that it must be a nice place to live, in a quiet sort of way. By the looks of it, about a quarter of the population was

American or Canadian. From time to time, he'd run into an artist sketching one of the old landmarks, or seated before an easel painting the street market, or whatever.

He went back to the Zócalo and down the line of taxis at the stand there, asking each of the drivers if he spoke English. One did and Rick climbed into his cab, sitting next to him in the front seat.

He had the mystified driver take him out of town on each of the three main exit roads for a short way. He asked occasional questions. Querétaro was about forty miles south, Celaya was about thirty-five miles farther on, and Dolores Hidalgo was not quite thirty miles.

Finally satisfied, he brought forth his directory, looked up the name Pavel Meer, and instructed the cabbie to take him to Calle Nuñez 32.

From outside, the house was on the unprepossessing side, but as a result of his walking, Rick Venner had already found that this was as meaningless in Mexico as it was in Spain or Morocco. On several occasions there had been large doors, open. Inside could be spotted extensive gardens, impressive-looking patios, expensive-looking Spanish colonial homes. No, you couldn't tell from the outside what was beyond the walls. It might be a ruin or a mansion.

Rick got out and said to the driver, "How much, chum-pal?"

"Forty pesos, *Señor*."

Rick grinned and brought forth a coin. "Double or nothing?"

The driver's eyes widened in surprise, but he said, "*Sí*, okay."

"You call it," Rick said.

"Heads."

Rick flipped. It came up tails.

"Tough luck," Rick said sympathetically and turned and headed for the door.

There was an iron knocker, rather than an identity screen or even a bell. Rick knocked. It was answered by a girl who was very neatly, very colorfully dressed, but in cheap styles from north of the border, not traditional Mexican ones. Her jet-black hair was waist-long and in braids, with red yarn braided into the tips. She was possibly eighteen years of age and had just enough Spanish or Norte Americana blood in her to avoid heavy Indian features.

Rick said in the atrocious Spanish he had picked up over the years in Spain, Argentina, and Uruguay, "*Por favor, quiero* uh, *hablar con Señor* Meer."

She flashed him a smile and held the door wide open.

Beyond was a long patio, complete with waterless stone fountain, with two fabulous mats of bougainvillea, one red and one purplish, running up the walls. There was also a huge iron cage in which a hyacinth macaw swung on a perch.

The macaw said, "Hello, Pancho."

Rich said, "The name's Rick. But hello."

"Quiet," the bird told him.

Rick followed the girl through the patio into a living room. Besides the heavy, obviously local furniture, the room was notable for a monstrous fireplace and a multitude of oils, watercolors, lithographs, etchings, and charcoal sketches—all seemingly crafted by the same hand. The walls were covered with them.

The girl led the way through to the next room, a library. Save for the space allotted to bookshelves—filled mostly with volumes on art—and a smaller fireplace, the walls were also devoted to the graphic arts. The next room was for dining, small and obviously not often utilized; it too had its quota of art, in profusion. A kitchen walled in tile could be seen off to the side. There was a small table in the kitchen; Rick suspected that most of the household eating was done there.

They went out a back door into another patio, this one dominated by a large shade-giving mesquite tree, and across it to a separate building. The girl knocked softly.

The man who answered wore denim pants, Mexican leather huaraches on his feet, a paint-bespattered smock and, of all things, a beret on his head. He had a paintbrush in one hand. He was somewhere in his early sixties and affected a graying beard in an era when facial hair was out of style. His eyes were a bit rheumy, but wise, and his cheeks were as red as those of Santa Claus, though hardly as a result of any cold weather.

He looked inquiringly, rather than speaking.

Rick said, "My name's Rick Venner. I'm interested in purchasing some of your work."

The other eyed him questioningly, and murmured in a small, womanish voice, "You do not look like a collector, sir. However, I have a show currently at *La Galeria*, down on the square."

Rick smiled. "I like to avoid the forty percent, or whatever it is those gallery robbers extract from you."

"I see. Very well, come in. I am cleaning my brushes. *Gracias; es todo*, Octoviana," he said to the servant girl.

She smiled, not quite curtsying and, her pigtails aswirl, turned and went back to the house proper. It occurred to Rick, now, that she must have posed for several of the nudes he had seen down below. The old boy still had an eye for beauty—or something for sex.

The high-ceilinged room beyond, into which he was ushered, was an artist's madhouse. Aside from oils and watercolors, finished and otherwise, there was lithography equipment, engraving tools and raw materials and, in one corner, looking as though it hadn't been used for a considerable time, even a potter's wheel. Not that Rick recognized most of the tools of the artist.

On an easel was a painting, possibly four feet square, depicting a San Miguel *fiesta*, complete with Indian folk

7

dancers. It was hardly more than begun. Bright reds and yellows predominated in color.

Pavel Meer said in his feminine voice, "Sit down, if you can find a clean spot, Mr . . . uh . . ."

"Venner," Rick said, carefully removing a sketch and several painter's rags from a cane and leather chair. "Rick Venner."

The other dipped the brush he was holding into a dirty glass of turpentine, then rubbed it onto a cloth.

He said, "What can I really do for you?"

"The maid . . . or anyone else . . . can't hear us?"

The other's shaggy eyebrows went up. "She speaks no English, and there is no one else in the house."

"No chances of a bug?"

"I see," Meer said, putting the brush into a dirty water glass and taking up a different one. "A bug, in Mexico? In the home of an established artist? *Please*, Mr . . . uh, Venner," he added wryly. "Besides, I have an electronic mop. Believe me, we are not being monitored. Now, what did you wish to see me for?"

"I want to become a worker in the Island at Lagrange Five." Rick grinned at the man's odd glance. "You know— the space colony near the moon."

The other squinted at him quizzically. "I see. And why not simply apply for a job?"

"I don't seem to have the qualifications."

Pavel Meer put down the brush and turned back to his visitor. "Why come to me? I'm an artist."

"I know," Rich said. "And the best. You're The Penman. Damn nice cover you have here." He indicated the studio with a sweep of an easy hand.

"It's authentic," his host told him. "I am a reasonably successful artist. I have shown internationally. There are none to say that my income is not all derived from my artistic sales. Now then, who in the hell sent you?"

"Paul Lund in Tangier."

"I see. And how is Paul?"

"His TB's still bothering him. He told me to tell you that the Funked-Out Kid was sneezed in London. It seems as though he didn't properly cool off a Winchell he'd taken a score from. Three years in the nick."

Meer nodded. "The Kid was never much of a brain, as grifters go. In the old days, I was on a couple of, ah, assignments with him. Let's go into the house and have a drink."

"I was hoping you'd ask," Rick said.

The artist shed his smock to reveal a white Yucatan shirt, somewhat wrinkled, and led the way back toward the house proper.

"Nice place you've got here," Rick complimented.

"Bought it some years ago, back when I was on the run, for only eight thousand dollars," Meer said absently. "Renovated it a bit, over the years, whenever my taw was in good enough shape. Really old. The three basic rooms are older than the Pilgrims."

Rick looked at him in surprise. "The Pilgrims? You mean in New England?"

The other skirted a flower bed on his way to the back door. "That's right. San Miguel's a really old town. The Spanish were up here founding it only twenty years after Cortés, ah, liberated Mexico City from the Aztecs."

In the main house they found Octoviana dusting in the library.

Meer said to her in Spanish, "Why don't you do the marketing now, *chica*? I have business."

She did her little half-curtsy and darted from the room.

The artist opened a cabinet door and brought forth a square, squat bottle and two three-ounce glasses.

"Tequila all right?" he said. "I believe in drinking the local product. Scotch in England, brandy in France, schnapps in Germany, bourbon in the States."

"Wizard," Rick said, taking a chair.

The other poured and brought the drinks over. "Would you like lime and salt?" he said.

"Not necessary." Rick sipped the fiery spirits. In actuality, it was smooth, as tequila went; the best he'd ever had.

Pavel Meer sat on a couch, looked over inquiringly, and said, "When were you in Tangier?"

"About ten days ago."

"I see." The other knocked back about half of the two ounces of tequila in his glass, then said, "How'd the romp work out, Rocks?"

The blue-green eyes went icy. "The name's Rick Venner."

"The name is Rocks Weil and you just pulled off the biggest romp of your career two weeks ago."

"How'd you make me? I don't like that. I planned this get with a hell of a lot of care."

The artist said easily, "You had to be some kind of a celebrity or Paul wouldn't have sent you. Our code for an introduction is for you to mention the Funked-Out Kid. Two weeks ago, in London, somebody knocked off three pendeloque-cut, colorless diamonds. The biggest was 69.42 carats; both of the others were about half that size. The romp had all the earmarks of a Rocks Weil job. Now, two weeks later, you turn up with an introduction from Paul Lund, the town crier of the grifter's world. And you want me to supply you with papers to get you into Island One at Lagrange Five, the most perfect place to go to ground that's ever been dreamed up. And you're here, and that's smart, and Weil is *very* smart. I'm betting that you're Rocks Weil. How'd the romp work out, Rocks?"

Rick sighed, finished his drink, and put the glass down on a side table.

He said, "The heist itself was routine. It was flogging

the stones that needed the finesse. You've got your work cut out, usually, getting rid of a couple million dollars' worth of diamonds, especially unflawed colorless stones of any size. Every one of those in the world is known to every jeweler worth his salt."

"Of course," the artist nodded. "How do you plan to fence them, Rocks?"

"They're already sold. To an Arab. They're one people who don't give a damn about the source. Nobody outside his harem will ever see them again. He paid in gold, about one-third of the real value, which is good, of course. I worked out a way to get the gold into India and stash it. It can sit there for the five years I'm in Lagrange Five. When I root it out, no matter what's happened to the world's currencies in the way of inflation, it'll still have at least the same true value it has now. I'll take the gold to Switzerland, flog it, and put the whole score into an International Credit Account. By that time, I'll largely be forgotten, and Rocks Weil will never pull another job."

Pavel Meer gave a sigh for his yesteryears. "A beautiful romp, Rocks. I can only envy you. Well, let's get down to cases. The papers will cost you ten grand."

"Ten! Holy smog, Meer, I can buy an authentic Swiss passport, absolutely authentic, for two hundred dollars."

"You need more than a passport to get into Island One as a space colonist or contract worker. I know Island One better than you do, scammer. The whole ten thou doesn't go to me. Not by a damn sight. The grease job goes all the way from New Albuquerque to Island One. I wind up with less than half of it."

"How sure is it?"

"Sure. That project is being milked every way from the middle. This is just one of the smaller rackets, a sideline so to speak, but there are no glitches." The artist got the tequila bottle and replenished their glasses.

"Okay," Rick said, shrugging acceptance. "Let's start it going. The sooner I get completely out of sight, the better. Interpol must have half their force on my trail." He took up his refilled glass.

The older man opened a drawer beneath one of the bookshelves and brought forth a pad and pencil. He said, "How good's this Rick Venner moniker?"

"A-1. My Dossier Complete, in the American National Data Banks, is absolutely McCoy. I've been working on this cover for ten years, just in case."

The other began making notes. "Great. Got any education?"

"I took a degree in engineering when I was a kid. It's all in the data banks. Electrical engineer."

"Well, hell, Rocks, that's perfect. This'll be a cinch. Ever do any work?"

"No. In this day of computers and automation? Nine people out of ten up in the States are on Negative Income Tax."

"I can fake some experience. Could your training be applied to electrical engineering in construction work?"

"I suppose so."

They spent approximately an hour while Pavel Meer got the information he needed.

Toward the end of that time he said, "You're not going to be able to take that shooter with you, you know."

Rick sighed and brought the 7.65 mm Gyrojet from its rig beneath his left shoulder. "I didn't expect to," he said. "You want it?"

"Hell, no. Ditch it somewhere. I'm clean here in Mexico. This is the best cover a penman ever had. I can buy engraving equipment. I can buy any kind of ink or paper. Nobody blinks an eye. I'm an engraver and a lithographer, as well as a painter. But I don't want a shooter in the house. You never know."

Rick returned the gun to its holster. "All right, I'll ditch it. What else?"

"Do you have an American Universal Credit Card?"

"No. That's why I have to stay in countries that still use currency. Like Mexico."

"Okay. I'll do you up one, but it'll be for identification only. When you go up to New Albuquerque, you'll buy your passage here with pesos. You won't be able to make a single dollar purchase with your credit card in the States. If you tried, they'd be on you before the hour was out."

"I know that," Rick said impatiently. "How do I get from the New Albuquerque airport to the space shuttle base? I suppose that's where I have to go."

"That's right," the artist told him. "You'll have to hitchhike or something. Once there, your papers will read that you were hired in New York. You'll have your health examinations and all. You don't have any disease, do you? Especially syph or clap?"

"Hell no. Do I look stupid?"

"You'll be having various physical examinations at the base. They'll keep you there for about a month in a training course before you're shipped out. Keep a low profile. Avoid getting into conversations with electrical construction engineers, or any field-related people. Among other things, they'll teach you Esperanto in a crash course."

"Esperanto?"

"That's right. The International language. One of the eggheads who first dreamed up the Lagrange Five Project realized that there'd be a multitude of different nationalities in space, so he suggested that all colonists be given courses in basic French, basic German, even basic Japanese. He didn't have the imagination to come up with the obvious answer. Train everybody in one international language."

Rick said, "Look, if I have to stay at the space shuttle port for a whole month, how am I going to do without an American Universal Credit Card? I couldn't buy a beer or a stick of gum without one."

"As soon as you're on the base, you go on the Lagrange Five Corporation payroll. They issue you a special credit card of their own. No problem."

"Wizard. Another question. As soon as I get up there to Island One, they'll spot me as a phony. It was nearly fifteen years ago I took that engineer's degree. That's a long time the way technology goes these days. I wouldn't know a fuse from a power pack. They'd grab me by the scruff of the neck and ship me back."

The other shook his head and chuckled. He scratched his thinning beard with a thumbnail and said, "That's where we'll fox them. Your papers will read that your field is construction—deep-water rigs, bridges, skyscrapers, that sort of thing. In short, the kind of work they'd put you on at Island One would be construction out in space. But the first day they suit you up to go outside the Island, you take one of the pills I'll give you. As soon as you get out into space you'll get deathly sick. You'll vomit, you'll shit in your pants, you'll stream cold sweat. So they'll haul you back in. It's not too uncommon a reaction on first being exposed to deep space. So, great; after a couple of days of rest, they'll suit you up again for another try. But you'll have taken another pill. They'll try three or four times before they give up. But you'll simply turn out to be allergic to space, so to speak."

"Sounds great," Rick said sarcastically. "Especially that part about loading my pants. But then they'll ship me back to Earth."

Meer shook his head again. "No, they won't. They're too short-handed up there, and they'll have paid your freight. Hardly anyone ever comes back from Lagrange

Five." He scowled, his moist eyes puzzled. "It's kind of strange. I don't believe I've ever heard of an ordinary construction colonist coming back. Some of the big mucky mucks, yes. The project directors, the security men, the big scientists and so forth, but not the rank and file. They all sign up for a five-year contract or more, but since the very early days, when they were building the moon base and getting the construction shack out to Lagrange Five, typically the workers don't come back."

"They must like it up there."

"Perhaps. Besides, they don't get their king-size bonus unless they stick out at least a full five years. At any rate, that's where you'll have to start finagling. You'll have to get yourself some job, preferably nothing to do with electrical engineering. You'll have to play it by ear. Wind up working in the community kitchens, or something."

"Holy Ultimate," Rick said. "I've never worked in my life. I'm a grifter born."

The other fixed his eyes on him. "Believe me, for the next five years, you work, chum-pal. You've picked the best thing in the way of going to ground in the solar system, but you'll work up there, like everybody else, or your cover is blown."

Rick Venner gestured with both hands in resignation.

Meer said, "Where's your luggage?"

"At the bus station."

"You'd better get it and move in here with me. I've got a spare room. It's just as well you not be seen on the streets in San Miguel. Somebody might make you. There are a lot of gringos here in this art colony, and a lot of tourists going through."

"There are damn few people who know me . . . anywhere."

"You never know, Rocks. Let's play it safe. It'll take me three or four days to do everything I've got to do.

15

You'd best lie low. Now, the ten thousand. Your taw is in pesos, I assume."

"Yeah." Rick shrugged out of his jacket, pulled out his shirttail, and unzipped the money belt. He opened one of its compartments and began counting out five-thousand-peso notes.

"Ten thousand dollars," he muttered. "What's that in pesos?"

The artist figured it out with his pencil on his notepad and told him.

Rick said, "How about double or nothing? We'll toss for it."

The other favored him with a look more negative than any headshake.

Rick shrugged and handed over the high-denomination notes, returned the money belt to its place about his waist, and rearranged his clothes.

He came to his feet saying, "I'll go get my bag."

*   *   *   *

It was about a month later that Octoviana answered the door and returned to the library where Pavel Meer was seated, peering through granny glasses at a volume of sketches by Leonardo da Vinci. Two strangers followed her.

They were well dressed in conservative fashion, approximately forty years of age, and absolutely empty of expression.

The artist looked up above the glasses. Pavel Meer was not a young man and he was old in his profession. He knew the type.

The first of the two made a minute gesture with his head.

Meer said in Spanish, "That will be all, Octoviana."

The cute little *criada* disappeared in the direction of the kitchen.

Without invitation, the two strangers seated themselves.

The first one said, very evenly, his voice that of an Ivy League graduate, save for the use of one term, "You were warned. No more lammisters sent to Lagrange Five, Penman."

There was trepidation in the old eyes. The artist said, "I know, but . . . well, it was Rocks Weil. He's talent."

"Shit," the other said. "Rocks Weil got it in a shootout with the French *flics* six months ago in Nice. He was trying to heist some countess's emeralds."

"That's what the *flics* said. It wasn't Rocks."

"It doesn't make any difference. We don't care if it was Jimmy Valentine or Jesse James. We don't want any more grifters on the run in Island One or on Luna or anywhere else in space."

The artist said quickly, "Look, boys, I'm an old man. I've been building up my taw for years. I've got a little over a hundred thou. You know, for my retirement. It's all yours. I've got it stashed right here in the house."

The second of the two looked at him with amusement.

The first said, "What do we look like, a couple of cheap punks? You've been messing around on the sidelines of a really big operation, Penman. Way out of your league. Your operation irritates some of the biggies. Now, what's the name of the stupid bastard on the Island end of your penny-ante game?"

"I don't know," Meer said. An old man he was. A small-time operator in most eyes he might be. But Pavel Meer was no fink. However, he added, in a hopeless defense, "It wasn't necessary that I know."

"Who was handling it at the shuttleport in New Albuquerque?"

"I don't know that either."

"Then I'll tell you. It was Monk Ravelle, the silly cunt. It seems as though Monk is no longer with us."

The second of the two brought a small-caliber Beretta from an inner pocket, brought forth from a jacket pocket a device that looked like a small muffler. He screwed it onto the end of the pistol's barrel, his face holding no more expression than it had held when they had first entered.

Pavel Meer licked his lips. He was no coward, but on the other hand, he was an aged man and no longer brave to the point of not fearing death.

The first one said, "Nothing personal, Penman, but you were warned. Do you have somebody you'd like us to write to? Any last business, a will, or anything like that?"

"I have a son I haven't seen for fifteen years," the artist said, a tremor in his feminine voice.

The spokesman of the two motioned with his head in the direction of the desk.

Pavel Meer got up wearily and went to it. He took up a pen and brought a sheet of paper from a desk drawer. He thought for a moment and slowly began to write.

The second of the two, gun in hand, came up behind him and shot him twice in the back of the skull. The silenced weapon made no more sound than *spat*.

The other stood as well and made a motion with his head in the direction of the kitchen.

The gunman went through the dining room and disappeared through the door that led to the right.

There was the beginning of a scream, in the midst of three more *spats*, and then silence. The second of the two returned, unscrewing the silencer from his weapon. It was only a .22.

The first one said, "Let's get going. It's a long drive back to Mexico City."

"... the end of the 1970s will see the beginning of Russia's manned Moon program. Cosmonauts will explore the lunar surface and set up their own bases. Would Americans concede the Moon to the Soviets? Neil Armstrong planted the American flag there. Would the country accept the fact that the only men on the Moon speak Russian? Science and engineering follow, not lead, political considerations. And the space politics of 1980 will compel our return to the Moon."
—Captain James E. Oberg, USAF, specialist in Astronautics.

Chapter Two

Leonard Suvorov, Leon to his few intimates, was a compulsive eater. Not a glutton, since sheer tonnage did not interest him; nor a gourmet, since he had neither the time nor patience to devote to becoming a real connoisseur of the art of haute cuisine. Perhaps gourmand would be the term. Whatever, a lover of good food Leonard Suvorov most certainly was. If nothing else, his stocky figure gave credence to that, not to speak of the shine that came to his blue Slavic eyes upon being presented with a superlative dish. He was perhaps fifty, and the endless hours spent in the sedentary occupation of the scholar had led already to middle-aged spread, thinning of his reddish hair, and weakening of eyes to the point of his affecting anachronistic *pince nez* glasses.

Right now, Leonard Suvorov was playing hookey. On his way to an international conference on bionomics to be held in Vienna, he had sidetracked for a few hours to put down in Prague. His motivation? The black beer and hot Slovakian sausages that were available nowhere else in the world save the *U Fleka*, at 11183 Kremencova, in the capital of Czechoslovakia. Given the caramel-dark brew, which had been made on the premises of the ex-monastery since 1499, and the unique spicy hot sausage of the establishment, paradise could wait, so far as Suvorov was concerned.

His order placed, he sat in anticipation in the spacious garden, admiring the medieval motif, including murals of peasant scenes, and the exuberant efforts of a troupe of Bohemian folk dancers and musicians. He sat alone at one of the smaller, heavy wooden tables, the evening still young. In an hour or so, he knew, the place would be crowded, the community tables jammed with beer-swigging revelers. The thirteen-percent brew came in heavy mugs, none smaller than one liter. A bibber could actually, if he wished, order steins as large as three liters, the better part of a gallon.

The plump, blonde, peasant-dressed girl came, beamed hospitably at the foreigner, and placed before him a plate with one huge sausage, a jar of mustard, a plate of toasted garlic bread, and his stein, creamy head slightly overflowing.

He sighed and set to, Vienna far from his mind.

A stranger slipped into the chair opposite him. There was no call for being annoyed; all vacant seats at the *U Fleka* were fair game. Leonard Suvorov didn't even bother to look up.

The stranger took a leather folder from his inner coat pocket, opened it, and politely pushed it across the table for inspection.

He said, once again politely, "Colonel Vladimir Dzhurayev, Comrade Academician."

Leonard Suvorov took in the identification less than happily. Not that he had anything to fear, save his sausage cooling.

He said emptily, "Of the *Chrezvychainaya Komissiya*—in

21

short, the Cheka. I was of the opinion, Colonel, that the Cheka had been dissolved some decades ago, even before that unspeakable monster Yezhov superintended the great purges. My memories of the Cheka are not fond ones, Comrade. Ai, ai, but they are not."

The other looked rather young to be a colonel in the Soviet ultra-secret police. Efficient looking, yes, with perhaps a touch of ruthlessness. The scar he affected on his left cheek, running down to the side of his mouth, could easily have been removed by cosmetic surgery in this day and age; evidently, he valued it.

He said now, with all due respect in his voice, "The *Komissiya* was never truly dissolved, Comrade Academician. You might say that it went underground in the face of popular disgust at that period some named *Yezhovshchina*, the same period in which your illustrious grandfather, Alexei Suvorov, the right arm of Lenin, uh, disappeared into Stalin's Lefortovo Prison."

Suvorov said harshly, "He was rehabilitated under Khrushchev and his remains are now in the Kremlin wall with the rest of the Old Bolsheviks."

"Of course, Comrade," the counterespionage officer said hurriedly. "Nor has there ever been any question about the loyalty of your esteemed father, nor of yourself, so far as the Party is concerned. You are a third-generation Party member and without doubt might even be a candidate member of the Central Committee, were your efforts not so appreciated elsewhere."

Suvorov grunted at that. He took a bite of the sausage, a bite of the garlic bread, rolled his eyes upward in appreciation, and washed the food down with a lusty swig of the black beer.

"What do you wish, Colonel?" he said grudgingly. "I must admit I am somewhat surprised to be accosted here by a high-ranking officer of your evidently phoenix-like organization."

The colonel said, "I had intended to meet you in Vienna, Comrade, and was surprised to find you had interrupted your trip with this stopover in Prague."

Suvorov took another sampling of his food, another swig of the strong beer. "I stopped off for a sausage," he said.

The colonel nodded. "For my purpose, it is possibly even better. One can never be sure. Wherever you might be, in Vienna, there is always the possibility that the imperialist spies might be monitoring your conversations."

Suvorov grunted contempt of that. "Who in the espionage world, East or West, would be interested in the words of a biologist?"

The other said, still respectfully, "They might not be interested in your words, Comrade, but they most certainly would be in mine."

The biologist took another pull at his beer and said sarcastically, "You seem to have delusions of grandeur, Colonel."

The colonel shook his head. He caught the waitress's eye, pointed to Suvorov's beer mug, and held up two fingers. She beamed back at him and took off for the order.

He said, "Tell me, Comrade, have you much interest in the space program?"

"Which one? That of the West, the so-called Lagrange Five Islands, or our own space platforms?"

"Both."

"Why, I suppose I have the normal interest. I follow the news. The capitalist world seems to be in a frenzy of enthusiasm over Doctor Ryan's project, but . . ."

The colonel demurred a little. "It's beginning to wane a bit," he said.

". . . but our own seems to go more slowly," Suvorov finished.

"But more surely," the colonel said.

The two fresh steins of beer arrived just in time. The food-loving scientist had drained his first liter. While he had the waitress, he ordered another sausage.

"You should really try one of these," Suvorov said. "We haven't the like in Moscow, or anywhere else for that matter."

"All right," the colonel said. "Thank you."

"I didn't offer to buy it," Suvorov said ungraciously. "Put it on your expense account. I still don't like the Cheka."

The colonel pretended to chuckle, as though a joke was meant. "All things change, Comrade," he said. "I doubt if I would have approved of the organization at the time of your illustrious grandfather's trouble."

"What's this about the space programs?"

Dzhurayev took a swallow of his beer and nodded approval. "The Czech *pivo* has always been superior," he said. Then he leaned forward. "From the first, the space programs of the Soviet complex and of the West have differed. Not in goals, since we both have realized since the nineteen-seventies that the domination of space will ultimately mean the domination of Earth itself, but in the method utilized to achieve such domination."

Suvorov raised his eyebrows skeptically and took another pull at his stein.

The other nodded again, this time with emphasis. "Ultimately, the conquest of space will mean unlimited solar power to replace depleted fossil fuels. Ultimately, it will mean all but unlimited supplies of raw materials, now nearing exhaustion on Earth. Ultimately, it will mean manufacturing under circumstances far superior to those prevailing on Earth."

"Perhaps there is room for both East and West in space. There would seem to be a great deal of it."

The colonel didn't accept that. He said, "In which

case, the world revolution that we look forward to might never transpire. If the capitalist system is given a reviving shot in the arm, such as would be brought about by the successful exploitation of space, we might never see the day when communism prevails."

Suvorov began, "I fail to see what . . ."

But the Cheka man went on. "Early in the game, the Americans, then working alone, concentrated their efforts on reaching the moon, seeking to regain their lost prestige when we launched Sputnik One. With the advent of Solomon Ryan's revolutionary project to build a space island at Lagrange Five, utilizing Luna raw materials, all of their efforts were devoted to this end. Hundreds of billions of dollars have now been plowed into it. Their basic idea is ultimately to build satellite Solar Power Stations, or SPS's to beam microwave power to receiving stations on Earth."

"We've spent a few hundred billion rubles ourselves," the biologist said mildly.

"Yes," the other said. "But on an entirely different approach. In actuality, the Yankees and the balance of the West have been fools in directing all of their efforts toward the moon and their island space colony. We have concentrated instead on building space platforms. Module by module, they continue to grow, but we do not attempt to use Luna raw materials for their construction. Our modules are prefabricated on Earth and rocketed up to geosynchronous orbit. Already, our people there are at work building space tugs and space barges, preparatory to heading out to the asteroids. We are stealing a march on Ryan and his colleagues. And eventually this will lead to our triumph."

Suvorov wasn't sure he had gotten that. He said, "How do you mean?"

The colonel was emphatic. "I mean that the moon is comparatively barren and worthless. Yes, it has oxygen, silicon, calcium, titanium, aluminum, and magnesium, but in forms fairly expensive to extract, as the Lagrange Five Corporation is discovering. The moon also has gravity—one-sixth that of Earth, but gravity. And it must be fought to get the raw materials from Luna to Lagrange Five and the island being constructed there. But the asteroids are ninety percent carbonaceous chondritic and not only have all the metals boasted by the moon but are rich in hydrogen, carbon, and nitrogen, all of which must be brought up from Earth for the moon base and the construction of Island One. In actuality, the Lagrange Five Project is a farce. Ultimately, perhaps, such islands will be practical, but at this point we have insufficient scientific knowledge to build a successful one. When such is built, it will be Soviet, not Western, and the materials will come largely from the asteroids."

"Are you so sure that Ryan's Island One is doomed to failure?" the academician murmured. "There is certainly a great enthusiasm for it."

"All our experts say that it is doomed. They are pouring their hundreds of billions down the drain into what is sometimes called a gigantic boondoggle, because they are so blinded by their high hopes. Practically none of the basic ideas with which they started have worked. Their moon-based mass driver has never become really operational. They've wound up smelting moon ores on Luna and sending them to Lagrange Five by space tug. Their smelters in space are driving their technicians out of their minds. Their closed-cycle ecology in the island has them stumped. But you, of course, know more about that than I. What is your opinion, Comrade Academician?"

The biologist took another swig of his beer and looked thoughtful. "I have been following their efforts, to the extent that they are published," he admitted. "And the problems of maintaining complex artificial ecosystems within the capsule are far from solved. The microorganisms necessary for the nitrogen cycle, and the diverse organisms involved in decay food chains must be established, as must be a variety of other microorganisms necessary to the flourishing of some plants. Unwanted microorganisms would inevitably be included with, or would evolve from, desirable ones purposely introduced. Furthermore, in many cases, the appropriate desirable organisms for introduction are not even known to us. Whatever type of system they are currently trying to introduce, there would almost certainly be serious problems with its stability. They have their work cut out for them, as the Americanism has it."

The other was gratified. "Their whole scheme revolves about their being able to establish a closed-cycle ecology. If they can't, then the project is doomed. They'd have to bring air, food, and water up all the way from Earth for their 10,000 population."

The biologist shrugged and considered ordering still another sausage. He decided against, it, though, and signaled the waitress again for one last stein of the dark beer.

He said, "Perhaps in time such a system will be possible. For the present, we have insufficient data. I would say that in this particular field of science, we of the Soviet complex are in advance of the Americans, Japanese, and Western Europeans. Perhaps by the time our own space program, utilizing materials from the asteroid belt, as you say, is ready to build a similar island, we will have solved the problems involved. But I fail to see, Comrade Colonel, what all this has to do with me and the here and now. I am on my way to an international bionomics conference in Vienna. In fact, I am scheduled to read a paper on ecology tomorrow."

Colonel Vladimir Dzhurayev leaned back and said softly, "Tomorrow, in Vienna, you will announce to the news media that you have defected. You will request political asylum of the United States. Upon arrival there, you will contact the Lagrange Five Corporation and offer your services to the Lagrange Five Project."

The biologist's face had gone slowly pale. "Are you mad?" he whispered.

"The Party requests this of you, Comrade Suvorov."

Leonard Suvorov said, an indignant rasp in his voice, "Colonel, I am a member of the Academy of Sciences, possibly the most prestigious scientific body in the world. There are less than two hundred of us, with perhaps three hundred candidate members. I am a Nobel Laureate and I also bear the Hero's Award of Soviet Science. I am not a spy or a saboteur!"

The colonel took a deep breath, but waited until the girl had served their two fresh mugs of beer and had gone again to reply.

He said evenly, "You are not being sent to Island One of the Lagrange Five Project as a saboteur, Comrade Academician. You are being sent to apply your best effort to their problems in establishing a closed-cycle colony."

The eminent scientist could only stare.

The colonel took up his beer, swallowed deeply, and set the mug down. He said, "Interest in the Western countries has been flagging, so far as the Lagrange Five Project is concerned. The financial drain has been unbelievable. Investors in the Corporation are beginning to have second thoughts. The program is years behind schedule. All phases of the operation seem to be going wrong. You are the most prominent ecologist in the world. Your joining the project will give rise to new hopes."

"But why?"

"It is really quite simple. We do not want the Lagrange Five Project to fail—as yet. We want it to continue. It is doomed to collapse, but the longer it continues the harder it will fall when it inevitably does. Tens of millions of investors in the Lagrange Five Corporation have put their savings into the promise of space. When the final collapse takes place, there will be disillusionment beyond any that has ever been known. Far beyond that of Vietnam and Watergate combined. No Western power or combination of powers will be willing to mount further space programs on such a scale for many years. Certainly not one of the magnitude of penetrating to the asteroid belt and exploiting it. The Soviet complex will be left alone in the field."

"It's diabolical!"

"Comrade Suvorov, you are a loyal and devoted member of the Party. Your father before you was the same. Your grandfather is a national hero. The Fatherland of the Proletariat is at a crossroads. If we can dominate space, milk it of its solar power and raw materials, we have triumphed and capitalism has failed. The Party calls upon you, Comrade Leonard Suvorov."

The older man sank back into his chair, unbelieving. "Ai, ai, my wife, my children," he whispered.

"Comrade Olga Suvorov is a Party member. She will be let in on the secret. It is a very well kept secret. Only a handful will be aware of the true nature of your defection. The children are too young to be trusted with it. They will have to bear up under the unfortunate pressures that will undoubtedly be released upon them, particularly from their contemporaries, when it is revealed that you have become a traitor. When all this is through, you will return to your country and recant. Much publicity will be given to the fact that you have rejected the West, after witnessing its shortcomings. You will be received with open arms by both the nation you love and by your family. Number One himself will greet you in the Kremlin and issue you a newly created, special decoration."

"I see," the scientist said weakly. "And you say my instructions are to cooperate wholeheartedly with my colleagues of the West in their efforts to maintain an artificial ecosystem in their Island One. But suppose that I am successful?"

"You won't be," said the other cynically. "But even if you are it will make no difference. There are too many, ah, bugs in the project. It's doomed to failure. At most you might prolong its life a fraction. And that is to our advantage, as I have pointed out." He paused before adding, "There is another aspect of your assignment. Undoubtedly, due to your prominence in the scientific world, you will be made privy to the innermost decisions made by Dr. Solomon Ryan and his closest associates. Possibly you will learn of matters that should be relayed to us. One of our KGB moles, located on Island One, will contact you upon your arrival."

The colonel snapped his fingers at the waitress for their bill.

"We will also need human institutions devoted to enforcing the rules and regulations. We will take our police forces, security forces, and military/naval forces into space with us. Initially, they may well be like Pinkerton men. They may be the company guard force. In any event, they will be there to enforce, by physical force if necessary, the property rights of the corporations, individuals, or nations involved in space industry. . . . The security groups of the Third Industrial Revolution will also be an interesting human institution to watch develop. They may begin as private groups. Or as mercenaries . . ."
—*G. Harry Stein*, The Third Industrial Revolution.

Chapter Three

Roy Thomas entered the small room tucked to one side of the famed Oval Office. He was looking thoughtful and displeased.

The expression was far from rare on the face of the man who had been the alter ego of three consecutive presidents. In his early fifties, Roy Thomas was a painfully thin man, gaunt of face, weary of eye, ulcer-prone, and sour. He dressed with a scorn for fashion befitting a man who gave not a single damn what others thought of his appearance. He gave not a damn about that or about anything else others might think about him, including his boss, if boss he could be called. Thomas was little-known outside government, and even in it, only by the highest echelons. He never talked to the media. The American in the street would have to think twice to even remember his name, and then it would be to recall, vaguely, that he had something to do with being a presidential assistant, or something like that. He bore no specific title.

Gertrude Steiner, the gray-haired, middle-aged, veteran presidential secretary, looked up from her desk and awarded him a harried smile. She flicked off the phone screen she'd been talking into and said, "Good morning, Mr. Thomas."

"Good morning," he told her. "Is the chief available?"

"It's his half-hour of morning meditation." She knew very well that the other was aware of this. Nothing short of a Hot Line message from the Kremlin was to interrupt the President during his half-hour of meditation. In actuality, it wasn't the first time that Roy Thomas had ignored this sacred cow.

"Right," he said. "We won't be interrupted."

In disapproving resignation, she flicked on her interoffice screen and spoke into it, apology in her voice. "Mr. Thomas requests to see you, Mr. President." And then, tight-lipped, "Yes, sir, I told him."

She looked up at the Chief Executive's one-man think tank, with continuing disapproval. "Very well, Mr. Thomas."

He was already on his way to the door that opened on the Oval Office.

Behind the huge desk, the Chief Executive of the United States of the Americas had pushed his chair back and was staring expressionlessly at the floor. He said aloud, but not as though to anyone in particular, "You can still see the holes made by his golf shoes. He must have been the only president in history to have made a permanent mark in the White House."

Roy Thomas took one of the heavy leather chairs, saying, "There have been alterations, additions, and reconstructions by various incumbents, including Truman."

"That's not the same thing," President Paul Corcoran said testily, moving his chair back nearer to the desk.

Roy Thomas looked at his superior and wondered how long it had been since the country had had a competent president. Roosevelt? He had been a consummate politician and, as chief executive, had at least the ability to surround himself with able aides. The fact that he was senile toward the end was beside the point. Hoover had probably been the better man, but he'd had the luck of the Irish to take office when he did. Still, in those days government had been another thing. Today, it was an impossibility for a single man to handle the job of chief executive. It wound up being an office more similar to the monarchy of Great Britain than to that once held by such as Lincoln. A chief of state, but a figurehead. Tri-Di and TV image was more important these days than brains and executive ability. And you couldn't fault Paul Corcoran there. Had he gone into show business rather than politics in his youth, he would have now been making more money than he was as the supposed leader of the nation.

"What was it, Roy?" the President said.

Roy Thomas nodded, and the unhappy expression returned to his gaunt face. He said, "I've been mulling over various odds and ends for some time. I want to pry into them further, Paul."

"One of your famous intuitive premonitions?"

His closest aide was impatient of that way of putting it but he said, "Something like that."

The President sighed inwardly. He hoped that it wasn't anything similar to Thomas's discovery that the agnostic vote had grown beyond that of the fundamentalists and that it behooved the chief executive not to drop so many mentions in his talks of the powers above. Paul Corcoran hated anything controversial, particularly anything as controversial as religion. He had a gut feeling that almost anything you said on such subjects lost you votes.

He said, "Well, out with it, Roy. What's roaching you now?"

"The Lagrange Five Project."

"The Lagrange Five Project! Good heavens, man, what's wrong with the Lagrange Five Project? That's like saying you're having second thoughts about mom and apple pie."

The other shifted his slight frame in his chair. "That's one of the things that's so upsetting. Its untouchable."

Paul Corcoran could visualize votes shedding away like dandruff. "Now look here, Roy, we can't go prying into the Lagrange Five Project."

"Why not, Paul?" his aide said, his voice very level.

"Now don't get your dander up. You know damn well why not. Why, I'd wager that half the people in this country own at least one share of Lagrange Five Corporation stock."

"You see, that's what I mean. You don't know. You're just guessing. We haven't the vaguest idea of the exact amount the American people have invested in LFC stock. And what's more, no government in the developed or developing nations does either. Only the Soviet complex knows how much money its citizens have invested in Doctor Ryan's dream—because their investment is zero."

"Well, you know that's perfectly explainable. LFC is incorporated in the International Zone of Tangier. If they'd incorporated anywhere else, then that nation would have had access to their records and they would have been subject to national laws. Some such laws can really be a burden for a corporation. Look at what might have happened had they incorporated here, with our anti-trust laws. They're a monopoly—except for the Soviet complex space program, of course. For all practical purposes, there are no corporation laws in Tangier, no banking laws, and practically no taxes. It was an ideal place for such an ultra-multinational corporation to base itself."

Roy Thomas nodded ironically. "Ideal for them. But it

means that nobody can take a close squint at their data-bank contents. Paul, do you realize that the La-grange Five Corporation has probably become the largest Cosmocorps in the world? It's probably now bigger than General Motors or AT&T. I say probably because actually we don't know. Nobody really knows just how much they've sold of those par one-hundred-dollar shares of theirs, Tangier laws—or lack of them—being what they are. But they've peddled them in at least fifty nations. It's been the softest sell—the easiest sell—of all time. *Everybody* wants to be in on the space dream. Even kids save their allowance until they have a hundred bucks to put into a share. Even the really poor, those on Negative Income Tax, somehow manage to scrape together enough to buy at least one share. How much have you put into it, Chief?"

Paul Corcoran said grudgingly, "Thirty thousand. And I suspect Molly has invested too. She has her own money. How many shares do you have, Roy?"

"None."

The president looked at him impatiently. "See here, Roy. Just what do you have in mind?"

The top aide said, "I was against taking this out of the hands of NASA and letting the Lagrange Five Corporation take over in the first place. We had a head start on the Russians in space, once we'd made the moon landings, and especially once the shuttles were operative. We could have handled the financing through such elements as the Space Transportation System, going it alone. Now we have precious little concrete knowledge of what's going on at all."

"That decision was made before my administration. But it was in the cards. The Reunited Nations practically demanded that all nations be allowed to participate. The roots of it were in the European Space Agency. Twelve nations, especially the Germans, pooled together and developed the ESA Spacelab our shuttle put into orbit. They built the labs, we built the shuttles. In doing it that way they gave up an autonomous space program. So now they wanted all the way in. What could we do? We're the head of the West. World opinion was for it going private, in the free enterprise tradition. Practically every world figure in government, business, science, spoke up for it. Some of the biggest names living became charter members of the LFC."

Thomas's face was askew. He said, "We must have turned over what amounted to billions in NASA hardware to it."

"And a very popular move it was, both nationally and internationally. Our party continues to profit by the good will obtained. Frankly, I don't understand what you're beefing about, Roy."

His assistant responded to that. "Take just one item. Back in the early days of the space program, when we were building the *Enterprise*, the first space shuttle, the big contractors included McDonnell-Douglas, Grumman, Chrysler, Rocketdyne, and North American Rockwell. Rocketdyne finally wound up with the contract to make the engines and North American Rockwell the main contract to make the shuttle. One by one they've been squeezed out of the picture by the Lagrange Five Corporation and johnny-come-lately contractors have taken over. Who in the hell is the Western Spacecraft outfit, for instance? Newcomers. Their contracts with LFC mount into the billions every year. And there are equivalent companies in England, Germany, France, and Italy. Who controls them is largely a mystery, so far as I can find out."

Roy Thomas had touched a sore spot there, as he had known he would. Paul Corcoran got excellent support from the American aerospace industries. The President thought about it. He had his lower lip in his teeth in a pouting expression that should have looked infantile, but was one of his trademarks so far as his Tri-Di audience and the political cartoonists were concerned. They loved it.

He said finally, "What did you have in mind, Roy? You haven't failed me yet, but this sounds pretty far out. You're butting heads with the most popular movement the world has seen since Christianity came along."

"Islam would be a better example," his aide said cynically. "LFC has taken the world like Grant took Richmond. What I want is for you to give me your go-ahead. I want some of my boys to start digging into this from every angle."

"Now, look here . . ."

"Oh, in a clandestine way, of course. Very undercover. And I want to send a man up to Island One."

"Why?"

"Just to see what he can find. All the information we get about what goes on up there comes from the Lagrange Five Corporation's PR men. Flacks. Either that, or from highly screened VIPs who go up, get the red carpet treatment, and come back even more enthusiastic than when they left. I find, by the way, that most of these VIPs are heavy stockholders in the corporation."

"Whom did you plan on sending?"

"I had in mind a competent investigator from the IABI. I thought I'd talk it over with John Wilson and let him decide."

The president nodded to that. "The Inter-American Bureau of Investigation would probably be best. But how would you get him in without spilling the frijoles? They'll smell a rat, leak the fact that the United States of the Americas is prying into LFC, and the fat would be in the fire."

Roy Thomas winced inwardly at all the metaphors, but said, "That's why I picked an IABI man rather than some other investigator. He can go up on the excuse of trying to find some fugitive from justice who is possibly hiding in the confusion of the construction of Island One."

"I suppose that makes sense."

"I have your go-ahead to take it up with Wilson?"

Paul Corcoran hated this, but he got out grudgingly, "I suppose so. But take this easy, Roy. If you don't find whatever it is you're looking for and the word gets out that this administration is monkeying with the Lagrange Five Project, we wouldn't get any votes in my own home town." He thought about it glumly. "Hell, I wouldn't get any votes in my own family."

* * * *

John Edward Wilson, director for decades of the Inter-American Bureau of Investigation, didn't like it. For that matter, he didn't like the man seated across from him in his office, and knew that the feeling was reciprocated. However, both of them were untouchables. Roy Thomas had made himself indispensable to the workings of the American government some fifteen years previous, and could no more have been replaced than John Wilson himself, though for different reasons.

Back before the FBI, the CIA, and the Secret Service had been amalgamated, John Wilson had begun his grand strategy. Today, in the data banks of the IABI were secret dossiers on every American politician of any standing whatsoever. They were thorough, even more thorough than they need be. And everyone in government knew that they were at the director's fingertips. In a matter of an hour or two he could have blackened the name of any person in politics to the point of ruining his career. For there was no man in politics without skeletons in his closet. One does not get ahead in that game without making compromises or soiling his hands. Even Roosevelt was nominated for the first time by Huey

Long, dictator of Louisiana. The Keyy-Nash machine of Chicago, the Frank Hague machine of New Jersey, the Pendergast machine of Kansas, the Curry machine of Massachusetts, all backed FDR. What had he conceded to them in return? No, there was not a politician in the land without his fear of John Edward Wilson.

Save one. If he could be called a politician. He had never been elected to any office.

And that one was now seated across from him. In all the years of Roy Thomas's power behind the throne of the presidents of America, John Wilson had been unable to dig up a usable scandal that he might have dangled over Thomas's head. The man was uncanny. He must have led the life of an egghead saint. He had never been arrested for so much as a traffic violation. He had married early, a childhood sweetheart, and there was no evidence that he had ever so much as pinched another woman's ass. And she was as clean as he. Patricia Thomas's dossier was as empty as that of her husband, and they had no children. The president's ultimate aide received a comparatively modest salary and lived modestly on it. With all his opportunities, there was no record of his ever accepting even the mildest kickback. And all presents sent to him, even on Christmas, save those from his family, were promptly returned, no matter what their nature.

No. Roy Thomas was clean, and John Wilson hated the fact.

The short, tubby man who wielded so much police power was now in his mid-sixties. In his youth he had probably been thought of as baby-faced. Now porcine would be more accurate. And his character came through in it. His eyes were small and invariably suspicious. Knowing himself, he could only believe that all men were similar. His few friends he had gathered close around him in the upper reaches of the Bureau. They all had fabulously paying jobs, they stuck together no matter what the emergency, and they were all as queer as chickenshit, including Wilson himself.

Now he said, "I'll be damned if I get this, Roy. What in the hell does the Chief want me to send a man to Lagrange Five for?"

Roy Thomas said easily, "He seems to have sort of a bee in his bonnet. I wouldn't be surprised if some of his chum-pals in the aerospace industry have put up a beef about losing so many of their formerly lucrative contracts. Western Spacecraft, unknown a decade ago, seems to be getting most of the gravy."

"That's probably it, all right," Wilson growled. "The Chief never would have been elected if it hadn't been for some of the fancy campaign contributions the aerospace corporations kicked in. You'd be surprised, some of the information I have on those deals."

"No, I wouldn't," Roy murmured.

"It's not the easiest thing to get a man into Island One," Wilson said. "Their security is really tight. The KGB tried to infiltrate one of their operatives last month. L5 Security nabbed him before he was halfway between the low-orbit space station and Lagrange Five."

Thomas accepted that and nodded. "That's one of the reasons I suggested we use your bureau, John, rather than some other possible investigator. Your man will have cover. He can pretend to be looking for a fugitive from justice. You'll be able to figure out the details."

"Oh, it was your idea, eh?" the IABI director said nastily.

"I'm paid to have ideas," the other told him evenly.

"God knows, the Chief doesn't have many of his own."

Roy Thomas raised his eyebrows. It wasn't acceptable that even John Edward Wilson say things like that about the nation's leader. Especially if it was true.

"All right, damn it," Wilson muttered, giving in. "What does my agent do once he gets there?"

"He plays it by ear. He gets whatever inside information he can about the LFC and its workings. He looks for hanky-panky. I'll go into it further with him."

John Wilson began to reach for the switch on one of his interoffice communications screens. He said, "I'll call in Steve and we'll figure out who to send."

"No," the presidential aide said quickly. Then, "Who's Steve?"

"Steve Handley. He's one of my top assistants. A very dear chap. He's got our best operatives at his fingertips. He'll know who'd be best to send."

"No," Thomas told him definitely. "See here, John, the president wants this to be held down to the smallest number possible. No one at all, save himself, myself, you, and the man you select to go. You, personally, will handle the details of his going. I'll personally talk to the man and explain his mission to him."

The IABI head didn't like it, but he shrugged. He flicked on one of his desk screens and said into it, "Is Peter Kapitz available for an assignment?" Then, "Very well, give me his address, please." Wilson made a note on a pad with his desk stylo. He said into the screen, "Very well, tell him to go home and wait to be contacted there."

He turned back to Roy Thomas, after tearing the note from the pad. He handed it over, saying, "Here's Peter Kapitz's address. I assume that you'd rather talk to him away from headquarters here."

"Yes. It's best that no one see us together. Who is Peter Kapitz?"

The IABI head said, "I'm not acquainted with many of the field men. I obviously work on a different level. But I know of Kapitz. He's been used on various foreign assignments. So far as I know, he's a good man on extraordinary matters."

Roy Thomas took the piece of paper, looked at it briefly, tore it up and threw it into the other's disposal chute. "Wizard," he said, coming to his feet. He hesitated a moment before saying, "Please remember, Wilson, discuss this with absolutely no one. If there's a leak, you're the only one—you or this Kapitz fellow—who could have made it. Needless to say, if this got to the media, that the LFC was being checked up on, there'd be hell to pay."

Wilson glowered at him, his pudgy face looking like that of a bulldog. He said, "Listen, Thomas, are you sure this all comes from Paul Corcoran? I get the feeling that stirring finger of yours is in the batter."

Roy Thomas looked at the other scornfully and motioned with his head at one of the other's TV phone screens. "Give Paul a ring."

He turned and left, neither of them bothering to say goodbye.

When he was gone, John Edward Wilson opened a desk drawer and brought forth a special model tranceiver. He set it before him and dialed.

The screen didn't light up, but he said into it, "Get me Al Moore in Island One, Lagrange Five. Scrambled and completely muffled."

* * * *

Peter Kapitz scowled and said, "What the devil is there to be investigated about the Lagrange Five Project? Hell, I've got twenty shares of their stock. By the time I retire, I figure I'll be getting more dividends from it than my pension will amount to."

Roy Thomas said acidly, "I doubt if there's a multinational corporation in the world that couldn't stand investigating."

"The Lagrange Five Corporation isn't in the world. It's up in space and it's the dream."

The president's one-man brain-trust nodded to that and said reasonably, "And nobody wants to kill the dream. However, one way not to kill it is to make double-sure it's a dream, not a nightmare. Possibly as many as a billion people would be affected if the L5 Project bombed out. It's not just the banks, the pension funds, the trust funds, the mutuals, that are going into the Lagrange Five Corporation. It's the candy money of kids being put into school-sponsored savings accounts; it's the life savings of middle-aged people looking forward to retirement; it's . . . hell, you know what it is. One item I ran into was about a lottery in Argentina. People so poor that they go to bed hungry almost every night, scraped up a few pesos to buy a ticket. If they hit, the payoff is a thousand shares of LFC. Nine-tenths of the population of the Argentine would give their right arms for that amount of dream stock."

Peter Kapitz said, an edge in his voice, "And why not? Suppose back about 1870 some corporation came along that had a monopoly on the exploitation of the American West. Can you imagine what it would have meant to have gotten onto the ground floor of that? What would the shares have been worth even ten years later, not to speak of twenty? Not to speak of what they would have been worth by the turn of the century. Anybody who had invested as little as a thousand dollars in a monopoly like that would have been a millionaire by the year 1900."

Roy Thomas cocked his gaunt head to one side and said, "That's a good example, perhaps. Look back and you'll find that millions of people did invest in the conquest of the West. Hundreds of thousands even took to their covered wagons or flatboats and trekked out to the promised land. But by the year 1900 the wealth of the West—and that of the East as well—was largely in the possession of a handful of what we call robber barons."

In his younger days, Roy Thomas had been a great fan of the suspense stories of several decades before. It came to him that the man in whose living room he was seated had little resemblance to Philip Marlow, Travis McGee, or Archie Goodwin, and certainly none to Mike Hammer. He was a very average-looking type. Indeed, dull. He was the sort of fellow you were introduced to three or four times before you finally remembered his name. He didn't look as though he had ever heard of the word karate, seen a gun, been in a fight since grammar school. When it came to girls, he was the type who got the dregs. He was possibly the most colorless thirty-year-old Roy had ever met. For a brief moment, he wondered if John Wilson had foisted this nonentity off on him in pure spite.

His host said, "Well, a job's a job. Even if it does sound like bullshit. What's the story?"

"Your cover is that you're looking for some top crook. Somewhat to my surprise, Wilson mentioned the fact that L5 Security was very efficient. I didn't even know that they had a security force. What would they need with a security force in space constructing a colony?"

Kapitz said, "Beats me. Would you like a drink?"

"The doctor says no. My ulcers come and go. Right now, they're gone. But with this thing, I wouldn't be surprised at a return. You have one if you want. I'll just sit here with my tongue hanging out."

Peter Kapitz got up, went into another part of his small apartment, and returned with a plastic of beer.

He sat down again and said, "I didn't know they had a security force up there either. I don't imagine it's very big. But I suppose there's always the chance of some crackpot. Can you imagine how much damage a terrorist with his eggs scrambled could do out in space? But what's that got to do with the assignment?"

Roy Thomas said, "You've got to look right to them. Your story has to hold water. You'll actually have to make the motions of looking for this gunman, or whatever he is. Have you a good prospect in mind?"

The IABI man took a slow sip of his beer and thought about it. He said finally, "A couple of times I've worked on looking for Rocks Weil. He's an American, but usually operates in Europe or South America. Jewel thief. He's never taken a fall. We don't have any photos of him that we're sure of. Every cop in the world has heard of him. On my last assignment I was working with the French Sureté. We thought we flushed him on the French Riviera, caught him in the act. Some trigger-happy local cop plugged him. The French were sure it was Rocks. I have my doubts; so have some of the other boys."

"Why?" Roy Thomas wasn't up on modern crime. There was comparatively little of it since the advent of the Universal Credit Card in the United States and the International Credit Card of Common Europe. Without cash, a criminal had his work cut out making a living.

Kapitz said, "Because, just recently a romp was pulled off in London where . . ."

"Romp?"

"A caper, a job, a heist," Kapitz said impatiently.

"All right, go on."

"It had all the earmarks of a Rocks Weil job. And, as usual, the criminal disappeared, complete with loot. In Rocks's style—no clues, no nothing. I think perhaps it was Rocks."

"Why would he go up to Lagrange Five?" Thomas asked. "What excuse could you give them for looking for him there?"

"The score was a big one. Bigger than Rocks has ever knocked over before. He's not stupid. With a score like that, he could retire. He might decide to go to ground and sit it out for a few years before trying to flog ..."

"Flog?"

"Fence. Sell the loot. He might just hide it somewhere and wait for the air to cool. Lagrange Five might be the perfect place, if he could get there. At least, the story would sound plausible. Like you, I didn't even know they had a security force. If they have, I don't imagine they spend much of their time looking for international jewel thieves."

Roy Thomas worked it over as the other sat and sipped at his beer. It made sense to him.

"All right," he said. "Let's use that for your cover. Director Wilson, himself, will take care of the details of sending you to Lagrange Five. Make arrangements to leave as soon as possible. Here, I'll give you my high priority number. Keep in touch with me and when anything at all comes up, use it."

Kapitz frowned. Doesn't this go through the Bureau?"

"No, you are working directly under the President. For obvious reasons, none of it must come out."

The other was taken aback. "Well, how about Mr. Wilson?"

The President's trouble-shooter shook his head. "Only me. I suggest that you phone President Corcoran. I'll give you his top priority number. He'll confirm what I have said about your mission, and the desirability of you reporting to me alone."

"Holy smog," Kapitz said. "The President himself, eh? I ought to ask for a raise."

"You'll get one without asking," Roy Thomas said. "Be sure that you earn it."

"I feel that we have done little enough with our present world to warrant our going off and putting soft-drink signs all over Mars and cluttering up the moon with oil rigs. These places are not ready yet for such advanced achievements."
——Walt Kelly, of Pogo fame.

Chapter Four

Mary Beth Houston was quite overwhelmed by it all. It might be said that Mary Beth overwhelmed easily, but at least on this occasion she had an excellent excuse. So far as she knew, she was the first member of the Friends of Lagrange Five ever to be invited to visit Island One. Most certainly, she deserved the honor. As secretary of the gung-ho organization, no one worked harder to push the space dream than did Mary Beth.

She was in her late twenties and still had enough of the effervescence of youth to be somewhat attractive. When youth was gone, it was seemingly in the cards that Mary Beth Houston was going to settle down into being a rather plain woman, a bit gaunt of figure, a bit drawn, if not washed out, of face, and a little buck of tooth. But enthusiasm carried her now.

At the space terminal at the New Albuquerque shuttleport, she went through the standard routine. Her personal things were taken from her suitcase and replaced in a special, practically weightless bag which had been designed for space. This was weighed in and found to be correct to the ounce. Mary Beth had been preparing for weeks. She then went into the locker rooms, where she showered thoroughly, using the prescribed antiseptic soaps, washed her hair thoroughly, all this under the careful scrutiny and aid of a uniformed nurse, and then returned to dress in the standard space coveralls. Her own clothes, as was her suitcase, were stored away awaiting her return.

Properly sterile—she had finished her lengthy medical examinations the day before—Mary Beth was escorted to the little electro-steamer shuttleport bus. There were three others in it besides the driver. All were in light-weight coveralls similar to her own.

She said, breathlessly, "Are you all going too?"

One of the three men, an easy-going type, grinned and said, "I'm afraid so. It's too late to back down now. I'm Rick Venner. You mean to Lagrange Five, undoubtedly."

"I'm Mary Beth Houston. Oh, who'd want to back down!"

"That's a good question," one of the others said, even as the bus took off. He smiled too, though rather faintly. He reminded Mary Beth somewhat of Kirk Douglas in the movie revivals. Even had the dimple in his chin. Possibly he was a little chunkier than the old movie star, she thought, and he seemed very quiet and reserved. He said, "I'm Bruce Carter."

Her eyes widened. "Not the *writer*?"

"I suppose so."

"Good heavens."

They were proceeding over the tarmac at a good clip now toward one of the launching pads. She looked at the third of the three.

He was about the same size as Rick Venner, but all resemblance ended there. Although he couldn't have been thirty, he wasn't young. His face was stolid, swarthy,

51

his eyes sleepy—something like those of Robert Mitchum, she decided—but he wasn't nearly as handsome as the revival movie actor. Not nearly. More like George Raft in those early gangster films.

He said laconically, "Joe Evola."

They were coming up on the *Russell Schweickart*, the space shuttle that was to take them up into Earth orbit.

Mary Beth said, "Good heavens, I had no idea that they were that big. I've seen them a hundred times on Tri-D but it never came through to me that they were so big."

The driver said over his shoulder, his voice bored, "They're not as big as all that, Lady. Only a fraction goes into orbit. That big fuel tank the shuttle is riding piggy-back and those two booster rockets drop away after you get about twenty-five miles up."

She knew all about that, of course. No one need tell Mary Beth anything about space shuttles. She'd read everything available about them long years since. And everything else that wasn't so technical that she couldn't understand, about the Lagrange Five Project. It was practically all she did customarily read, except some of the science fiction dealing with aspects of space colonization. Mary Beth Houston had the dream with a vengeance.

They met Captain Ames briefly. Clipboard in hand, he didn't have time for them in the midst of last-minute checking with the harried ground crew chief.

One of the other crew members, who didn't bother to introduce himself, took them into the cabin, assigned them four of the bunks, and saw they were belted down.

He said, "Any of you want to go to the bathroom?"

Rick Venner said, "They just gave me the most thorough bath I've ever had, even had my toenails cleaned out. But thanks for the offer."

The spaceman wasn't amused. "You know what I

mean," he said. "It's possible to do it in free fall, of course, but it's more trouble."

Mary Beth said, "They warned us back at the Terminal. At least they warned me."

"They told us all," Joe Evola said flatly. "It's part of the routine." He had belted himself down, without need of assistance.

The crewman looked at him. "You've been up before, eh?"

"Yeah."

"Construction worker?"

The other looked at him for a moment, as though considering whether or not to answer, but then said, "Security."

Another crew member came in with their four pieces of luggage and put them into a compartment.

The cabin of the *Russell Schweickart* was on the barren side, but not as small as the three space neophytes had expected. It was actually on two levels, and boasted such amenities as a toilet and heavy blue glass portholes. Up above the pilot's and co-pilot's places before the controls was a fairly sizable TV screen. The crewman who had seen them to their acceleration bunks went over and flicked it on.

"You'll be able to see the take-off," he told them. "It's pretty exciting the first time."

The screen lit up and they watched the last minute preparations.

Captain Jim Ames came in with the co-pilot and all the crew took their places. The captain looked at his four passengers briefly and said, "You people all set?"

"Oh, yes," Mary Beth told him. The three men nodded.

"Wizard," Ames said. "Let's get this kettle spaceborne." He began going through his cockpit check with the co-pilot.

Bruce Carter looked over at the crewman who had got

them into their bunks and said, "Do you mean to tell me that you've taken some ten thousand construction workers and colonists up to Lagrange Five like this, four at a time?"

The other shook his head. "Before, we used to have one shuttle with the whole freight compartment converted for passengers. We'd take 'em up a hundred or so at a time. Christ, you should've smelled the stench by the time we got to the *Goddard*."

Mary Beth blinked. "What stench?" she said.

"Vomit."

She blinked again. "Oh."

The co-pilot turned and said in disgust. "Goddammit, Freddy, what are you trying to do, give them ideas?" He turned his eyes to Mary Beth. "Don't let it worry you. It's unlikely you'll get space sick. The trouble with lobbing them up a hundred at a time, all jampacked into that windowless compartment, was that if one got nauseated, it set off almost everybody else. It's like seasickness. You see somebody else tossing their cookies and it's monkey see, monkey do." He added absently, "And the smell of vomit doesn't help any." He turned back to the cockpit check-out.

"Okay," Ames sighed. "Let's go." He began fiddling with buttons, switches, levers.

On the TV screen they could see the fireworks begin. It was difficult to realize all that explosion was going on immediately beneath them. It was dramatic and in full color. The space shuttle stirred.

"Oh, heavens," Mary Beth bleated. "I should have gone to the bathroom again."

The g-forces weren't nearly as bad as any of the three space tyros had expected. At tops it was about three gravities, and, on the cushions of their bunks, they could still move their limbs. To the crew and to the security man, Evola, it was all obviously routine.

On the TV screen, they could watch themselves disappear into the sky, most impressively indeed. In free fall, Mary Beth could understand what the crewman called Freddy was talking about. Initially, her stomach did a bit of churning. But she suppressed it with some effort.

The shuttle trip was surprisingly short for the first-timers. Through the ports they could see themselves coming up on SP *Goddard*, the Space Platform. Largely, they had been occupied in staring out the ports on the way up, but prolonged silence was simply not in Mary Beth, even as she stared.

She had said to the taciturn Joe Evola, "You know, I've been a member of the Friends of Lagrange Five for years, but you're the first actual space colonist I've ever met. It's so exciting to meet one of your heroes." She actually managed a faint blush and her gaze dropped.

"Yeah," he said. "Not many of us around." He hesitated, as though that seemed inadequate, then added, "We're all up in the colony mostly."

"Oh, I can understand that. Who'd want to leave, once you'd made it?" She took a quick breath. "How is it? How is it living in Island One?"

"Boring," he told her flatly.

"Oh, you're pulling my leg," she said, laughing her rejection of the idea. "It's the most exciting thing ever." And then, apropos of nothing that seemed to apply, "I remember watching *Star Trek* when I was a mere child." She turned back to her porthole and gasped at the appearance of Earth.

A few minutes later she said to Rick Venner, "Are you going to be a colonist?"

"Not exactly," he told her. "I'm an electrical engineer. I signed up for five years."

For some reason, Joe Evola gave a low snort at that.

"Oh, I'm sure they'll let you remain," Mary Beth reassured Rick.

A few minutes later, she said to Bruce Carter, "I've read some of your things and one of your books, Mr. Carter. I'll bet you're going up to write some wonderful articles about the whole space colonization program."

"Bruce," he said. "Something like that."

"I'm only surprised you didn't come up ages ago. If I was a writer, I can't imagine not immediately heading for the most important story since the Resurrection."

Bruce Carter cleared his throat and touched his cleft chin with a forefinger. "It took me three years to swing it," he said.

Rick Venner looked over at him. "How do you mean?"

The writer shrugged. "Obviously, I couldn't afford to pay my own way. Or, for that matter, to goose some publication into financing it. I don't think the price has ever been figured out. Round trip fare, expenses while in Island One, all that sort of thing—I imagine at least a million dollars would be involved. But, even if I could have swung it financially, no tickets are being sold. Evidently, they're not quite ready yet for tourists and such."

Mary Beth said, "But . . . then, how are you here?"

He smiled his rueful smile. "I twisted arms."

Joe Evola looked at him. "What do you mean by that, chum-pal?"

Bruce grunted amusement. "I'm supposed to be a muckraker. I began to toss around remarks about the fact that no freelancers had thus far gotten to Lagrange Five. Finally, I got through to Solomon Ryan himself and gently hinted that all the news that came out of Island One was from Lagrange Five flacks. That I was figuring on doing an article about the fact. He evidently got the message. So I'm here on invitation."

"You'll love it. You'll never want to leave," Mary Beth assured him. "There'll be things you could write about forever, up here in space. Oh, look, there! It's the *Goddard*."

From a distance, the *Goddard* looked like a jerry-built construction surrounded by a space junkyard. It wasn't. It had been planned and put together with the greatest care and skill, piece by piece, with materials brought up by the earliest shuttles. The space platform proper consisted of what looked like two crossed barbells, four large modules at the ends. From this projected a long stem, at the end of which was a V-shaped structure that housed the nuclear generating plant. The docking port was located at the point where the barbells crossed. All about were drifting Lagrange Five shipments from Earth, waiting to be picked up by the passenger freighters that plied back and forth from low Earth orbit to Island One or the Luna base. There was also quite a bit of space debris—remnants of satellites, fuel tanks, and second stages of rockets used years before in the infancy of space travel. Some of this was to be shipped out to Lagrange Five, some returned via shuttle to Earth. Here and there could be spotted tiny spacesuited figures working at various jobs, propelled about by small jet outfits attached to their shoulders, remarkably similar to the equipment Buck Rogers had utilized in the comic strips of more than half a century before.

Docking was a simpler matter than the neophytes had expected. Captain Ames was obviously an old hand. Contact was made without an appreciable jar.

The crewman named Freddy who had belted them in now helped them out of their bunks. He said, "We're still in free fall, here at the hub. The modules rotate so they have gravity, but not here at the hub. Follow me and do as I do. You won't have any trouble. Mike will bring up the rear."

He was right. They had no great difficulty learning to pull themselves about in zero gravity. Inside the docking compartment, once they had left the shuttle, they found rails to pull themselves along. There was a natty looking nurse, garbed in white, there to meet them. Captain Ames and his copilot were already too busy to bid them goodbye, bon voyage, or whatever. It would seem space personnel had little time for the amenities.

The nurse beamed at them and checked her clipboard. "Ms. Mary Beth Houston, Mr. Rick Venner, Mr. Bruce Carter, Sergeant Joseph Evola. Hello, Joe."

The first three nodded to their names. Evola said, "Hello, Ruth. Got anything on for tonight?"

"My pajamas," she said. "This way, folks."

Pulling along one of the rails, she led the way to what looked like a narrow metallic tunnel and then along it. As they progressed, they began feeling weight returning to them. Shortly they were able to walk—shuffle would be a better word. They still needed the rail to steady themselves. By the time they reached the module that was their destination they were walking normally.

"How exciting," Mary Beth gushed. "Isn't it exciting, Bruce, Rick?"

They both said, "Yes," and Rick added, "Sure is different."

The nurse led them along a metal corridor. "You'll stay here until the arrival of the SS *Konstantin Tsiolkowsky*," she told them. "You're lucky. She's scheduled for tomorrow. Quarters are a little cramped in the *Goddard*."

Bruce said, "How many people do you get into this, uh, compartment?"

"It was designed to have accommodations for 186, but since the numbers coming up have fallen off so much, it's almost empty. Now, here is the wardroom. Over there is the galley, rather small as you'll note—about 300 square feet. Here's the dining area, almost 800 square feet."

There were two men in the small dining room arguing

over cups of coffee. They looked up as the newcomers passed and one of them gave a little wave.

Ruth, the nurse, said, "There are several other passengers waiting for the *Tsiolkowsky*. You'll meet them later. Now, here are the bathrooms and showers. You don't have private baths with your cabins. This is the ladies' bath, and this the men's. Down here is the medical area. As soon as you've moved into your quarters you must return to it for a check-up." She looked at the security man. "Except for you, of course, Joe."

"Check for what?" Rick Venner said. "They've been checking me inside and out for the last month. I couldn't smuggle a single crotch crab in, even if I wanted to."

"Very funny, Mr. Venner," she told him briskly. "For any signs of space sickness. If you're susceptible, you don't get any farther than the *Goddard*. They don't need anyone prone to space sickness out at Lagrange Five. You'd be sent back on the next shuttle. Now here's your cabin, Mary Beth, dear. Someone will bring your bag shortly." She opened a metal door.

Mary Beth blinked. "Good heavens," she said. "You mean you people live in a space no bigger than that?"

"It's 54 square feet," the nurse said briskly. "Just large enough to sleep in, change your clothes in, that sort of thing. You can spend most of your time in the wardroom or dining hall. We of the permanent crew have quarters in one of the other modules. We have larger allotments of space per person. The officers and scientists, visiting technicians, and other VIPs are in still another module. By these standards, their quarters are quite spacious. Now remember, as soon as you're settled in, report to the doctor."

She led the three others on down the corridor.

Mary Beth closed the door and involuntarily shuddered. Of course, it all made sense. Travelers from Earth to Lagrange Five or the Luna base were brought up from

Earthside by shuttle and then remained here until one of the passenger freighters that never landed on Earth, or Luna either for that matter, arrived to take them on the next lap of the journey. You were only here for a few days at most. This room was no larger than a bathroom, with only a toilet and washstand, about seven feet by seven and a half. But she didn't really need more space, she told herself again. However, as soon as the bag came, she was going to get out and, after her medical checkup, go to the wardroom and find the others. She thought both Rick and Bruce were rather cute.

The wardroom, she found later, was just as austere as her cabin, or nearly so. Certainly, no effort had been made to decorate it. Evidently, weight considerations were such that frivolities like paintings, drapes, or artificial flowers were scorned. There was a TV screen set into the wall. There were two tables with chairs around, and several other chairs. There were half a dozen men in the place, including Rick and Bruce. They waved to her when she entered. She came over.

Rick grinned and said, "Sit down and join the rest of the sardines. We were just talking about you. In view of the trouble Bruce had getting an invite to visit Island One, how in the world did you swing it? From what we understand, you're not a colonist."

Mary Beth sat in the light plastic chair. She said happily, "Oh, I'm the secretary of the Friends of Lagrange Five. You've heard of the FLF, haven't you? You must really join when you return, Bruce. You could help us with publicity."

"Vaguely," Bruce said. "Didn't you have some kind of a parade in Washington, not so long ago?"

"*Did* we? I'll say. That's how come I'm here. Doctor Ryan himself invited me. There was a proposal for the government to donate a billion dollars to the Lagrange Five Project, no strings attached, and President Corcoran was vacillating. Well, the FLF was having none of that, so we marched on the White House, delegations from every state in the Union. The detachment of the FLF cadets from New York alone numbered nearly fifty thousand young people, all in their space cadet uniforms. There were over a million of us, in all, but, of course, that included the Spacists."

Rick said cautiously, "What are the Spacists? I'm not up on some of these things. I've been, uh, working abroad."

"They're kind of a sister organization, only more political than the Friends of Lagrange Five. They believe in Spacism."

In pain, Rick Venner refrained from asking what Spacism was. He was sure he didn't want to know.

But the freelance writer was fascinated. "What happened?" he said. "I've been busy researching the whole project since I got notice that my request to visit Island One had gone through. I'm not up on the current news."

"Well, good heavens, what do you think? The President couldn't ignore that many voters. He had to stand on a platform out in front of the White House as we marched by and then he gave us a speech and said all sorts of nice things about the Lagrange Five Project and our organizations and how high-minded we were and all."

"And the appropriation went through, of course," Rick said.

"Of course."

"No wonder Ryan invited you to Island One," Bruce said. "One billion bucks. There go my taxes up again. I'm surprised he didn't invite a whole delegation of you."

She looked unhappy. "That's what we expected and wanted, at first, but they were very nice and explained how horribly expensive it is to bring somebody up and

61

then take them back and all. And they're trying to watch every penny for the sake of the stockholders. So the National Committee decided I'd be the one to go. I'm only to be there for a few days. Everyone's so busy, you know. They don't have time to have earthworms underfoot."

"Earthworms?" Rick said.

"It's a term we use in FLF. As soon as the new Islands begin to be finished and there's room for more colonists, we're all going to apply. We're going to be space colonists, not earthworms. Have you read the article Dr. Ryan wrote about it for one of the magazines? He said the first 10,000 colonists would be carefully selected, but as time goes on, he expected that it would develop into a situation where anyone who wants to, goes."

"What?" Rick said, grinning. "Including lepers, Mongolian idiots, Texans, Californians, and people like that?"

"Oh, you're pulling my leg."

Bruce Carter had been looking over at the other side of the room and frowning. There was a rather heavyset man there, poring over some papers he had on the tiny writing desk the wardroom provided.

He came to his feet and said, "Pardon me, for a minute. I think I know that fellow."

He walked the few feet over to the other and said politely, "Excuse me, sir, aren't you Academician Leonard Suvorov?"

The other looked up over the top of his *pince nez* glasses as though momentarily confused at being taken away from his concentration. "Why, yes," he said, in only slightly Slavic-accented English.

"My name's Bruce Carter, sir. I'm a freelance writer, sometimes a journalist. I saw some newscasts about your defection but I didn't know about your coming to Lagrange Five."

The chunky man looked uncomfortable, but he said,

"Do sit down. I hardly expected to have news media following me all the way to Island One."

Bruce sat and said, "A coincidence. Is there a story in it?"

"I rather doubt it. Just before leaving, the fact that Dr. Ryan had welcomed me into the ranks of his inner circle of specialists was released to the media. In fact, once I have become oriented, I am to head the ecology department. But I daresay that may take some time. There are some very good men already on his staff."

Bruce said, exploring, "Are they having problems with the closed-circle ecology system?" In his cramming on all things pertaining to the L5 Project, Bruce Carter hadn't gotten a very clear picture of that phase of the overall program.

The ex-Soviet scientist looked uneasy. He said slowly, "In actuality, the establishment of the O, C, N, S, and, of course, H cycles largely depends on the establishment of proper soil conditions, together with the requisite macro and micro flora—that is, everything from earthworms to bacteriophages and back again by way of fungi and molds. It seems to me that this will be a major problem; that is, the conversion of lunar dust, which is predominantly volcanic rather than chondritic, into soil suitable for rapidly establishing a self-sustaining biosphere."

"I think I got most of that. Are you saying you're going to have your work cut out for you, the way it looks now?"

"Frankly," the Russian said carefully, "I am not as yet acquainted with what Ryan's ecologists have come up with, thus far. But it has always seemed to me that in a space colony it is prudent to have the bulk of the oxygen ultimately generated from algae in ponds and carbon dioxide from soil-bacterial complexes. I would consider it unsafe to attempt to simulate livable environments from our present biological knowledge."

Bruce Carter was no biologist, and only part of this got through to him. He said, "But I'd gained the impression that they had already set up their closed-cycle ecology system. That there might be a few bugs in it but that it was already operative."

"Not to my knowledge, young man," the Russian scientist said, pursing his lips. "However, as I say, I am as yet unacquainted with just what they are doing. I suggest that you postpone this interview until after our arrival in Island One. I assume that you are to be there for a time. In only a few days, I should have a better idea of just how things stand. Ask me then."

Bruce nodded. He said, "Thanks, I'll do that. Tell me, sir, your reasons for def—uh, leaving the Soviets. You're opposed to the present regime in the Soviet complex?"

Leonard Suvorov was unhappy again. He said, "I would rather not discuss my motivations. I am not political. I am a scientist. Besides, my family still remains in Leningrad, so you will appreciate that I must guard my statements to the media. However, I might say that as a biologist, I am tremendously interested in the ecological problems that manifest themselves in Island One. I simply couldn't stay away. Since the Soviet government refused me permission to leave with the intention of joining Dr. Ryan, I . . . well, I simply defected."

"They are making a great deal of it in the West, sir. Academician Suvorov is a respected name in the world of science."

"I suppose so. You refer to the Nobel Prize, of course. However, there is no manner in which I can control the propaganda. And now, Mr. Carter, if you will excuse me, I am perusing some of the work of my colleagues in Island One and, as the Americanism goes, time is a-wasting."

"Certainly, sir," Bruce said, coming to his feet. "And I'll contact you again after a few days at Lagrange Five."

He returned to the table where Mary Beth and Rick were seated, to find the girl looking indignant and the electrical engineer grinning at her.

Bruce said, "What spins?" as he took his chair.

Rick said, "Mary Beth won't believe the reason I signed up for a five-year contract at Lagrange Five. She thinks my motivations are contemptible."

Bruce looked over at him. "As a matter of fact, what does motivate a man to take on a five-year exile voluntarily?"

"Money," Rick said.

"Exile!" Mary Beth said indignantly. "That's not the way to put it."

Bruce regarded Rick questioningly. "It would seem to me that an engineer qualified enough to land a job with the L5 Corporation could get a pretty good job Earthside. If not in the States then, say, Iran or Saudi Arabia, or perhaps the Amazon region of Brazil."

"Sure," Rick admitted. "I could make at least fifty thousand a year, possibly lots more, on one of the more remote or dangerous jobs. But what happens? First of all, I'm single. The taxes slapped on me are ferocious. And the cost of living in those places is sky high—not to mention local hazards like radiation in Iran. At the end of the year, I'd be lucky to have put away five thousand. And even that would be eaten up if I was very long between jobs."

"So?" Bruce said. "In what ways is a job with the L5 Corporation different?"

"First of all, you needn't spend a penny in Island One, or at the Luna Base. Everything is supplied. Food, clothing, shelter, medical care, entertainment, even education for your children, if you have any. The standard contract for a construction worker is ten thousand a year and . . ."

Bruce scowled surprise. "No more than that? I had thought . . ."

"Wait a minute," Rick told him. "Plus a bonus of twenty thousand a year in shares of Lagrange Five Corporation stock, *if* you finish out your full contract. Contracts are for five years, ten years, or life, if you're a colonist. Figure that out. Suppose I spent half of my ten thousand a year on extras, gambling, wenching, or whatever's available in the way of living it up, and save the other five thousand. Suppose I stick it out for ten years. At the end of that time, I'd have a quarter of a million dollars coming to me. And tax free, mind you. Every country in the Reunited Nations has pledged not to tax the wages and salaries of space workers. With a quarter of a million dollars, Bruce, I can retire in comfort in some comparatively cheap country like Mexico or Morocco."

"I suppose it makes sense, at that," the freelancer admitted. He smiled his slow smile. "You don't suppose the Corporation needs any writers on their payroll, do you?"

"Oh, you two are impossible," Mary Beth said. "You seem to think that there's nothing in the glorious conquest of space but money." She came to her feet.

"It's been known to help in various causes, glorious and otherwise," Bruce said mildly.

She said, still indignant at these two clods, "Well, I'm going exploring. I wonder if it's allowed to go to the other modules. I'd like to see those nicer quarters where the officers and scientists live."

"It's worth trying," Bruce said. "We're only going to be here until tomorrow, but there sure doesn't seem to be much to do except to wait for mealtime."

After she was gone, the engineer said, "As a matter of fact, you're right." He looked over at a small table upon which sat chessmen and checkers, along with boards, and various other games. He went over to it and returned with a deck of cards and a container of chips.

"Poker?" he said to Bruce.

The freelancer said, "A favorite game of mine, but it's not much fun two-handed." He looked about the small wardroom. "Possibly someone else might be interested."

Rick grinned at him, even as he began to count out chips. "I'll tell you the best way to get a poker game going," he said. "What you do is start playing. Pretty soon, you've got a kibitzer, then another. Then one asks if he can sit in. Before you know it, you've got a full table."

Bruce smiled. "You have the instincts of a con man, I'm happy to say. Let's see if it works." He took up the cards and began to shuffle.

Rick said, "Suppose we start with a hundred dollars. On the cuff. When we get to Island One and make our financial arrangements, the loser can pay off, making a credit transfer to the winner."

"Right." Bruce pushed the cards over for a cut. "Let's say the ante is one dollar."

"Wizard."

Bruce Carter won the first hand with three ladies, mildly surprised that the other had pushed the betting with no more than two small pairs. Evidently, his companion was the out-for-blood type.

Rick dealt and won with a full house.

It was two hands later, without any kibitzers materializing as yet, when Bruce said mildly, "You do that very well."

Rick looked up from his shuffling. He didn't seem to be a very good shuffler. "How do you mean?"

"The Louisville flip."

Rick Venner put the deck of cards down. His faded blue-green eyes were cold. "What the hell are you talking about?"

The freelancer said, deprecation in his voice, "You should have read my last book, Rick. It was entitled *Gambling Is No Gamble*. I spent over a year researching it. Spent a whole month with Dakota Slim on cards and dice. Hit the bestseller lists. There were some who thought it'd put Vegas, Reno, and Atlantic City out of business. But it didn't, a compulsive gambler being a compulsive gambler. What's the old story about the high roller who was asked why he gambled in a certain casino when he knew all the tables were crooked, all the cards marked, all the wheels wired? And he said, in despair, 'Yes, I know, but what can I do? It's the only place in town you can play.'"

Rick gave up, shrugging in resignation. He made a rueful mouth. "You know how it is," he said. "Construction gangs don't have anything to do in their time off but play cards, or dice, or whatever. And half the time everybody in the game is cutting corners. In self defense, you've got to do it too. So you get into the habit. Sorry, Bruce."

Before the freelancer could answer, a newcomer came up to the table. "Playing poker?" he said. "Could I sit in?"

Bruce looked up. "I'll be damned," he complained. "Pete Kapitz, the last of the G-Men."

The newcomer, an unpretentious type, looked surprised. "Well," he said mildly. "Carter. The hack to end all hack writers."

Bruce pretended to wince. "Being illiterate, you don't know deathless prose when you see it," he said. "Sit down, Pete. Don't tell me your gumshoeing takes you to Island One. Pete Kapitz, Rick Venner. Pete's an IABI agent, Rick; Rick's an engineer on his way to L5 on a contract, Pete."

Pete Kapitz sat, after shaking hands with Rick. "You two just get here?" he said. "I've been in this goddamned block of cells for three days. If we stuck convicted grifters in a place like this back Earthside, a reformist howl would go up that'd raise the undead, Dracula and all." He looked at Rick. "What do the chips cost?"

Bruce said, "We just decided not to play. The hell with it. Come on, Pete. What sends you to Island One?"

Wryly: "Would you believe wanderlust?" He searched the writer's face as if looking for credibility, then shrugged. "Or I could tell you the truth. You wouldn't believe me, of course, and if you did it wouldn't matter much . . ."

"Are you *trying* to be mysterious?"

"Off the record?"

"If you insist," Bruce answered.

"I'm following a hunch; a certain international jewel thief seems to've dropped off the face of the Earth. Matter of fact he's *the* classic jewel thief, and maybe he *has* left the face of the Earth."

The freelancer stared. "Be damn. You must mean Weil." He paused in thought. "But I thought I read that Rocks Weil had caught a Sureté bullet somewhere in the South of France."

"Who did?" Rick said it as though mystified.

Pete looked over at him. "Rocks Weil. He's found some new wrinkles in an old trade, and it's made him a legend before he's forty."

Bruce put in, "With universal credit cards, there's so little cash and so many records that old-style heists don't seem to be popular anymore. So Weil's a computer thief?"

"Nope. He's a thief by contract. He locates some rich sonofabitch, Arab or Indian, whatever, who's willing to make a credit transfer or to pay gold for some gems that belong to someone else. Sometimes they tell him exactly what it is they want. It's up to Rocks to pull off the romp and deliver the goods."

"And everybody's happy but the owner of the stones—and the insurance company," Bruce said. "Now then: what makes you think he's on Island One?"

"Sorry," Pete said; "trade secret."

"Well, it's an interesting yarn," said Rick. "But it has to be cover story number one, right?"

"That thought had crossed my mind too," said Bruce, smiling. "If it were true you wouldn't be telling a professional blabbermouth about it."

Pete smiled at some inward joke. "You don't understand, gentlemen; this operation is no more secret than a police barricade. If our Mr. Rocks Weil has come to Island One, he has checked into prison."

"It doesn't have a prison," said Bruce.

"It *is* a prison," said Pete. "Weil, if he's out here, is in a trap. He can't get out without retina and fingerprints, and it's only a matter of time before we've checked every last mother's son in the colony. Ours is a big net, but it's narrowing."

"Could be a hell of a story," Bruce murmured.

"Rocks Weil; Rocks Weil," Rick repeated, rolling the name over his tongue. "Never heard of him. . . ."

"*The very idea of Space Colonies carries to a logical—and horrifying—conclusion processes of dehumanization and depersonalization that have already gone much too far on the Earth. In a way, we've gotten ready for Space Platforms by a systematic degradation of human ways of life on the Earth ... Walter Gropius designed a major living space for students (at Harvard). Every room was a unit space for a unit student, small and forbidding, lined with cinder block. One couldn't even drive a nail to hang a picture. In the open space outside is a Bauhaus object d'art: a stainless steel Tree of Life. It looks like an umbrella stand. A young woman student once said to me, 'On moonlit nights in the spring, Radcliffe girls dance around it, dropping ball bearings!'*"

—*George Wald, biologist, pacifist, Nobel Laureate.*

Chapter Five

The arrival of the passenger freighter *Tsiolkowsky* at the docking bay of Island One was a bit on the confusing side for Bruce Carter. Among other things, he was expecting to be met by Doctor Solomon Ryan, or at least by someone in the higher ranks of his organization. However, it turned out that the passenger list of the *Tsiolkowsky* boasted the names of various VIPs carrying considerably more prestige than that of a freelance writer. Among them were Prince Abou ben Abel, of the Arab Union, Academician Leonard Suvorov, of course, and even Mary Beth Houston, secretary of the Friends of Lagrange Five. The greeting of incoming celebrities in a space island docking compartment, in free fall, has its aspects, particularly when the VIPs in question are space tyros unused to zero gravity. The flowing robes of the Arab, for instance, had their disadvantages. He had evidently refused to wear the standard space coveralls, worn by both men and women. Money gave him that power of refusal; the prince was the only VIP among them who could have bought the *Tsiolkowsky* outright.

Bruce Carter had managed to get to a rail where he supported himself as best he could while the receiving committee was milling around those who really mattered.

Eventually a young fellow, managing to look natty even in coveralls, pulled himself over to Bruce and said, with a pleasant enough smile, "Bruce Carter?" His name was stitched over his breast pocket: Carl Gatena.

"That's right," Bruce said.

"I'm Carl Gatena. Ron Rich sent me over to take you to the L5 Hilton and get you organized. He'll see you as soon as he can. He's ass-deep in some of these new arrivals."

Gatena, somewhere in his mid-twenties, was the Madison Avenue type. Slight of build, clean cut, obviously anxious to please, obviously a flunky of some sort or another. He was darkish of complexion, brown of eyes, and his hair, worn slightly longer than was fashionable these days, was very black and straight. Probably Greek or Italian background, Bruce thought. Perhaps Spanish.

Bruce said, "Who's Ron Rich?"

The other smiled again. "He's our public relations chief. You'd be surprised how much PR routine we have to go through. I'm one of his staff."

"Wizard," Bruce said. "Let's go. Look, I thought Island One already had gravity. Don't tell me that I'm going to have to float around like this for my whole stay. What's this about the L5 Hilton?"

"Follow along behind me," the other man told him. "There's a monorail over here to take us into the colony proper. Yes, we've got simulated gravity in Island One, but not much of it here at the docking bay. This is at the axis. It has its advantages; nearly zero gravity for loading and unloading. We call it the L5 Hilton as kind of a gag. It's the only hotel in the Island. Pretty nice, too."

The docking bay was sizable. In it were parked several small spacecraft and endless piles of boxes, machinery, sheet metal, and whatnot. Bruce was taken aback to see a nonchalant worker, using his rocket harness to shove around a chunk of machinery that must have weighed several tons. But then, of course, here it didn't weigh anything at all. The longshoreman's job was a natural in a place like the docking bay: no heavy cranes necessary. Bruce noted, though, that massive cargo got moved very slowly because, once nudged into motion, it had to be stopped again.

As they progressed along the rail, he could see what was obviously the Arab's luggage coming off the passenger freighter. Seemingly, the Prince had brought everything but his tent, camels, and harem with him. Bitterly, the freelancer recalled his own limited luggage.

They reached the monorail, which looked like nothing so much as some ride in an amusement park back Earthside. As a matter of fact, now that he thought of it, it was probably where they had gotten the idea.

The vehicles were of varying sizes; in fact, some were obviously for freight, rather than human transportation. He and Carl Gatena got into a two-seater.

Gatena said politely, "Have a nice trip up?"

"Let's say interesting."

The younger man sighed. "I haven't had a vacation for six months. I've got a fiancée in Philadelphia. I wonder if she remembers me."

Their little vehicle started. They held onto a brace before them. Zero gravity was still in full effect.

Bruce said, "If she's an average American girl, she's thrilled to death being engaged to a spaceman. She could no more forget you than if you were currently the top-ranking Tri-Di star, or, say, the current mafia *Capo di tutti capi*, assuming there still is one."

The public relations man looked over at him. "What do you mean by that?"

Bruce frowned, not getting it. "I just meant that you're a celebrity, Earthside. Anybody in space is a celebrity. I imagine that when you go down on vacation, the girls swarm all over you."

The other's smile returned. "Not with Alicia around. She'd cut their hearts out."

Gravity was beginning to evince itself, to Bruce Carter's relief. The passenger freighter that had brought them up from the Space Platform *Goddard* had spun, making existence normal. He wondered how in the hell those early astronauts and Russian cosmonauts had ever existed in their zero-gravity, months-long manning of the Skylabs and—what had the Soviets called their equivalent—the Soyuz?

He said to the publicity man, "How often do you colonists rotate?"

The other's eyes shifted as they approached a station. "Not very often," he said. And then, as though that was inadequate, added, "Too damned expensive."

"But you said six months ago."

"Yeah. Well, here we are."

The terminal where they left the monorail resembled in many respects a subway station. There were a few people coming and going, all dressed in the standard coveralls, names stitched over the right chest pocket, serial number stenciled on the back.

The PR man led the way toward a corridor.

Bruce said, "Everybody in the Island dresses the same?"

The other looked over at him. "Mostly. You see, thus far we have no textile industry up here. It'd involve too much; we'd have to grow the cotton . . ."

"Why no synthetics or wool?"

Carl Gatena said in deprecation, "You're not thinking it through. Most synthetics are based on petroleum or

75

coal. We'd have to bring them up from Earth. We don't have sheep. The only animals we have, so far, are rabbits and chickens; per pound of feed, they're the most efficient there are. Anyway, we'd have to grow the cotton, or linen; then gin it, make thread, weave cloth, dye it, then sew it up into clothing. There's a project to spin glass filaments from lunar ore. But in any case, it takes one helluva factory and employs people we need elsewhere. So we have to bring our own textiles up from Earth. Very expensive, of course. So we standardize clothing and use the most durable available. These coveralls wear like iron."

Bruce had never thought of that angle. "Must apply to shoes, too."

"Of course. We have no leather, or anything else suitable, and no shoemaking machinery."

They came to a door before which stood a husky young man whose overalls were a dark green, rather than the usual faded blue.

Gatena said, "Hello, Joe. This is Mr. Bruce Carter. He's going to be staying at the hotel. Special guest."

Joe took the newcomer in. "Yes, sir, Mr. Gatena." He touched a finger to his cap, which resembled that of a railroad engineer Earthside. "Good morning, Mr. Carter." He opened the door for them.

They went through and into what would pass for the lobby of a moderate-sized hotel on Earth. Bruce was somewhat surprised that the hotel had an entry directly into the subway station.

He said to his guide, "Who was that?"

"Joe? One of the security men."

"Security men? What in the world do you need security men for?"

The other hesitated, almost as though irritated, but then said, "The L5 Hilton is restricted. If we allowed everyone into it, the place would be jammed, and the guests, and those who work here, such as Professor Ryan and his top aides, wouldn't be able to get anything done." He hesitated again, then added, reasonably, "The bar and the dining room would be overflowing and visiting VIPs such as yourself would have their work cut out getting anything to eat or drink."

"I see. So you haven't exactly established the classless society here in Island One."

Gatena shrugged at that.

The sparsely-peopled lobby of the L5 Hilton was obviously meant to look as much like an Earthside establishment as possible. But there were some aspects that didn't come off. There were no rugs on the floor, no paintings or other decorations on the walls, no drapes at the windows. The furniture was all metallic, with rubbery plastic seats and no signs of wood. There were no cushions, leather or otherwise. It gave an antiseptic effect, something like that of a hospital. To Bruce's surprise, after what his guide had said about textiles, the few people in the lobby wore ordinary Earthside clothing, rather than overalls.

There was no reception desk, in the ordinary sense of the word. Only a girl who sat at an ordinary metallic office desk, with the usual office equipment, including a voco-typer and a TV phone, before her.

She looked up smartly at their approach.

Carl Gatena said, "Maggie, this is Mr. Bruce Carter, the noted writer. I believe Mr. Rich has already gotten in touch with you."

She smiled a standard receptionist's smile at Bruce and said, "Welcome to Island One, Mr. Carter. Please call on me if there's anything you need, or need to know. If I'm not here, one of the other girls will be." She looked at the PR man. "Mr. Carter has been assigned to Room 114."

"Wizard," Gatena said. "This way, Bruce." He led his charge toward the stairs.

"No elevator?" Bruce said.

The other looked at him in deprecation again. "Can you imagine the weight and space involved in shipping an elevator up all the way from the New Albuquerque shuttleport?"

They started to mount.

"Why not make it here?"

The other shrugged. "This is the only building high enough in Island One to call for it. To build just one elevator from scratch would involve one hell of a lot of time and material. And a lot of the things that'd go into it aren't available in Lagrange Five, so they'd have to be shipped up."

"I guess that makes sense," Bruce admitted.

His room, though neat enough and spacious enough, carried on the sterile motif of the lobby and halls. The inflated bed looked comfortable, however, and the bedding had obviously been chosen for quality. As in the lobby, there were no rugs and the furniture was of metal. The bath had standard fixtures and its towels were the only other textiles besides the bedding that the room afforded. Taking up a considerable section of one end of the room was a TV screen, a Tri-Di, and a surprisingly large file of video-cassettes. At the other end of the room was a small bar.

Bruce's guide smiled wryly. "Kind of spartan, eh? The amenities are on the sparse side, I'm afraid. They all take up precious space in the shuttles or the heavy lift launch vehicles from Earth up to orbit and then in the passenger freighters from the *Goddard* to here. They'll all come in time, of course. Or, later, we'll make some of them here. As a matter of fact, I understand there's a shipment of art materials scheduled. Some of the colonists have gobs of talent. There's no reason why they can't start doing paintings in their spare time to hang on some of these bare walls."

Bruce nodded. "I can see there are a lot of ramifications to the Lagrange Five Project that have never occurred to me," he said. "However, in all the various Tri-Di programs, TV and movies, I never quite got the picture of things being so . . . spartan, as you put it."

The other made a gesture with one hand. "That's the way public relations goes. Those people down below who have the dream don't want to see anything but the brightest side of it all. So that's what we give them."

"You sure do," Bruce said, remembering some of the programs in question.

The other said briskly, "Make yourself at home, Bruce. Your bag should be along at any time. There's guzzle over there on the bar, if this isn't too early for you. And I assume that you're familiar with the workings of the entertainment equipment. Ron said he'd work you in as soon as possible. Probably an hour or so."

Bruce said, "Isn't there anything I could be doing until then?"

The PR man looked at him. "I think that Ron would rather check you out first. Let you know what the drill is. Assign you a guide."

"I'm not much for guided tours. I like to wander around on my own."

Carl Gatena frowned. He said, "Well, that's up to Ron. But some places, where construction's going on, can be dangerous if you're a greenhorn. And other places you could get in the way of busy workers."

Bruce said in irritation, "Damn it, I'm not the type that goes tripping over electric cables on some movie set, or getting himself shot in one of those African bush wars, or having a wall cave in on him in some earthquake. I've been around."

The other said placatingly, "I'm sure you have, Bruce.

But just let us play it Ron's way, at least at first, eh? So long, I'll be seeing you later." He hesitated. "Oh, if you get hungry, just go on down to the dining room. They'll do you up proud."

"So long," Bruce said sourly.

The publicity man left and Bruce went over to the window and stared out. And then *really* stared.

He'd gotten the impression, in researching the Lagrange Five Project, that the idea was to make the interiors of these Islands as much like Mother Earth as possible. If that's what they had attempted, it evidently wasn't very possible.

He assumed that the L5 Hilton was located in the center of Lagrange City, as the largest town in Island One was called. Before him now stretched an area of what would be called three or four city blocks, back on Earth. Houses, most of them two or three stories in height, lined quite narrow streets. The streets bore no traffic save bicycles and pedestrians, all coverall garbed.

It came to Bruce that they looked more like convicts in a prison than citizens of a community. The buildings had a stark look that at first didn't come home to him. Then he realized what it was. They were all metal, brick, cement, and clear plastic; there was no wood. None were painted. But that, he supposed, made sense. The ingredients of paint were expensive in Lagrange Five. He supposed that this was one of the amenities Gatena had mentioned that would have to be postponed. There must be a multitude of them.

On some of the terraces of the apartment houses, attempts had been made at a touch of gardening. But somehow it didn't seem to come off. At this distance, at least, he could see little, if any, color of flowers. There were some sad greens, even one attempt at a lawn, but it was rather unsuccessful.

Beyond the city limits he could make out less-developed

areas. To each side of the narrow strip of living space were equally wide strips of what he knew to be panes of coated high-impact plastic stretching on like gigantic picture windows to the other end of the 3,300 foot-long cylinder that was Island One. He looked up and, yes, there beyond the panes were other strips of living space and he could actually see other buildings, other soil areas, and even small people moving about—*upside down*. Island One's interior was composed of three such strips of living space, alternating with three strips of windows. He had read all about it, of course, and examined endless photographs, watched endless programs devoted to the project, but now it came home to him in all reality.

Suddenly impatient with the inadequacy of his viewing point, he turned and hurried to the door. He went down the stairs to the lobby and headed for the front entry, leading out to the town. From her desk, the girl Gatena had called Maggie frowned worriedly at him, but said nothing. The doors were open and he headed through.

There was a green-coveralled husky there. He touched a finger to his cap and said, "Where were you going, sir?"

Bruce scowled at him. "Why, I was going for a walk."

"Do you have a pass, sir?"

"A pass? What in the hell do you mean, a pass? I'm Bruce Carter. I just got in an hour or so ago. I'm not acquainted with procedure. What do I need a pass for?"

The other said politely, but not *too* politely, "You have to have a pass from Security before you can go out on your own, Mr. Carter."

"See here," Bruce told him, putting on an air of indignation. "I was invited to Island One by Doctor Ryan. I'm a journalist. I came up to do some articles. I'll go wherever I damn well please."

"Yes, sir. But not without a pass or a guide. That's the rule, sir. I didn't make it up."

Bruce glared at him for a moment, then gave up. The cloddy was obviously just doing his job. The freelancer turned and headed back into the lobby. He ignored the sorrowful look that Maggie bent on him.

He headed across the thinly peopled room just in time to witness the arrival of Prince Abou ben Abel, attended by three or four coverall-clad Lagrangists and followed by a dozen docking bay workers carrying luggage. They swept across the lobby toward the stairs. It would seem that the Arab need not be checked out by Maggie, the receptionist.

While all eyes were on the princely party, Bruce Carter slipped through the door leading to the monorail station.

Joe was still posted outside the hotel door. He said, "Mr. Carter! Where were you going? Looking for your luggage? It oughta be here any time."

Bruce sighed deeply and said, "Oh no. I'm in no hurry. I've got to see Carl Gatena's boss, Ron Rich, shortly. But I thought I'd stretch my legs and take another look at the subway station. Interesting transportation setup, that. Just what a place like this calls for."

The other hesitated. "You want to leave the hotel—without a guide?"

"It's not that," Bruce said, complaint in his voice. "I just want to stretch my legs. I've been cooped up in that damn spaceship for days. And I can't just parade up and down the lobby. I'd look like a dizzard."

"Oh, well. Go ahead. But don't leave the station. You're not supposed to go out without a guide."

Bruce headed down the corridor.

What in the hell wasn't he supposed to go out without a guide for, damn it? Right here in Lagrange City, how could he be expected to get in the way of construction workers—he hadn't even seen any out the window—or get himself into some dangerous position because he was a greenhorn to space. Safety precautions are great, but you can carry routine too far.

He entered the station, just in time to see a monorail car pull in containing Mary Beth Houston and Rick Venner, along with four others. He waved to them but didn't go over. Instead, he headed for what was obviously the main entrance to the terminal.

There was no Security man at the entrance and he issued forth into the street. He knew he was being childish. When in Rome, you should do as the wops do, and if the powers that be thought it best that he not be wandering around on his own without a guide the first time he went out, he should have gone along with them. However, both Gatena and the guard at the entry to the L5 Hilton had irritated him. He was going to spend the next half hour or so seeing the town on his own, or know reasons why.

The first impressions he had gained looking out the window of his hotel room were now largely borne out. Lagrange City had an artificial quality far and beyond anything he had ever seen before. All buildings were in metal, cement, plastic, or a sort of gray or chalky colored brick, which predominated. There were no signs of wood. Come to think of it, most plastics, like synthetic fibers, were derived from hydrocarbons, usually petroleum, but weighed less than glass. In Island One the stuff would have to be shipped up from Earth. And in shipping, weight was at a premium.

The streets were narrow, in view of the lack of vehicular traffic, and there weren't as many colonists on them as he might have expected. About half of those rode on bicycles.

There was a good deal of prefabrication in the architecture, but it wasn't universal. Some of the houses were largely of brick, perhaps of compressed slag. The single houses, in particular, were quite small, with a basic area of about 23 feet by 23 feet. Most of them were two-storied, but he passed two or three single-story dwellings. Whoever lived in the latter must have had about as much space as in a medium-sized trailer back Earthside. The next-sized house seemed exactly twice the area of the smallest ones and they too were usually two or even three stories. The next size was three times the size of the smallest ones.

And then it came to him. Each colonist was probably allowed a set amount of living space—by the looks of it, about 500 square feet, the area of a moderate-sized living room. If you lived alone, that was it, and if you wanted more space, you had to go up. But if two people lived together, they had a thousand square feet of ground area to work with. He passed a rather large dwelling, and there were two coverall-clad children, the first he had seen in Island One thus far, playing out in front of it. That fitted in. Probably two, or even more, families had pooled their land allotment. There was even room out in the front for a small garden area, which looked as though it got insufficient care; at least such plants as there were looked on the dejected side.

He passed, from time to time, what were obviously community buildings of some sort. Either that, or office buildings. There were no signs. Obviously there was no need of them. Members of the community would know if they were restaurants, movie houses, stores, or whatever. As a matter of fact, that was one of the few desirable attributes of Lagrange City. No signs. They were a pet abomination of his back home.

He tried to sum up his first impression, and decided on drab. But that wasn't exactly it. The buildings were all new, the streets were all spotless, everything was neat. But . . . perhaps the word was colorless. There was an unlived-in feeling.

Lagrange City was far from extensive. He had no way of knowing just how many residents there were, but it couldn't be many, certainly not over a couple of thousand. Though you never knew about some of those community buildings. They might have been dormitories for single men and women, with several hundred living in each.

He came to the end of the buildings area in short order and to what he assumed was supposed to be a park. There was a bandstand in its center, various walks, and benches spaced along them. A few people strolled through, and there were a few kids. Some of the benches were occupied, though not many. It came to Bruce Carter that there was a comparatively small span of years in the colonists he had seen thus far. Aside from the children, most of whom seemed to be about ten years of age, everybody looked somewhere between thirty and forty. There didn't seem to be any teenagers and no elderly folk. But that probably made sense. Younger people wouldn't have the education and experience to qualify for a job at Lagrange Five and elderly ones would only be a drag on the community's resources, consuming but not producing.

It was time he made some personal contact. He sat down on a bench that had a sole occupant, a man of about his own age. On his breast pocket was stitched *Pal Barack*.

Bruce said in Esperanto, in which he had taken a crash course, "Mind if I sit down?"

The other looked over at him indolently and in the same language, with a slight European accent said, "You can fall down as far as I'm concerned." But then he grinned mischievously, to take the edge off his words.

He was on the short side, swarthy of complexion, and with a nervous quality. He projected the impression that he could become excitable very easily, though right now he was leaning back, his arms over the back of the bench and his legs stretched out before him. He had been staring lazily up above.

Bruce's eyes followed the other's. There, above them, was one of the alternating strips of land area. Bruce, of course, was as yet far from adjusted to the sight.

The other said idly, pointing to a man in a field, "Look at that stupid funker up there. Only 328 feet away. I've been here four years, eleven months, three weeks, six days, and four hours, but I still can't get over the feeling that if nature called and he answered, I'd get a shower down here and it wouldn't be rain."

Bruce laughed.

The other was gratified. He said, "You know, off and on I've wondered: if I could get hold of some heavy rubber bands, I could make a sling shot and hit one of those upside-down cloddies or maybe break some of the windows in those isolated houses."

Bruce laughed again. "At that distance?"

The other looked over at him, pretending indignation. "Why not? It's 328 feet, but you've got to remember that the higher the stone gets, the less gravity there is. When it hits the halfway mark it begins to be attracted by the gravity up there and begins to fall." He looked over at the newcomer to his bench, seemingly noticing the lack of a name on the breast pocket of Bruce's overalls. He said, "You must be from the hotel."

"That's right," Bruce said. "I just pulled in this morning."

"How come you haven't got a couple of those Security funkers trailing around with you? They don't usually let an earthworm out of their sight."

Bruce frowned at him. "Why not?"

"Because they don't want outsiders to find out what a farce this whole thing is."

Bruce said softly, "Such as what?"

The other grunted sour amusement. "Such as what we were just talking about, for instance. The diameter of this island is 328 feet and it's 3,280 feet long. Like a dizzard, I didn't bother to figure that out before I signed up for this stupid job. That means we've got a circumference of 1032 feet. We're divided into six strips, running from one end of the cylinder to the other, alternating solar strips and living space. So how wide does that make each strip—171.6 feet. In that initial propaganda of his, old Ryan was describing towns, rivers, lakes, woods, and what not, even in this Island One. Ha! How big a lake or river can you have with a working space only 171 feet across? How big a town? The L5 Hilton isn't as big a hotel as all that, but it stretches all the way across this strip. And that river bit. How in the hell can you have a river flowing along through lunar lava dust?"

Bruce scowled at that. He said, "Well, after trees, bushes, grass, and other vegetation were growing, it'd be just like any other stream. The vegetation holds the river banks. Humus accumulates, all that sort of thing."

"What vegetation?" the other said scornfully. "You mean you think we're going to turn this whole island into one big hydroponic tank? And how about all that crud those physicists gave us about fish in the rivers and lakes, and ducks and even swans swimming around? What in the hell would the fish eat and the ducks and swans? You'd have to go out and feed them every day by hand and toss fish food into the ponds and streams. What shit!"

"Wait a minute, now," Bruce said. "I'm green up here but I've read about it. The idea is a closed-cycle ecology. The animals eat the plants and breathe out carbon dioxide, and their excrement is fertilizer. And the plants give off oxygen. Everything is recycled; the water, the air, the human refuse—everything. It's a closed system."

The other nodded, wearily. "Yeah, that's the theory they started off with, but it'd never been tried on this scale. And we haven't been able to make it work." The other turned and pointed at the dozen or so trees planted around the park. "See those fruit trees? I planted them myself. I'm a landscaper, a gardener. You know what a gardener starts with down Earthside? Good black earth, with vegetation in it, rotting leaves and so forth, and with worms and bugs in it, some of them microscopic. You know what we start with here? Breccia, lava dust from the moon. Sure, you can grow plants, even trees, in lava dust, given water and the correct nutrients. You can do it with no soil at all, in a hydroponics tank. But it means that you've got to tend each plant each day. It's a job, keeping a hydroponic tank going. The damn plants will die on you at the drop of a hat. Ah, the hell with it. You couldn't understand."

He turned and pointed out one of the stunted little trees in the park. "I've got to water 'em every day. But what good is it going to do? That's supposed to be an apple tree. Back on Earth, it takes about eight years to get an apple tree to bear any amount at all. But in eight years, if it survives that long, where's that tree going to get room for its root system? The soil's about a yard deep. What are the roots going to find down in that soil? You're going to have to continue treating it like it was in a hydroponic farm for the rest of its existence. Ah, the hell with it." He thrust his feet out farther before him, in disgust.

Seemingly, the other was on his pet peeve. Bruce Carter changed subjects. He said, "What was that about you having been here four years, eleven months and . . ."

The other grinned suddenly. "That's right, and three weeks, and six days, and four and a half hours. And tomorrow my contract's up and I'm getting the hell out of this overgrown submarine."

Bruce was interested. "Don't figure on signing up again, eh?"

The other gawked over at him as though he'd gone completely around the bend. "Do I look drivel-happy? I've never even *heard* of anybody who wanted to stay up here as soon as he got a chance to leave. Five years ago they shortened the minimum contract period from ten years to five, trying to attract more qualified workers. And now, along in here, the five-year boys are beginning to see their contracts expire."

The other was obviously a malcontent, Bruce decided. "What's wrong with it up here?" he said. "I can see that it's no paradise, but. . . ."

Pal Barack laughed bitterly. "What's right with it? We get some food from our hydroponic gardens, but all the fertilizer has to come up from Earth, along with carbon for carbon dioxide, and nitrogen for air. So mostly we eat dehydrated food. A man can live on about a pound a day. It's Godawful. All the fresh meat we get is rabbit and chicken. For all practical purposes, there is no booze, except a little jungle juice we ferment ourselves. It's so expensive to ship up it's prohibitive. Some bootleg, of course, but it's nearly as expensive. Then there aren't enough women, not nearly enough. And there isn't enough entertainment, except the canned stuff. And the only tobacco is black market. And . . ."

Bruce brought forth a pack of cigarettes and said, "Smoke?"

Pal Barack contemplated him, then reached out and selected a cigarette with a sigh. He said, "You haven't got a match or a lighter, have you? I've given up carrying them."

"Sure," Bruce said. "Here, take the pack." He handed it over and reached for his book of matches.

The other's eyes bugged. "Listen, chum-pal," he said, as though hating to reveal the fact to his new acquaintance but being forced to through conscience. "In Island One a package of butts costs fifty dollars and up, *when* you can find them. You sure you want to give these away? How long you going to be up here and how big's your supply?"

"It's all right," Bruce told him. "I don't smoke myself. Down at the shuttleport in New Albuquerque one of the employees there told me to use up my baggage allowance with liquor and cigarettes. That they were worth their weight in gold up here. So I didn't even bring my portable voco-typer. I figured I could borrow one in Island One. By the way, my name's Bruce Carter."

They shook hands. Pal Barack sucked in smoke blissfully. He said, "My name's Barack. Pal Barack. I'm a Hungarian gypsy. Don't ever trust a Hungarian and especially don't trust a gypsy. Did you hear the one about the Hungarians being the only people in the world who can go into a revolving door behind you and come out ahead of you?"

Bruce laughed and said, "The way I heard it, they're the only people who can go into a telephone booth and leave by a rear door."

The Hungarian gardener said, "Look, are you the writer? I've read some articles by a Bruce Carter."

"That's me. I've got permission to come up to do some freelance articles on the workings of Island One."

"Well, Bruce, you sure as hell aren't going to get any straight material from that gang at the hotel. What you ought to do is attend the meeting of the WITH-AW-DOH Club tomorrow night."

"The *what* club?"

"WITH-AW-DOH. It consists of persons who have the WITH-AW-DOH syndrome. The letters stand for What

90

In the Hell Are We Doing Out Here? We'll give you something to write about."

Bruce laughed still again. "All right," he said. "I'll try to make it. Where is it held?"

His new acquaintance turned and pointed down the street from which Bruce had entered the park. "See that big grayish building? It's the auditorium. We meet at nine. Watch out for the Security funkers. I doubt if they'd want you to come. In fact, I know God-damned well they wouldn't."

A voice from behind them said, "Mr. Carter?"

They turned. It was one of the green-coveralled Security men.

Bruce said, "That's right."

The other said, politely enough, "Would you mind returning to the hotel with me? Mr. Rich is looking for you."

Bruce stood and said to the Hungarian, "Nice meeting you. Hope to see you again."

The other nodded, looking a bit apprehensively at the Security man. "Likewise," he said.

The Security man looked at the gardener's name on his pocket before turning to go with Bruce back to the L5 Hilton.

"*My negative feeling about such a project revolves around the kind of 'Pie in the Sky' vibration which I feel. Given the problems we are facing from population overload and its attendant horrors—famine, land rape, water pollution, dwindling resources, etc.—I wonder at the wisdom of putting before the people the idea of 'getting out of here,' when here is where the work is, here is where the problem is. At that level it seems like escapism, and as such the last place where we should put our energies.*"
—Steve Durkee, Artist

Chapter Six

The introduction of Peter Kapitz to Island One was almost identical to that of Bruce Carter. He was met at the docking bay by a young fellow wearing a dark green space coverall with the name "Mark Donald" stitched on the left breast pocket. It sounded like a Scottish name but there must have been others besides Scots in the family woodpile. Either that or he was a fanatic on sunbathing. He was friendly enough and boasted a beautiful set of very white teeth when he smiled.

He smiled and said, "Mr. Kapitz?" then frowned a little, as though perhaps he'd made a mistake. This wasn't exactly what he'd expected Mr. Kapitz to look like. Mr. Kapitz was supposed to be a topnotch IABI operative.

Pete was used to the reaction. He said, "That's right. Peter Kapitz."

"My name's Donald, sir. Mark Donald. Mr. Moore sent me to meet you."

"Wizard," Pete said. "Who's Mr. Moore?"

The other made a rueful mouth, as though Pete should have known. "Alfred Moore. He's the Lagrange Five Security Commissioner. We've been expecting you. I assume you've had a little experience in free fall by this time. If you'll just follow along behind me on this rail, we'll get down to gravity."

"How about my bag?"

"I've made arrangements to have it sent to the hotel." Mark Donald began expertly to pull himself along the guide rail and in the direction of the monorail cars.

"You have hotels up here?" Pete said, following along as best he could.

"One hotel," the other told him over his shoulder. "We're not exactly ass-deep in traveling salesmen and such. It also kind of doubles as city hall and the headquarters of the Lagrange Five Project. It's the biggest building in the island."

They reached the monorail and shared a four-seater with a couple of docking bay workers going off shift. Pete Kapitz half listened to them as the little vehicle headed inward. They were bitching about the food at the community mess hall. Evidently, they were tired of rabbit and chicken to the point that, in spite of the fact that it was the only fresh meat available, they sometimes refused to eat it.

One of the space colonists at least had a sense of humor. Pete heard him say, "That poor French chef cloddy. Here he is, one of the best cooks in France, and they lure him up here with the best pay he's ever heard of. And what happens? Everybody hates him because the food is so shitty."

"Yeah," the other one chuckled sourly. "It never occurred to him that you could cook without such little items as butter and cream. I'll bet he can hardly eat his own food himself."

Pete looked over at his guide from the side of his eyes.

He said lowly, so the two workers seated behind couldn't hear, "Surely the meals can't be that bad."

Mark Donald grunted. "Did you ever hear of construction workers out in the boondocks, or soldiers, or sailors, who didn't spend half their time complaining about the chow?" He turned in his seat and looked back at the two. They went silent.

At the terminal, they had adequate gravity and the Security man led the way. Pete Kapitz recognized several of those who had accompanied him on the passenger freighter over from the *Goddard*, including Rick Venner; but everybody seemed in a hurry and there was no opportunity to say anything.

Pete continued to duplicate the experiences of Bruce Carter, who had come this way only a few minutes before him, though Pete, of course, had no way of knowing that. They passed by Joe, the Security man, at the entry to the L5 Hilton and crossed the lobby to Maggie's reception desk. Pete even got almost identical reactions to the hotel as had his predecessor; sterile, hospital-like, colorless, naked of decoration.

Maggie was her bright self and gave him his room number, 116. Once again, he couldn't know it, but he was quartered next door to the freelancer, Bruce Carter.

The interior of the room was bleak. Mark Donald sat in one of the unupholstered chairs and watched him, faint amusement in the back of his eyes, as the space tyro checked out the accommodations.

The IABI operative looked out the window down the long cylinder which was Island One for minutes before saying, "I thought it'd be bigger than that."

"Yeah," Donald said. "So did I when I first saw it."

Pete turned and looked at him. "How long have you been up here now?"

"A few years. Since just after they pressurized it and had enough living accommodations to move in."

"How do you like it?"

The other wasn't thoroughly comfortable at the questioning, but he shrugged and said, "It's a job." That didn't seem to be enough so he added, "I like the money piling up."

Pete frowned at him. "But if you're a colonist, how are you going to spend it? What is there up here you can spend it on? I suppose that if you were Earthside you could do the usual with all the pay you're undoubtedly accumulating. That is, a bigger house, complete with servants, a bigger car or two, perhaps a boat. Or possibly you like to travel. But suppose you accumulate a quarter of a million, or whatever it amounts to, up here. What do you blow it on?"

The other still seemed uncomfortable, as though they were in a forbidden field. He said, grudgingly, "I can always go Earthside and spend it." He showed his white teeth in a quick smile. "A quarter of a million makes quite a splash in a place like, say, the Bahamas."

Pete looked at him strangely. He said, "It sounds something like those Rocky Mountain men, the fur trappers who in the early 19th Century would go out after beaver for a couple of years at a stretch and then come back to the rendezvous with their catch and blow everything in a three day binge." He thought about it and scowled. "It doesn't seem like much of a motivation to come out into space. If all the things you want to spend your money on are down Earthside, why come up at all? Why not just stay down there?"

The other shrugged it off, as though he took it that Pete was kidding.

But the IABI man pursued it. "Does everybody else feel the same way?" And then, thinking it through a little further, "I thought most of you up here had the space dream. That you were colonists, here for good. That the money part of it wasn't particularly important."

The Security man seemed to be on happier ground. He said, "I suppose different people look at it different ways. Most of those who've signed up are here for good. Colonists. But some signed contracts for only ten years, some only five. They can always extend their contracts, of course, and stay on. But some figure on making their piles and returning and retiring down below." Donald cleared his throat and made a motion toward the small bar. "How about a drink?"

The IABI agent shook his head, saying, "It's a little early for me," but he walked over to the little bar and inspected its offerings.

"Holy smog," he said. "This is the most expensive collection of guzzle I think I've ever seen. I couldn't afford this kind of scotch and cognac if I were the director of the Bureau himself, John Wilson."

The other said, smiling on a bias, "Sure, but it'd be stupid for it to be otherwise. The expense in Island One isn't in what's *in* the bottle. It's the cost of bringing it up. It'll go a couple of hundred dollars a fifth for transport. Why send up rotgut?"

Pete picked up a bottle and looked at it. "As a matter of fact, I'm surprised to see it at all. I got the impression that such luxuries were practically unknown in Lagrange Five and at the moonbase. That the freight sent up was strictly limited to utilitarian items—fuel, machinery, raw materials you can't get from the moon, such as copper, and so on."

Mark Donald was uncomfortable again and looked as though he wouldn't have minded changing the subject, but he said, "It's contraband. We seize it and then, of course, it'd be a crime to destroy such things, so we consume them here in the hotel." He added apologetically, "There's not enough to go around, so we keep it for visitors like yourself, or for VIPs on junkets up from

Earthside. And, of course, for top ranking members of Doc Ryan's staff, visiting scientists, and so forth."

Pete had turned back from the bar, staring at him. "Contraband?" he said. "You mean from smugglers?"

"Well, sure, kind of. No matter where you are, given shortages, there'll be characters who'll take any risk to smuggle in contraband either for themselves or a black market—if the price is right."

"Black market!" Pete got out in his surprise. "You mean there's a black market in Island One?"

"Yeah, kind of. Not very big, of course, but one way or the other things are smuggled in. Hidden in pipes, in heavy machinery, that sort of thing. You'd be surprised at some of the ingenious places they figure out to run in guzzle, tobacco, cosmetics, food delicacies."

That brought back to Pete Kapitz the complaints of the two workers who had ridden in the monorail vehicle with them. He said, "You mean that the colonists will pay sky-high prices to supplement their diets?"

Donald shifted in his chair, as though being put upon with this conversation. "That's not exactly the way to put it; but say that somebody is fond of sardines. He builds up an absolute neurosis for sardines, which are, of course, not available at all—except here at the hotel, if we've intercepted some. So, figure it out for yourself. He's making ten thousand a year with nothing to spend it on. Wizard, finally he gets to the point where he's willing to pony up fifty dollars or so for a small can of sardines. Crazy as a bedbug."

The Security man looked relieved when his pocket transceiver buzzed. He took it out, flicked it on. Pete politely turned his back and went over to the window again and looked out over the streets of little Lagrange City with its sad attempts, here and there, at a bit of greenery.

Behind him, Mark Donald said, "That was the Chief.

He's got some time open and can work you in now. Shall we go on up? Your bag will probably be here by the time we return. You can unpack and then we can have lunch."

It seemingly hadn't occurred to the Security man that Pete Kapitz might wish to dine alone. Pete said, "Fine. Let's go."

The offices of Alfred Moore were on the uppermost floor of the L5 Hotel. And Pete Kapitz had some surprises coming. The upper floor was a far cry from the one that embraced his room.

They mounted the steps and Mark said to the green-clad Security man at their top, "Hi, Dean. This is Mr. Kapitz. Al is expecting us."

The guard touched a finger to his cap. "I've been notified. Go right on, Lieutenant."

The Security force seemed to have military ranks, Pete thought. He wondered how many of them there were. Surely, with labor up here at a premium, everyone involved in some sort of crucial effort, they couldn't devote many to such unproductive tasks as whatever it was that Security did, besides intercepting contraband.

He was vaguely surprised at the identity screen on the door before Alfred Moore's quarters. The mechanism could hardly have been manufactured out here in space; too much bother. It would have had to be shipped up from Earthside. But then, so would the rug on the floor of the hallway. It was the first rug or carpeting of any sort he had seen thus far in the island.

Donald stood before the screen and said, "Lieutenant Donald and Mr. Peter Kapitz to see Security Commissioner Moore."

The door opened and Pete followed the other in.

The room beyond was a reception office with two girls at the desks. The place was considerably different from Pete's hotel room. In fact, it differed only from an ultra-swank Earthside corporation office in the view from the windows. Wall-to-wall carpeting, paintings hanging, and drapes at the windows. The desks were either wooden or very good imitations; they most certainly weren't metal.

Nor were the girls attired in space coveralls. They were done in the latest styles prevailing in such fashion centers of Earth as Paris, Copenhagen, or perhaps Budapest. They wore the first cosmetics Pete had seen in space and either of them could have been Tri-Di starlets. One was a brunette, one a redhead, and both were luscious. Pete Kapitz refrained from hissing appreciatively. The few women he had seen on the *Goddard* and here in Island One, thus far, had led him to believe that he was fated for less than pulchritude until he returned to mother Earth. But evidently all was not lost.

The redhead looked up brightly, in the best tradition of the receptionist, and said, "Mr. Moore is expecting you, Lieutenant. Go right on in."

"Wizard, Marie," Mark Donald told her, and led the way to the door set a few feet to the left of her desk.

The two girls looked Pete up and down contemplatively as he smiled at them in passing. He got the impression that a new face was always in demand in the L5 Hilton. And, in thinking about it, wondered. With ten thousand people up here, surely most of them men, there could hardly be a man shortage so far as a couple of good-looking mopsies such as these were concerned.

If he had thought the outer office was swank, it was nothing compared to that of the Security Commissioner's sanctum sanctorum. Pete Kapitz was far from a connoisseur, but he strongly suspected that those Renaissance paintings on the walls were originals. And he winced at the thought of what it must have cost to transport the couple of thousand or so beautifully bound books that filled the floor-to-ceiling bookshelves.

The desk was immense, an antique, and even on Earth must have been worth thousands. If it cost a couple of hundred dollars to bring a fifth of liquor up from Earth, what would that desk be worth up here, after having been lifted by space shuttle to the *Goddard* and then freighted over to Lagrange Five?

Behind the desk sat a high-echelon executive as steretypical as Pete Kapitz could have asked for. Except that he wasn't quite old enough, he could have been the chairman of the board of IBM, AT&T, or, say, Chrysler-Ford. His business suit was immaculate: his hair trim was such that surely he had stepped out of the barber's chair but moments ago. And in the chair he'd had both a manicure and a massage, and possibly a sunlamp while he had been acquiring them. In short, Alfred Moore was every inch of his five-foot-ten, one hundred-and-sixty-five pounds, the epitome of a prosperous business executive. To Pete Kapitz, he most certainly didn't look like a head of Security. He had been expecting something more in the way of a Chief of Police, possibly complete with belly and florid Irish face.

The charm went along with the appearance. Lagrange Five's Security Commissioner came to his feet and extended his perfectly manicured, dry, firm hand across the desk to Pete Kapitz.

Smiling, he said, "You must be our representative from the Inter-American Bureau of Investigation."

"Peter Kapitz," Pete said, shaking and nodding acknowledgment.

"Alfred Moore," Mark Donald said in introduction, needlessly. He brought up a chair for the visitor and then took one further back for himself.

When they were seated, the Security head beamed and said, "A drink, Mr. Kapitz?"

Pete said, "Theoretically, it's early for me. I haven't had anything alcholic since leaving the New Alburquerque shuttleport." He twisted his mouth. "No alcohol in space. Actually, I thought that applied up here too."

Alfred Moore smiled again, this time in deprecation, and said, "They ban it in space because there's nothing quite like a hangover in freefall. But here, inside the island, we don't consider ourselves actually to be in space. This is our own Brave New World and we try to carry on as similarly to Earthside as possible. Mark, will you do the honors?"

The lieutenant got up and went over to an elaborate bar up against a wall. It, too, was obviously of antique wood. He looked back at the seated men and raised his eyebrows. "Whiskey?" he said.

"Scotch sounds good to me," Pete told him.

"Wizard," Moore nodded.

Pete said to the Security head, "More confiscated contraband?"

The other frowned. "I beg your pardon?"

Donald said quickly, "I told Mr. Kapitz how we confiscated any products brought up surreptitiously and that rather than destroy them, in view of their value, we used them here in the hotel."

"Oh. Oh, yes, of course," Moore said, taking the glass his underling proffered.

Pete sipped at his. It was easily, smoothly, the best whiskey he had ever tasted.

Moore said, "Well, now, as I understand it, my old friend John Wilson has sent you up in pursuit of a more than ordinarily wily fugitive from justice. I must say, you don't fit the usual picture one has of a dedicated and highly experienced sleuth, if you'll pardon my saying so."

Pete Kapitz had heard much the same before. He said now, "Possibly that's one of my attributes." He grinned. "Who'd ever suspect that I was a cop?"

The other chuckled. "Throws them off guard, eh?"

Then, "But frankly, I am somewhat surprised that John would go to the expense involved in sending a man to Lagrange Five simply to apprehend a single fugitive."

The IABI agent nodded seriously to that end, after taking another swallow of the superlative Scotch, went into his well-rehearsed story. "It's more than just putting the arm on Rocks Weil himself. It's a matter of image and prestige. Rocks usually operates abroad but he's known to be an American citizen. If we still had the 'ten most wanted' system, he'd undoubtedly be Public Enemy Number One. It's a black eye for the bureau that he's never taken a fall. In fact, so far as we know, he's never been arrested on even a minor charge. It's bad business allowing him to continue to operate. It gives other would-be grifters the idea that they, too, could pull off romps equivalent to his. So we're going all out to make an example of him."

Moore nodded wisely. "I suppose that makes considerable sense. You said Rocks Weil. Up here we don't keep up with the latest police affairs too well, but it seems to me that I've heard of him—a jewel thief, isn't he?"

"That's right," Pete told him. "Undoubtedly the most competent of this century."

The other grimaced in thought. "But wasn't he reported shot, somewhere in France, not too long ago?"

"We think that was a case of mistaken identity. You see, for one thing, we're not sure of his appearance. That crook shot in Nice might have been somebody quite different."

"But if you're not sure of his appearance, how in the world do you expect to apprehend him, Mr. Kapitz?"

"Call me Pete, everybody does." The IABI man opened his small attaché case. "I've got old partial prints, probably his, and three photos, one of which might be of him." He brought them forth and placed them on the desk before the Security head.

Moore looked down. "And please call me Al. We're very informal here at Lagrange Five," he said. And then, "But these are obviously three different men."

Pete nodded and said, in self-deprecation, "Yes. But if I can locate anyone up here that looks like any of those three, and find a match for the partial fingerprints, we're in business."

The other sighed. "But just what led you to suspect that this Rocks Weil fellow is in space? A colonist must be highly qualified to be taken on, you know. And the qualifications of a jewel thief are hardly the ones we need."

Pete grinned wryly at that. "We've got our methods," he said. "And they've led to a strong suspicion that Rocks made it to Island One, or perhaps the moon base. For one thing, just shortly before I left we got word that Pavel Meer, the Penman, was killed down in Mexico, where he had evidently set up shop."

"Penman?" Moore said.

"Pavel was probably the top forger and counterfeiter of our time; he even cast fake latex finger masks to pass a print check. For the past five years or so he's been on the run, sought by every police force that makes any difference, including Common Europe's Interpol. He went to ground in an artists' colony in Mexico and kept a low profile, passing himself off as a second-rate artist. When he was killed, the Mexican police found equipment in his house that indicated he had the capability to forge documents that would get a man, or woman for that matter, into Lagrange Five as a colonist or construction worker on contract."

The Security head's eyebrows went up; he looked at Mark Donald and then back to his visitor. "Good grief, now you mean to tell me that other fugitive criminals might be hiding here in Island One?"

"That's right," Pete told him. "We were able to follow

a man we suspected might be Rocks, with the assistance of Interpol, as far as Mexico. He disappeared there, probably heading north by hoverbus and other public transportation of the type that wouldn't necessitate reservations and hence create any records in the data banks. We suspect that he might have been heading for Pavel Meer with the intention of getting papers to hide out here in Lagrange Five."

"Holy smog," Donald said. "What do you think, Chief?"

The Security Commissioner shook his head. "We'd better put some people on it, soonest. Offhand, I can't think of anything they might do. Certainly there isn't anything worth stealing, and, even if there was, they'd have no way of getting their loot back Earthside. But if there are any such, I'd feel happier if we rounded them up."

"Righto, Chief," his underling said.

Al Moore turned back to Pete. "So, where would you like to begin?"

"I suppose the first thing would be to go through your files of colonists and contract workers, especially those who've been Earthside recently, and see if I can match up any of these photos. I assume that whatever kind of records you keep on your people include portrait shots."

"Certainly, and our data banks are right here in the hotel." Moore chuckled. "In fact, practically everything that makes any difference is right here in the L5 Hilton. Some of our visitors, very big mucky-mucks from Earthside, never leave the hotel. They can see all they want of the island through the windows. You might keep that in mind, Pete. We've got everything you might wish right here. If you want to interrogate any of the colonists, we can have the boys round them up and bring them in. No need for you to go out. If you do leave the hotel, be sure the lieutenant here is along."

"Wait a minute," Pete said. "I don't need a nursemaid. The way I work. . . ."

Al Moore held up a hand and smiled ruefully. "Pete, you don't think we'd run the chance of anything happening to you, do you? Suppose you ran into this Rocks Weil and he took a dim view of the fact. Do you think that anybody with that Public Enemy Number One label on him would just give up? And what would happen to us if John Wilson got news that one of his top operatives had been killed in Island One? He'd send up so many men the place would be swamped. And what would our investors think, down Earthside, when they found out that some of the world's top criminals were hiding at Lagrange Five? No sir, I don't believe that there are any such fugitives here, but I'm not taking the chance. Everywhere you go, the lieutenant goes."

Pete Kapitz sighed resignation.

The Security head looked at his desk chronometer and said, "I've got an appointment. Mark, you see that Mr. Kapitz is fixed up—in all ways, of course." He turned his eyes back to the IABI man. "There's going to be a party tonight in honor of Prince Abou ben Abel. Doctor Ryan and everybody else of importance in Island One will be there. You're invited, of course." His smile was inverted. "I doubt if your Rocks Weil will make it, but it'll be a chance for you to become acquainted and get the feeling of the place."

"Wizard," Pete said, coming to his feet. "Thanks for the cooperation, Al. I ought to be able to check this out in short order and be back on my way Earthside, with or without friend Rocks, in a few days."

Al Moore got up and shook hands. "See you at the party, Pete. Good luck."

On the way back to his room, Pete looked over at his companion and said, "Mr. Moore doesn't exactly look like a cop."

The other shrugged in amusement. "He's not ... exactly. I don't know how we got the name Security hung on us. Actually, Al's basic job is more like that of an expediter. Keeping all the strings together—kind of a traffic director." He hesitated, then added, "There's a lot of angles to building one of these islands."

Back at the room, Pete found that his bag had been delivered. He put it on the bed with the idea of unpacking the few belongings he'd been allowed to bring, but the Security man looked at his wrist chronometer and said, "It's lunch time. You must be hungry after the kind of food you get on the way up here. Why don't you leave your unpacking until later?"

"Okay with me," Pete told him, straightening up. "Lead the way. I haven't the vaguest idea where the dining room is." He took his attaché case along with him again.

The main dining room of the L5 Hilton wasn't quite as austere as the lobby, but nearly so. There weren't any tablecloths, for instance, which made sense, of course. They would have to have been lobbed up from Earth at God only knew what expense. Evidently, the lunch hour wasn't as yet well underway. There were only a dozen or so other diners. About half wore space dungarees; the rest were in Earthside dress of invariably the best quality. Pete supposed that made sense. It was the same as the guzzle. If you were going to go to the expense of shipping it up, you might as well start with the best available.

To his mild surprise, the dining room was not automated. Instead, there were neatly uniformed waitresses, each of them a potential runner-up for Miss Universe. He snorted inwardly in amusement. He supposed the same thing applied here, too. If you were going to go to the expense of lobbing it up, you might as well start with the best available.

Their waitress turned out to be Irene, and Irene was stunning enough that Pete couldn't keep his eyes from her, both face and figure. His companion did the ordering, knowing the ropes, and was obviously amused at Pete's bewitchment with the girl.

He said, when she was gone, "You like Irene? I'll fix it up for you, if you'd like."

Pete was again surprised. He said, "Is there any place to take a girl on a date? Come to think of it, I suppose there must be. Movie theaters and so forth, dance halls. You can't have ten thousand people and no entertainment."

The other waved a hand negatively. "No use going to those colonist joints. The best is right here in the hotel. Pretty damn good nightclub, a cocktail lounge, a sizable bar. Movie theater, too, for that matter. Like the Chief said, there's no reason to leave the hotel at all."

The surprise continued. The meat course was the best lamb, by far, that the IABI man had ever laid lip upon. It was so much a better rack of lamb than he had ever eaten before that he couldn't believe it.

He said to Mark Donald, after washing the first mouthful down with a swallow of excellent French rosé that came chilled in a long-necked bottle, "I thought you didn't have anything but rabbit and chicken up here."

Donald laughed in deprecation. "The Imperator of Basra sent it as a special present to Doc Ryan. Whole carcasses of it."

Pete eyed him. "The Imperator? Hell, he's in oil. When Island One and the islands that followed really get into production with those SPS's microwaving power down to Earth, the Iraqis will be up the creek with no means of propulsion."

Donald laughed lightly again. "Wizard. But he's also got the space dream. Absolutely around the bend about it. From what I've heard, he's stuck a couple of billion-odd dollars into Lagrange Five Corporation stock. Hedging his bets, I suppose. The oil can't last forever anyway.

He might as well get in on where the real action is going to be."

Pete took on some more of the superlative lamb. It wasn't just the lamb. The vegetables and the salad were equally superb.

He said, "These vegetables you grow up here are really in there."

"Eh?" the other said vaguely. Then, "Oh, yeah. We grow a lot of our vegetables hydroponically."

"Not all?"

"Well, no," the other admitted. "Not as yet. We even have to send up some dehydrated."

Pete said, "What you say about the Imperator and all the stock he's bought gives me heart. I've got a few thousand in LFC common myself."

The other nodded to that. "I suppose just about everybody Earthside has."

Pete said, "How'd you get into this, Mark? I mean, what's your background for being a Security lieutenant?"

The other frowned slightly before saying, "I took my doctorate in the social sciences at New Kingston. Anthropology."

Pete regarded him, taken aback. "Doctorate? At New Kingston, eh? The first university to edge into the Ivy League in a century. It's Doctor Solomon Ryan's school too, isn't it?"

"That's right. Try some of this wine. The Rothschild people sent it up from their own vineyards. Yeah, Doc Ryan and his colleagues first dreamed up the whole Lagrange Five Project at New Kingston. The Alma Mater still doesn't get quite as many of the government and foundation grants as, say, Yale and Harvard, but we're coming up fast."

Pete said, still murmuring pleasure at his dish, "Anthropology, eh? That was a favorite of mine when I was a kid. But there's damn little future in it. Teaching is

110

about all you can do on graduation. I dropped out when I got a chance to get into IABI. I used to specialize on the Aztecs and the other pre-Colombian Mexicans. Did you ever get into Lewis Henry Morgan's *Ancient Society*, or his shorter work, *Montezuma's Dinner*?"

"Who?" the Security man said.

Pete looked at the other, frowning. "Morgan. The Father of American Ethnology."

"Oh, him. Well, not much. Father of American Ethnology. Kind of old hat these days, isn't he?"

"I wouldn't say so," Pete said stiffly. "His comparisons of Aztec society to the gens system of Ancient Rome are revolutionary. Besides. . . ."

The Security man said, "About this afternoon. Would you like to take a crack at the data banks and see if you can locate your man from those photographs?"

Pete put down his fork and sighed in repletion. "I suppose so. The sooner, the better. If that lead falls flat, damned if I know where to start, otherwise."

After a fantastic pastry dessert and a black cherry liqueur, Pete was feeling no pain as they took off for the data rooms.

The offices could have been in the IABI building in Greater Washington: that was Pete Kapitz's first reaction. Room after room of files and humming business machines, a dozen or so young men and women, all in white smocks, working over them, not bothering to look up as Donald and his charge passed through.

They wound up in a small office equipped with the usual in scanners, boosters, a voco-typer, several screens, all clustered at one metallic desk.

"Here you are," the Security man told him. "Ask for anything you want in this screen here."

Pete sat himself at the desk, put his attaché case before him. He sighed, "I suppose this'll take me the rest of the day, and probably into at least tomorrow."

Mark Donald nodded at that. "Look," he said, "you won't be leaving the hotel. Suppose I go do some things that have accumulated. I'll meet you in the dining room at eight-thirty. Then later we can go to the party. It should be quite a fling. The Prince has brought up everything except some of his mopsies, or his boys, or whatever he's into."

"Wizard," Pete said, opening his case and bringing forth the three photos he had showed Al Moore earlier.

"See you then," Donald said and left.

Pete Kapitz looked after him for a moment and then down at the photos. They were fakes. The Inter-American Bureau of Investigation had no photos in its archives of Rocks Weil, nor any other clues to his identity. Nor did he, Peter Kapitz, have any belief whatsoever that the international jewel thief was in Island One. In fact, for all he knew, it *had* been Weil who had been shot by the French in Nice. If it hadn't been for that romp in London that looked so much like a Rocks Weil job, Pete would have been inclined to write the other off for all time. But it was as good a cover as he could think of. Obviously, both Mark Donald and his superior, Commissioner Moore, had swallowed the story.

For half an hour, he went through the motions of checking out the dossiers of the space colonists. Then he decided the hell with it. He might as well go out on the town and find what he could find. He still thought that Roy Thomas, the President's brain-trust, had holes in his head when it came to the Lagrange Five Project. But an assignment was an assignment and he'd been promised a bonus. He'd pry into anything up here that looked as though it could use some prying into. Personally, he still had the space dream and thus far he'd seen precious little to chill it.

He put the photos back into the attaché case and came to his feet preparatory to leaving.

*   *   *   *

On the top floor of the L5 Hilton, Mark Donald re-entered the office of the Commissioner of Security. Sergeant Joe Evola had just come in before him and was standing before Al Moore's desk.

"Sit down, boys," Al told them. He looked them over. "Wizard," he said. "You got anything to report on the trip up, Joe?"

The taciturn Security man shook his head. "Not really, Al. It was standard routine. I sat around with this Kapitz and the little group he hung out with as often as possible."

"Who were they?" Donald said, taking out a notepad and stylo.

"That writer guy, Bruce Carter. A new contract man, some electrician named Rick Venner, and that soft-headed mopsy Mary Beth Houston, the secretary of the Friends of Lagrange Five. Then there were a couple of others that'd come and go, sit in for a hand of cards or something."

"What'd they say about the project?" Al Moore said, his eyes narrow.

"Standard stuff. The broad evidently thinks Lagrange Five shit doesn't stink. Carter asks questions and listens, but doesn't say much on his own."

"And Kapitz?"

"He's not as hot for it as the girl, nobody could be; but he's obviously pretty keen about space colonies himself."

"He is, eh?" Moore mused. "Could be a bluff. He looked at Donald. "Where's the bastard now?"

"I left him in the data rooms, supposedly checking out Rocks Weil."

Moore nodded. "Now he thinks you're out of his way, he'll probably take off on his own, snooping." He turned his eyes to Joe Evola. "Keep on him. We want to see if he makes a contact. The sonofabitch must have somebody up here. If the KGB has an operative in the island, there's no reason to believe the IABI hasn't."

"The first space community would house 10,000 people; 4,000 would be employed building additional colonies, while 6,000 would be producing satellite solar power station." —"Space Colonies: The High Frontier," by Gerard O'Neill, The Futurist, *February 1976.*

Chapter Seven

Rick Venner's reception at the docking port of Island One had differed considerably from that of the others, who'd been taken to the Lagrange Hilton. Rick and two other construction workers who had come in on the *Tsiolkowsky* were met and checked out by an arrogant clerk, who read off their names flourishing his clipboard like a sceptre. Carrying their own bags, the new-hire workers were led to the monorail and taken through the tunnel to the terminal; but their destination was not the island's sole hotel. They were led out the main entry into the street and, making their way on foot, proceeded to a fair-sized building a few hundred feet along the pavement.

One of the three, the youngest contract worker, looked around as he progressed. "Sure doesn't look like the Tri-Di shows," he said, a touch of dismay in his voice.

"Nothing ever looks like Tri-Di shows it," the clerk said flatly. "In real life, did you ever see any mopsies stacked like Tri-Di starlets? What the hell did you expect, sour cream in your borscht? You came here to work, not gawk."

Rick gave him the once-over from the corner of his eye. With that slight, carefully deliberate exaggeration of gentleness that spells "menace" he said to the clerk, "What's the matter, chum-pal—don't you like us poor people? Or is it that we're new up here; or friendless?"

"That's my business," the clerk sniffed.

"Let me tell you something about the construction business," said Rick, making an educated guess into a veiled threat: "We won't long stay poor. Or new. Or friendless. That's because we have good memories."

The clerk looked up nervously at Rick. All three of the new workers looked as if they'd been around and kept in shape—and they all outweighed the clerk. His adam's apple bobbing, the clerk looked away. "This way, gentlemen," he said with respect.

He led them to a dormitory that had space for a hundred men. The quarters weren't exactly reassuring; in fact, they were stark. The sole bedding consisted of two off-white sheets over a thin, hard mattress, and a small pillow covered with the same material—some durable synthetic almost as heavy as denim.

The clerk said, "This is the induction center. You'll be here until you're assigned to your jobs, and until you make arrangements for permanent quarters. Some of the men, singles, prefer to stay—I suppose for the companionship," he sniffed. "The location is up to you. Pick your own bunks."

The metal bunks were three high along the walls. None of the top ones and only a few on the second level were strewn with the magazines, clothing, or other articles that indicated occupancy.

Rick and a tough, rangy Texan he'd met glancingly on the way up, simultaneously swung their bags onto the sole unclaimed lower-level bunk. The Texan, with a level look at Rick, said, "I had it first."

Rick shrugged. "I make it a dead heat. Tell you what: I'll match you for it." He brought a coin from a coverall pocket. "Or are you a short sport?"

The other grinned, then gave a curious glance at the coin. "What's that thing?"

"A half-dollar. You know; currency, like your grandpaw used." Rick showed it off. "A head on one side, and the other side is called "tails." I flip it, you call heads or tails. If you're right, you get the bunk."

"Huh. I remember somethin' about that. Well, I say you'll flip heads up."

Rick flicked the coin, let it fall to the floor. It came up tails. "Sorry," he murmured. "Lady Luck's a fickle bitch."

The other glowered but took his bag and slung it to the bunk just above.

"It's just as well," Rick said affably. "You wouldn't want me above you anyway. I'm a bed-wetter."

Beneath each bunk were three small drawers. Rick unpacked, crumpled his flimsy luggage up and stuck it in, too. He kicked off his shoes, climbed into the metal bed, put his hands behind his head, and stared up at the bottom of the bunk above. It was so near his nose he could barely focus his eyes on it. Rick had never been in a prison, but he suspected that most prisons had more spacious quarters than these.

"Home was never like this," he muttered. He thought back about some swank hotels he'd known. "Neither was the Paris Ritz," he added.

He relaxed, waiting for developments, until he had almost dozed off. He could hear the clerk showing others around, pointing out the showers, dining room, and assembly room, which doubled as a library and Tri-Di room. Rick didn't bother; in his true profession, you got your bearings in moments.

He was aroused by a voice calling, "Venner? Rick Venner? Is there a Rick Venner here? Speak up, lad."

Rick tried to sit erect, banging his head on the Texan's

bunk and swearing. He swung his legs to the floor, got into his shoes, came to his feet. "That's me," he called.

The man who came up to him, beaming, was possibly forty-five and obviously an old pro construction man. He shook hands with controlled energy. "You're a sight for sore eyes, lad," he said. "Been waiting for you. Waiting for half a year, in fact."

Rick let his arm be pumped and said, "But I only signed up a month or so ago."

The other stepped back a pace and eyed him enthusiastically. "Wizard, but I've needed a half-dozen more experienced lads for so long I can't remember. Haven't worked in space before at all, have you? Down in low-Earth orbit, or wherever?"

Rick shook his head. He tried to recall the details of the papers Pavel Meer had forged for him. "Mostly oil rigs, bridges; a couple of tunnels."

The older man was clearly disappointed, but ready for that disappointment. He was a bluff, friendly, loud-voiced sort, banged-up of face, rough as unaged tequila. He had a flash of gold in his mouth in a day when cosmetic dentistry could hide the fact that you had any dentures at all. Two of the man's front teeth were solid, gleaming gold. Rick had the damndest feeling that, at one time or another, the man had willingly hocked those gold teeth when he needed money between jobs.

"No deep-sea experience?" The question held forlorn hope.

" 'Fraid not. Why'd you ask?"

"You'd be surprised how similar diving suit work is to working in a spacesuit. Some of our best lads are deep-sea men. Oh, well, you can't ask for every—oh, the devil! I'm Davis. Freddy Davis, Rick; your supervisor. Should've said that first, eh?"

They had moved over to the benches that lined the long metallic table in the center of the sleeping room. Davis looked around and said, "A helluva place to pad out, this. As soon as possible you'll want to team up with a buddy or two; get an apartment or a house. They aren't much better, but at least you get privacy. At least they're someplace you can take a mopsy—if you can find one."

"I'll keep it in mind," Rick said. "Where'll I be working?"

"Ah. Outside on the hull, at present. Lots of bugs out there, lad. Whoever designed this thing down Earthside may have been a great pastry cook, or tap dancer, but he was sure as hell no engineer, for my money."

"I can hardly wait to get to it," Rick said, hoping it was what the older man wanted to hear.

Davis, beaming at his new assistant, shot a glance at his wrist. "I'm between shifts now. You can get processed and suit-fitted and start tomorrow. Meanwhile, long as you don't have to work a full shift in a bad fit, we can rustle you a borrowed suit so you can go outside the hull." The gleam in Davis's eyes was that of a teenager. "Want to pop outside for a look at the job? Lunch isn't for a couple of hours."

An excuse was on the tip of Rick's tongue, but it was high time he learned what those pills really did. "Wizard," he said, "soon as I get a drink of water." And the pill that goes down with it.

*   *   *   *

An hour later, after the brief excursion outside multiple airlocks and the pill-induced nightmare, Rick Venner found himself half-dragged to a metal stool in the innermost airlock. He struggled to sit up, his face greenish, panting like a dog. Tears ran down his cheeks, and those weren't the only signs of distress.

Freddy Davis unsealed a gauntlet and laid a friendly hand on Rick's shoulder. "You'll be all right, lad," he soothed.

Rick managed to say, "Jeee-*zus!*"

"Let's get you out of that suit and clean it—and you—up."

Rick followed the other to the suit-up room, staggering. "Holy Jesus, Freddy; what happened?" It shamed him that he knew.

"Just a touch of space sickness. Somebody once said if you combine vertigo with paranoia, this is what you get. Not all that uncommon for a first-timer, lad. Go on, get into that shower. You know how spacers shower?"

"I'm not sure."

"Like showering in a ship in the old days when fresh water was short. First wet yourself down. Turn off the water, lather up good, then rinse it off quick."

Rick stared at him. "Water shortage? Up here?"

"Durn tootin'—we're short on everything good up here," said Davis grimly. "Oh yeah, we were supposed to have plenty of everything, soon as the closed ecosystem recycled it all. Wizard; only they haven't got it working yet. We get oxygen from refining lunar ores, but to get water we have to combine it with hydrogen, and that has to come from Earthside. And large-scale recycling isn't quite perfect. Sometimes it reminds you that you're drinking recycled piss. You earn your pay up here, lad."

Rick cleaned up. The effects of the pill weren't quite as bad as Meer, the Penman, had warned. But he'd vomited and was drenched with sweat. His bowels, at least, hadn't come unglued. So far, everything was going as planned, discounting a nagging guilt that Rick seldom knew.

He returned to the dressing room to find that Davis had found him a fresh set of coveralls. As he dressed, the other tried to reassure him. "This isn't all that rare, lad. Hell of a lot of guys got space sick when we first started this project. These days, Earthside medics and at the *Goddard* catch most of those too prone to it. They get rotated back fast. But cases like yours usually get adjusted after two or three tries."

"Two or three?" Rick's anguish was plain. "I have to go through that several times? I mean—you're out there without anything solid under you, and there's Earth with nothing between you and it but about a million miles of falling."

Davis's smile was on a bias. "Actually only a quarter-million miles. Just rest up, and in a couple of days we'll give it another try. You'll be surprised how much easier it'll be."

"I can't believe I'm a flop," Rick said. "After looking forward to this for so long, and now look at me."

Davis patted his shoulder roughly, in man-to-man affection. "Don't believe that. You'll make out. I know a good worker when I see one, and Lord knows I need some good electrical engineers. You'll get used to free fall."

"It didn't bother me on the way up. But out there . . ." He shook his head. "A hundred dollars says I can't hack it."

"I'll take that bet," Davis told him, "just to show I believe in you. Come on. Let's get back to your dorm so you can get some lunch, such as it is."

Back at the induction center dorm, Freddy Davis pointed out the dining hall. "I won't be eating there," he said. "I've got my family here and we have our own place."

Another coveralled man, already seated at the long community table, looked up sourly. "You forgot to mention that you're a supervisor, so you don't have to eat this swill."

Freddy Davis, a veteran at handling construction workers, pretended to take the slur as a joke, though there was an unhappy element of apology beneath his words. As Rick took a place at the long metal table, Freddy said, "You know how it is, lads. It took me a good many years to work myself up to supervisor."

"Yeah," the disgruntled one said around his food.

"And things aren't so bad for you bosses. From what I hear, they live like fucking gods over there in the L5 Hilton."

Freddy Davis ignored him and gave Rick a last clap on the shoulder. "I'll see you in a couple of days, Rick," he said. "Get yourself oriented and try to line up some buddies so you can get into a private pad."

"Wizard," Rick told him, making his voice sound embarrassed. "Sorry I made such a spectacle of myself."

"Forget it." The other turned and left.

About twenty were eating. The places were set with aluminum plates, knives, and forks. There were large metal bowls and plates in the center of the table. Rick reached out for one of the bowls.

Across from him, a fellow diner said sourly, "Eat hearty, mate. Today's treat day. We've got shit-on-a-shingle for the main course. At least it's better than everlasting stringy rabbit and scrawny chicken."

Rick looked at him.

"Shit-on-a-shingle," the other said. "I can see you've never been in the military. Dried beef, cut tissue-paper thin, and cooked up into a gravy with dehydrated milk and flour. You get it on toast. I sure as hell never thought I'd live to see the day I'd think it was a treat."

One of the other said, his voice just as lemonish, "Stop your whining, Jeff. When you signed up, did you figure there'd be a branch of *Antonio*'s New Orleans restaurant up here? Shucks, today we've got fresh carrots from the hydroponic farm."

Rick filled his plate from the unappetizing-looking bowls of food and set to. He had never eaten dehydrated food before in his life, save a small amount of it on the spaceship coming up. Except for the carrots, which proved to be on the tasteless side, this was all dehydrated, save for the bread. He assumed that there was no manner of dehydrating flour beyond its already dry state. He looked down at the food in dismay and realized, upon looking up, that the other newcomers, including the Texan whose bunk he had done him out of, were doing the same. A universal laugh came up from the older hands seated. Seemingly, it was a standing joke, watching space tyros eating their first meal in Island One.

Projecting his usual good humor, Rick said, "It's obviously pretty rugged here in Island One, but I imagine when the larger islands get built, things will soften up."

"What larger islands?" one of the old-timers scoffed.

Rick looked down the table at him. "Islands Two and Three, and, later on, even Four. The big ones. Holding millions of space colonists eventually."

Almost all of them laughed at that.

The one named Jeff, a scrawny little man with complaint built into his wizened face, said, "Island Two, ha! We'll never finish Island One. They can keep pouring money down the drain until the Sahara floods over, but they'll never finish this one, let alone ever get around to starting Island Two."

The Texan, who was seated across from Rick, was scowling. He said, complete with a drawl that could only have come from the vicinity of San Antonio, "What-all's wrong with the way this island's going? I can see there's a lot of work to be done, but . . ."

He'd set several of them to chuckling anew.

Jeff, who seemed to be the most talkative, shook a fork at the larger man and said, "Everything's wrong with it. And most of it shoulda been seen before it was ever started. The eggheads who dreamed this whole Lagrange Five Project up were a bunch of college professors and scientists. Damn few, if any, of them, had any practical experience. When they got out of their own fields, they supplied the missing parts off the tops of their heads. Everything's gone wrong. That moon base where they're supposed to lob up raw material for us to smelter up here and use to build everything is a laugh. The Solar Satellite Power Stations aren't reliable. At least, not yet. The microwaving of power down to Earth has so many bugs in it they oughta spray it with insecticides. The ecology system here in the island hasn't gotten off the ground and practically everything has to be shipped up from Earth; hydrogen, food, nitrogen. The ore smelter here in space don't work. The radiators can't get rid of all the heat they generate. In short, everything's fucked up."

The Texan was looking unhappier by the minute. He said, "What's wrong with the moon base? I'm supposed to go over that way."

One of the other complainers took over. "We call it Siberia," he said. "From the first, it was a balls-up. The plans set by Doc Ryan and the others called for 200 men to run the moon base. Two hundred men, shit. First they were supposed to be landed there and set up a community. Then they were to build that eleven-kilometer mass-driver monorail, all lined up to a fraction of a fraction so the packages of lunar ore they lobbed up would hit the Catcher, 35,000 miles off. The Catcher is only 100 meters across, about three hundred feet. How'd you like to hit a target that small from 35,000 miles away? That gives you an allowable error of .00017 percent."

"What went wrong?" Rick asked. He was irritated by all this. Damn it, if he was going to be out here for five years, he didn't want the project to be a fouled-up mess.

"Everything," the other said. "Take that figure of 200 men. Break it down. Say you have a steward department of a dozen people. They cook the food, they serve it, they make the beds, they do the laundry, they sweep the floors, and all the rest of it, like on a ship. Then you have the medical department—the doctors, the nurses, the clinic attendants, the X-ray and other technicians. You think you could get by with a smaller medical department on a danger spot like the moon? Don't kid yourself. They have to be ready for everything. On an oil rig, off the coast, if a man gets hurt or sick and they don't have the facilities to take care of him on the rig, they send him by helicopter to shore and to the nearest hospital. But not at the moon base. He'd be dead before they got him to Island One or Earthside. They've got to take care of every medical eventuality on the spot. Then there's the office workers, including the communications people, also working three shifts every 24 Earth hours. There's a lot of paperwork, computer work, supervising, and all involved. That's another 25 people, at least. Then there's the maintenance people, maintaining everything from the computers and the communications equipment to the vehicles and all the equipment devoted to air, water, solar power, the nuclear plant, and even the electric typewriters and kitchen stoves. Don't think there isn't a lot of machinery involved in that damned moon base. And don't think that just anybody can repair it. A lot of it's awfully sophisticated. There goes another 25 men."

"Holy smog," the Texan protested. "You've already hardly got anybody left."

"Yeah. And there's another small item or two. How about broads? Are you going to have two hundred men up there for periods of at least a year or eighteen months at a stretch, as the egg-head saw it, without any kind of relaxation? You know what happens to guys who are locked up without mopsies in prison or in concentration camps, or labor camps like in Siberia? They go queer, that's what happens. Hell, even sailors have a bad reputation. You'd better have at least ten broads up there, willing and able to put out. Maybe some of them could double as waitresses and so forth in the reception hall, but they'd have to be available for getting laid when a man wanted some nooky."

"Jesus," Rick laughed.

"There's another item," the other pursued. "With two hundred men, you better figure on five percent being on the sick list. That's a conservative figure for a dangerous location like the moon. That means you've got ten men in the sick bay at any given time, some of them waiting to be shipped back to Earthside, some of them waiting for broken arm or leg to heal. Oh, ten men is a conservative figure."

"Is there anybody left at all to mine the ore and send it off?" Rick said.

"Add it up," Jeff told him. "But just a minute. That's not all. We're not through yet. How about the spaceship field? There's one hell of a lot of space shuttles, space tugs and so forth, coming and going from the moon base. You've got to have pilots, engineers, mechanics, men to handle the freight, refuel the ships, control tower technicians, and all the rest. Let's say twenty-five again, which is low, always remembering that everything goes on a three-shift Earthday basis. Now that totals 145 people, including the broads who are working at things other than mining that ore, freighting it over to the mass driver, packaging it and loading it into the mass driver buckets. So we've got 55 men left to handle the basic operation, lobbing ore into space. Working three shifts, that's 18 men on a shift. Remember that monorail, so carefully calibrated, is 11 kilometers long—about 6.5 miles. If you had your men stationed along that delicately balanced, carefully aligned monorail, one every third of a mile, for adjustments, lubrication, and troubleshooting in general, you'd use up all 18 of your men. You could also use up the whole number packaging and loading up the mass driver."

"How about automation?" the Texan said unhappily.

"Sure, automation. Everywhere it makes sense. But machinery on the moon is another thing. Big swings in temperature, one-sixth gravity, and so forth. Lava dust all over the place to gum up anything mechanically delicate. If you boost your automation, you're sure as hell going to have to boost that 25 maintenance men."

A newcomer lowered himself into the place next to

Rick. Rick glanced over at him. A man about his own age and physical build, seemingly a bit shifty of dark eyes but with an ingratiating little smile.

He grinned and whispered to Rick, "The usual beefing brigade in full voice?"

Rick said, "Yeah. I guess so."

"I'm Tony Black."

"Rick Venner," Rick said. "I just got in. Is there anything in what these characters are saying?"

"Some. You'll hear it all, a hundred times over." The other reached for food. "How're things going, Rocks?" His voice was still low, as though avoiding disturbing the controversy.

Rick's face froze.

Tony Black grinned a small grin and whispered, "I'm your contact up here. We'll talk after lunch."

Rick had nothing to say to that. What contact? He hadn't known anything about contacting anyone in Island One. He thought that he was completely clear now.

The Texan was still bravely holding forth. He demanded, "Why not just up the crew working on the mining and the mass driver? Send in, say, another fifty men?"

A newcomer to the conversation, who had finished his food, or, at least, that part of it that he managed to get down, said with a bitter laugh, "Sure. And when you do, you up everything else. First you've got to construct bigger living quarters, make arrangements for more grub, air, water, and all the rest. You've got to increase the size of the hospital, the steward department, everything, including the number of broads. To feed all these new additions, you've got to send up more spaceships from Earth. And an extra fifty still isn't enough men."

"Why not?" one of the other space tyros, who hadn't spoken up thus far, said. He was the youth who had pointed out on the street on the way to the dormitory that Lagrange Five City wasn't exactly as portrayed in the Tri-Di shows.

Jeff, who seemingly carried half the conversation load at the community table, took over again. "Because the fucking mass driver doesn't work, and the fucking smelters here in Lagrange Five don't work. Practically nothing the eggheads dreamed up works. We've had to improvise. First of all, the ore doesn't get to us, because the catcher doesn't catch it, even when it gets off the moon okay. Not all of it, at least. Some gets through. But with the smelters a disaster, we've been doing the smelting at the Luna base, then shipping up sheet metal by rocket to moon orbit, and then pushing the stuff over here to Lagrange Five by space tug. And if you think that's not a damn sight more expensive than they originally figured, you're drivel-happy, and if you think that it involves less than a couple of thousand people, you're crazier still. It's still cheaper than sending everything up from Earth, but it's nothing like the original idea."

The Texan was flabbergasted.

Rick said, ignoring his new contact for the moment, "you mean out of the ten thousand workers up here, two thousand are on the moon base? I never heard that down Earthside."

"What ten thousand?" one of the others growled. "That's another one of those egghead goof-offs. They said there'd be ten thousand people here; four thousand would be employed building additional colonies, while six thousand would be producing satellite solar power stations. Wizard, but who was supposed to be running the island? Who was going to be keeping the hydroponic farms going, regulating the air and water, running all the equipment involved in maintaining a space colony? Who was going to be teaching the kids? Who was going to be taking care of the hospitals? Who was going to handle the office work? It's the same story as the moon base; you're lucky to get half of your people out doing

129

the actual work you came to do. But there's something else involved here in Island One. The original dream Ryan and his Lagrange Five Corporation sold us on was that we were going to be space colonists, not just temporary contract workers. We could bring up our families. Wizard, some of us did. And when you bring a family, it includes kids and even some old folks. Swell. They don't work. They eat, but they don't work. And neither do quite a few of the wives. Supposedly, the married couples that came up were both to have jobs. But many women can't do anything but white-collar jobs, medical jobs such as nursing, or maybe restaurant work. And when they're pregnant, or the baby's small, they can't even do that. And, like Jeff said, there's always five percent or more of everybody on sick call." The speaker snorted. "If anybody thinks there's 10,000 highly trained workers up here, all working their asses off building more space colonies and SPS's, he's around the bend."

Both Rick and Tony Black had finished eating. They got up together and the new acquaintance led Rick into the assembly room and to an isolated corner of it where they took chairs facing each other.

Rick said, "Now then, what's all this jetsam about being my contact?"

The other smiled and said, "It was a three-way operation, Rocks. The Penman, down in Mexico, Monk Ravelle at the New Albuquerque shuttleport, and me up here. It had to be handled all the way along the line."

"What do you mean, it *was* a three way operation?"

"The Penman's dead, Rocks. So is Monk Ravelle."

Rick fixed his eyes on him, they were pale and cold. "Who killed them?"

"I don't know," the other said. "Somebody Earthside evidently took a dim view of our little operation. It couldn't have been something else because that was the only scam the two of them were involved in together."

"Holy Zoroaster," Rick snorted. "And on top of everything else, there's a damn IABI man came up with me on the shuttle and then the freight passenger spacecraft. Guess who he's looking for? Rocks Weil. Thank sweet Jesus he didn't make me."

Tony Black looked less than happy. "You're going to *need* a contact up here, Rocks. By the way, you owe me five thousand dollars."

The other eyed him. "Why?"

"It's my share of the deal."

"Pavel Meer said the tab was ten thousand. I gave it to him."

Black shook his head. "That doesn't count me. I take care of this end for five thousand."

"I haven't got that much left."

The other looked at him unbelievingly. "What was the score of that last romp of yours, Rocks?"

"It's stashed. I haven't fenced the stones yet. I planned to lay doggo for five years before trying."

"There's no hurry. You're making ten thousand a year up here, not counting the twenty thousand a year bonus payable in LFC stock when your five years are up. I can wait."

"What good can you do me?" Rick said coldly.

The other grinned his sly grin. "You'd be surprised." He motioned with his head toward the dining room. "How'd you like to eat that slop for the next five years? And sleep in a bunk like they assigned you?"

"I wouldn't."

"Wizard. Get your things. I've got a two-person house. You're moving in with me."

"Why?"

"My former housemate found himself a mopsy working in Commissary and moved in with her. I've got to find another guy to take his place or move into either smaller quarters or into a dormitory. No thanks. You'd

131

better take the offer. It's more comfortable than most pads."

Rick eyed him suspiciously. "You must know other people better than you do me. Why give me the break?"

Tony Black grinned his weasel grin again. "Because you're Rocks Weil, one of the smartest operators to come down the track for years. And there're various profitable operations in this island. Now that my deal with the Penman is off, I'm going to have to go even further into them. I wouldn't mind a helping hand from a talent such as yourself." He grinned wider. "Besides, I've got to protect my investment. You owe me five grand."

Rick thought about it. He said, "Look, I'll tell you what I'll do. The Penman didn't tell me about five thousand for you. The deal was for a flat ten thou. But I'll match you for it. Double or nothing."

Tony Black laughed in open admiration. "By Christ, Rocks, you're a card. Why do you think I want you in with me? Paul Lund, in Tangier, gave me a rundown on your career once. You must've been no more than ten years old when you started off, conning the kids in the neighborhood out of their lunch money. Before you got into heists, you were a pro gambler, then a grifter specializing in the big score. Then you worked out your own system of putting the snatch on important stones and flogging them to offbeat millionaire winchells. That's where you got the moniker Rocks. Well, Rocks, I wouldn't match pennies with you."

Rick had to grin back at him. "I'll get my things," he said.

He went back to his bunk and began reassembling his belongings.

The Texan came over and said, "Y'all leaving already?"

"That's right. So the bunk's yours after all. Be seeing you around, Tex."

"Probably not," the other said gloomily. "They'll be sending me over to that there moon base the boys was telling us about."

Rick took up his bag. "They were probably exaggerating," he said, with an attempt at comfort.

As they walked along the narrow street, Rick said to his newfound house companion, "Your place very far?"

The other grunted. "Nothing's very far in Island One," he said. "The length of the whole cylinder is less than a mile. You get used to it after a while." He thought about that, then said, "Like shit you do."

Rick had been eyeing the buildings they passed and decided that the only word was grim. Come to think of it, so were the expressions on most of the pedestrians they passed.

He said, "Been here long?"

"Three years."

"Pretty rugged?"

The other looked over at him. "Rugged enough, Rocks. But there're always angles. And there're always people like us to find them."

Rick inwardly accepted that. It had been his own experience.

Tony Black came up on a small, two-story house. "This is us," he said, in deprecation. "The Maison Black."

They entered, Rick noting that there was no lock on the door. The whole ground floor was taken up by a living room, rather sparsely furnished. There was a dark blue rug covering most of the floor, of a material the newcomer had never seen before.

Black saw the direction of his eyes. "Beta-cloth," he said. "They make it out of woven glass fiber. It was originally used by the Apollo astronauts because it's fireproof. We're beginning to make it up here now. Not much, though. Can't spare the time and labor."

"How'd you get some, then?"

Black grinned. Rick was beginning to dislike the other's

version of a smile. It had too much of a sly, furtive quality.

Black said, "Like I said, I've got angles. Come on upstairs. I'll show you your room."

They went up the stairs. On the second floor there were two rather small bedrooms. Rick was led into one of them. It was austerely furnished. There was a bed, admittedly with more comfortable-looking bedding than the dormitories boasted, and obviously brought up from Earthside. There were a table, one straight chair, one more comfortable chair, a bedstand with a lamp on it, a small chest of drawers. There was also a small closet.

Black said, apologetically, "Roony took most of his things with him. We'll get you fixed up as time goes by."

Rick said, "No TV or Tri-Di?" He hadn't seen any such equipment down in the living room either.

"Are you kidding?" Black snorted. "They have them over in the L5 Hilton and in some of the community recreation halls, but private sets aren't for such as us. These items have to be lobbed up from Earth. Plenty expensive."

"Where's the bathroom?"

"What bathroom? There's a community bathhouse down the street—toilets and showers."

Rick took him in. "Where's the kitchen?"

"What kitchen? We eat at one of the community dining halls. Smarten up, Rocks. They can't ship in thousands of flush toilets, bathtubs, kitchen stoves, refrigerators, kitchen sinks, and all the rest of such items as go into bathrooms and kitchens. And we sure as hell can't tool up to make them here; not yet. The only places they've got such things, in private quarters, is in the hotel and in some of the homes of the big shots who keep their own places, rather than living there."

Rick whistled softly. He put his bag on the bed. "Five years, eh? I suspect I'd rather serve it in New Alcatraz."

"You shoulda thought of that before you signed up, Rocks."

Rick sat on the bed and eyed the other. He said, "You better start remembering to call me Rick. Rick Venner. Especially with that IABI man pussyfooting around looking for me. What's this about the L5 Hilton?"

His newfound companion sat in the more comfortable chair. "It's the showplace. It's where the Lagrange Five Corporation has its headquarters and where Ryan and the top executives live. It's where all the politicians and the other big shots stay when they come up from Earthside. It's got everything—mopsies and all. From what I hear, they're going to have a big party tonight, undoubtedly with champagne and such. Some Arab sheik or something came up on the same passenger freighter you did. I don't know why. And some big shot Russian scientist."

"How do you get an invite?" Rick said.

"You don't." Tony Black grinned his sly grin. "And you don't sneak in, either. Not in those space coveralls. In the Hilton, they dress like they were down Earthside, in some swanky resort. You'd stand out like a hard-on in the showers. Look, I got some things to do. They'll keep me out until late. The community dining hall is down the street about eight houses. Turn right when you leave the house. We'll get together in the morning and work this all out—get you registered as living here and all."

He stood and nodded to Rick. "Make yourself to home, Rocks . . . uh, Rick."

After he had left, Rick looked about the sparse room again. He muttered, "And the Waldorf Towers was never like this, either."

He waited ten minutes, then came to his feet, went out into the hall, and let himself into the other bedroom.

It was considerably different from his own, to his surprise. There were drapes at the windows that must have come up from Earthside. There was carpeting on the floor. There was also more, and more comfortable, furniture—including a chest of drawers that doubled as a bar, with several bottles on its top. The liquor represented was the best. Rick poured himself a double Scotch and knocked it back.

He whistled softly to himself and then went to the closet. Inside were three Earthside suits that looked as though they had been tailored in London. Rick Venner knew London styles and London labels. In his time, he had been flush often enough to invest in them. He ran his tongue across his upper lip. Come to think of it, they'd fit him very neatly. Friend Tony was almost his size. There was also a considerable collection of packaged, canned, and bottled food, obviously Earthside. He thoughtfully peeled a bar of chocolate and almonds and munched on it as he pried around.

He turned back to the bedroom and investigated his host's dresser drawers. There were shirts, socks, silk underwear, and dress shoes. There were even some of the currently faddish Byron revival cravats.

Rick Venner's eyes went easy. "You know," he said softly, aloud. "It looks as though there's going to be an additional guest at that party tonight."

"My impression is that there are cheaper ways, ways less demanding of capital, to satisfy any goal put forward by the L5 effort—to do that on Earth rather than to do it in space. . . . What are needed to solve these problems on Earth are different values and institutions— a better attitude toward equity, a loss of the growth ethic, and so forth. I would rather work at the root of the problem here."
—Dennis Meadows, co-author of The Limits of Growth; Dynamics of Growth in a Finite World.

Chapter Eight

Carl Gatena was awaiting Bruce Carter when the freelance writer returned to the L5 Hilton with the Security man who had found him in the park talking with Pal Barack. In fact, the flack was pacing up and down in agitation.

When Bruce entered, the other came up and said, "My chum-pal, I turn my back for a few minutes and you disappear."

"I got bored," Bruce shrugged. "And I guess I was anxious to get my first look at the island."

The other scowled puzzlement at him. "But the guards. How the hell did you get out without a pass or anybody to go with you?"

Bruce in turn seemed surprised. "I just walked out," he said in all innocence.

Carl Gatena closed his eyes wearily, opened them again, and looked at the Security man who had found the missing writer.

The Security officer said, "I found him in the park, talking with one of the workers."

Gatena said to Bruce, "What did he have to say?"

"Nothing much." Bruce shrugged it off, lacking interest. "I only spoke with him for a few minutes. He was one of the landscaping men. Largely, he told me his contract was up tomorrow and he was looking forward to returning to Earth."

"Didn't like it here, eh?"

The freelancer shrugged again. "He didn't seem to want to renew the contract."

The flack said, "Well, Ron's waiting for us. Shall we go on up?" He looked over at the Security man. "Be sure and check that other matter out."

"Yes, sir," the other said, touching the brim of his cap.

The publicity offices of Lagrange Five Project were on the second-to-the-top floor of the hotel. And they were on the extensive side. There must have been at least a dozen young men and women going about their business or seated at desks in the several rooms Bruce passed with his guide. Only two or three of them wore coveralls; the others were attired as they might have been in any office Earthside. At least there was some decoration here, the freelancer noted. It consisted largely of photographs and paintings pertaining to the Lagrange Five Project, including some depictions of the Luna base. As a matter of fact, Bruce had seen some of the color shots in Lagrange Five Corporation publicity down on Earth.

They wound up before a door a bit more ornate than usual. Gold lettering on it proclaimed simply, *Ron Rich, Director*. There was no identity screen. Carl Gatena knocked briskly and, without awaiting a response, took the knob in hand and opened the door, ushering Bruce through.

"Here he is, Chief," the flack said. "Elusive sonofagun."

Ron Rich was every inch the PR Man. He came to his feet, smiling broadly, absolutely beaming pleasure, and rounded his desk to shake hands. He was possibly five years older than Bruce and had the dynamic projection that the freelancer had long since come to associate with Madison Avenue publicity pros.

"So," the Chief of L5 Corporation's public relations happily said, "the famous Bruce Carter. I've been reading your stuff for years, Bruce. A real follower of yours."

"Thanks," Bruce told him. He smiled his slow smile, even as he took the extended hand. "Would you have told me if you hadn't liked it?"

"Hell, no," the other grinned. "I'm a flack by trade. We're all born liars. Sit down, Bruce. I recognize you from your book jacket covers, of course, and I've seen you from time to time on Tri-Di and TV panels. But it's a treat to meet you personally."

Bruce thanked him again and sat.

When the two publicity men had also taken seats he said, "It wasn't the easiest thing in the world to get up here. I've been trying to make it for years. It wasn't until I got next to Doctor Ryan himself, by phone, on one of his trips down Earthside, that I finally got permission."

The other nodded and looked very frank. "Yeah," he said. "And, to be truthful, it was no accident. We made every effort to keep you out—along with all other freelancers."

Bruce took him in, somewhat surprised at the admission. He said, "Why?"

"Because we can control most of the media. Among other things, we're big advertisers. Besides that, the same rich mucky-mucks who control the press and the airwaves are often big investors in the L5 Corporation. So just about all the coverage we get is upbeat. And that's a challenge to any freelance writer. If you could publish material really giving us the old boot, you'd hit the jackpot. So you come up with that in mind."

Bruce crossed his legs and said mildly, "By definition, a freelancer isn't necessarily a bastard. I don't make a practice of falsifying my material. If you've read as much of my stuff as you say, you would know that."

The publicity man sighed before answering. "You wouldn't have to falsify, Bruce. It would take precious little digging around for you to find material for a dozen anti-Lagrange Five Project pieces. Hell, you could do one of your famous muckraking books."

Bruce Carter felt his eyebrows go up in surprise. At least Ron Rich was pulling no punches.

"It's like this," the PR man went on. "To any layman, this project looks like a madhouse. For the pros—the scientists, the engineers, the technicians—sure, they have their problems every day, but they have the overall picture, and to them its just one hell of a big job that'll eventually be all wrapped up."

"I can see a certain amount of validity in that," Bruce admitted. "However, I'm not exactly green. I don't go dashing around throwing mud at things I don't understand."

Ron Rich pressed his point. "Suppose you were in an operating room, witnessing some long, complicated surgery—say, a heart transplant. There are a dozen doctors there and nurses and various medical technicians all over the place. It's a crazy bin. Everybody is scurrying around, there's blood all over. People are chanting out readings from all sorts of gismos. They all seem comparatively cool, but it's a madhouse from your viewpoint. Nurses slap gruesome-looking tools into the hands of doctors, other nurses swab the sweat off the foreheads of those surgeons in there with blood up to their elbows. Needles on dials up on gobbledygook devices keep swaying this way and that, and their readings are repeated by technicians watching them, flicking switches, pressing buttons. A real nut factory, so far as you're concerned."

Bruce began to say something but didn't.

"All right," the PR man said, "That's Island One of Lagrange Five. To you it looks like a lunatic asylum. Everything's going to pot. Everything looks like it came out of a science fiction horror Tri-Di show. But, you see, that's not the way it looks to Sol Ryan and the top technicians and engineers of the world. They know what's going on. They know when they do something wrong and it has to be rectified. And frankly, lots of things that go wrong, often through sheer stupidity on the part of somebody, can run into tens of millions of dollars. This is the biggest operation that the world has embarked upon. *Ever.* It makes the Great Wall of China look like a child playing with building blocks."

Bruce still held his peace.

The publicity man was breathing deeper now, in his earnestness. "Can you begin to see, Bruce, why we don't want muckraking, ambitious laymen up here? We can't even tell you what's going on—you don't have the background to understand it. You'd have to have a dozen degrees in half a dozen sciences to get the overall picture. Frankly, we're scared shitless of people like you. We can keep going in the science, the engineering, the technology of building these islands, but we can't adequately handle the problem of informing the public of just what's happening. The public doesn't have the know-how to understand and, let me be sincere, neither do you."

He laughed bitterly. "As a matter of fact, neither do I."

Carl Gatena, seated off to one side, laughed softly at that.

Ron Rich looked over at him for a moment, then said, "Carl, why don't you go look up that Mary Beth Houston girl, the perpetual emotion one, and butter her up a little?"

It was obviously a dismissal. Gatena came to his feet,

as always smiling, and said, "Sure, Chief. See you around later, Bruce."

Bruce said, "Yeah, sure, Carl."

When the underling had gone, Bruce turned back to the PR head. "Wizard," he said. "What's the answer? You don't want unknowledgeable writers around, sticking their feet in their mouths. But here I am. And my reputation is that I write it like I see it."

Ron Rich sighed deeply. He said, "Bruce, there are hundreds of billions of dollars involved. And it's not just the money we get from grants from governments and foundations, or the billions that come from big investors buying into the corporation, or the union pension funds, or the mutual funds. It's the millions of ordinary people investing money they often can't afford. We can't let somebody come along and, for a few lousy bucks, throw a lot of shit in the fan that might disillusion half the world."

"Wizard," Bruce said again, recrossing his legs. "So what is the answer?"

The other leaned forward earnestly. In his day, Bruce Carter had never met anyone who could be so earnest as a publicity flack.

Rich said very slowly, "Bruce, you've got to come out of this assignment with copy. That's obvious. You have a name, especially among the liberal, progressive element down Earthside. However, let my boys handle it. We'll come up with the story material. All you'll have to do is release it to your markets under your byline. You'll be taken care of, beyond your dreams of avarice, Bruce. Let's put it that way."

"I've got some pretty extensive dreams in that direction," Bruce said, smiling softly. He shifted in his chair again. "There's one difficulty, Ron. It'd never do for your flacks to write my copy. I've got fans. In fact, I've got millions of them. My last book stayed on the bestseller list for nearly a year. With no false modesty, I'm probably the best-read writer in my particular field since Vance Packard. They know my work. Even with computer matching, you can't fake my style without some gung-ho fans spotting it. I have to write it myself. Sure, I'm a professional freelancer. I make my living at it. And it's like Samuel Johnson once said, 'Anybody who writes for any reason except to make money is an ass.' But I doubt if you taking over would be worth my throwing away a reputation that's taken me half my life to build."

Ron Rich said softly, "I'm talking about a guarantee of at least one million, Bruce."

"That's a lot of guarantee," Bruce said, nodding. "But, in actuality, I make enough as it is to lead a very comfortable life. Besides, if a million dollars were tossed into my lap in a lump sum, you know what'd happen to it? I'm single. The tax people, these days, would hit me for nine-tenths of it. I'd be in the highest bracket with no excuse for special deductions."

Ron Rich said, very softly indeed, "Deposited to an unnumbered account in Geneva, Switzerland."

The writer had to laugh, in deprecation. "And then you'd have me by the balls for the rest of my life. If I refused to jump through your hoops, you'd leak the information and I'd be in the banger for twenty years for tax evasion. And I'd lose every reader I've accumulated, in their sheer disgust. No thanks, Ron."

The other was irritated. "We don't operate that way," he protested, then sighed deeply all over again. "Sure, you'll find things to set up a howl about. Hell, I can think of half a dozen right off the cuff. The dehydrated food most of the colonists eat now is god-awful. If we gave it to the scientists and top technicians, they'd drop out like Italian soldiers in combat. We've got a million problems. But you've got to see our point, Bruce. This is the biggest project of all time. We'll lick our problems, we're licking them now, but we can't have some free-wheeling, half-assed writer—if you'll pardon the expression—trying to make a quick buck throwing shit in the fan."

Bruce nodded. "I get the message. I got it the first time around," he said. "Let's let it ride for the present. Let me look around, initially. Maybe we'll come up with something that makes sense to both of us in a few days. One thing: your boy, Carl Gatena, was pretty keen about my not going out without a guide. I was stopped at the entrance to the hotel by one of the Security men. When I finally did mosey around a bit in the town, it wasn't more than fifteen minutes before another Security lad picked me up and brought me back to you. I don't particularly appreciate this kind of surveillance, Ron."

Ron Rich sighed and held his two hands out in a gesture of it being out of his control. "I'll see what I can do, but policy is not to allow casual visitors from Earthside to go around tearing up the pea patch."

"I'm not a casual visitor," Bruce said coldly. "I can see where you wouldn't want that big-shot Arab to go out on his own and trip over his robes and break his ass, or something, but I'm a writer, not a VIP on a junket."

"We'll see," the other said again. He looked at his wrist chronometer. "Sol Ryan ought to be free by now. He's another big fan of yours. So is Annette. I told them I'd bring you up, soonest."

"Who's Annette?" Bruce said, coming to his feet, as his host did.

"She's Sol Ryan's Person Friday. His brains behind the brains. She runs interference for him, straight-arming anybody who gets in the way. You'll love Annette Casey. Everybody loves Annette. Sometimes I wonder why."

"Person Friday?"

"Yeah," Ron grinned. "Nobody ever thought women's

lib would get to the point achieved by Annette Casey. It used to be Man Friday."

On the way up to O'Malley's office, Bruce said casually, "These Tri-Di and TV movies you release to the public Earthside. Where do you make them, Ron?"

The other glanced over at him. "How do you mean, Bruce? Largely, we film them up here, or at the Luna base, or out in the space showing the construction going on."

"Yeah, largely. But those shots taken inside Island One. The beautiful town. The kids running around playing in the parks on the grass, climbing the trees, swimming in the river. The lovers strolling hand in hand through the fields of flowers. The happy family, sitting around the table groaning with the abundant food you grow in the island. The big community dances, complete with orchestra and with the guys standing around the bar with big steins of beer. Everybody happy as a pig in shit."

"Hell," the other said, after snorting. "We have a mock-up of parts of the interior of the island, the way it's going to look when all the bugs have been solved and it's all finished. It's located in Saudi Arabia. Really remote, so the chances of its existence being discovered are nil. See, I'm not pulling any punches with you, Bruce. You know how publicity is. To keep the people happy we've got to kind of emphasize the positive. They wouldn't understand if they saw some of the rough edges."

"Ummm," Bruce said mildly. "Some of the early publicity you people put out really did bring out the imagination of some of your illustrators. I remember a painting of what the interior of Island Four was going to look like. In the foreground was a scene in the countryside. There was a big boulder in a big field. It was the size of a two-story house. How in the hell were you going to get a boulder of that size up from the moon? Using that mass driver, with its ten-pound buckets firing Luna ore up to Lagrange Five? It'd be unlikely you could get a boulder much larger than a man's head off the moon's surface with that super-catapult. But what really got me in that depiction was that in the far background was an enormous lake, looking somewhat like San Francisco Bay. And across it was a bridge, looking like the Oakland-San Francisco bridge. Now, how silly could the designers of that Island Four be, to build a bridge costing possibly hundreds of millions, when they could have just redesigned the land-scape so that no bridge was necessary."

Ron had to laugh. "Touché," he said. "Some of the early publicity was pretty far out. However, that boulder makes sense. You've got to realize that by the time we're building Island Four, we won't be dependent solely on materials from the moon. We'll be mining the asteroids. It wouldn't be very difficult to send down a small asteroid and work it into the interior of the island. If you brought it in before you started spinning the island for artificial gravity, a single man could shivvy it around into position, since it'd be weightless."

"You got me there," Bruce admitted.

They arrived at the offices of the ultimate head of the Lagrange Five Project. The quarters of Ron Rich, as publicity director, had been far from austere, but they were nothing compared to those of Solomon Ryan. The reception room was as luxurious as any Bruce had ever seen in Greater Washington or New York. Obviously, all furnishings, equipment, and decorations had been lobbed up from Earth.

Ron Rich flipped a hand at the pert-looking office girl behind the reception desk and said, "Hi, Ruthie. I think Sol's expecting us."

"Certainly, Mr. Rich," she tinkled at him. "Professor

Koplin's in there now, but Annette says for you and Mr. Carter to come right in as soon as you arrive." She flapped eyelashes at Bruce. "I just love your books, Mr. Carter."

"Thanks," Bruce said. The inane thought came to him that he had never expected to find readers of his a quarter of a million miles or so from home, but here everybody was claiming to be a fan of his.

Meeting Dr. Solomon Ryan for the first time had its shocking aspects. The man was uncanny. His personality reached out across the room and grasped you. Bruce Carter had heard of the phenomenon before. It was said that Dwight Eisenhower had it, and Churchill and Hitler, for that matter. His charm captivated you, even before words were exchanged.

He was seated behind a desk overrunning with papers, books, pamphlets, charts, blueprints, and even a break-away model of Island One. The other two occupants of the room were an energetic, albeit sensuous-looking brunette seated to the side and behind a smaller desk, and a short, rounded, somewhat clown-like man in rumpled, poorly fitting Earth clothing and wearing thick-lensed, steel-bound spectacles in an age when old fashioned eyeglasses were passé, contact lenses and eye surgery having taken over.

The fat man was bent over Ryan's desk, excitedly pointing to a paper and squeaking out a protest.

Dr. Ryan looked up and grinned at the newcomers. "Sit down, boys," he said. "I'll be with you in a minute. I remember talking to you on the phone, Bruce, but we didn't meet. This is Professor Rudi Koplin, my scientist of all trades, and my built-in gooser. And, oh, yes, Doctor Annette Casey, my brains, arms, and alarm clock."

"Your feet would be a better description," she said tartly. "You keep mine working running your errands." She looked at Bruce and said, "Likewise," before he could get out his, "Pleased to meet you."

Ron Rich and Bruce took chairs and held silence while Ryan wound up his interview with the professor.

Rudi Koplin was saying excitedly, ignoring the newcomers as though they weren't there, "Doctor, it would seem to be something that no one has thus far considered. And I have dire fears it might well doom the prospects of ever building the larger islands."

Ryan smiled his doubts of that and said, "You've had dire fears before, Rudi. I sometimes suspect you Poles are born with dire fears. Very well, what is this new crop?"

"Sol, Sol," the other objected. "Always you laugh. Very well, it is this. Humans must have phosphorus in the form of phosphates in their food. But the lunar phosphorus content is not as high as we once estimated. So phosphates for fertilizer in the space islands will have to come from Earth."

"So," Ryan said. "We'll bring it from Earth, along with the multitude of other things that will continue to be needed from there."

"Ah, so, but that is it," the rounded man said in despair. "On Earth we are already in phosphate trouble. The best estimates put us all but completely out of phosphates between the years 2010 and 2030."

Solomon Ryan pushed back in his chair and looked at the other for a moment. The other stared back, as though apologetic for bringing bad news. His deep affection for the younger man was obvious in his face.

Ryan said, "Rudi, when we get these SPS's really going, we will have at our disposal an infinite amount of power."

"But power isn't phosphorus, Sol!"

"Strangely enough, it is. For decades, Rudi, we've had transmutation of elements in the laboratory. The Philosopher's Stone, long sought by the Alchemists to turn base metals into gold, has been found. To date, it has not been practical, since to change, say, lead into gold, is such an expensive undertaking that the cost is much, much more than the value of the gold realized." He chuckled. "I don't actually have the figures, but I understand that to create ten cents worth of gold from lead would cost at least a million dollars. However, practically all of the cost is power."

The Polish scientist's face fell as realization came to him. "And given infinite power, all but free from the sun. . . ."

"Yes," Ryan said. "We'll create not only our own phosphorus, but will export it to Mother Earth."

"Sol, you are a genius," Rudi Koplin said with emotion in his squeaky voice. He gathered his papers from the desk, bowed at the newcomers and to Annette Casey, and trundled to the door and out.

Annette looked at her superior skeptically. "Now that's really something to come off the top of your head at a minute's notice," she told him.

Ryan grinned at her. "You'd better put a few of the boys on it," he said. "It's a problem for the future but the sooner it's looked into, the better."

She said, "Are you sure that you can create phosphorus in the laboratory from other elements?"

His contagious grin widened. "If they can make gold, why not?"

He turned to Bruce and the PR head. "Draw up closer, boys," he told them.

Solomon Ryan was a slight man and gave the impression of being unflappably, perpetually optimistic. And, above that, he had the power to bring out the same quality in those who met him. He projected confidence.

As Bruce brought his chair up nearer the desk, the space pioneer reached over and shook hands, his blue eyes registering sincere pleasure in meeting the newcomer.

"Bruce Carter," he smiled. "For us, possibly the most dangerous man alive."

"We could always shoot him," Annette said. "I read your last book, Mr. Carter. Is there anything left of the gambling industry?"

"Unfortunately, yes," Bruce smiled back. "And there's no percentage in shooting me. I left notes with various friends and my bank, to be opened in case of my death. The notes read simply, *Annette done it*."

She snorted at that. "You hadn't even heard of me ten minutes ago."

Bruce said, carrying it on, "*Au contraire*, m'dear! Ron, here, told me all about you fifteen minutes ago. He said everybody loved you. And then added that he didn't know why."

Annette's dark eyes went to the flack, who winced. "My chum-pal," she said.

Ryan was chuckling at the banter. He said, "Well, in spite of appearances to the contrary, this office is a very busy one. Should we get down to the nitty-gritty? Bruce, here, is a famed writer, highly respected, who has come to dig into our Lagrange Five Project garbage."

"Not exactly," Bruce protested mildly. "But that brings up a question. What do you do with your garbage in Island One?"

"We recycle it," Annette said flatly. "And then eat it."

The three men laughed. The girl made good company, obviously completely at ease with her superior and with all else in the L5 Project, no matter what their rank.

Bruce looked at Solomon Ryan and said, "I suppose the nitty-gritty starts with you, as head of the Lagrange Five Project."

But the other smiled his charm at the freelancer and said, "To the contrary, I have no position with the Lagrange Five Project whatsoever."

Bruce Carter was not the type to have his jaw drop. Had he been, his jaw would have creaked.

151

Ryan smiled deprecation. "Most people don't know it, but I am not on the Lagrange Five Corporation payroll. I am on leave of absence from my position as a professor of physics at New Kingston University. I am here as an advisor. I am neither an employer nor an employee. I receive my expenses only."

Bruce, flabbergasted, got out, "But . . . but . . . you're the Father of the Lagrange Five Project, the colonization of space."

Ryan smiled his charming smile, which was a little on the rueful side. "In actuality, the better term would be the Jewish mother of the Lagrange Five Project. Long since, the technological aspects of the endeavor have gotten beyond me. I actually have no time for research these days, Bruce. I'm kind of a figurehead. Something like royalty in England, you might say. I have to do with raising money, making speeches, public relations, writing, or. . . ." he smiled ruefully again, "having things ghost-written for me, articles and pamphlets, even books, appearing before governmental committees in a dozen different countries, or at international meets. Oh, I simply have no time for actual research."

"But, this stuff about you not having any connection with the L5 Project, that simply doesn't make any sense at all."

"It makes sense, all right," the other told him, a touch of grimness in his voice for the first time. "You see, as it is, there is no one, not even the redoubtable Bruce Carter, who can point a finger at me and say that I am profiting by the L5 dream. In that respect, I am untouchable. I earn nothing whatsoever of the hundreds of billions being expended on space colonization. I live on my salary from my university, which is still paid me in spite of the fact that I am on leave. That makes sense, too. The Lagrange Five Project was boosted at New Kingston; basic research is still being conducted there by hundreds of scientists and engineers. In fact, New Kingston University is the heart and soul of the project but, of course, is a non-profit institution. In short, Bruce, my position here is an honorary one. I have a voice, but no vote, in the management of the Lagrange Five Project."

"A damn loud voice," Annette put in cynically.

Ryan grinned at her. "Admittedly."

"Well," Bruce said, "That's a story in itself. And certainly an untold one, down on Earth. Just what do you do?"

Still smiling, Sol Ryan thought about that for a moment. "I suppose," he said, "that we of New Kingston stand around with whips in our hands watching with eagle eyes that all goes well with the dream, seeing that there is no hanky-panky."

Ron Rich said, "Is it too early for a drink? It occurs to me that Bruce just got off the *Tsiolkowsky*. He must have a week-long accumulated thirst and I've never even heard of a freelancer who didn't have writer's disease."

"That's the advantage of being here in space," Annette said. "The sun is always over the yardarm."

The PR man went over to the rather ornate bar and began bringing forth ice and glasses.

Bruce said, "I had gotten the impression that guzzle was all but unknown up here, due to the cost-of-shipment factor."

Ryan frowned and explained. "You'd be surprised at the number of gifts sent up, usually to me or my immediate staff. The Corporation allots a certain amount of room and weight for packages, charging fantastically, of course, to keep such non-essentials down. But cost means nothing to some. On the same passenger freighter you arrived on, came a case of vintage champagne from the French. We could hardly turn it down and insult some of our staunchest political backers."

"Heaven forbid," Annette said. "Especially since it's Pol Roger '91."

Ryan was saying, "And on the freighter before yours came over from Earth orbit, a Scottish distiller sent us four cases of prehistoric whiskey. And on the same spaceship arrived ten kilos of caviar. It's embarrassing, in a way. Obviously, there isn't enough to go around. Even four cases of Scotch wouldn't be enough to supply each space colonist with a single sip."

Ron wound it up for his chief very briskly. "So we keep it all here in the hotel. Rank has its privileges. So what'll it be, folks?"

Ryan said, "At this time of day, let's have some grappa."

Bruce looked at him in horror. "Grappa! You mean that Italian liquid H-bomb made from leftover grape skins?"

Ryan laughed. He said, "I have a strong belief that the best potables are still those that are home-produced rather than commercially made. The best guzzle to come out of Ireland is poteen, when it's made by an expert. The best whiskey in America is moonshine that's been properly aged up in the mountains of Tennessee by a devotee. The best applejack is made in illicit stills in the Catskill Mountains of New York. And, in my belief, the best brandy in the world is not French cognac but properly distilled grappa from the hills of Siciliy. This grappa is at least forty years old and is never seen in a bottle meant to be sold in a liquor store."

"And why the Father of the Lagrange Five Project doesn't have a nose as red as that of Rudolf the Reindeer's is a mystery," Annette said.

"Oh, come now, my dear," Sol Ryan said, taking the glass of water-clear spirits that Ron passed him. "I don't drink anything thick enough to eat."

Bruce laughed at that. Actually, he was surprised at the degree of camaraderie that seemed to exist in the highest ranks of the L5 Project personnel. He took his own glass and sniffed at it. It smelled like grappa, all right, forty years old or nay.

Ron held his up in toast. "To the rapid completion of Island One," he said.

"And the beginning of Island Two," Bruce added.

The three space colonists knocked theirs back, stiff-wristed, evidently old hands at taking stone-age grappa down. Bruce sipped his and was amazed to find it as smooth and delicious as Sol Ryan had claimed.

The Lagrange Five leader had raised his eyebrows. "So, Bruce, from your toast it would seem that you, too, have the space colonization dream."

Bruce said in a voice of self-deprecation, "I have had since I was a boy. You people seem to have jumped to the wrong conclusions about my purpose in wanting to come up here."

"I'll be damned," Ron said, going around with the bottle and refilling the glasses. "Here I was trying to put you on the payroll, and your services are available for free."

"That's not exactly how I'd put it," Bruce told him, accepting more of the Italian brandy. "However, it's not my purpose to throw monkey wrenches in the machinery. It's my belief that man's fated to go into space. Who am I to attempt to buck the tide?"

"Cheers," Annette said, holding up her glass. "A new recruit. It's a damn shame that he probably doesn't know how to buck a rivet gun."

Ryan said, after laughing, "We ought to go easy on this stuff, in view of the party tonight." He turned his eyes to Bruce. "We're having a shindig here in the hotel tonight in honor of His Highness. You're invited, of course. It'll give you a chance to meet a selection of our top people."

"Wizard," Bruce said.

"You can be my date," Annette told him. "I just love fearless journalists. We can rake a little muck together."

"If the space colonies are sold to the American public as a way of escaping the juggernaut of apocalypse, of escaping the internal contradictions of our industrial civilization, and of not having to face those contradictions but simply to extend, extend, extend always to a new American frontier, then I think we will overextend ourselves to a point of deserved collapse. I think the space colonists excite the Faustian imagination of the managers and technocrats, for it offers them a way of continuing their existence without going through the pain of a transformation of consciousness."
—William I. Thompson, *author of* At the Edge of History.

Chapter Nine

Only minutes after entering Solomon Ryan's party in honor of Prince Abou ben Abel with Annette Casey, Bruce Carter came to the conclusion that a cocktail party at Lagrange Five differed not at all from a cocktail party Earthside. In his time, he had once attended one in the White House, hosted by President Paul Corcoran. In his time, he had attended one in Chad, hosted by His Imperial Majesty, Aflu Aflu. In his time, he had attended one in the Kremlin, hosted by Number One. There was precious little difference.

There were perhaps fifty or sixty present, two-thirds of them men. Of the women, most were on the youthful side and the average degree of pulchritude was surprising. Their median age must have been twenty years younger than that of the men. Then it came to the freelancer. The men present were top-echelon L5 Project scientists and engineers; the women, largely office workers. What was it Ron Rich had said? Rank had its privileges. Bruce had no idea who it was in the Lagrange Five

Corporation's organization who was in charge of feminine personnel, but that worthy had a sophisticated taste when it came to exotic young women. With three or four exceptions, any of them could have been more expected at some Hollywood bash than at a staid gettogether of space scientists and engineers. The exceptions, he decided, were probably high-ranking women scientists. The suspicion came to him that the usual applied here. Given a community with women in the great minority, those that were available gravitated to the influential. When champagne and caviar were available to the few, why put up with dehydrated eggs?

"Women's lib hasn't gotten as far as all that," he said to Annette, testing out his theory as they headed for the bar.

She looked at him from the side of her eyes and it occurred to Bruce Carter that she was probably not only the most beautiful woman present, but the most expensively gowned. Her jet-black hair was done up in short curls, meant to have hands ruffled through them, as though distractedly, without effect on the hairdo. She looked absolutely and literally edible.

"How's that, Comrade?" she said.

"I'll bet the twenty most beautiful women in Island One are in this room."

She looked about. "Could be."

"Why aren't any of them out in the colonist beer joints, or clubs, or whatever the colonists have, making out with big, strong, handsome construction workers?"

"Because they haven't got any extra holes in their heads," she said, taking a glass of champagne from one of the bartenders. "They don't confuse muscles with power. Have you ever drunk jungle juice?"

"Jungle juice?" He took a glass of the bubbly wine as well.

"They make it from potato peels . . . and stuff."

159

Bruce looked around at the assemblage. Almost everyone, save the bartenders and waiters, were in evening dress. Those that served were in the dark green coveralls of Security. Bruce himself had been loaned formal attire by Carl Gatena. He spotted Carl across the room chatting with a gorgeous blonde. Then he remembered her. Ruthie, the receptionist at Ryan's offices.

He said to Annette, "You mean the colonists get nothing to drink but home brew made out of leftovers?"

"On special occasions—Christmas, for instance—they are issued rations of 190 proof alcohol, which they usually mix with concentrated fruit extracts. They say that the lemon flavor is quite good."

They had drifted away from the bar, their glasses in hand. He looked at her wryly. "They say, eh? Then you've never tried it?"

She gave her little snort. "Do I look like a masochist?"

He grinned at her. "If you are, I'll gladly play sadist with you. But why do these construction workers put up with it? I'd think they'd be on the rough and tough side."

"They are," she said, her eyes checking around the room, as though she was not particularly interested in the subject. "But what can they do? It's not as though they could just quit, drop their tools, jump in their cars or jeeps, and drive home."

"Couldn't they strike for better working conditions—better food, more tobacco, a reasonable amount of guzzle?"

She sighed and said, "You really are a prying freelancer, aren't you?" She took a sip of the wine. "There's a no-strike clause in their contracts. If they break it, their bonuses are forfeit. And that's what brings most of them to Lagrange Five and what keeps them here. Even the least paid gets a twenty-thousand-a-year bonus, in L5 Corporation stock. Tax free."

160

"I suppose that makes sense," Bruce said. And then, after looking around, "At the rate this champagne is being poured, that case the French President sent up won't last very long."

"Oh, there's more available," she told him. And, switching subjects, "Have you met the Prince, the guest of honor?"

"Not yet."

"He seems to be alone for the moment. Shall we go over?"

Prince Abou ben Abel, as ever in spotless white Arab robes, wore the traditional *agalas*, a headdress of braided black ropes worn over white kaffiyehs. He was bearded, the black hair just touched with gray, his eyes were sharp, and his nose beaked in the family facial characteristic. He held a glass of wine in his hand.

Annette said, "Your Highness, may I present Mr. Bruce Carter?"

"*As-salaam alaykum,*" the Prince said graciously, bowing his head slightly but not offering his hand. The true Near Easterner, like his fellow Orientals, doesn't like the Western personal contact of a handshake.

"*La bas,*" Bruce said politely.

"What in the devil are you two jabbering about?" Annette said. "Why don't you speak Esperanto, like everybody else here?"

Abou ben Abel smiled forgivingly at her. He said, Eton and Oxford in the background of his perfect English, "The traditional Islamic greetings. It would seem that Mr. Carter has visited the Arab Union in his time, I shouldn't wonder. I am afraid that my trip to Island One was planned so quickly that I had no time to take the customary crash course in Esperanto. Alas, I fear I am ignorant."

Annette said, a glint in her eye, "Your Highness, I was of the opinion that Moslems were forbidden, ah, strong drink." She eyed his glass of champagne.

His own dark eyes sparked back at her in amusement. "It is no coincidence that "alcohol" is an Arabic word. But in my case, Allah has created an amazing miracle. Whenever I bring a glass to my lips which contains the forbidden *Al-kohl*, it turns to water."

She looked at him and snorted. "That'd be worse than that golden curse of Midas," she said. Then, "Gentlemen, I see my lord and master, Sol Ryan, beckoning to me. A man works from sun to sun but a private secretary's work is never done. If you'll excuse me."

When she was gone, the two men looked after her. "I say, what a beautiful woman," the Prince murmured.

"I wouldn't recommend her for your harem, Your Highness," Bruce said.

The other raised his eyebrows. "Why not, old man?"

"She'd have it in an uproar before the first day was out. Women's rights and all."

The Prince laughed. "You're Bruce Carter, the writer, I take it. I've enjoyed some of your things."

"I seem to have more of a following up here than I do Earthside," Bruce said. "Thanks."

He saw someone about to pass them and said, "Pete. Have you met Prince Abel?"

The IABI man came to a halt. Where he had acquired the ill-fitting evening clothes, Bruce hadn't the vaguest idea, but he suspected that it was the first time Pete Kapitz had ever been in formal wear. The colorless agent looked as though he had been wrestling in them.

Bruce said, "Your Highness, Mr. Peter Kapitz, of the Inter-American Bureau of Investigation."

For the moment, the Prince had his drink in his left hand and couldn't avoid having his right taken and pumped up and down.

"Ah," he said. "I say, a G-Man."

"I'm afraid that term is kind of out of date, Your, uh, Majesty," Pete said.

The Arab smiled at him, taking the edge off the mockery in his voice. "I'm afraid that one is too, I shouldn't think. Especially since I am not the king but only one of his many sons."

Mark Donald, the lieutenant of Security, came up apologetically, nodded to Bruce and Pete, and said, "Pardon me, Your Highness. I dislike to interrupt, but Doctor Ryan and Mr. Moore would appreciate a few moments of your time in the library, if possible."

"Certainly," the other nodded. He turned back to Bruce and Pete Kapitz. *"Trig esslama,"* he said and then followed after the Security man.

Pete said, "What in the hell's that supposed to mean?"

"May the road lead to salvation," Bruce told him.

"Sounds kind of fruity," Pete said. "You think he's queer? I've heard about these A-rabs."

"Let's go get another drink," Bruce said. "How're you doing on your search for Rocks Weil?"

"Haven't had much time, so far," Pete said as they wound in and out among the other guests on their way to the bar. He snagged a canapé from a tray being carried about by one of the Security men and popped it into his mouth. "Jesus, that was good," he said.

"Probably sent up by the King of England," Bruce said. "You'd think this party was being held in Beverly Hills, rather than a half-finished, overgrown tin can floating in space."

They got their drinks. Pete said, "Half-finished? I thought it was just about through and that pretty soon they were going to start on the next one, Island Two."

"Well, it's not, by a damn sight," Bruce told him. "From what I've been able to pick up so far, every wheel and its cousin has come off."

The IABI operative looked at his watch. He said, "Look, I'd like to get together with you some time and check notes, but I've got something to do now."

"Wizard," Bruce said. "I'm here at the hotel."

When the other was gone, the freelancer drifted near a couple of middle-aged, scholarly looking types who seemed to be having an argument. They were, of course, talking shop, just as everyone else seemed to be.

One of them was saying, "What I'm asking is what would happen if a real disaster struck an island. Any island ranging from a population of 10,000, like this one, to the millions sometimes projected by Sol Ryan."

"What kind of a disaster?" the other said.

"Any kind. On Earth, we can flee war, floods, hurricanes or tornados, earthquakes, even a plague. But no island would have available the spaceships to handle the refugees involved. How long would it take to move a million colonists from their island to one only fifty miles away?"

The other said sarcastically, "Look, John, I rather think that such disasters as floods, hurricanes, and earthquakes are unlikely to occur on even the largest island proposed."

"Ah? But we have our own potential disasters. Suppose something suddenly happened to an island's air supply? Suppose one was struck by that king-sized meteor that nobody expects to come, given percentages. Suppose there was an attack by some crackpot terrorists, such as the religious cranks who are sounding off against our flying up God's nostrils by penetrating the heavens. And a plague is always possible; some new strain of bug escaped from our laboratories, perhaps. On Earth, doctors and nurses can be brought in to a disaster area from a nearby country in short order. Even mobile hospital units. But suppose your island was stationed out in the Asteroid Belt. It takes a year to get there from Earth or from Lagrange Five."

The other took a pull at his drink and scowled. "A plague doesn't sound very likely."

"But possible, damn it. And how about a war? Do you know how vulnerable one of these islands would be to an enemy spacecraft armed with nothing more destructive than, say, even a French 75 of the First World War? A few shells would rip an island apart, the atmosphere would flush out into space. And where would the population flee?"

"They could take to spacesuits," his companion said grumpily.

"Balls," the other said in disgust. "What spacesuits? I doubt if there're more than two thousand space suits in Island One. And how long can you live in a spacesuit even if you were able to find one in a hurry?"

Bruce moved on. The idea had never occurred to him. A major disaster in a space colony. The guy was right. It'd have to be one king-sized rescue operation.

Across the room, cigars in hand rather than drinks, Leonard Suvorov, the Russian ecologist, and Rudi Koplin, the once-Polish biochemist, were worriedly discussing subjects dearest to their hearts. The two men were of a type—both middle-aged, both rotund, both sincere men of good will, but on the naive side when out of their own fields of endeavor.

The Soviet Nobel Laureate was saying, "The biologist, Howard Odum, one of your Americans, I believe, calculated that it would take about 2.5 acres of ecosystems combining water and land to sustain safely one person in a space colony. If my crude estimate of this first colony's potential biotic area of one hundred acres free of structure, machinery, storage, and what have you is correct, Island One can support 40 people, not the 10,000 that it supposedly now contains. If Odum is right, that means that the other 9,960 people will have to continue to bring their own gases, food, and waste disposal units. Not to speak of all the other necessities."

Rudi Koplin wet his lips and blinked his eyes many

times. He said, "My dear Academician, surely Odum's figures are exaggerated."

The Russian shook his head. "I do not know. But even if he is way off the mark, as the Yankees say, I cannot see how one hundred acres could support 10,000 colonists. Besides, as yet, a valid, closed-cycle ecology system has not been devised."

The other pushed his steel-rimmed glasses back on his nose and attempted a chuckle. "But, now that you have arrived, we shall see about that, my dear Suvorov."

"Call me Leon, my friend," the Soviet scientist told him. "But though I have been here but a single day, the magnitude of the task overwhelms me. I have been led to believe that my colleagues already on the job had gone far toward solving the problems involved. I had expected to find the celebrated Nils Petersen and Professor Chu Sing, both of whom have laurels as great as my own in the field of bionomics."

Koplin said with a sigh, "Doctor Petersen met with an unexpected accident when all air, suddenly, and in a thus far unexplained manner, flushed from the hothouse in which he was working. Our Chinese comrade was rather hot-headed and could get along with but a few of us. I am glad to say that I was one of the few. However, finally, in high agitation, he argued with Sol Ryan over some point evidently above my head and insisted upon being returned to Earth. From the story that has come up to us, he had seemingly become used to the lack of vehicles here in Lagrange Five and was struck by a car in the streets of New York before being able to return to Peking."

"I heard nothing of this in Leningrad," Suvorov grumbled.

Koplin was apologetic but said, "I understand that the Soviet news system is somewhat different than that in the West."

The Russian drew hard on his cigar. "That doesn't apply to the sciences," he said coldly. "In the Academy of Sciences, we keep up as well as is done anywhere. Possibly better. At any rate, those ecologists remaining on the project's staff give me a first impression of being dolts. With Nils Petersen and Chu Sing, I would have at least had a team."

Koplin said placatingly, "Many of our research people are at New Kingston University doing much of the work where there is more adequate equipment, such as the very latest computers."

"We shall see," Suvorov said, "However, at this early point, prospects look grim to me." He glanced down at his cigar. "This is as good as I have ever enjoyed."

"Havana," Koplin beamed. "I shall tell Sol you appreciate them. He will certainly send you a few boxes."

At the other end of the room, Mary Beth Houston said, in surprise, "Why, it's Rick Venner. I didn't expect you to be at this party, Rick."

Rick, champagne glass in hand, looked quickly to right and left before answering her. None of the Security waiters seemed to be in the immediate vicinity. "Why not, honey?"

She looked embarrassed. "They told me that it was for the most influential people in Island One—Doctor Ryan, the Prince, Academician Suvorov, and all those other scientists. And you're only an electrical engineer, aren't you?"

"Oh, I'm more of an engineer than you'd think," Rick said. He was immaculately dressed in evening wear that he had thoughtfully borrowed from Tony Black an hour before while the other was gone from the house the two occupied.

"Isn't it exciting?" she gushed. "Imagine, a real, live Prince."

"Yeah," Rick said, turning so his face wouldn't likely

be seen by any of the Security-men-cum-waiters, and taking more of his wine appreciatively. It was damn good champagne.

"Oh, look," she said. "There's Joe Evola over there. The Security fellow who came up with us. They've made him be one of the waiters. Isn't that funny? He's such a gloomy Gus."

"Yeah," Rick said. "Hey, let's take a crack at the buffet. That looks like caviar to me."

They made their way to the lengthy buffet table and Rick, in particular, shoveled a huge amount of the delicacies onto his plate. "I missed lunch," he told her. "I'm on kind of a diet. What do you say we go out onto the terrace to eat this?"

"Oh, that sounds terribly romantic. Imagine being at a party in Island One with Doctor Solomon Ryan and a live Prince and going out onto the balcony with a real space construction engineer."

He ushered her onto the terrace. There were only a couple of other guests. He took Mary Beth down to the far end and, as much as he had noticed thus far, besides Joe Evola, the only others present who would be aware of the fact that he had crashed the party were Bruce Carter and Pete Kapitz. He doubted if either of them would call him on it. However, it was just as well if they didn't spot him. At least, until he had gotten as much of this superlative guzzle and food under his belt as possible.

"Is this caviar?" she said. "I've read about caviar all of my life, but this is the first time I've ever had any." She tasted it and frowned. "Goodness, is that caviar? Tastes like salty fish eggs to me."

Rick Venner closed his eyes in pain.

He said, "Are you staying here at the hotel?"

"Oh, yes. And I'm having the most wonderful time. I've just always got one of Mr. Rich's publicity men, or one of the Security fellows dancing attendance on me.

Tomorrow one of them is going to take me into space in what they call a space taxi, so I can see the men at work on the SPS's. That's the great big mirror that they're going to use to collect solar power and beam it down to Earth. Oh, they're going to occupy every minute of my time, until the next passenger freighter leaves for Earth orbit. Gosh, I'll sure hate to go."

"Ummm," Rich said thoughtfully. "I'm staying in private quarters I share with a friend. How does the hotel work? For instance, how do you pay in the dining room?"

She looked at him in surprise. "Nobody pays anything," she told him. "Didn't you know that? In Lagrange Five practically everyone except for a few visitors like myself and Bruce Carter and the Prince, are either space colonists or contract workers and they get everything they need for free."

"So, in the dining room you just sit down and order. They don't look at your identification or anything?"

"And the food is just delicious," she gushed. "You're lucky. You'll be eating this wonderful space food for the next five years."

"Yeah," he said. "Imagine."

She looked at him mischievously. "Longer than that, I'll bet. You'll probably sign up to be a life-long colonist, after your five years are over."

He looked upward in appeal. Not that there was anything to see upward. Evidently, the mirrors had been so warped that the solar rays were cut off and the equivalent of night had fallen in Island One.

She said, "Come to think of it, there were few in the dining room who were dressed in space coveralls. I think that the waiters did ask them for identification, or something. I don't know why."

He looked thoughtful again. "Oh, they did, eh? They expect you to be in Earthside clothing."

After they'd finished their food, they stared down at

the town for a while. There wasn't a great deal to see in the darkness, save for occasional lights in the windows of the houses and other buildings.

Rick cleared his throat and said softly, "You know, Mary Beth, I'm going to hate to see you leave after just a short stay. I wish I had told you sooner, but I suppose I'm shy."

"Told me what?" she said. "Why, you're the least shy man I've ever met."

"I just, uh, cover it over. I should have told you I built up quite a crush on you. And now, here you are, leaving in a few days or so and I'll be here all alone." He managed to work a small sob into the end of that.

She looked at him in surprise and caught her breath. She said, a hitch in her voice, "I didn't know that you felt that way, Rick."

"Well, I do. And, well, I've never even kissed you. And you're leaving."

"Why, you poor man." She put a hand on his arm, lowered her voice demurely, and said, "Rick, darling, I'd put out for any true spaceman."

The bluntness of that set him back momentarily, but he said, "Sweetheart," and took her into his arms. Her teeth, slightly bucked, were a hindrance to his kissing technique.

She said, "We can go to your house, darling."

He cleared his throat. "I think it's better if we just went to your room."

Mary Beth pouted. "But I'd just love to see where you're going to live for the next five years. If you're important enough to be at this party, you must have a really scrumptious place."

"Tell you what I'll do," he said with a little laugh. "I'll match you for it. I'll take this coin and you call heads or tails . . ."

Back at the party, Bruce Carter strolled up to where

Ron Rich was listening in on a several-way discussion, an impatient and somewhat frustrated look on his usually open face.

"Nice party," Bruce told him, under his breath.

Ron looked at him quickly and said, "Let's go back to the bar and get another drink."

"I just got one," Bruce told him. "And, besides, I'd like to listen in on this."

Ron wasn't happy.

One of the debaters was saying in a demanding voice, "Where in the devil does Sol expect to get qualified space colonists to fill up these future islands of his? Who'd be silly enough? The kind of people he needs have to be tops, in the best of physical health, well educated, experienced, highly trained. The very sort of people that hold down the best jobs on Earth. The unemployed need not apply. If they were the capable workers he needs, they wouldn't be unemployed. In the depths of the worst depression the United States, or any other advanced country has ever had, the type of person needed for space colonization was not looking for work. There's always work for that type of man who seeks affluence and security for himself and his family. Say he's making 25,000 dollars a year and up, Earthside. How much would you have to pay him to leave his job behind and colonize space?"

His opponent, a somewhat younger man who had "engineer" written all over him, broke in. "The adventurous type of man. The enthusiastic and dedicated. The type of men and women who explored, then conquered, then colonized the New World from Europe. The Columbuses."

The first one chuckled. "I can see that you're no historian, Bob. It was the unemployed, the dregs of the ports of Southern Spain, that crewed Columbus's ships. Most really competent sailors of the day wouldn't have dreamed of going, in view of the dangers that lay out in the reaches of the Atlantic. Columbus himself was motivated by avarice. The contract he drew up with Queen Isobel made him Admiral of the Western Seas. His crew dragged their heels all the way. They even threatened mutiny at one point. And the Spanish Conquistadores? A bunch of cutthroats out for gold and silver. When they got it, most of them returned to Spain to live it up there."

One of the others cut in. "That didn't apply to the North, to what later became the United States and Canada."

"Like hell it didn't," the other laughed. "There were a handful of gentlemen out to seek their fortunes, but mainly North America was settled by the dregs of Europe, by criminals on the lam, sometimes by convicts. The State of Georgia, in particular, was settled by convicted criminals, like Australia was. They were given their chance of being either executed, or imprisoned, or becoming colonists. The great waves of immigration later on weren't brought about by much higher ideals. The blacks, of course, didn't want to come at all. The poorest, most illiterate Irish came to escape the potato famine. The more successful Irish, the better educated and more prosperous, remained in Ireland. The Germans came to escape the anti-Social Democratic laws of Bismarck. The Italians immigrated from the poverty-stricken conditions of Sicily and southern Italy; the better educated, better adjusted, more highly trained Italians of the north largely remained at home. The Jews fled in escape from the pogroms in Poland and Russia and later the gas chambers of Hitler. The Puerto Ricans came to escape the poverty of their home island and the Chicanos to get jobs that couldn't be found in Mexico. No, my friends, the New World wasn't settled by the elite of the Old World, it was settled by those who couldn't make the grade, for whatever reasons, including racial and religious ones in Europe. Even the pilgrims were malcontents who were indignant at not being allowed to inflict their religious beliefs on their neighbors."

Ron Rich said to Bruce, "Come along, I'll introduce you to the more interesting personalities here tonight. It might be quite a while before you have a chance to meet some of them again. Possibly never. They're usually pretty busy."

Bruce whispered back, "Maybe later. I want to hear this."

The debater named Bob snagged a drink from a passing Security man's tray and said, "It'll be different in space. Why, that secretary of the Friends of Lagrange Five was telling me a little while ago that every member of her organization wants to sign up as a space colonist. Along with the so-called spacists, they must number into the millions."

"Sure," the other said sarcastically. "A bunch of kids who were weaned on *Star Trek* and *Space War* and the comic strip *Star Hawks*. All raring to go. But, once again, the need is for highly educated, trained, and experienced persons. And you don't achieve those qualities while you're still in your teens or twenties. You're well into your thirties or even forties before you have such qualifications. And by that time you're settled down with family and job and adventure isn't so high on your list. The good life and security have taken its place."

Ron Rich got into the act, as though reluctantly. "You've got to keep the population explosion in mind. There's room for millions, eventually, in the islands. Even billions in the farther future."

But the other was shaking his head in rejection. "Ron," he said, "you're always in there pitching, but in this case, it doesn't wash. For one thing, what population explosion? In the advanced countries it began petering out in 1976 when Germany was the first to *lose* population. She lost some 22,000 that year, and the next year it was even more. She was soon followed by Switzerland, the Netherlands, the Scandinavian countries. Even the United States by the end of the '70s had a birth rate, among women of childbearing age, that's less than it takes to maintain population. Sure, the populations continued to increase in India, Indonesia, Africa, and Latin America, although the rate has been slowing for some time. But those are exactly the people not needed in the space colonies. Usually, they're even in bad health, as a result of diet and so forth. And, most certainly, they do not have education, training, and experience. They usually don't even have an average I.Q., due to protein deficiency during the mother's pregnancy and during childhood. That minority in India, Africa, and the other underdeveloped areas who do have the qualifications needed for space, wouldn't want to go, population explosion or nay. They're already happy. But suppose you did get them to Island Three or Four, or whatever. Then that'd rob their home nations of the people they need the most, a type of brain-drain that would be disastrous."

One of the others of the group, who hadn't spoken as yet, said glumly, "There are other elements that are going to be involved that will discourage space colonization. There are millions of well-educated, well-to-do folks on Earth now who won't even get into an airplane because they're afraid to fly. How many others, even those qualified, will be leery of coming into space?"

Ron said to Bruce Carter, "Look, see that girl over there? The redhead? She's been telling me she'd like to be introduced. You know, she's hot to meet such a famous writer. To tell you the truth, I can recommend her. She fucks with her underwear on."

Bruce had to laugh. He hadn't heard that expression since he'd been in high school. And even then he hadn't been sure of what it meant.

174

The PR man took him over to the girl, who smiled expectantly at their approach.

"Bunny Bahr," Ron said. "This is Bruce Carter, the freelancer you were asking about."

"Oh, sure," she said brightly.

She was stacked, as the expression went, like a brick Kremlin, Bruce told himself. A lifelong bachelor, Bruce Carter just loved girls who were red of hair and stacked.

He smiled and said, "It's nice to meet you. How long have you been up here?"

She smiled a smile that would have given an erection to a eunuch and said, "About a year, Bruce. What do you write? I just love comic strips. I was simply raised on *Flash Gordon*."

Bruce glowered at the flack. "My chum-pal," he said.

Ron said defensively, "Well, she's a redhead. I didn't say she could read."

* * * *

Solomon Ryan, Prince Abel, Al Moore, and Annette Casey entertained in Ryan's library. The Prince and Ryan were talking even as they sought comfortable seats.

The Prince was saying, "The Arab Union is willing to continue on the present basis. That is, we will continue to contribute five billion a year, secretly deposited to your unnumbered account in Berne."

Al Moore, idly, and as though automatically, had taken what looked to be a pen from his breast pocket. He flicked a stud on its side and began to stroll about the room. Annette went over to the library's bar, took stock of the offerings, and began to reach for glasses.

Al Moore came to a sudden halt. His face went empty. For a moment he stood stock-still, as though unbelieving. Then his forefinger went to his lips. The other two men and Annette stared at him, shocked. He continued around the room, pointing his device here, there, and everywhere. He shook his head in lack of understanding. Finally, he

175

approached Annette, who was continuing to bug-eye him. Then he turned to the two men who had resumed their feet. He pointed the device at each of them in turn.

A faint humming, which all could hear now, became louder as he pointed the gismo at the Arab. He came closer still, going over the Prince's whole body until finally the electronic mop was directed at the other's sash. His eyes narrow, Al Moore dipped his left hand into the sash before Abou ben Abel could step back. The Security head came up with a small black metallic object, no larger than a button. His expression flat, he held it out in his open hand for all to see.

"God damn," Sol Ryan blurted. He reached out and grabbed the thing, dropped it to the floor and ground it beneath his heel.

The Security man was staring at the Prince. He rasped, "Were you taping this conversation?"

"What?" the Arab said, surprise and a bit of indignation at being so molested. "I say, what in the bloody hell is going on?"

Al Moore pointed at the floor. "A bug. You had an electronic bug in your sash. Somebody's listening in, or were, on everything we've been saying."

The Prince was indignant. "Don't be ridiculous, old chap. Certainly nothing to do with me. I already know what is being said, wouldn't you know? I'm here and I need no record. If anybody should be accused of taping the conversation, it might be you chaps, though for the life of me I can't see a reason for it."

Ryan, still looking aghast, said, "No. No, we have no reason for wishing such a recording. We've got just as much or more desire to keep our transactions with the Arab Union a secret as you have." His eyes went to Annette's and then to Al Moore's. "But who?"

The Security chief shook his head. "Let me think, dammit. It had to be planted at the party. Earlier, when we were all together in your office, I automatically used the mop. I always do when entering a room where something offbeat might be said. There was no bug then."

Annette said, or, at least, began to say, "But there's nobody at the party. . . " And then she stopped.

Al Moore looked at the Prince, all but glowering. "Damn it, who got near enough to you to plant that bug in your sash?"

Abou ben Abel shook his head in turn, obviously at a complete loss. "But at a party of this type one meets just about everybody present, especially the guest of honor."

Annette said, "You attempt to avoid being touched. I noticed that when I introduced you to Bruce Carter."

"Bruce Carter!" the Security man spat out. "That damned prying writer. The busybody to end all snoops! The goddamned muckracker!" He glared at the Arab. "Could he have planted the bug?"

"I . . . I couldn't say, old chap. I . . . I wouldn't think so, you know. I didn't even shake hands with him, as Miss Carter just pointed out. Oh! Half a moment, now. That other chap he introduced me to, the uh, what did I call him? The G-Man. I'm afraid I have forgotten his name. An uncouth type, you know."

"Kapitz," Moore growled. "Peter Kapitz, of the IABI."

"That's the fellow, I'm quite sure."

"Could he have planted it?"

"I'm not really sure, don't you know. But he's the only chap I recall shaking hands with. A ridiculous custom. Two total strangers pawing each other."

"It had to be one of them," Moore muttered. He glowered in turn at Sol Ryan. "You were a fool, inviting that writer up here."

"Sorry, Al," Ryan said uncomfortably, his cheerfulness for once gone.

The Security head looked at Annette. "Get out into

that party and see if they're both here. Get close to Carter and stay close from now on."

"What do you mean, get close, Uncle Al?"

"As close as possible, for Christ's sake. Into bed with him at night. In his pocket as much as possible during the day. Don't bother to search his things. I'll have some of the boys, who know more about it, do that. Meanwhile, I'll check out that damn federal cop. We'll put somebody else on him."

He bent and picked up the crushed, electronic bug. His eyes went to Ryan in disgust. "I could have deactivated it without mashing it like this. I'll see if the boys can figure out where it came from, if it's police, military, or if any ordinary citizen could obtain one."

"Sorry, Al." Sol Ryan shifted his eyes again.

"Let's get back to the party," the other muttered. "I want to see if they're both still there. If they are, that means whoever planted the bug has at least one accomplice in this island."

Ryan turned to the Prince, his smile inverted. "Your Highness, I'm truly sorry about this."

The other smiled, displaying a fine set of teeth. "Actually I enjoyed it immensely, old man. Very exciting, don't you know? Right out of a thriller. But of course it's most important that the chap be found. It wouldn't do at all for the news to leak that the Arab Union is subsidizing the Lagrange Five Corporation."

To Al Moore's surprise, both Pete Kapitz and Bruce Carter were still at the party. He gave quick orders to Mark Donald to search the rooms of both, on the off chance that one of the two had some sort of automatic recording device tuned in on the destroyed bug. He doubted that, though. Such equipment would of necessity be impractical to bring up from Earthside, particularly considering the luggage searches.

Later in the evening, in her room, which was not

quite so sterile as those of Carter and Kapitz, Mary Beth Houston was happily shucking her dress.

She said enthusiastically to Rick Venner, who was climbing from his own clothes, "Don't you just love fucking?"

He cleared his throat. "Well, yes, I have since I was about thirteen."

"Oh, I didn't start nearly as soon as that," she admitted in sadness. "I must have been almost fifteen. I liked it fine the very first time I did it." She dropped her panties and looked over at him. "Gosh, I'm glad you're not circumsised."

He didn't know what to say to that. Was she anti-Semitic or something?

She came over and, as they stood there, took him in hand and looked down, pushing his foreskin back and forth.

His erection was already raging. "You know," he said huskily. "You keep that up and the party's going to be over before it ever gets underway. I'm a once-a-night man."

At that exact moment, Bruce Carter was beginning to climb into the bed that already held the nude Bunny Bahr; the redhead, he had decided, to end all redheads.

Just as he was making the preliminary grab for her, a knock came at the door. The freelancer looked up, scowling surprise. But before he could arise to answer it, the door opened and Annette Casey entered. She closed the door behind her and took in the scene.

"Revolting," she said, shaking her head. She fixed her eyes on Bunny. "Take it on the heel and toe, sister. He's my date."

"Yes, Doctor Casey," the redhead squealed. In record time, she had scrambled from the bed, zipped into her dress, and, carrying the rest of her clothes, had hurried through the door.

"Good night," Bruce called after her sadly.

Annette Casey had her hands on her hips. "Some sadist you turned out to be," she said nastily.

"I beg your pardon?"

"And well you should," she told him, beginning to get out of her evening gown. "You told me earlier that if I was a masochist, you'd gladly play the sadist for me. Now, if that's not a proposition, I've never heard one."

She climbed into the bed and rolled over on her stomach. "You can spank me a little, if you don't do it too hard."

"In addition to full disclosure prior to the onset of an experiment, there should be agreement concerning the conditions under which an experiment (space community) could be halted by the participant. Inherent in the community, there would have to be reserved freedom for the individual to change his mind ... 'Stop the extraterrestrial community—I want to get off!' "
—Carl R. Vann, Extraterrestrial Communities—Cultural, Legal, Political, and Ethical Considerations.

Chapter Ten

Pal Barack, humming happily to himself, a small sheaf of papers in his right hand, entered the side door of the L5 Hilton, which led into the offices of the Security Division of the project. He had never been in them before, for which he was satisfied. Construction workers and Security didn't exactly see eye to eye in various fields; besides which, the small Hungarian was noted for his volatile temper and being short-fused. And it certainly didn't do you any good to get on Security's shit list.

There was a green-coveralled girl at a desk near he door. Pal waved his papers at her triumphantly and chortled, "Where do I get my discharge, sweetie? I've served my ever-loving time."

She looked up from the booster screen she had been scanning and said, "That'll be Captain Borgia. Room 4, down that hall."

"Borgia?" he said. "Jesus, if I had a name like that I'd change it to Brown."

She didn't bother to smile.

Humming again, he made his way down the indicated hall to Room 4. The door was open. Inside, behind a metal desk, was obviously Captain Borgia and, Pal Barack decided, he looked the name. He was dark of complexion, flat of eye, and had mustaches been currently in vogue, and had he sported a flowing black one, he could have passed neatly as a pirate.

The captain was talking to a blue-coverall-clad construction worker who looked sullen. Pal Barack took one of several straight chairs that sat near the door, crossed his legs, and waited patiently for his turn.

The construction worker was saying disgustedly, "Wizard. I give up, damn it. Where do I see about the new contract?"

The captain scribbled on a note pad, ripped the paper off, and handed it over. "Room 7, Miller. And congratulations."

Miller took the paper, grunted contempt, got up and left.

As he passed the Hungarian, Pal said, "You must be out of your mind, chum-pal." He vaguely remembered having seen the man once or twice before. A deep-space construction worker.

"Yeah," Miller growled ungraciously.

Pal Barack got up, went to the desk, and put his sheaf of papers before the Security officer. "Pal Barack," he said. "Five-year man. The contract is up, as of three-and-a-half minutes ago."

"Sit down, Barack," the other told him. He scanned the contract. "Landscaping, eh?"

"If you can call it that," Pal said. "For five years there's been no land to scape. I used to specialize in golf courses back Earthside." He laughed bitterly. "They used to say we Hungarians were the only people in the world who could put a dime in a pay toilet and hit the jackpot, but not even a Hungarian is going to landscape a golf course, or anything else, starting with lava dust."

The captain ignored that, switched on a desk screen, and read Pal's name and serial number into it. He looked at whatever came onto the screen contemplatively. Finally, he switched it off.

He looked up and said, "Figure on signing over for another five years?"

Pal looked back at him. "No."

"We've got a new policy," the other told him. "You're due for a special re-enlistment bonus of twenty-five-thousand dollars. And your base salary is upped five thousand a year. Both payable in LFC stock, of course, when the contract is terminated."

"I want to go home."

"We're short of your type of worker."

The Hungarian snorted at that. "So far as I can see, you're short of all types of workers. Tough shit. I'm heading Earthside on the first passenger freighter and that's the *Armstrong* and it's scheduled for tomorrow."

The captain sized him up, weariness there. He said, "You should know better than that, Barack. Haven't you read your contract? When your five years are up you are given transport back to Earth on a standby, space-available basis."

The feisty Hungarian gypsy eyed him coldly. He said, just as coldly, "What is that supposed to mean?"

The captain leaned back in his swivel chair and sighed. "Barack, if you've been here five years, you should know the facts of life as pertaining to the Lagrange Five Project. Travel between Earth and Island One is largely a one-way thing. Except for a few shuttles, almost everything sent up from New Albuquerque is in unmanned, heavylift launches. They take everything we've got to have into Earth orbit to the *Goddard* space platform. From there, it's sent in the passenger freighters, such as the *Armstrong*, either here to Island One, or to Luna orbit, where it's transferred down to the moon base."

"What the hell's that got to do with my going back to Earth now that my contract's up?" Pal Barack said, his voice ominously low.

"Don't you see? Sending you back by passenger freighter to the *Goddard* in Earth orbit is no problem at all. There's lots of room. But getting you down from there, the last 0.1 percent of the return trip, is the thing. The only human transport from the *Goddard* to New Albuquerque are the shuttles, there aren't that many of them, and they can take only a few passengers apiece."

"Okay. I'll be one of the few."

The captain nodded agreeably. "You'll be placed on standby, space-available. Unless, of course, you change your mind and sign up again."

"I won't change it. How long do I have to wait?"

The captain smiled a smile devoid of humor. "That's up for grabs. You've just got to wait until there's room for you. I suggest you sign up again. By the time you've put in another five years, you'll be rich."

Inwardly, Pal Barack was beginning to boil. "Rich with what?" he said. "With LFC stock? In five years that stock won't be worth its weight in toilet paper."

The Security man took him in for a long moment. Finally he said softly, "Your dossier lists the fact that you're a troublemaker, Barack. That you're inclined to sound off. Including talking to that Earthside freelance writer, Bruce Carter, yesterday. You know that island workers are supposed to steer clear of visitors at the L5 Hilton."

"You're damn right they are," the Hungarian snorted. "You're afraid we'll let them know some of the real facts."

"That's enough, Barack. I suggest that you sign a new contract. If not, then you're on standby and we'll advise

185

you when there's a passenger freighter with room available."

"Don't worry about that," Pal told him with some heat. "I'll pop by here every day to check, until there is. Meanwhile, I'm short of funds. Like everybody else, I've spent my pay as fast as I could get my hands on it. Mostly in the Luxury PX, bar, and restaurant. I want an advance on the 100,000 dollars I've accumulated Earth-side."

"I'm afraid that's not possible, Barack. You are issued that bonus when you return to Earth. Besides, it's in the form of stock, not cash credits. When you get it, you'll have to sell it if you want cash."

Pal Barack stared at him. "You mean to tell me I'm stranded up here, now that I'm off the payroll, with no funds at all?"

The other said patiently, "You should have thought of that when you were blowing your pay, Barack. From what you say, you've gone through ten thousand a year just for frivolities. All your food, clothing, shelter, medical care, and entertainment are provided. It's sheer stupidity that you've left yourself short."

Pal was still goggling at the other, disgust in his eyes now. "Frivolities! Love of Jesus, do you think that there are any of us who could keep from going drivel-happy if we didn't have our occasional blowoffs? At the end of the month, when we get our pay credited to us, we make a beeline for the Luxury PX, the Luxury restaurant, and the bar. Three hundred dollars for a mediocre meal. But at least it's food. A hundred bucks for a couple ounces of raw alcohol. A couple of hundred for enough cheese or ham, or whatever, to make yourself a sandwich or two. And those of us who don't have a woman? All the single mopsies in the island are lined up with the higher echelons, the supervisors, the Corporation staff, the scientists, and you Security funkers . . ."

"Watch your language, Barack," the captain snapped dangerously.

"So what do we ordinary slobs do? We go to the Everleigh House and treat ourselves to a paid-for piece of ass. Frivolities! How I've remained sane for five years, I don't know."

The captain didn't bother to reply.

Pal Barack said, breathing deeply, "This standby routine. How come all of the bigwigs and you Security people all take trips back and forth to Earth every six months or so, and we contract men can't even get passage when we want it after we've served our time?"

The other said wearily, "Once again, you should've read your contract before you signed it, Barack. The more important employees of the Lagrange Five Corporation are guaranteed periodic rotation and rest leave. Due to space limitation, the same cannot be granted to others. There are thousands up here; if everyone wanted a two-week vacation Earthside every year, we wouldn't have the spaceships to bring up anything else. And, now, if you don't mind, I'm rather busy."

"What makes Security personnel important employees?" the Hungarian snarled, as he took up his papers. "They're the most useless people in the island. You haven't heard the last of me, Borgia." He turned and stormed out.

Captain Borgia looked after him thoughtfully. He finally flicked on one of his desk TV phone screens and said into it, "Pal Barack. Keep an eye on him. He looks like a potentially active malcontent."

Pal Barack, seething, left the Security offices and the hotel and crossed the street to a larger than average building, given Lagrange Five City standards. Island One's Luxury PX was in three sections; the PX proper, looking like a small Earthside supermarket, a restaurant that would possibly seat two hundred, and a bar that could handle about a hundred customers at a time.

The Hungarian made a beeline for the sole public drinkery in the island. At this time of the day and at this time of the month, there were few customers. Rather than taking a table, he went right to the bar and to one of the two bartenders. He climbed up onto a stool, ignoring the other customers next to him, and snarled at the bartender, "An ounce of straight and some cola to stick it in."

The bartender said, "Don't take it out on me, chumpal. I only work here. Credit card?"

Pal handed over his credit card. The bartender put it in the payment slot, deducted the amount, then handed it back. He reached under the bar for an unlabeled quart bottle and carefully measured out an ounce of the colorless contents into a tall glass. He reached down again and came up with a bottle of cola mixer and put it before Pal to mix his own.

The Hungarian knew the other was right. The poor cloddy had his own troubles. Everybody who worked in the Luxury PX was moonlighting, save for a few Security men. It gave you a chance to make some extra credits to expend on luxuries, so called, for yourself. Pal suspected that it also gave you an opportunity to do a little ripping-off. What would keep this bartender, for instance, from cadging a few drinks when no Security officers were around? However, Pal Barack was still steaming in indignation. He poured cola into his straight alcohol, then took a third of the drink down in one long swallow.

The man on the next stool said, "I've never seen anybody come out of an interview with Borgia who wasn't sore."

Pal looked over at him impatiently. It was Miller, the construction worker who had preceded him in the Security office.

The Hungarian landscaper said, "You'd be sore, too.

188

My contract's up. I've been looking forward to this day since the first few days I arrived in Lagrange Five. And now what does he tell me? I might be sitting around here on my ass for weeks before I get a berth to go home."

"You dreamer, you," Miller said.

"What's that supposed to mean?"

"I caved in after six months."

Pal Barrack gaped at him. He brought up his glass quickly, took another long pull at his drink, and then stared again. Miller drank some of his own drink. He was a big man, in the construction worker's tradition. Big, strong-looking, tough-looking. He didn't seem the type who'd allow himself to be put upon.

Miller said, "I suppose I must have been one of the first to sign up on the new five-year contract. It ran out six months ago. They put me on standby for passage home. So I stood by. They twisted my arm to sign up again. Not too hard, but too long. I got to figuring it out. In the six months not working, I lost fifteen thousand tax-free dollars, counting the bonus. So I took the hint and caved in."

"Holy smog," Pal said in protest. "Why didn't you put up a howl? Why didn't you beef to everybody and his cousin?"

"Because I wanted to play it smart," the other said, gloomily staring down into his drink. "I didn't want to antagonize the Security boys, and they antagonize easily. I figured that if they got sore enough, I'd never get my transportation."

The Hungarian finished his drink and pushed the glass toward the bartender, who had retreated down the bar to talk to his mate. He came back, took Pal's proffered credit card, and put it in the payment slot. He took it out again and handed it back, saying apologetically, as though he knew how it was, "Sorry, chum-pal, you don't have enough credits for a repeat."

189

The landscape man stared at the card in disgust. "I didn't know I was that low," he muttered.

Miller said, "Have one on me. I'm back on the payroll."

"Well, thanks," Pal said in surprise. It was the first time the small man could remember anyone buying him in a drink in the five years that he'd been at Lagrange Five. Guzzle was just too expensive for a man to be generous.

When the bartender had served them both and drifted off again, Pal said, "See here. Do you know anybody that's served their term and got back home?"

The other shook his head. "No. And I've looked into it. The first four whose contracts expired were given a bang-up party in the hotel. Lots of real guzzle, good food, even mopsies. Hell, even pot to smoke. When they woke up in the morning, they found they'd signed over again. That smartened the rest of us up. And when our contracts expired we refused invitations to a similar party, but we might as well have gone."

"Didn't any of you put up a beef?"

The construction man looked around first and then lowered his voice. "Yeah, a friend of mine. It got him beaten up by characters unknown. But even that didn't shut him up. So he was found a few days later drifting around outside. There was a king-size leak in his space-suit and the suit's emergency system was on the blink."

Pal Barack was boggling again. "You've got to be shitting me."

The other applied himself to his drink.

Pal said, "Listen, have you ever been to one of the WITH-AW-DOH Club meetings?"

"No. I've heard about it. It's that sour grapes outfit. Security takes a dim view of them, so I've always steered clear."

"Well, you've got nothing to lose now. Why don't you come along to the get-together tonight? There'll be some people there that'd like to hear what you have to say."

"I think I'll take you up on that," Miller said. "Somewhere along in here, us worms gotta turn."

When Pal Barack and Jeff Miller arrived at the public auditorium that evening, it was to notice two Security men standing across the street from the entrance.

"Sons of bitches," Pal muttered. "Al Moore would like to crack down on the WITH-AW-DOH Club, but he can't find an excuse. It presents itself as a kind of tongue-in-cheek organization. What In the Hell Are We Doing Out Here? Not really serious. He doesn't have any valid reason for folding it up. There's too damned little entertainment as it is. Beginning to crack down on what few things we have to do would be too damned blatant even for him."

"You know," Miller told him, "in all the reading I did before coming up here, and in all the Tri-Di shows I saw about the Lagrange Five Project, I never saw anything about the Security police. There's no mention of it in the public relations propaganda that Ron Rich puts out."

Inside the fairly sizable hall, they found that at least a hundred members had already arrived. Largely, they were standing around talking with soft drinks in hand. Occasionally, off to one side, you could see one of them bring a pint bottle from a coverall pocket and spike his drink. Pal shuddered. Bootleg. Bootleg guzzle might be passable down Earthside, but with the materials they started with in Island One, it was grim.

Adam Bloch met them at the door and shook hands with Pal. "Didn't expect to see you," he said in his soft, rather empty voice. "I thought you'd be packed and waiting at the docking compartment."

"Yeah," the Hungarian said sourly. "Give me a violin and I'll play you some gypsy music that'll have the tears running down your face."

Adam Bloch was a sad, gray-faced man somewhere in

his early forties. He gave the impression of realizing that life had largely passed him by. That somewhere along the road he'd made the wrong turn, so far as happiness was concerned. His space coveralls looked somehow incongruous on him. He should have been dressed in a conservative suit, complete with forgettable tie.

He cocked his head slightly to one side. "Something go wrong, Pal?"

The Hungarian indicated his new friend. "Meet Jeff Miller. You know those rumors we've been hearing about difficulties getting passage home when contracts expire? Well, Jeff's got the whole story and it'll freeze you."

Bloch shook hands with the newcomer. "I'll be interested to hear it," he said.

"I think it ought to be brought before the Central Committee," Pal said.

The construction worker scowled and said, "What Central Committee?"

Adam Bloch said quickly, after looking at the Hungarian in surprise, "Perhaps we'll tell you later, Mr. Miller. Meanwhile, make yourself at home. You'll find that most of us with the WITH-AW-DOH syndrome are compatible people. There's punch over there at that table."

Pal sighed and said, "Non-alcoholic, of course. Once a year, we throw a big bash, combine our resources and buy a half gallon of straight one-ninety at the Luxury PX, or maybe from one of the black marketeers, but this isn't it."

Even as Jeff Miller wandered off, Adam turned to Pal Barack. "Was that intelligent?" he said.

"Yeah, I think so," the other told him. "He's going to be a good recruit. Really bitter and it's all boiled up inside him. And basically, he's tough. He's been playing it quiet, making no waves until he gets out of here, but now he's had it."

Bruce Carter came in and looked around with interest.

"I'll be damned," Pal said to him. "So you made it. I didn't think Security would let you out."

Bruce smiled his askew smile at the smaller man. "I foxed them," he said. "In that hotel they've got Security men at each door I checked save one. It evidently has never occurred to them they'd need one there."

Adam Bloch frowned. "Which one is that?"

"The door that leads from the Security offices to the street. You enter the corridor from the hotel proper, simply walk down the hall briskly, as though you had business, and then slip out the door into the town."

"I'll have to remember that," Adam murmured. "It sounds as though it would be just as easy to enter."

Pal said, "You've probably already guessed, but this is the writer guy I told you about, Bruce Carter."

The two shook hands.

Pal said to the newcomer, "This is Adam Bloch, Bruce. I guess if we had a head of the club, he'd be it."

"I've read quite a few of your things, Mr. Carter," Bloch said. "Particularly your books."

"Oh?" Bruce said, looking about the room. Most of the occupants were standing around in groups chattering away in much the same manner as they had at the party he had attended the night before. "Which ones did you like?"

Pal interrupted by saying, "I think I'd better go and introduce Jeff around." He left Adam and Bruce to continue their conversation.

"I liked them all," Adam said. "But I think that I'm going to like your next one best of all. It'll be your masterpiece."

Bruce took him in. "I don't even have a next one in mind."

"It will be about the Lagrange Five Project," the other told him. "You will reveal it to be the greatest catastrophe in history."

"I will?" Bruce said coolly.

"Yes," Adam nodded. "Since never in history have so many people been caught up and put so much of their resources into a disaster."

Bruce was irritated. He said, "Are you so sure that it's a disaster? It's already been admitted to me that there are still a lot of bugs, but isn't that to be expected in a project of this magnitude?"

"It's more than just a few bugs, Mr. Carter. The whole concept has been idiotic since its conception. Some aspects of it so much so that one can only suspect sabotage."

"Wizard," Bruce said impatiently. "Let's have just one of those aspects."

"There are so many that I hardly know where to begin, but I'll take a simple example. In one of the early books on space colonization, the author points out, rather in passing, that most likely it will be necessary to import soap from Earth, at least for the first island or two. He goes no further in developing the ramifications of that."

The writer was puzzled. "Well, what are they? Obviously, you're not going to be able to make much soap up here if your only animals are chickens and rabbits. Even when you get pigs, you'd have to have one hell of a lot of them to obtain enough fat to supply ten thousand people with soap."

"Quite correct. Picture ten thousand people using a bar of soap or its equivalent every day."

Bruce said indignantly, "A bar of soap a day? Nobody uses the equivalent of a bar of soap a day."

"I'm afraid a modern, civilized person does, Mr. Carter. I wasn't just thinking in terms of washing one's hands and face and taking a bath or shower. There is also shaving, washing dishes, laundry, scrubbing floors, washing windows, and so forth. So we have 10,000 bars, or the equivalent in other forms of soap. That's 3,650,000 bars a year. If you figure four bars to the pound, roughly, that means 1,912,500 pounds a year, or about 456 tons. All to be brought up by spaceship every year."

Bruce whistled. "That sets me back."

"Ummm," Adam Bloch nodded. "Seemingly a minor matter, but there are a thousand similar, minor matters that add up to the catastrophe I was speaking of. Tell you what; let's circulate a bit."

Bruce fell in beside the sad-faced man as they left their position near the door and entered the hall proper. He was beginning to get used to the sterility of the interiors here in the island. No rugs or carpeting, no drapes at the windows, no art on the walls, the sparse furniture all of metal.

He said, "You don't look exactly like a space worker."

The other smiled wanly. "We're not all construction men, you know. We have everything from health workers to garbage disposal people. I'm a teacher. Many of the community who signed up as colonists brought their families. There aren't a great many children, as yet at least, but on the other hand, they aren't rare."

They approached a lean, tired, frustrated-looking man, leaning against a wall, glass in hand.

"Ah," the teacher said. "Here we have someone who can tell you about another far-out aspect of the Lagrange Five Project."

The man stood erect as they approached. "Hi, Adam," he said. "What spins?"

"Cris," the teacher told him, "This is Bruce Carter, the well-known author. He's doing a book on Lagrange Five." He smiled wanly at the freelancer. "He might not know it yet, but he is. This is Cris Everett, Bruce, a window washer."

Bruce shook hands. "A window washer? You're right, Adam, you do have a wide variety of professions represented here. It wouldn't have occurred to me that window washers would be one of them."

"Are you kidding?" Cris Everett said indignantly. "We're one of the most numerous classes of workers up here."

Bruce looked at him blankly.

"Tell him about it, Cris," Adam said.

"What the hell is there to tell? This cylinder is 3,280 feet long, with a circumference of 1,030 feet. It's divided into six strips, half for living space, half in windows, to let in sunlight. Each one of the strips is about 170 feet wide, and, of course, runs the full length of the cylinder. Figure it out; three strips of windows, 170 feet wide, over 3,200 feet long. We start out at one end, hundreds of us, and by the time we get to the other end, it's time to go back to the beginning and start all over again. Whoever designed these islands evidently didn't figure that the windows would need washing. Well, they don't on the outside, but they sure as hell do here on the inside. They intended to install automatic cleaning apparatus. They didn't."

Adam put in, looking at Bruce, "Ryan and his colleagues talk about islands eventually that will be several hundred square kilometers in area. They, too, are to be half in windows, half in living area. Window washing doesn't lend itself to automation. Even in the most modern skyscrapers on Manhattan, the windows are washed by hand." He said to the indignant worker, "See you, Cris. I'm showing Bruce around."

As they continued on their way, Adam said, "There are some other interesting angles to those islands of a couple of hundred square miles or so. By the way, there are four European sovereign nations with land areas much less than that. Andorra, Liechtenstein, San Marino, and Monaco. Andorra is the largest with 175 square miles."

"I've been in all of them," Bruce said.

"Ummm. Now, the way Ryan and company picture it,

there will be rivers and lakes on such islands, complete with swimming, boating, fishing, and other water sports. I submit that to have a river or lake permitting such activities, you're going to need water at least six feet deep with, I'd say, soil beneath the water at least another foot deep, if you plan on aquatic vegetation for the fish to feed on. Then you'd have to have the land level a foot or so higher than the water level. So the land level would be eight feet in all. Now, I ask you to imagine transporting enough lunar soil up to your island to fill several hundred square miles to the depth of eight feet. I might point out that the mass driver now on the moon was designed to propel into space about 150 tons of lunar raw materials daily. How many additional mass drivers would be needed to put up the millions of tons necessary to build an island that big and then to fill it, eight feet deep, with lunar-derived soil?"

Bruce regarded him from the side of his eyes. Surely there were engineering solutions for these problems; but it made a man wonder. . . .

They came up on a group of four or five who were evidently going into lighter elements of the problems of Lagrange Five. The two newcomers to the group held their silence and listened in.

One of them was saying, "I tell you, some of these double-dome agricultural scientists must have learned their farming in a laboratory. One of them came up with the bright idea of bringing up a ton of earthworms. It must have put fishing in the States back a few years. At any rate, they dump them onto one of the patches where they're trying to get vegetation going outside the hydroponic areas. A ton of earthworms, mind you. The poor little bastards probably all got bloody noses bumping them against the island's metal shell, the soil only being a foot thick at that point. But the thing is, the simple cloddies who dreamed up the idea evidently never considered what those worms were supposed to eat. What in the hell could they find to eat in that incompatible luna dirt?''

The others laughed and one said, "If you think that's bad, how about the wildlife specialist? The one who brought up the ducks and turned them loose. After a while the ducks decided they wanted to migrate and broke their damn necks flying up against the windows.''

They laughed again. It would seem this group had a supply of bootleg with which to spike their punch.

Across the room, Pal Barack and his new friend, Jeff Miller, were the center of another group.

"I mean to say," Pal was declaiming dogmatically, "It's like joining the army. Even worse. In the army, supposedly you can get out if you have some medical reason, or some personal matter like family problems. You know, you've got to take care of your sick mother or something. It's not easy to get discharged, but it's possible. Well, it's not possible if you work for the Lagrange Five Corporation."

Tony Black, who was standing to the rear of the group, demurred grudgingly. Rick Venner's contact man in Island One said, "Hell, Pal, a lot of the early construction workers went on home after their particular specialty was no longer needed."

"Yeah, sure," the little Hungarian admitted. "But those were the early days at the moon base and in the Construction Shack and everybody knew how rugged it was up here. In fact, all the Tri-Di shows and all stressed the fact. Kind of took pride in it. But now the story line is that Island One is just about completed and everything is hunky-dory and any day now the happy colonists will start building Island Two and start mass producing SPS's wholesale once a few more wrinkles are ironed out. Ha! No wonder they don't want any of us going back Earthside and telling everybody what it's really like up here. Who the hell'd buy any more LFC stock?"

The others in the group stirred restlessly and looked at each other unhappily, almost furtively, from the sides of their eyes.

Jeff Miller said softly, "You might not believe what Pal says, but I can vouch for it. Nobody who might shoot off his mouth, Earthside, gets to return. Those big-name scientists and engineers, the executives of the project, and the Security men, sure. They're safe. Hardly any of them ever leave the L5 Hilton anyway, and even if they did know what was really going on, it's to their interest to keep their traps shut. But we working-type joes, we simply don't leave."

Tony Black said, "I've known several guys who went home after their contracts expired."

"Like shit you do," Pal Barack said nastily. "What do you know about anything? You work in Supply and your itchy fingers latch onto anything not nailed down. No wonder you're the best source of black-market items around."

Adam Bloch and Bruce had drifted around between groups for a time and then settled down to a couple of chairs against one of the auditorium walls.

Bruce was thoughtful. He said, "Some of these complaints seem valid enough, though I'm only a layman in each field. However, I met Doctor Ryan and some of his intimates yesterday, and they admitted that there were all sorts of holes that needed plugging. But they certainly didn't see any point in scrapping the whole space colonization program."

"The thing is," Adam said urgently, "that it's all premature. We simply don't have the theoretical background yet. We're going off half-cocked. I don't have anything against Sol Ryan personally. He's one of the most charming men I've ever met. But he's a scatterbrain, a dreamer. His basic ideas don't hold water."

"Once again, such as what?"

"You've read his famous book?"

"Certainly. I've even met one of the men who wrote it."

Adam Bloch looked at the freelancer. "Now that never occurred to me. You mean Ryan didn't write that bestseller that introduced the whole dream to the man in the street?"

Bruce sighed. "Adam," he said, "whenever you see a well-written book with a non-pro's name on it as author, you can be sure it was ghosted by an old-timer. It takes years, plenty of them, to learn the tools of the trade in the writing game. President Eisenhower's *Crusade in Europe* was written by Quentin Reynolds. President Nixon's *Six Crises* was done by a ghost named Berlin. And did you think Mohammed Ali's autobiography was written by a doggerel-spouting boxer? Or that Lindberg wrote *We*? They might all have been capable men in their own fields, but they were not writers."

Adam Bloch accepted what the other said, scowled in thought, and evidently came to a conclusion. He said, "See here, Bruce, obviously you are gathering material for your writing, whether or not you write a book, which I hope you do. And obviously, to secure your material, you're going to have to seek out other sources of information than you'll get at the L5 Hilton. Ron Rich will give you little beyond his standard publicity releases. Very well, without even consulting my associates, I am going to reveal to you that the WITH-AW-DOH Club is actually a front for what might be called an underground organization."

Bruce eyed him in surprise. "Underground!"

"That's what it amounts to. We are organized for the purpose of subverting the present administration of the Lagrange Five Project. One of our greatest difficulties is that we have no manner of getting any of our more articulate membership back to Earth to spread our message. But with you on the scene, it's another thing. If we can convert you to our way of thinking, when you return, no one is in a better position to reveal the true nature of the Lagrange Five Corporation."

Bruce was taking him in as though the sad-faced, older man had gone around the bend.

The teacher pressed on. "Tomorrow there is to be a secret meeting of our Central Committee. I'd like to have you attend."

"I'd love to attend," Bruce said evenly.

"Very well. I live on the edge of the park, just on the outskirts of town. My home is a small, two-storied one, and is constructed entirely of gray moon brick and plastic. It will immediately come to your eye. Take all precautions not to be followed. I'll be waiting for you at four o'clock. I suppose you've already found that we keep Greenwich time here. I'll take you to the meeting. Meanwhile, I suggest that you continue to circulate around here. Almost all the conversations you will listen in on will concern shortcomings of the L5 Project. That's supposedly the purpose of the Club, to get together and exchange complaints, supposedly in a humorous way."

"So I've already found out," Bruce said mildly.

The teacher stood and said, "I'd just as well not be seen in your company any more tonight. It's almost certain that Security has an agent or two present and it might look suspicious if I spent too much time with a writer."

"Wizard," Bruce told him. "I'll see you and this mysterious committee of yours tomorrow."

Pal Barack was one of the last to leave that night. He had spent the whole evening sounding off about Security and the conspiracy to keep contractees from returning to Earth when their time had elapsed. He'd had no difficulty in getting ears to listen.

Now, on his way home, he was mulling over the position he was in. He had no doubt that Jeff Miller had been right. Captain Borgia could keep him on standby indefinitely, as he had Jeff. And meanwhile he had no funds whatsoever. He could continue to occupy his quarters and eat the unappetizing food in one of the community dining halls, but the prospect of continuing to survive without any funds for extras was bleak. As he walked through the darkened streets an instinct, perhaps an ESP manifestation going back to his Romany heritage, caused him to suddenly spin in alarm. It was too late. There were three of them and they came into the attack fast. The first struck the little man heavily in the belly, and when he doubled over in pain, the second clubbed him brutally on the back of the lower skull with a blackjack. Two of them grabbed his arms before he fell to the sidewalk.

"Wizard, there's nobody around," the leader of the three snapped. "The disposal chute's a couple of hundred feet up the street. If we run into anybody, and that's unlikely this time of night, we're all drunk and he's passed out and we're carrying him home."

"Great," one of the two supporting the victim growled.

There was no difficulty in shoving the unconscious Pal Barack into the chute.

The three stepped back and the leader said in satisfaction, "That's the advantage of recycling everything. Tomorrow, the bastard will be fertilizer, along with all the other shit. Antonio, you go to his house and get his things. All of them. If any of his friends get to wondering about him, it'll look like he got his passage to Earthside."

"On the economic side I think that (the space colony advocate's) vision fails. We must always measure proposals like his against Hitch's Rule, which says that a new enterprise always costs from two to twenty times as much as the most careful official estimates . . . (He) says his space program will cost hundreds of billions of dollars. Applying Hitch's Rule we can be sure it will cost thousands of billions. Would such a venture push the economic system past the flop-over point?"
—*Garrett Hardin, author of* Nature and Man's Fate.

Chapter Eleven

Peter Kapitz had awakened the morning after the party for Prince Abou ben Abel to find himself momentarily disoriented. He stared up at the unpainted metal ceiling and for a moment wondered if he was in a battleship. Obviously not. Now it came back to him. He moved his eyes to the right and there was the blonde head of Irene, the girl who had waited upon him and Mark Donald, the Security lieutenant, at the L5 Hilton dining room the day before.

Mark Donald was a man of his word. He had promised to fix the IABI man up with Irene. Somewhat to Pete's surprise, the waitress had attended the party and, before it was over, Donald had gotten them together. Pete had memories of too much guzzle and too much rich food after more than a week spent in deep space under austere conditions. And evidently it had never occurred to the girl *not* to come to his room when the party broke up. It couldn't be his good looks and he rather doubted it was his charm. Peter Kapitz had few illusions about himself as a romantic figure.

She came awake at almost the same time he had and was the type who could smile as though meaning it at the first sight of the new day. A repulsive characteristic, in Pete's estimation.

She said, "Good morning, darling."

"Good morning?" he repeated. At least she looked as attractive the morning after as she had the night before. Which didn't always apply. In fact, it rarely did. She was one scrumptious mopsy, he told himself. One of her coral-tipped melons popped up from under the bed sheet and and it came back to him that they'd tumbled into bed nude and that her figure was as gorgeous as her piquant face.

"Why?" he said.

"Why what?"

"Why'd you bother to come to bed with me last night? I'm not exactly a Tri-Di super-jock."

She grinned at him. "It all comes under the head of public relations. Mr. Moore said that you were to be given VIP status."

"You mean that you work all day in that restaurant and then at night you perform, ah, public relations duties? You need a union."

She shrugged shoulders that were as round as her heels, brought her arms up, and stretched hugely, revealing the other melon as the sheet slipped. "Extra pay," she said. "A girl's hard-put at Lagrange Five to afford any of the goodies unless she takes every opportunity to, uh, improve herself." She took a deep breath. "Besides, they never would have let me come up if they hadn't known I was cooperative."

He took her in, all over again, and said, "You don't exactly look like a space construction worker, or even some scientific type. Why did you come to Island One? I'd think a girl like you could make a small fortune in Vegas or the Bahamas. In Lagrange Five, it must be a little rugged for a girl who likes her goodies."

She hesitated momentarily, then shrugged the magnificent shoulders again. "I *was* in the Bahamas, but I got a little warm and, uh, a friend made arrangements for me to come up here."

"A little warm?"

"I shot a man a little."

"How little?"

"He's a little bit dead. He was my husband, the bastard."

He fixed his eyes on her. "Didn't you know I was a cop? I'm an IABI operative."

"Oh, yes. Mr. Donald mentioned that," she said carelessly.

"Well, for Christ's sake, girl, suppose I arrested you? If you're on the run it wouldn't be very hard for me to check with the Bahamas police, get the details, and haul you back down."

Her blue eyes widened a little, but there was a touch of mockery there. "You have no jurisdiction in Island One, Mr. Kapitz, darling. You're from the United States of the Americas."

He was indignant at her. The damn fool, letting him know she was a fugitive. He said severely, "I could work through the Reunited Nations."

"They don't have any jurisdiction here either. Neither has any Earthside government. Only Lagrange Five Security has. And there's no extradition from Island One, Mr. Kapitz."

"Pete," he told her in disgust. It hadn't occurred to him before, what she had just revealed. But she was obviously right.

He said, a certain amount of compassion in his voice, "Then you're up here for good? Not just a five- or ten-year contract."

She sighed. "That's right. I'm a colonist, not just a contract worker. And after a few years, when my looks have gone, I'll be limited to my income as a waitress. It's not much of a prospect. Perhaps I can get one of the big shots to marry me, or at least take me on a full-time basis."

Pete scowled. For all he knew, Irene's husband had deserved the shooting. He said, "I suppose, at least, when they've finished the larger islands, say Island Three, you'll be able to move over there and living won't be so rugged."

She gave a little snort. "I'll believe Island Three when I see it. Who do you think's going to populate the place and run it?"

Bruce Carter and Rick Venner had come up against this aspect before, but Pete Kapitz hadn't. Scowling still, he said, "All those people down Earthside who want to become space colonists."

"Anybody who wants to become a space colonist has solid bone in his head where brains ought to be," she told him sarcastically. "When it comes to living the good life, this is the end of the line."

Pete Kapitz still largely had the space dream, as he'd explained to Roy Thomas before taking the assignment. He said, "It'll be different when the big islands get underway. With all that high pay the colonists get, life'll be pretty rosy."

Her snort was more definite this time. She said patiently, "Look, suppose you have some engineer who makes maybe 40,000 dollars a year, tax free, and a wife who's a doctor, and makes the same. A family income of 80,000 a year up here. Fine. What do they spend it on?"

He eyed her blankly.

She spelled it out for him. "If you had eighty thousand a year, tax free, Earthside, you could live it up. Nice home, a maid maybe, gardens, a boat, nice cars, vacations. The works. But you've got to remember that in Island Three, if it's ever built, everybody else is going to be making big pay, too. So who'd want to be a servant? That big house is out unless you're willing to do all the work yourself. So are the gardens, unless you do your own gardening. The boat is out, unless it's so small you don't need to crew it. Cars, big or otherwise, don't make sense in an island. There's no place far enough away to call for them; besides, it's one of the few real reasons for going into space at all—getting away from the automobiles that have loused up Earth. Vacations? To where? Other islands all but the same as yours? Or back to Earth? If you want to be on Earth, why leave? If you've got enough on the ball to work in space, you can make a good living Earthside. The second-raters are all on the 'nit,' Negative Income Tax, or the equivalent in other countries, but if you've got any real ability, you can earn a good living."

"Wizard, I get the message," Pete said. "You don't think anybody in his right mind would become a space colonist."

"I sure as hell wouldn't, darling," she said. She smiled again. "Would you like a repeat this morning or did you lose your repeater?"

He looked at his wrist chronometer, which was all he wore, and said, "Don't think I don't appreciate the kind offer, lady, but after that hectic party . . . ," he cleared his throat, ". . . and what happened after, I find it's getting late and I have a lot to do. Besides, I've got a slight hangover."

"Don't apologize," she said, her smile inverted. "I assume you didn't arrive in Island One just to see the sights. There aren't any. Did you want me to come again tonight?"

"At least half a dozen times," he said, swinging his feet to the floor.

Irene laughed. "It's a date," she said. "See you here tonight then, if not sooner in the restaurant."

Pete was on his way to the dossier files in the Security offices on the ground floor. He was going to make a policy of checking out everybody he met and, on the excuse that he was in the files looking for Rocks Weil, no one could complain. However, on his way he stopped off. Peter Kapitz was a strong believer in the fallacy that a hair of the dog that bit you was a cure for hangover.

The main bar of the L5 Hilton was immediately off the lobby and Pete made a beeline for it. At this time of the morning, it was empty save for a single customer and a bartender. Peter took a stool.

He looked hopefully at the bartender and said, "I don't image you'd have a very cold beer. Too much weight involved in sending up such an item."

"Why not, sir?" the barman said briskly. He turned and went to a refrigerator.

The other customer, a middle-aged, rugged-looking type, said sourly, "Nothing too good for the Hilton. Most construction workers can't afford twelve ounces of straight alcohol a month. Here, you drink the same amount of beer in one go. What's more, you don't even have to pay for it."

Pete looked over at him again. The other was wearing space coveralls and on the pocket was stitched, *Fred Davis*, and under that, *Supervisor*. He didn't look the type that would be in the L5 Hilton. The bartender returned with a chilled, beaded bottle of Tuborg and a thin pilsen glass. He poured carefully down the side of the glass until it was a little over half full, then more steeply to bring up a beautiful head, and then set the glass and beer bottle before Pete.

"Cheers, sir," he said and began to return to the place down the bar where he had been polishing glasses that already sparkled like crystal.

"Here," Fred Davis said, holding up his empty glass. "Let me have a refill."

The bartender frowned just a bit and ungraciously came back. He took up a bottle of twenty-year-old rye whiskey from the well-stocked shelves behind the bar and poured and served the drink before returning to his job.

Fred Davis grinned at Pete and said, "Ever notice what snobs waiters and servants are? He calls you sir, but he knows damn well I don't belong in here and he hates to have to serve me, even though it's no skin off his nose. Everything's free in the hotel."

This was a new one to Pete. After taking a life-giving pull on the brew, he said, "How come you're in here if you don't belong?"

"I've got an appointment with Sol Ryan and I'm waiting to see him. As long as I have a legitimate pass to be in the hotel, I rate the same things as everybody else." He laughed a hard-hat construction worker's laugh. "I hope the hell he doesn't get around to seeing me for hours. You know what this guzzle would cost me in the Luxury Bar, across the street?" He grimaced. "Hell, they wouldn't even have it there, no matter what you'd be willing to pay."

Pete said, "You're a construction worker?" Thus far, he hadn't met any of the rank-and-file employees in Island One.

"That's right," the other said. He grinned. "And poor Sol Ryan hates to see me enter his door."

Pete took down some more of his beer. This was interesting. "How's that?" he said.

The other had obviously already had enough of his unaccustomed rye to be on the loose-tongued side. He winked broadly, a burlesque of a wink. "Because I'm bad news. I'm one of the *real* space construction men. When I show up, it's because something's gone plenty wrong."

The IABI man held out his hand. "Pete Kapitz," he said. "I'm temporarily up from Earthside."

The other shook gravely. "One of these one-only special jobs, eh? I'm Freddy Davis. I'm one of the supervisors working in space on the hull."

"Glad to meet you," Pete said. "What's the emergency now?"

"I got several of them," the other said owlishly. "But this one involves one of the basic impossibilities of this whole fuck-up of a job."

"Such as what?" Possibly, Pete realized, here was some of the material of the type Roy Thomas had sent him up to get.

"Such as the vanes, the mirrors on the outside that reflect the sun's rays into the island. You know anything at all about the vanes?"

"Well, vaguely," Pete told him, taking another grateful pull at the Danish beer. "I remember one of the articles Doctor Ryan had in a magazine. He was describing changing the weather by opening and closing the mirrors. He said you could control the average temperature, even chilling it down to the point where there'd be snow."

The other grinned and sipped at his whiskey. "Snow is right. I'll never forget the damn freeze when the mirrors got stuck a couple of years ago and it took us several days to repair the whole complicated shebang. Froze every body of water in the island solid. That was back when they were still trying to introduce fish and wildlife, birds and all. The houses, of course, are all without heating and air conditioning. We weren't expecting to need them. The only way we colonists and contract workers stayed alive was by wearing every stitch of clothing we had and jerry-rigging heating devices."

"Holy smog," Pete said. "I never heard about that."

Freddy Davis smirked in deprecation. "Ron Rich doesn't release that kind of news," he said. "At any rate, here's the thing about the vanes. When the cylinder is revolving at speed enough to get centrifugal forces equal to one G on the inner surface, the movable vanes also feel the one G folded flat. Fully extended, they experience forces averaging over one G. And these vanes are supported only at the hinge end. To give you an idea, you only have to ask what is the longest structure that we can make down Earthside, parallel to the surface and supported or cantilevered at one end. Maybe fifty yards. So, the way the original plans went, if you built the island and started it rotating, it wouldn't be long at all before the vanes would begin to bend, fan out, and soon break off."

Pete was ogling him. He said in protest, "But those mirrors. They're one of the basic things. Can't the vanes be supported by cables or something?"

"It's bad enough in this island," the other told him. "It's only half a mile long. But when you start talking about the big islands, which supposedly we'll start building shortly, then you're talking about vanes that are miles long. You're not going to be able to support them without a whole new design to support many miles of their own length against such forces, to say nothing of the weight of the vanes. It'll be back to square one—or almost."

Pete said, "Wizard, but the fact remains that they are working. All you have to do is look out the window and see. And last night it got dark, just as though we were Earthside."

The space construction engineer and supervisor chortled and said, "For that you can thank yours truly and a couple dozen of my lads who have been improvising, jerry-rigging and patching things up with stickum paper and baling wire. Right now we're working on the possibility of building the mirror support structures as fixed assemblages on which the mirror panels are mounted in the fashion of venetian blinds. But, like I said, it's one thing chasing our tails around like crazy trying to keep this little island more or less operating. But it'd be another thing with any structure as large as Island Two, not to speak of Island Four or Five with their supposed hundreds of square miles of interior area."

Unbeknownst to either Pete Kapitz or Freddy Davis, the bartender, supposedly intent on his glasses, had been taking most of this in. Now he went down to the far end of the bar, flicked a stud and spoke softly, unheard by the two, into a mike set into the wall. Then he returned to his glasses and resumed polishing.

Pete said, finishing his beer, "Being on the practical construction end must give you a viewpoint we laymen can't even comprehend. But you mentioned that this was just one of the basic problems involved. What'd be another one?"

The other looked down into his glass as though pondering the desirability of ordering another, and evidently deciding against it, at least for the time being.

He said, "With Murphy's Law operative, I have a certain misgiving about our island gravity machine, as you'd probably call it. It's not my particular responsibility, but one hell of a lot of things are going to start getting all jolted and fucked up—people, bicycles, soil, water, compost heaps, and what not—when the spin equipment that maintains exact pseudo-gravity gives a big burp because of some defective parts, or whatever. I'm not saying it's going to happen today, or tomorrow, but given time, any machinery throws a red light."

It was then that Annette Casey and Bruce Carter entered the bar. Ryan's Person Friday raised her eyebrows at the sight of the construction supervisor and Pete Kapitz chewing the rag at the bar. The two newcomers came over.

Bruce said to the IABI agent, "Hitting the bottle

already, at this time of day, eh? Once a cop, always a cop. Any chance to freeload . . ."

Pete said, "Hi, Bruce. What spins?" He waved at the bartender for another beer.

Annette said to Davis, "Hi, Freddy. What're you doing off the job? I thought you were the only really reliable man we had in this tin can."

Freddy grinned at her. "I'm not playing hooky, Annette. I have an appointment with Sol. Maybe he's forgotten me. Not that I mind. I have a chance like this at decent guzzle about once in six months. How about having one with me?"

"Before lunch? Heaven forbid. My sainted father died of the shakes. Come along, I'll take you up to the office. Without me on the scene, you're probably right; he's forgotten the appointment."

She turned to Pete, smiled, and said, "You must be Peter Kapitz. Doctor Ryan has been trying to fit seeing you into his schedule, but we've been rather busy." She put out her hand.

They shook, Pete appreciating her brunette beauty. "I've been kind of busy myself, not that I've accomplished much. I saw you and the doctor at the party last night, but you were always so occupied, I didn't want to intrude."

She bent a smile on the IABI man and said to him and Bruce, "I'll see both of you later. Meanwhile, let's go, Freddy."

After they had left, Bruce said to the bartender, "Is it possible to get a cup of coffee in here?"

"Certainly, sir. Right away." He went down to his mike at the end of the bar and spoke into it.

Bruce said to Pete, "Let's go to a table. If I sat here, staring at those bottles, I'd probably succumb and start drinking myself."

Pete picked up his fresh bottle of beer and followed the other to a table.

Bruce said, "I got the damnedest feeling that our girl didn't like the idea of you talking to that guy."

"Oh?" Pete said, surprised. "Why not?"

"Damned if I know. What were you talking about?"

Pete laughed and poured half of his bottle into the pilsen glass with less than the finesse the bartender had displayed earlier. He said, "What seems to be the inevitable topic in Island One? What's wrong with it and why the whole L5 Project is going down the drain."

Bruce squinted at him. "Oh, you've been getting that song and dance too, eh?"

"Yeah. To hear them talk, I'm surprised that they've gotten this far."

"For that matter," Bruce said wryly, "I can't seem to find out just how far they have gotten. When I left Earth, I had the impression from Lagrange Five Corporation publicity that Island One was practically finished and that some ten thousand space colonists were already happily established."

The coffee came, brought from the dining room by one of the inevitably cute waitresses.

After she was gone and Bruce had stirred sweetener into his beverage, he said, "Where in the hell do they get them all? You'd have your work cut out judging a beauty contest up here. They'd all deserve to win. I haven't seen a plain-looking mopsy since I arrived, unless it was a couple of these women scientists last night."

Pete said sarcastically, "They work a double shift. Waitresses or whatever during the day and public relations all night. And for that kind of public relations work, you can't have second-rate bimbos."

Bruce raised his eyebrows. "I'll be damned. I assume you're speaking from experience."

Pete drank some of his beer. He was feeling better by the minute.

Bruce said nonchalantly, "Why don't you pick up Rocks Weil, Pete?"

The other took him in indignantly. "I just got here yesterday. Who do you think I am, Nero Wolfe or Charlie Chan?"

The freelance writer said, "Come off it, Pete. I've seen you work before. Appearances to the contrary, you're a damned good operative. If you were really looking for Rocks Weil, you would have disappeared into the wallpaper after him long before this."

Pete Kapitz was indignant still. "What in the hell are you talking about?" he said. "Long before this. We got here yesterday. I've just started to go through the dossiers, checking out the photos of every male in Lagrange Five. I'll start on the Luna base next."

"Bullshit," Bruce said earnestly. "You could have arrested him in the *Goddard*. Rick Venner is Rocks Weil."

The IABI man bug-eyed him.

The freelancer was taken aback. He said, in surprise, "You can't be acting. You're really flabbergasted, aren't you. I'll be damned." His eyes went thoughtful. "You know, I don't think you're really looking for Rocks at all. There's probably a story in this. What in the name of hell are you doing in Island One, Pete?"

Pete Kapitz said, "Why do you think Rick Venner is Rocks Weil?"

"I'm not absolutely certain," Bruce told him. "But it adds up. If Rocks is in Island One, then he's Rick Venner. Check it out. According to what you told us on the *Goddard*, when we were waiting for the passenger freighter to bring us out here, Rocks pulled his most recent romp in London, taking a very nice score, as the grifters call it, in diamonds. About six weeks later, a forger in Mexico named Pavel Meer was found murdered and in his possession was equipment that indicated that he'd been involved in forging papers that would allow an ordinarily unqualified person to get into the Lagrange Five Project. Wizard. A new contract man has to spend one month at the New Albuquerque space shuttleport getting checked out, going through simulated space experience, learning Esperanto, and so forth. So, figure it out. If Rocks pulled his romp in London six weeks ago and immediately headed for Lagrange Five, he would have had to spend a month in New Albuquerque."

"So what?" Pete said.

"That means he had to arrive here within the past couple of weeks and, most likely, even less time than that."

"Even given that," Pete said skeptically, "it doesn't mean that Venner is. . . ."

"All right, here's more," Bruce told him. "On the way up, Rick tried to take me at poker. Stacking the deck. A real pro card sharp. Last night, he crashed the party, evidently after getting his hands on some formal clothing. In short, he's a fast operator without a conscience. So, just because I'm nosy by trade, I made a call for his dossier in the National Data Banks down in the States. The dossier seemed to be on the up and up. I suspect that it's genuine and that Rocks Weil's real name is Rick Venner. But there was one thing offbeat. He was educated as an electrical engineer, but there was no record of his ever working at the profession. In fact, there was practically no record of him after his graduation. He had no criminal record, not even a traffic violation. He never applied for Negative Income Tax. He seemingly just disappeared."

"That's still not evidence that Venner's. . . ."

Bruce went on. "Intrigued, I checked and found out that yesterday Rick was taken out into space. He became deathly space sick. That's pretty rare, these days. The doctors down in New Albuquerque, at the *Goddard*, and even on the way over in the passenger freighter checked us all for proneness to space sickness, but especially the three who came up to be construction workers because that'd take them in space, while you and I and Mary Beth would remain solely inside the island. It was very handy, Rick getting sick that way because now the L5 people will never know if he's really an experienced construction engineer or not; they'll have to find some other job for him here, inside."

Pete was eyeing him. "What else?"

"I did some research into Rocks Weil once, thinking I might do an article on him. I had to scrap the idea because there wasn't enough authentic information. However, I went through Interpol's files and Rick is in the right age group and physically resembles Rocks Weil from the admittedly inadequate descriptions given by some of his victims."

Pete finished his beer with one long gulp. "Damn it," he said, meaninglessly.

"So," Bruce said smoothly, "he's one of the very few new contract men to come up in the past two weeks. And *if* Rocks is in Island One, he would have had to come up during that period. So why don't you snag Rick and grill him? Surely, Security would cooperate. Obviously, they're collaborating with you, or you wouldn't be up here."

Pete gritted his teeth. "Damn it," he said again.

"Yeah," Bruce said, looking at him over the rim of his cup as he sipped his coffee.

"Look, Bruce," Pete said looking the other full in the face. "Off the record, you've got it right. I wasn't even looking for Rocks Weil. It made a good cover story, but I didn't really think he was up here. I can't even legally arrest him. If I tried my supposed reason for coming to Lagrange Five would be accomplished and they'd send me back on the next passenger freighter, maybe along with Weil."

"So why'd you really come up?"

"I can't tell you, damn it."

Bruce sighed. "That's a helluva thing to say to a writer, Pete. Now I'm really curious. So suppose we tell the story this way. Suppose that I expose the infamous Rocks Weil myself. It'd make a damn fine article for me: Bruce Carter, fearless muckraking author, shows up Interpol, the IABI, Scotland Yard, and the Sureté by making a citizen's arrest of the notorious international jewel thief."

"Holy smog, Bruce," the other said in protest. "That'd end in my having to go back too. My supposed reason for being here would be over."

"Yeah," Bruce said. "So what're you really doing up here, Pete?"

"Now, look, Bruce," the IABI operative said earnestly. "You're an American. You have certain responsibilities as a citizen."

"Stop it, stop it, you're striking sparks off my heart."

"Look, Bruce. I'm on an assignment working directly under President Paul Corcoran. It's very hush-hush."

"Tell me more."

"I can't."

"Then I don't believe you," Bruce told him reasonably. "And in exactly two minutes I'm going to get up out of this chair and start steps to arrest Rocks Weil. I'll teach that sonofabitch to stack a deck on me. I take my poker seriously."

The nondescript agent registered despair. "Look," he said. "This has to be off the record. It can't get out. Certainly not for the time being."

"You'll have to leave that up to me, Pete. But I'm cooperative. You know that. What are you up here for?"

"I'm on an assignment for Roy Thomas, for Christ's sake."

Bruce whistled softly. "I've met Thomas. He's a good man," he said. "Doing what?" Pete groaned in despair. "Digging into what's going on in the Lagrange Five Project."

It was Bruce's turn to boggle. "What in the hell are you talking about?" he said.

Pete groaned again. "The President's brain trust thinks that something stinks about the Lagrange Five Corporation. He evidently thinks it's some sort of a rip-off."

"Some sort of a rip-off! Holy jumping Zoroaster, you cloddy, if there's anything off-color about the LFC, it's the biggest news and the biggest world disaster since the flood."

"I didn't say I thought there was something wrong," the other said defensively. "Hell, I own stock in the corporation. I said that Roy Thomas thinks he smells a rat. He's working on it Earthside. He sent me up here to root out anything I could. I came, not expecting to find anything to root." He swallowed the last of his beer. "But now I'm not so sure."

Bruce Carter's eyes narrowed. "Why? I came up to do some stories about the project, maybe a book. I had an upbeat viewpoint, but now I have a few second thoughts, too. Roy Thomas is no dizzard. In fact, he's the smartest man in Washington. If he thinks something's wrong about the LFC, it's four chances out of five that he's right."

Pete shook his head in misery. "It's a lot of the little things about the place that I've noticed. This island, for instance, is a far cry from what we see on Tri-Di and TV down Earthside."

"It sure as hell is," Bruce said grimly. "See here, Pete, what do you say we continue on the present basis? I continue to gather my material for my articles or book, you continue to supposedly look for Rocks. We'll get together and exchange notes periodically. All we can do at this stage of the game is play it by ear."

Pete stood. "Wizard, Bruce. God only knows what we'll eventually come up with. Meanwhile, I'll get down into the Security files, pretending to look up Rocks, but actually checking out anything I can think of."

"Right-o," the freelancer told him.

Pete Kapitz went on out to the lounge and turned to head for the Security offices, but then came up abruptly. On the far side of the lobby, he spotted someone he knew. Someone wearing the dark green coveralls of a Security man. He scowled, not having expected to meet anyone in Island One that he was acquainted with. But who was the man?

Then it came to him. Natale Lucchese. In the old days, Pete supposed, they probably would have called him a *caporegime*, of the Biamco family of Philadelphia. Pete vaguely remembered the man as disappearing a couple of years ago, for unknown reasons. But here he was, seemingly hiding out in Lagrange Five. Well, if a criminal talent like Rocks Weil could pick a remote place like Island One to go to ground, there was no reason why a minor cog in what they used to call the Syndicate, such as Natale Lucchese, couldn't.

The other hadn't spotted Pete. In fact, the IABI man rather doubted that Lucchese would recognize him. They hadn't ever really come face to face. The other had been pointed out to him a couple of times back Earthside. Pete continued on his way to the files. Seated at the same desk he had used the day before, he first checked out the personnel files of the Security department. He was surprised to find the number of them, more than two hundred. What in the world did they need with that many police on a project like Island One? And, yes, here was the less than handsome face of Natale Lucchese. Only his name was listed as Nat Luke. And, of all surprises, he had a master's degree from New Kingston University and in, of all things, the humanities. Well, he supposed that would have helped the other to secure a job with Security in the Lagrange Five Project.

One by one, he checked out all the other persons he had thus far met in Lagrange City, not excluding Al

Moore or even Annette Casey. Moore, he discovered, held a doctorate in the social sciences, and the young woman one in physics. As a matter of fact, she had an impressive list of accomplishments. She certainly didn't look the double-dome she obviously was.

When he had finished his checking, he left the Security offices, arousing no more attention than had his arrival, and returned to the lobby. The Syndicate man was no longer present. Pete took to the stairs and continued upward until he had reached the roof.

It provided an excellent view out over the town and, indeed, the whole cylinder, since the L5 Hilton was the tallest building in the island. Some of what he had been hearing was borne out. The interior, at least, of Island One was far from being completed. He could see considerable numbers of workers in the distance and assumed that they were landscaping. They seemed to have some small land movers, and some trucks, but larger equipment wasn't in view. He imagined that there'd be problems involved in bringing really king-sized vehicles to Lagrange Five.

He walked to one corner of the roof and sat on the parapet, facing the door so that he could see anyone emerging. He brought from one of the coverall pockets his specially issued transceiver, flicked both the scrambled and muffled studs, and then dialed the high-priority number Roy Thomas had given him in Greater Washington. He was surprised at the clarity of the other's voice when it came through. Somehow, he'd had the feeling that communication would be difficult in view of the distance involved.

He said, "Kapitz here."

The delays in their messages were barely noticeable, and Roy Thomas's brisk voice was . . . brisk. "Very well. What have you to report, Kapitz?"

Pete gave it all to him concisely, including the fact

that Rocks Weil was evidently really in the island and that he'd had to come to terms with Bruce Carter. That irritated the Presidential advisor, but there was nothing for it.

Thomas said, "Give me that about Prince Abel again. This simply doesn't make sense. He's high in the finances of the Arab Union."

Pete said, "I thought it was funny he should be seeing Ryan, so at the party I planted a bug in his sash. Then I went into the men's room and sat in a booth and tuned in on it. I wasn't able to listen long before somebody found the bug. The big news was that the Arab Union was willing to continue to subsidize the L5 Project at the rate of five billion a year."

"He said *to continue*? Implying that they've been doing it already for some years?"

"Yes, sir."

The voice of the faraway governmental troubleshooter was puzzled. "That simply doesn't make sense at all. If there's anything the Arab Union wouldn't want to see, it's a successful Lagrange Five Project. Given solar power, the value of their oil would drop disastrously."

"Yes, sir. That's what I thought."

"Anything else, Kapitz?"

"Nothing much definite. However, I've only been here two days, but I can already see that this thing isn't coming along as fast as the L5 Corporation would want the public to believe. There seem to be more bugs than they figured on."

"Anything else?"

"Well, one thing. Evidently, Rocks Weil isn't the only one to pick Island One for a hideaway. Last night I met a call girl who's wanted in the Bahamas for homicide. And today I spotted a, uh, Syndicate member. Natale Lucchese, who's hiding under the name Nat Luke. He's even got a job in the Security force."

"Syndicate?"

"Yeah, what they used to call the Mob, the Cosa Nostra."

"See here, Kapitz, aren't you being a little romantic? There is no Syndicate these days. The era of Al Capone and Lucky Luciano is as gone as those of Blackbeard and Henry Morgan."

"Not quite, sir. Of course, they don't rob banks or bootleg guzzle any more, but there are still remnants of the organization in such unions as are left and in gambling and resorts. Even when you do run into them, they're usually legit. This one even has a college degree in humanities."

"Not of a great deal of importance, I suppose. Look, Kapitz, there's one thing you might look into. In my investigations at this end, I have been surprised that I haven't been able to locate any construction workers who formerly worked at Lagrange Five. I've had to proceed very cautiously, of course, but I've found none at all. Check about and see if you can find a reason for this."

"Yes, sir. Oh, just one other thing. Probably has no significance, but I've checked out in the Security archives everybody I've met so far, mostly top executives, scientists, and engineers. What strikes me is that it's not just Doctor Solomon Ryan that comes from New Kingston University; so do practically all the rest of them. They've all taken their degrees at New Kingston except a few like Academician Leonard Suvorov, from the University of Leningrad, and Doctor Rudi Koplin from the University of Warsaw. They're both defectors, of course."

There was a pause while the President's right-hand man thought about it. He said, "I suppose it's understandable. This whole project originated at New Kingston, and most of the research goes on there. Obviously, they'd put their own people in. It's one of the most prestigious schools in the country. I would think they could supply as many competent men and women as are needed. That'll be all, then. Continue to report every time something comes up. Down here, we're beating our heads against a stone wall trying to find out anything about the inner workings of the Lagrange Five Corporation in Tangier. It's worse than trying to get inside banking information in Switzerland." The other's voice hesitated. "And, Kapitz, ah, take care of yourself. There are some aspects of this that make me nervous."

"Yes, sir. I usually do."

At about this same time, Irene was being interviewed in the office of Al Moore by the Security Chief, Mark Donald, and Joe Evola. Al Moore was furious, Irene abject in her apology.

Moore was saying, "You goddamned fucking mopsy, you must've known that room was bugged. It's bad enough you letting that stupid cop know you're on the run. He'll get the impression that not only is Rocks Weil up here, but half the lamsters Earthside."

"I'm sorry, Al," she wavered, her eyes going nervously from one of the grim visaged men to the other.

"Call me Mr. Moore, you stupid cunt. And that's not all. What the hell did you think Mark told you to show Kapitz a good time for? Your job was to give him an upbeat picture of Island One. Instead of that, you shoot off your fucking mouth about what a rough go it is and how nobody in his right mind would ever come up here as a colonist."

"I'm sorry, Mr. Moore," she said fearfully. Then added, in hope, "I got another date with him for tonight. I'll . . . I'll be different."

"You're goddamned right, you'll be different. Joe, emphasize what I've just said to this stupid broad."

Joe slapped her hard with the back of his right hand

over her lips, bringing blood, then reversed his hand and struck her brutally again.

She moaned, "Not my face, Joe. Not my face. He'll notice tonight."

"Get the hell out of here," Mark Donald said. "And if you think you're going to get any kind of bonus for last night, next time I'll have Joe kick some of your teeth in."

When she was gone, Al Moore said to Joe Evola, "Where in the hell's the funker now?"

"He went on up to the roof; I couldn't have followed him without his seeing me." Joe hesitated. "I'm kind of surprised. If he's an IABI man, he ought to be experienced enough to make me, especially since we came up together. But he doesn't seem to realize he's being followed."

The Security head looked at Donald. "What in the hell would he be doing on the roof?"

His lieutenant said, "He could be just taking a look-see out over the town. On the other hand, he could be making a report Earthside."

"If he's reporting," Moore mused, "his equipment's probably both scrambled and muffled. Is there any way we can bug in?"

"I'll put the electronic boys to work on it," Donald said.

Moore looked at Joe Evola. "Get on back to the job. We want to know where that bootlicker of Roy Thomas is every minute."

"I think that when people talk of colonizing space they really don't have any genuine perception of what it will involve. All the present support for space comes from Earth and until we learn much, much more about contained ecosystems, it will continue to do so. It won't be the kind of knowledge that a crash program of space biology will generate."
—John Todd, Biologist, co-founder of the New Alchemy Institute.

Chapter Twelve

Academician Leonard Suvorov pushed his *pince nez* glasses back higher on his nose and looked about the opulent office. He said, "Only a few decades ago the little dog Laika became the first Earthling ever to enter space. And already we have such as this. It is hard to believe I am hundreds of thousands of kilometers away from the planet of my birth."

Solomon Ryan laughed ruefully and said in deprecation, "I am in the hands of the Public Relations Department of the Lagrange Five Corporation, Academician. Our Ron Rich insists that my office be as magnificent as any that might be found in the World Trade Center, or the Sears Tower in Chicago. Mine not to reason why."

Annette Casey, seated at her own desk to one side of that of her boss, said cynically, "Investors plowing tens of billions of dollars, Common Europe marks, francs, and pounds, South American pesos and what not, into the Lagrange Five Project, would be set back seeing you seated on an orange crate behind a desk jury-rigged from a packing case."

The Soviet bionomics authority nodded and said, "I am afraid that I am over my head in this field of publicity." He ran a chubby hand back through his thin, red hair. "As I am in so many fields pertaining to the project. Indeed, though I have only been here two or three days, I find myself increasingly confused."

"I am truly sorry that I have taken so long to get around to properly greeting you, Academician," Ryan told him. "It is a feather in our cap to be able to add the prestigious Leonard Suvorov to our ranks." He smiled his charisma again. "What are your first impressions?"

The Russian thought about it. Then, "Possibly not very sound ones, Doctor Ryan."

"Sol, please. Here in space there are no formalities. We are peers without qualifications regarding race, creed, color, class, title, rank. . . ." He looked at Annette, smiled his little rueful smile and added, ". . . or sex."

Annette gave a small snort. "Oh, there's a little sex in Island One, but you're right, no discrimination against it."

Leonard Suvorov chuckled in appreciation. He liked the atmosphere. "You must both call me Leon," he told them.

The father of the Lagrange Five Project said, "But I am truly quite interested in your first reactions. You may think them premature, but in actuality, first snap impressions often have a surprising validity. I would say that a newcomer here has three periods where his opinions are of particular interest. The first, when he has been on the scene only a few days. The next, when he has been here perhaps six months. And, finally, when he has worked on the project for several years."

The other adjusted his somewhat heavyset body in his chair and sent his habitually tired eyes to a far corner of the room in consideration. He said musingly, "I see what you mean. A newcomer might spot things that you

229

veterans would miss through familiarity. Well then, my first impression, and one that I did not particularly nurture until my arrival, is that the project is premature."

Ryan frowned. "How do you mean?" he said.

The Russian nodded. "Let us suppose that at the turn of the century, in 1900, a government had approached the pioneers of heavier than air flying."

"In actuality, the Wright brothers didn't fly until 1903," Annette said pertly.

He looked at her. "I wasn't thinking in particular of Orville and Wilbur Wright."

Annette was irrepressible. "Sorry, I forgot. The first powered flight was made in the Ukraine, or Siberia, or somewhere by somebody named Ivan Ivanovitch, or something."

The Russian scientist was amused. "Ai, ai," he said. "Chauvinism rears its head. I am surprised at you, Doctor Casey."

"Annette," she said, "or I won't call you Leon."

"Annette," he said. "It is the old story. We have an international gathering. A Russian mentions in passing that his people were the first to develop the submarine. An American laughs. The Russian looks at him huffily and says, 'Then, who did first develop the submarine?' And the American informs him that it was Simon Lake or, perhaps, J.P. Holland. Whereupon, both the Dutchman and the Greek laugh in turn. Perhaps the Greek with the most validity, since I understand there are records of a submarine in Ionia going back to the era before Christ."

Annette was not one to be sat upon. She said, in a touch of irritation, "Oh, come now, Leon. It is rather commonly accepted that the Wright brothers were the first to accomplish powered flight. Nobody is running down the other pioneers in aviation, but the Wright brothers were the first."

"According to you Americans," Suvorov nodded. "In actuality, I suppose that possibly the French have as good a claim as any, in this nationalistic prestige game. Clement Adlet achieved powered flight for a hundred or possibly a hundred and fifty feet in 1897, six years before the Wrights. He was, by the way, the first aeronautical engineer to receive a government subsidy. However, he didn't seem to press on after his initial success. Henri Farman, another Frenchman, was the first to achieve a flight that might be called complete. He took off without assistance, that is without an initial push such as given the Wright craft, made a circle of more than a kilometer, and then landed without damage to his airplane, at the same spot from which he had ascended."

Annette looked at him sourly.

But Leonard Suvorov was not to be put off. He said, "The Wright brothers are somewhat comparable to Columbus. He was by no means the first European to discover the Americas. It is known today that they had been discovered many times over the centuries, without permanent result. But circa 1490, the day of the New World had come. Even if Columbus had not made his epic journey, a dozen others would have done so within a few years. It was in the wind. So it was with the Wrights. A score of men were working on the project contemporaneously with them. The Canadian Horatio Phillips, Lilienthal in Germany, J. J. Montgomery in the United States, Percy Pilcher and Sir Hiram Maxim in England, Alberto Santos-Dumont of Brazil. Maxim, by the way, was another who flew, in his steam-engined aircraft, before the Wright brothers, but his airplane cracked up on landing. At any rate, it was the Wrights who made the breakthroughs that precipitated the birth of aviation."

Annette said, "How in the world can you remember all that?"

231

The Russian pushed his glasses back onto the bridge of his nose and sighed. "I am cursed with almost complete recall," he told her.

Solomon Ryan was amused. He said, "How did we get off on this tangent?"

Suvorov looked over at him and said, "I was building up to saying that I feel the Lagrange Five Project is something as though one were to go to the . . . ," he flicked his eyes at Annette, ". . . Wright brothers in 1903, and offer them a hundred billion dollars to embark upon a project to build an aircraft that would carry three hundred passengers at a time across the Atlantic at a speed exceeding that of sound."

Ryan rubbed the end of his nose with a forefinger and screwed up his face. "Oh, come now, Leon," he protested.

But the Russian was shaking his head. "And then, when they were thwarted on a dozen fronts, parlaying it up to two hundred billion, then three hundred billion."

Annette said in exasperation, "What in the hell are you getting at?"

Suvorov said slowly, "My point is that no matter how much you were willing to contribute to the building of such an aircraft, the Wright brothers were in no position to do it. Nor would anyone be for half a century and more. My first impression, upon spending two or three days in Island One, is that the Lagrange Five Project is in the same position. That it is premature. We do not as yet have the knowledge to build a valid space colony."

"But it is here!" Ryan blurted.

"Is it?"

Sol Ryan drummed his fingers on his desk unhappily. He said, "Admittedly, there are a lot of problems, Leon. But, one by one, we're licking them."

"Are you?"

Ryan stared at him.

232

Suvorov said, "Some things there are, in science as elsewhere, that do not admit of crash programs, infinitely funded or not. For instance, we have yet to defeat cancer; indeed, it continues to grow. We have plowed hundreds of millions into the fight, but as yet without success. Some things do not concede to money alone. Time is an element. The Wright brothers would have needed the jet engine, among other things, to build that supersonic aircraft and the world's technology was not up to jet propulsion at that time."

The other two were eyeing him emptily.

He said slowly, "I am out of my depth so far as your other problems are concerned. But so far as ecology is concerned, the world's technology is not up to space colonies at this time."

Solomon Ryan said, "Are you admitting defeat before beginning?"

The academician shook his head. "No, I accept the challenge. I will do all possible to achieve a self-sustaining biosphere, a closed-cycle ecology system here in Island One. The problem intrigues me endlessly. And I understand that you have facilities and resources available such as are undreamed of Earthside. I shall do my best. You asked me, however, for my first impressions. I have given them to you. In this field, we are in our infancy, much as the Wrights were in aviation in 1903. Frankly, I would rather see this project begin possibly twenty years from now."

Solomon Ryan shook his head sadly. "I suppose," he said. "I asked for it and you've certainly laid it on the line." His irrepressible grin came to his face. "And I suppose that the sooner you get to this all but impossible job, the better." He looked at his assistant. "Annette, suppose that you take Leon down to his new office. Find out his needs. Get his nose to the grindstone."

"Wizard, Sol," she said, coming to her feet.

Suvorov stood too and looked down at the project head. "Sorry, Sol," he said. "Perhaps you shouldn't have asked me. And, after all, it is but my first impression." He smiled heavily. "Ask me again in six months. And then, again, after a few years."

One of the screens on the desk of the L5 Project head buzzed, but before Ryan could answer it, the door burst open and Rudi Koplin hurried in, a sheaf of papers in his hand, and looking even more than ordinarily distraught.

"Doctor Ryan!" he got out. "Sol! It's madness."

"It sure is, Comrade," Annette murmured under her breath.

Ryan grinned and said, "What is it this time, Rudi?" And then, "Academician Suvorov, have you met our stormy petrel, Doctor Rudi Koplin?"

The Russian extended a hand to the Polish biochemist. "Of course. Not only at the party for the Prince, but various times Earthside at scientific conclaves. Rudi and I are old colleagues."

The dowdy Koplin shook his hand absently, saying, "Leon! You must hear this. It is madness."

"Very well, Rudi," Ryan said. "What disaster now faces the Project?"

The newcomer to the scene turned and faced him, his expression registering anguish. "It's Doctor O'Malley again. Do they present clods with doctorates at your New Kingston University? He is insane."

Annette sighed and said, "Aren't we all, or why are we all here? What's Barry up to now?"

Koplin slapped his sheaf of papers down onto Ryan's desk dramatically, and thumped them with the back of a fat paw. "He is again off on his tangent about the lack of need for nitrogen in our atmosphere. That we can do with oxygen alone."

Ryan nodded. "The subject has come up. O'Malley,

among others, has pointed out that long since, deep-sea divers and astronauts have proved that 78 percent of the air we breathe is nitrogen and unused by the human body. We have no need for it in our breathing."

The Pole looked at him aghast. "Sol! You are not siding with this maniac!"

The other grinned at him. "I haven't taken a stance as yet. But O'Malley correctly points out that neither humans nor most plants take their nitrogen from the air. We eat it in our food; plants take up nitrogen from their roots, from the soil."

Suvorov said mildly, "But where do the bacteria in the soil get it?"

Annette said, "Providing an Earth-normal amount of nitrogen costs us in two ways in space colony construction. Our structure masses have to be increased to contain the increased pressure that adding the 78 percent of nitrogen to our atmosphere involves. And, of course, nitrogen has to be brought up from Earth. Endless tons of it, even for a small island such as this one. For the larger islands, it'll be a sizable expense."

The rotund, disheveled Pole peered at her through his thick-lensed, steel-bound spectacles in continued agony. Then he turned to Leonard Suvorov. "Leon," he said. "It is more your field than mine. Tell them."

Ryan looked at the Russian ecologist. "What do you think, Leon?"

Suvorov shook his head ruefully. "It is childishness such as this that caused me to state I would rather see this whole project begin twenty years from now. Sol, an enzyme called nitrogenase is responsible for taking atmospheric nitrogen and changing it into high energy ammonia, NH_3. The ammonia is necessary for protein production. Now, here is the important thing. Oxygen must be kept away from nitrogenase. If there is too much oxygen, then there can be no ammonia and no protein. It is hard enough on Earth to keep nitrogenase without upping the amount of nitrogen in the atmosphere to eighty percent. I am afraid that your Doctor O'Malley—I have yet to meet the gentleman—isn't thinking in terms of the nitrogen-fixing bacteria. And, now that I think of it, I wonder if he has considered sources for the trace elements. For instance, molybdenum is needed to make nitrogenase. And while we are at it, we could mention such crucial elements as phosphorus. The universal energy currency of all living organisms is adenosine triphosphate, or ATP."

Ryan nodded. "Rudi has already been on our necks about the need for phosphates."

The Russian scientist pursed his heavy lips. "Sol, I suggest that if you wish no more than to grow hydroponic gardens that it can be done with your Luna soil with suitable nitrates to enrich it. Indeed, it could be done without the soil at all. However, if you wish finally to achieve a closed-cycle ecology system, then you had best continue to include, both in this island and those to come, from 78 to 80 percent nitrogen in your atmosphere."

Annette said, "Leon, suppose we go and introduce you to your new office and avoid the further dismal sight of Rudi beating poor Sol over the head."

The L5 head said, in mock wryness, "I'm going to put a sign outside my door, 'No Rudis Allowed.'"

"Ha," the Pole said, rummaging through the papers he had brought, looking for a particular page.

The office that had been allotted to Academician Leonard Suvorov was one floor below those of Solomon Ryan. The Soviet bionomics expert followed Annette down.

He said, on the way, "Your Doctor Ryan is a most charming man. It would seem difficult to maintain such a cheerful front in the face of so much adversity."

Annette gave her little snort. "He loves it. It's his life."

He contemplated her from the side of his eyes. Annette Casey was taller than he was by almost half a head. He said, "And what will happen to him when he finally confronts failure?"

"Are you so sure he will?"

He hesitated. "Perhaps it is a matter of time. Given sufficient time, I have no doubt but that a valid space colony can be built. But I am afraid that your publicity people have been a bit too—what is the Americanism— gung ho."

She looked over at him as they descended the steps. "How do you mean? Obviously, Ron Rich and his people get a little enthusiastic from time to time, but what's that got to do with the eventual success of Island One and the islands to follow?"

"Perhaps, Annette," he said heavily, "you have spent so much time up here these last few years that you have gotten out of touch with reality Earthside."

She repeated still again, "How do you mean?"

"There is still a great deal of enthusiasm on Earth for the L5 Project and billions are still being invested in the Lagrange Five Corporation, though as yet, of course, not a single dividend has been declared."

She said, a bit tartly, "Obviously, there is no income as yet. Only outgo. The SPS's are as yet inoperative. When they get underway, LFC stock will be worth its weight in blue diamonds."

He nodded skeptically: "*After* the bugs have been eliminated. But the point I was making is that the investors Earthside have been led to believe that Island One is now all but completed and that final success is all but here. From everything I have thus far seen and heard, it isn't. And I suspect that success, if ever it comes, will require many more years of arduous effort. Somewhere along here, disillusionment is fated to develop. And then, once again to use an Americanism, the fat will be in the fire."

They had reached the floor, one below the top, and Annette had led the way down the corridor to the office apportioned to the distinguished ecologist. She opened the door and let her companion pass through. A space coveralled worker was dusting the floor with a long-handled mop. Tall, blond, strikingly blue-eyed, Scandinavian in appearance, he bobbed his head awkwardly in greeting at their entrance.

The secretary said, "Ah, Alvar. You aren't through as yet?"

His blue eyes took her in admiringly as he straightened up. "Almost, Doctor Casey," he told her. "The place hasn't been touched since Doctor Petersen's accident."

Annette said, "Academician Leonard Suvorov, this is Alvar Saarinen. Alvar was brought up as a forestry authority, but since we aren't as yet ready to utilize his expertise, he has been devoting his efforts to sanitary engineering."

Saarinen laughed humorlessly as he shook hands with the Russian. "That means janitor," he said in Esperanto. "When I left Helsinki, I had no idea I would wind up sweeping floors."

The scientist nodded, only slightly set back. The Fatherland of the Proletariat the Soviet Complex might be, but an Academician of the Academy of Sciences in Leningrad did not usually shake hands with a janitor. It would seem the democracy reached its ultimate here in space.

Suvorov looked about the large room approvingly. It seemed more a study than an office. The bookshelves extended from floor to ceiling and monopolized the walls. The furniture, though all metallic, was well done and cushioned and the desk was large and workmanlike, rather than ostentatious, such as that of Sol Ryan. There were several sets of steel files along the walls.

He said to Annette, "Then this is the former office of

my old colleage Nils Petersen? Excellent; I look forward to perusing his notes. It should save me considerable time. It is my honest opinion that it should have been Doctor Petersen who received the Nobel Prize with which I was honored."

She said, "Well, yes. The doctor's death came as a great shock to all of us. The accident has yet to be explained. The blow to our ecology department was shattering. Thank heavens you've materialized in the nick of time." Her mouth twisted. "To use the Americanism."

The academician blinked his weary eyes at her. "Aren't you an American, my dear?"

"Hell yes, to use the Americanism."

He chuckled, getting her dig at him, and went over to one of the bookshelves and scanned titles. "Ah, excellent," he said. "Trust Nils."

She said, "I imagine that you'll wish some time to get adjusted here. This afternoon I'll take you over to the laboratories and introduce you to your fellow ecologists. There are only two offices here in the hotel devoted to your department."

He had drifted to a set of steel files and pulled open one of the drawers. It seemed empty. He pulled out another.

He said, frowning, "And who is in the other office?"

"It's the one adjoining this. Professor Chu Sing was there."

"Ah, yes." The second drawer was also empty. He pulled out a third. "I heard that the professor left, to my dismay."

"That's right," Annette said, almost apologetically. "He seemed a little short-tempered. He finally flew off the handle."

"To use the Americanism," Suvorov murmured.

She grinned and went on. "And returned to Earth. At first, Doctor Ryan had hopes that he'd reconsider and return. But then he was struck, by a taxi I think, in New York."

The Russian slammed shut the third drawer he had opened and said testily, "You seem to have a high mortality rate among your biologists. Where are the computer files and notes of Doctor Petersen?"

"Why . . . I don't know. Perhaps in his desk?"

"I'd think they would be more extensive than that. How long was he here in all?"

"The better part of a year."

The academician sat at the desk and opened all the closed drawers. "This desk has been cleared out," he said in disgust.

"I'll check," she said. "Probably, knowing that you were taking over, someone has removed all the documents of the doctor and stored them elsewhere."

"Please do," he said. "It is quite important, if he devoted his considerable genius to creating a viable closed-cycle ecology system here in Island One for a full year. His notes will undoubtedly save me many a day's work which I would otherwise expend duplicating his experiments. It is especially important in view of the fact that Professor Chu has also departed the scene."

She said, frowning, "But wouldn't his notes all be in Norwegian? Perhaps we can find a translator to. . . ."

"My dear Doctor Casey, I am thoroughly acquainted with the Scandinavian tongues."

She blinked, but then looked at her wrist chronometer and said, "I have an, uh, appointment with Bruce Carter. Suppose you take over here, Leon, and I'll check with you later on going to the laboratories and meeting those who will be working under you."

He grunted at that, even as he continued to investigate the desk. "I've already met some of them," he rumbled. "It's a tragedy that Petersen and Chu aren't still with us."

Annette left and the academician slumped back in his chair. He looked at Alvar Saarinen, who was still pushing his dust mop about the floor.

"Aren't you through yet?" the Russian said ungraciously.

The other straightened and put his forefinger to his lips in the universal gesture signifying silence. Suvorov stared at him in lack of comprehension. The Finnish janitor leaned his mop against a chair and approached the desk. He took up a stylo, drew a small piece of paper toward him, and wrote a single word on it. And then, with the scientist still staring at him, went over to one of the office's windows and opened it. He turned and gestured to Suvorov to join him. Mystified, the Russian obeyed.

Alvar Saarinen leaned out the window slightly and held up the paper so that Leonard Suvorov could see what he had written. It read CHEKA.

The janitor said in a whisper, "Softly; the office is electronically monitored."

The other was still staring. He whispered back, "Then you are my contact with Colonel Vladimir Dzhurayev? How in the name of hades did you manage to infiltrate this citadel of the Lagrand Five Project?"

The other put the piece of paper in his mouth and, very serious of face, chewed and swallowed. He whispered, "It was not overly difficult, in view of the fact that I have had plenty of time. I am what is called a mole. I have been placed without knowledge of what my eventual use might be. Perhaps I will not be called upon for some special duty for years—if ever. But I remain available just in case. Comrade Colonel Dzhurayev has informed me that I am at your disposal, though it is unlikely that you will need me. Have you any questions? Keep your voice very low."

"Why is my office monitored?"

"I don't know, but they all are. So are all of the hotel rooms. Surveillance is remarkably complete. Anything else?"

"Where are Nils Petersen's notes?"

"Two of Al Moore's goons came and got them this morning. I have no idea where they took them."

"Who is Al Moore?"

"Alfred Moore is the Security Commissioner."

"Police? You mean that they have police up here?"

The Finn looked cynical. "Per capita, we have more police in Island One than the KGB has at home. It is they who have placed the electronic bugs everywhere. Anything else?"

"No . . . not for the time being. Perhaps I will think of questions to ask you later. How do I make contact with you?"

"I will come here to your office every day shortly before noon, ostensibly to clean up. If you have any messages to relay to the Comrade Colonel, I will take care of it."

"I doubt if I will have. I am afraid that I am inexperienced in the field of espionage. Besides, it is not my primary task."

The other nodded and, without further words, turned, regained his mop, and shambled out into the corridor to take up his janitorial duties.

Suvorov looked after him for a moment, then shook his head and resumed his exploration of his new quarters. Examining the balance of the drawers in the files and desk, he found not a scrap of evidence that the ecologist Nils Petersen had ever worked here. He had a deep-rooted suspicion that Annette Casey would not be able to discover what had happened to the papers. Why, he couldn't imagine, but the suspicion was there.

There were two doors besides that which led into the hotel. He tried one and found it opened into a small bathroom. The other, also unlocked, led into an office almost identical to his own. That of Professor Chu Sing, the high-strung Chinese scholar? He entered and looked about. On the desk there were still piles of papers, graphs, sketches, notes. The thick eyebrows of Leonard Suvorov went up. He shuffled among them for a few minutes, his face going increasingly serious. All the writing was in Mandarin.

Thoughtfully, he turned and approached one of the steel files. It was full of the Chinese ecologist's work. All in Mandarin, the scholastic universal language of China. He took his time going through this file and then the others. From time to time he removed single sheets of paper, sometimes a sheaf of them.

The hobby of Academician Leonard Suvorov was linguistics. Since boyhood he had found his relaxation from his scientific studies in the acquiring of ever more tongues. As an undergraduate, he had studied English, German, and French as a matter of course. But then his hobby took over from duty and he found that with one Latin language, French, the acquiring of Spanish, Italian, Portugese, and even Rumanian were simple matters. German led him to both Holland Dutch and Flemish, and then to Danish, Swedish, and Norwegian. He was frustrated to find no relationship between the Scandinavian and Finnish and launched himself into the conquest of that strange language, unrelated to any other European other than Estonian and Hungarian, since all had originally come from far Central Asia. Finnish, Estonian, and Hungarian dispensed with, he turned to still more exotic challenges and became one of the few students of language to become proficient in Basque, a language related to none other on Earth and seldom mastered by anyone not born into the ancient tongue. Indeed, he had conceived a theory, which he never surfaced, not wishing to face ridicule, that Basque was descended from the language of Cro-Magnon man, whose cave art was still to be found in Southern France and Northern Spain, now the home of the volatile Basque people.

He gathered together his selection of Professor Chu Sing's months of work and returned with them to his own office. He decided, with inner satisfaction, that the goons of Al Moore, as the Cheka mole Saarinen had called them, would never suspect that the Russian academician, Leonard Suvorov, had extended his hobby to the Orient, after having mastered every language of Europe.

In short, Leonard Suvorov was thoroughly conversant with Mandarin. He sat at his desk and began perusing his finds. And as he read, his face became increasingly expressionless. When he had finished, some two hours later, he came to his feet, gathered up the notes, and returned to the Chinese scholar's office. He took great care in returning the papers to the exact place each had been found. Then he returned to his own office, sat at his desk, and looked unseeingly through a window that opened out on a long view of the cylinder that was Island One.

He said aloud, "I should have suggested to Doctor Ryan fifty, rather than twenty years, before this project should have been undertaken."

"I regard Space Colonies as another pathological manifestation of the culture that has spent all its resources on expanding the nuclear means for exterminating the human race. Such proposals are only technological requisites for infantile fantasies."
—Lewis Mumford, *author of* Technics and Civilization, The Story of Utopia, *etc.*

Chapter Thirteen

Rick Venner, immaculately dressed in an Earthside business suit, smiled across the table at Mary Beth Houston. They were having lunch in the main dining room of the Lagrange Five Hilton.

The waitress came up smiling, no menus in hand. She said, "Good afternoon, Ms. Houston. I hope that you are enjoying your visit."

"Oh, yes," Mary Beth said.

The waitress said to Rick, "My name's Irene, sir. I don't believe I've waited on you before."

He turned on his charm. "You'll be seeing more of me, Irene. Rick Venner. One of the new engineers. I came up with the Prince."

"Oh yes, of course. Now let's see. I hope you two have good appetites today. To begin with, the gazpacho soup?"

"From Andalusia, Spain," Rick told her. "It's a cold soup made of oil, vinegar, tomatoes, onions and garlic, with side dishes of fresh chopped green peppers, cucumbers, onions, and croutons of fried bread available to be

sprinkled on it. It's really quite good when done correctly."
He smiled up at Irene. "And I'm sure that the chef here
is an artist."

"Oh, yes, sir."

"Well," Mary Beth said. "I've never even heard of cold
soup. And I don't like garlic, but I'll try anything once."

"Two," Rick said smiling at the waitress.

"And then," Irene said, "we are especially recommend-
ing the Dover Sole. Antoine is quite enthused about it.
He claims it is the best sole that he has seen since the
Savoy in London."

"The Savoy is rightfully famed for its fish, Mary Beth,"
Rick told her.

"Actually, I was thinking about a steak and french
fries," she said doubtfully. "I like fried catfish, but I'm
not really much for fish."

Irene said, "Antoine does a wonderful filet mignon
with Bernaise sauce."

"The sole for me," Rick said.

"Oh, then I'll have it too," Mary Beth said. "I really
should try more things when I'm in restaurants. I always order the same thing over and over. It's hard to
miss on steak and potatoes in a good place."

"A tossed salad with, say, a Roquefort dressing?" Irene
suggested.

"Of course," Rick said.

"And a Riesling? The wine steward tells me that he
has just received a shipment of *Nachenheimer* that is
excellent."

"Fine," Rick said. "Should go wonderfully with the
sole."

When the girl was gone, Rick smiled at Mary Beth
across from him. "On the swank side for a space colony,
wouldn't you say? That "no menu" routine is really putting on the dog."

"Well, yes," she said. "Oh, it's very nice, of course, but

I didn't really expect so many imported things. I thought there'd probably be fresh fish, out of the island streams, and, of course, lots of fresh vegetables and fruits, and possibly some ordinary wine, like California wine, and all, or maybe beer brewed right here in the island. But this is so fancy."

Rick broke a bread stick and dabbed some butter on it. "I suppose it's a matter of good public relations, Mary Beth. It wouldn't do for a visiting Prince, for instance, to be presented with hamburgers and home brew."

"No," she said hesitantly. "I suppose not. And all the people here at the hotel are VIPs or top-notch scientists and everything. All except me. But, well, good gracious, I kind of get the feeling that I'm not seeing the real Island One at all."

"How do you mean?" Rick said sympathetically.

"I don't know. When I go back and have to tell everybody at the Friends of Lagrange Five what it was like, all I'll be able to tell them will be about the hydroponic gardens and the air plant and the recycling works and the hotel here. And, well, of course, I had my ride in the space taxi to where they're building the SPSs and that was thrilling, of course. All the men in space suits, out there working on it." She frowned. "But it wasn't nearly through yet, I don't think. And I got the impression, down Earthside, that it was just about to go into operation."

"Space taxi?" Rick asked.

She shrugged her somewhat bony shoulders and giggled. "That's kind of a joke they have, I guess. They're little four-place spacecraft and go squirting around just anywhere. Carl even let me handle the controls for a while. There's really nothing to it, but it's very exciting. Imagine, me driving a spacecraft all around."

"Carl?" Rick said.

They waited for a moment while Irene served them their Andalusian cold soup and the liveried wine steward brought an ice bucket complete with long, green Germanic wine bottle and dark red goblets. He politely showed Rick the label before popping the cork. Rick pursed his lips in appreciation at the vintage date and the vineyard. On the face of it, the L5 Hilton served nothing but the best.

When the servants were gone, Mary Beth said, "Carl Gatena. He's one of Ron Rich's publicity men and awfully cute. He's just with me every minute. And if not him, one of the others."

"You seem to be getting the royal treatment," Rick told her.

She watched him sprinkle the chopped salad vegetables and the croutons onto the soup and imitated him.

"Yes," she said doubtfully. "But I thought I'd be able to get out and meet the regular space colonists and talk to them and all. You know, and possibly go into their homes and see how they live. And maybe go to one of their parties, or entertainments, and that sort of thing."

"I see what you mean," he said sympathetically. "Actually, all you're really doing is meeting the big shots and seeing the tourist sights."

"That's right," she said, making a face as though she was ashamed to be criticizing just anything at all about the Lagrange Five Project. "I'm only going to be here a couple of more days and ... why, I get the darnedest feeling I'm being hurried around here and there, and not seeing the *real* space colony. Which is what I came for. I ... you'll never believe this ... I feel like I'm being *used*."

"Oh, come now," Rick scoffed.

Their fish was being served. It was elegantly presented, complete with fresh parsley.

When Irene was gone, Rick said, "Undoubtedly, it's

because of your limited time. They've probably gone far out of their way to show you the most important things. After all, a gang of men shovelling processed moon dirt around, half way up the cylinder, wouldn't be of much interest to you."

"I'd like to see it, though, and talk to them and all," she said stubbornly.

"Actually, I'm a bit busy myself," Rick told her. The fish was proving as good as Irene's buildup. Damn it. Who was going to be his contact when Mary Beth was gone? He'd have to see to making some more contacts among those privy to the L5 Hilton.

"I begrudge every minute I'm away from you," he said, smiling his shy, little boy's smile. "How about tonight for dinner and afterwards. . . ." He let his sentence dribble away.

She flushed a little and her eyes went down to her place, as though demurely, which hardly went with the sexual athlete she proved herself in bed. She said, "Why don't we go to your place tonight? I'm dying to see it."

He laughed gently. "I'll match you for it tonight after dinner," he said.

Someone sauntered up and stood next to their table. "So, here you are," the newcomer said jovially.

They looked up.

"Oh, hello Carl," Mary Beth said. "I was just having lunch with Mr. Venner here. We met each other on the *Tsiolkowsky* coming up. Rick Venner, this is Carl Gatena, who's been guiding me around. He doesn't give me a moment to myself."

The two men shook, Rick rising halfway from his chair.

The flack frowned slightly. "I don't believe we've met," he said. "I thought I knew everybody in the hotel."

"Sit down," Rick told him easily. "Have a glass of wine. The Reisling is excellent here. As good as I've had in the Rhone Valley. They don't export their best, you know, but this is certainly up to it for my taste, and I'm an old hock man."

Carl Gatena drew up a chair but continued to frown at Rick. "You're connected with the Prince's staff?" he said. "Now that I recall, I saw you at his party."

"Oh, no," Rick said, pouring himself some more of the wine and proffering the bottle to both Mary Beth and the publicity man, at whose elbow the wine steward had magically materialized a glass. "I'm an engineer. They brought me up to give a hand to Fred Davis."

"Oh," Gatena said. "I heard that Supervisor Davis was having some difficulties."

"Not insurmountable, I trust," Rick said grandly. "But you know how some of these old-timer construction men are. In actuality, all of them should be required to attend an upgrading school every couple of years. Time passes them by. Hardly a year unfolds but that some major breakthrough takes place in just about every field."

"I suppose so," Gatena said, evidently dismissing it. He turned to Mary Beth. "I have a pleasant surprise for you this afternoon, Ms. Houston. Mr. Moore is giving a cocktail party for the Prince."

"Cocktail party?" she said blankly. "But ... good gracious, Carl, my time is so limited. I thought I might tour the cylinder, see them planting the trees and all. Maybe go boating on one of the lakes."

The publicity man rubbed his chin as though checking his morning shave. He said, "In actuality, the lakes aren't quite ready for boating as yet."

She fixed her eyes on him in disbelief. "You must be pulling my leg. I definitely saw a Tri-Di show about Island One with a boat race."

Rick was inwardly amused. Obviously, it was all the flack could do to refrain from closing his eyes in suppressed grief.

Gatena said hurriedly, "Oh, *that* race. That was just sort of a preliminary try out, kind of. Just to see if we could do such things once everything was completed. At any rate, there'll be a lot of people you'll want to meet at the party. Big-name scientists and all. And Doctor Ryan has mentioned that he wants to see more of you."

"He has?" Mary Beth said, excited at last.

"Yes, he's very thankful for all the efforts of the Friends of Lagrange Five. And I heard the Prince mention that he thoroughly approved of your type of American girl and looked forward to talking to you again."

"Talking to me again? Why, I hardly more than said hello to him at the party."

"He was evidently impressed by you. You'll simply have to come to this cocktail party, Ms. Houston."

"Mary Beth," she admonished him. "But I haven't a thing to wear."

He said smoothly, "Annette will take care of that. But first, of course, you'll want to go to the beauty salon."

The Secretary of the Friends of L5 looked at him blankly. "Beauty salon? You mean that there's a beauty salon here in Island One?"

"Right here in the hotel."

Rick was wondering whether he should attempt to wangle an invitation to the cocktail party. It'd be a chance to make acquaintances with some of the hotel's permanent residents. He had to make some new contacts fast. It wouldn't do to be conspicuous around the place by eating and drinking alone, or crashing parties without a date. The way he sized it up, there were several hundred permanent guests in the L5 Hilton, the cream of the cream of the upper echelons of the project. If he could keep a low image and keep the suitability of clothing available, he should be able to milk this indefinitely, but to do so he needed some contacts, preferably one of the women office workers. But no, he'd better play it cool with this Carl Gatena. If the other got a glimmering of suspicion, he'd look Rick up; nothing could be easier. And nothing was more obvious, from the records, than that Rick Venner was not eligible for the goodies of the L5 Hilton.

After dessert, an overly rich Danish pastry, which the publicity man sat through patiently, Mary Beth was whisked off to the beauty salon. She had been taken aback by the presence in the island of such an establishment. Rick was amused. From what he had seen of the female space colonists on the streets, its services were hardly available to them. But, on the other hand, from the perfectly presented women he had noted at the Prince's party, they did have the best of beautician's care for the elite.

He thanked Irene graciously for her service—there was no manner in which to tip, obviously—and strolled from the dining room, looking every inch the well-fed, super-level executive.

His way led him to a side door of the kitchens. He strolled through them, hardly noticed by the staff. However, near the door, a salad chef looked up; his eyebrows rose as he took in Rick's attire.

Rick said easily, "Shortcut to the laboratories. Don't have to walk all around the front of the hotel."

"Oh, yeah," the other said. "I saw you come in earlier this way."

Hands in pockets, Rick made his way down the alley behind the hotel to the narrow streets of the small space town. Pedestrians in Earthside dress were on the rare side, but not unknown, and none of his fellow walkers bothered to glance at him. They weren't a happy looking lot, he told himself, but then, what in the hell did they have to be happy about?

Thinking about it now, he asked himself why he had come up here. He must have known, if only subconsciously, that all wasn't going to be apple strudel with sour cream. He could have taken a relatively small amount of his loot and gone somewhere like Tangier or Brazil and laid low for the five years. Paul Lund could have been instrumental in finding him a small place in the wide-open Moroccan town where he could have remained inconspicuous. Say in the Casbah area. He shook his head and grunted. But no. Every heavy in the world of the grifter would soon have known about his big score, as even Pavel Meer had. And some would have come looking for him. There are those who will go to any ends when over a million dollars are involved. Even had he been a gunman of renown, which he wasn't, sooner or later a hit man would have gotten to him. Here, deep in space, he was safe. But then he grunted amusement at himself. Safe? Hell, how far could he trust even Tony Black? And were there any others in Island One who knew about him? Face it, he hadn't actually come for safety. He had come because he wanted to see the last frontier, the very last frontier—space. He was a fucking romantic. He was actually here for the same reasons all these sucker space colonists were. He was just as big a sucker as they were.

He came up to the double-occupancy house that Tony Black had brought him in to share. Automatically, he looked up and down the street; for what, he didn't know. He saw nothing untoward and entered the living room.

Tony Black was there with a swarthy stranger dressed uncomfortably in cheap Western garb. A Levantine, Rick decided. What was there about Moslems that they never seemed at home in the clothes of the West? Give one a five-hundred-dollar suit and in fifteen minutes he looked as though he had slept in it.

Rick nodded at them unconcernedly and headed for the stairs.

But Tony Black said, "That's okay, Rick. Ahmud was just leaving."

Rick hesitated at the stair bottom. But the Arab, or whatever he was, avoided looking at him, bobbed his head at Black and, a slip of paper in his hand, turned and left the house.

"What in the hell was that?" Rick said, coming back to the sparsely furnished living room's center.

"Business," the other said, in an offhand tone. He indicated a suitcase on the low table before him. The top was up.

Rick looked into it. Its contents were motley, including, of all things, some fancy women's brassieres and a half-dozen watches. Rick sent his eyes over to the other.

Tony Black grinned his irritating sly grin. "Black market," he said. "One of the Prince's servants. Somehow the staffs of these visiting firemen instinctively know that they can pick up a small fortune smuggling in odds and ends for the local black market. The baggage of an Abou ben Abel goes through our equivalent of customs without search, obviously."

"Odds and ends such as what?" Rick said, staring down into the suitcase.

"Such as real hash, from India. Sure, some of the colonists grow a little weed of their own. But this is the real stuff. Indian's the best in the world. They've been using *cannabis* for five thousand years and more. Then there's nose candy and H. Ahmud brought up some of that, too."

Rick gazed disbelief at him. "Cocaine and heroin in Island One?"

The other snorted. "You can get anything in Island One, given the credits. Hell, you can get anything anywhere on a local black market if you're willing to pony up enough. I had a pal once who operated in one of the Antarctic bases. He got himself taken rich in a year and

255

a half." Black grimaced in memory. "Before some big Navy slob got irritated with him when he found out he was laying his wife. It took him three months and half of his take getting out of the banger."

He observed Rick's attire. "Where've you been?" he said. "I noticed my soup-and-fish outfit was missing last night. You must've been taking the party in."

Rick lowered himself into a chair. "That's right," he said. To his surprise, the other didn't seem to be especially upset. "And I've been to the hotel just now, having lunch."

The other nodded and sat down, too. "How'd you get in past the Security guards?"

"Professional secret," Rick said easily. "There're several entrances to that hotel besides the main one. What're you doing with these clothes, Tony?"

"Same thing you are. Earthside threads are like a badge or a uniform. Nobody wears 'em except the really big noises. There's no rule against it, but it's damn seldom you ever see an ordinary colonist in a suit or dress. Oh, sometimes for a wedding or something like that, an ordinary construction worker will borrow or rent a suit. But usually, well, for one thing, they're too damn expensive."

"Where'd you get them? You've got three suits upstairs besides this one."

Tony Black shrugged it off easily. "Traded around. Like I said, you can get anything up here if you've got the credits."

"And from time to time you get done up in them and go into the hotel?"

"I usually slip one of the Security guards a little something and he lets me past. But I've got to take it awfully easy. I don't exactly look the part. Now, you're another thing. You've got the air about you. You look like somebody important, in an easygoing sort of way.

You look like you belong. I suppose it's part of your stock in trade. You could hang around in those big resorts in Switzerland or the Riviera and nobody'd look twice at you. Okay, that's great. That's one of the reasons I brought you in with me."

"How's that?" Rick said, contemplating the other with care.

"The hotel's where the money is. If you can work your way in there, get established, accepted, on whatever terms, we've got it made. That's the place to make arrangements. So many opportunities, you can pick and choose."

Rick leaned back in his chair and said fretfully, "I'm not exactly anxious to stick my neck out, Tony. I can't afford to blow my cover for the sake of a few hundred dollars. Sure, it's one thing eating in the dining room for free and even sleeping with one of the mopsies in a decent bed. If they caught me, I could simply plead that I didn't know the hotel was for VIPs only and just happened to have this suit."

"With that cheerful, innocent-looking phizz of yours, you'd probably get away with it," the weasel-faced Tony Black said in admiration. "But I wasn't talking about a few hundred dollars, Rocks."

"Rick."

"Yeah, wizard, Rick. Sorry. Listen, you want to know what it costs to ship a pound of something up here?"

"Damned expensive, I'd guess."

"Yeah. Roughly one hundred dollars a pound."

Rick hissed through his teeth.

"Take a pint of whiskey," the black marketeer went on. "A pint's roughly a pound. But that's not all. The whiskey itself weighs a pound, but if you're running a class act, the weight of the bottle's there, too. Say almost another half pound. That brings the price up to about 150. But that's just the beginning. First you've got to buy the guzzle Earthside, then you've got to make arrangements to have it shuttled up to the *Goddard*. There you've got to make arrangements to relay it on to either Island One or the moon base. Then you've got to get it through customs. All the way along the line, the hands are out to be greased. You know what that bottle of smuggled whiskey finally sells for? Three hundred bucks and up, and usually up, when you can find it at all."

Rick hissed again.

"And that's just the beginning, too," the other told him, happy at the impression he was making. "You'd be surprised what these colonists and contract workers will pay for something they decide they've just gotta have. Cigarettes, cigars, pot, hard drugs, cosmetics, even chocolates and cashew nuts. Even things like sardines and crab or anchovies. And that's not all. Things like watches. You come up here with a watch and it goes on the blink. Where do you get it repaired? There's no repair shop and there's no spare parts. To send it to Earth and back would cost plenty. So you buy a new one. Things like mirrors for the mopsies. Things like shampoo and fancy-smelling soaps and perfumes. Even fancy clothes; I imagine half the broads in this island have, in their homes, just one really fancy outfit." He motioned at the brassieres in the suitcase the Arab had brought. "They'll pay almost anything for such stuff."

Rick said, "I thought the project had what they call the Luxury PX where you can buy things like that."

"Sure, a lot of it. But at sky-high prices. Even worse than the black market. The L5 Corporation doesn't miss a bet. They milk the suckers for all they can get. I doubt if there are two hundred workers up here, men or women, who save *any* of their ten thousand a year base pay. And probably if they could get their hands on the twenty thousand a year bonus that accumulates down Earthside, they'd blow that, too."

Rick said, "That presents a problem. How do your customers pay off? And, ultimately, I assume you want to take it back to Earth with you. How do you arrange that? These Lagrange Five Corporation credit cards we have up here aren't valid Earthside, except at the New Albuquerque spaceport."

The dark little man grinned slyly. "There are ways, Rick, there are always ways. When I said I could buy anything up here, given the credits, I meant *any*thing. Say, for instance, diamonds, an old specialty of yours. A diamond that might go for ten thousand on the wholesale market in Amsterdam might go for as high as twenty thousand up here. So, wizard, you accumulate twenty thousand credits working one of the rackets—the black market, drugs, guzzle, gambling, or maybe peddling your ass, if you're a good-looking mopsy. Then you buy a diamond and stash it away until you return Earthside where you can sell it. Sure, you lose half of your take, but that's better than nothing. It's just one of your business expenses."

Rick was thinking it over. He said, musingly, "What's your source of the stuff you peddle? You surely can't depend on characters like that Arab who just left, very often."

"No, he's an exception, but not too rare," the other told him. "He's probably been on the Prince's staff for some time, jetting around between countries Earthside. The Prince has a diplomatic passport, so his stuff is never searched, and old Ahmud has probably been smuggling hard drugs for years. When he got to New Albuquerque he greased a palm or two to find out who to contact in the black market up here. Somebody evidently knew my name and told him and also tipped him off to the best things to bring."

"But where does most of your stuff come from?"

"A hundred different sources. For one thing, I work in

Supply and I've figured out various ways to rip things off. Then I've got some buddies who work in the L5 Commissary at the Hilton and some in the Luxury PX. They've all got sticky fingers and funnel things through to me. Then there're crew members on the passenger freighters coming up from Earth. They tuck things away here and there on the spaceships and since they don't have any way of peddling it themselves, they use me as a middleman.

"Hombre, you have no idea how many ways there are to smuggle. Some tuck stuff away in pipes and machinery. Some get it into the dehydrated food that's shipped up. Some package black market items to look like tools, or chemicals, or fertilizer, or whatever. Oh, never fear, Rick, the smuggler is always one jump ahead of those out to stop the traffic."

"Yeah," Rick said. "But Security must intercept one hell of a lot of it."

The other grinned his rodent-like smile that was already rubbing Rick Venner the wrong way. "Sure. And then what do you think happens to it?"

Rick gave him the eye.

Tony Black made a gesture with his two hands. "They're all on the take, too. I don't know one of those Security bastards who doesn't have his hand out. Oh, the hotel grabs some of it, the better stuff, and the big shots use it there, like you know, they all do all right for themselves in the hotel. But most of it they intercept goes in the front door of the Security offices and what they don't take for themselves goes out the back. They can't usually peddle it on their own, very easily, so they pass it on to me and the other cloddies in my racket."

Rick thought about it for a while. He said finally, "And what was my end to be?"

The other nodded. "I see you as a top-notch front man. Get yourself organized over at the hotel. You won't be able to get a room; they'd go on the records and they'd spot you. But with your style you should be able to make your way around, acting like you belong, until the Security men and the waiters and bartenders and all accept you. Then you play it the way it comes. Try to get next to somebody who counts. Maybe some mopsy working in Commissary on a high level. Maybe some guy with an itchy hand working in logistics. We need contacts who can deliver. Say, be able to divert guzzle by the case into our hands. I used to have a source working in the hotel kitchens, a junior chef. Christ, he ripped off so much expensive grub, you'd think the guests would have starved to death."

"What happened to him when they finally caught up with his stealing?"

"They never did. He was a smart bastard. But he had the bad luck to be transferred over to the moon base. From what I hear, he's head chef out there. I'll bet he's robbing them blind. The black market's even worse over there than it is here. The poor fucking moon colonists are even more desperate than they are here."

Rick said slowly, "I'll think about it, Tony. Sure as hell, I don't want to spend the next five years eating, drinking, and sleeping the way most of these dizzards do. On the other hand, I've got too much to risk sticking my neck out in a penny-ante game. I've got a date with a girl at the hotel tonight. I'll probably stay the night and talk to you in the morning again."

Tony Black stood. "Lucky stiff," he said. "Wizard, Rick. I went over to Housing this morning and recorded the fact that you were staying here with me. How long's it going to be before you're out from under with Freddy Davis and his construction work?"

"Maybe a week. I've got to prove to him a couple of more times that I get space sick every time I get two feet out of a pressure lock."

His housemate nodded, making with his furtive grin. "At that time, I'll see if I can't make a deal to get you in with me working in Supply. With two of us on the scene, we ought to be able to take higher scores than just me working alone."

He snapped shut the suitcase the Arab smuggler had brought, took it up, and ascended the stairs to his room. Shortly he came down, waved at Rick, and said, "I've got some deals I have to see about."

"Yeah, but just a minute, Tony," Rick said. "I wanted to ask you something."

The other halted on his way to the door. "What?"

"Where're all the other guys Pavel Meer arranged to have come up here? There must've been quite a few of them to make the racket worthwhile for the Penman, Monk Ravelle at New Albuquerque, and you at this end."

The other shifted his eyes. "They're around."

"Am I going to meet any of them? It's just possible some of them might know me, being in the game themselves. That might be awkward over the next five years."

Tony/Black said, "Well, actually, I usually make arrangements to send them over to the Luna base. There's less chance there of anybody making them. Not so many people there and visitors to the project never go to the moon. No facilities for them, like the hotel here. I'll be seeing you, Rick." He turned to go again.

Rick looked after him thoughtfully. For some reason he couldn't put his finger on, he had his doubts about the other's answer.

When he was gone, Rick Venner thought his words over in detail. In actuality, with his gold stashed safely away in India, he didn't particularly need the black market money. On the other hand, he had no taste for living the average space colonist's life for the next half decade. Not by a damn sight. He was used to better things. There were some three or four hundred persons, he estimated, either living in the Lagrange Five Hilton or working there with above-average quarters on the outside, almost all of them in Earthside dress. There must be considerable coming and going—newcomers from Earth, visitors, scientists on short-term special jobs, upper-echelon officials and technicians going back and forth to the Luna base. Could he merge with them, unnoticed? He had a sneaking suspicion that he could. He sighed. Rick Venner had aristocratic tastes. Most certainly, he preferred Dover sole, washed down with Riesling, to dehydrated slop washed down with sterile-tasting, recycled water.

Without so much as a knock upon it, the front door opened and two brawny men entered. Both of them wore the green coveralls of Security. Rick looked up, startled.

The first one said, without inflection, "Rick Venner?"

"That's right," he said. "What's . . ."

The Security man said, "You're wanted over at head-quarters."

Damn it, he didn't know what this was all about. Probably just routine. Something to do with his being a newcomer. But they'd caught him in Tony Black's Earthside suit. What would they think about that?

"Wizard," he said, standing. "What's it all about?"

Neither of them bothered to answer. One held open the door and they let him precede them out into the narrow street. And they held their peace, walking one on each side of him, in the direction of the hotel.

They marched in the front entrance and headed across the lobby to the stairways. On the way, they passed Bruce Carter, who raised his eyebrows at them. Rick lifted and dropped his shoulders, indicating that he didn't know what it was all about. Which he didn't.

They took the stairs all the way to the top floor. There was a guard posted there who took them in without particular interest.

One of the two said, "Hi, Dean. What spins? The chief wants to see this guy."

Dean nodded without changing his position, leaning against the wall.

They made their way down the corridor. They stopped before a door with an identity screen and one of the two muttered into it. The door opened. Inside was a reception room office. Neither of the two girls there bothered to look up as they crossed to another door. It would seem that they were expected, since neither bothered to knock. One of the two police opened the door and motioned for Rick to go on through. When he did, the Security men didn't follow, but closed the door behind him.

Inside was as lavish an office as Rick Venner had ever seen, even in the Tri-Di shows. He doubted that even the Oval Office of President Corcoran was as ostentatiously rich as this. There were two men present, one behind the half-acre of desk, the other seated in a leather comfort chair to one side. They looked at him curiously.

The one behind the desk said, his voice brusque, "Sit down." While Rick was doing so, on a straight chair immediately before the desk, the other took up a paper before him and scanned it. He said, "I'm Al Moore, Lagrange Five Commissioner of Security." He nodded at the other man present. "And this is Lieutenant Mark Donald."

Rick said politely, "Pleased to meet you."

Moore read from the paper, "Rick Venner, electrical engineer on five-year contract."

"That's right," Rick said.

"I noticed you last night at the party given for Prince Abou ben Abel. You fill out evening clothes very nicely, as though you were born to them. You were talking with Ms. Mary Beth Houston. Later you went with her to her room and threw a screw into her. You work fast, Rocks."

Rick started to reply, then thought better of it.

Al Moore put the paper down and smiled wolfishly. He said, "We're not a bunch of cloddies up here, Rocks."

"I can see that," Rick said, his voice bitter.

"The thing is," the Security Commissioner told him, "that we don't particularly mind your going to ground here, other things remaining equal. There's no way you could operate here. No way you could hurt us."

Rick goggled at him, not able to believe what he had just heard.

Moore sighed. "As a matter of fact, under ordinary circumstances, we might even be able to use a man who can think on his feet the way you've proven you can. This is a big operation, Rocks. Bigger than you can imagine. It's not a small-time-peanuts deal, like heisting a few stones."

Rick was still gaping at the other.

Moore said slowly, "The trouble is, these are not ordinary circumstances. You've got an IABI man bird-dogging you. Did you know that?"

"Kapitz?" Rick got out. "Yeah. I met him at the *Goddard*, coming up."

"We got a rundown on Peter Kapitz. He doesn't look like much, but he's one of their top manhunters."

"I know," Rick said. "He's been on my tail before. But he's never seen me. Has no description—and no matter what he says, no fingerprints or retinals. He didn't make me on the *Goddard*, or later when we crossed in the *Tsiolkowsky*. There's supposed to be some ten thousand people up here, most of them men. He won't be able to pinpoint me."

"Don't be too sure," Moore said sarcastically. "He obviously has something in mind. Possibly, plain ordinary elimination. You've been operating quite recently Earthside. More than half the men up here have been in Lagrange Five for years. He undoubtedly knows you can't be one of them."

"I don't get all this," Rick said. "Why don't you just turn me over to him?"

The Security head shifted one shoulder in response to that and sighed. "Because we have reason to believe that Pete Kapitz has another job besides latching onto you, Rocks. He's snooping around. And we don't like snoopers. He could start a lot of waves up when he goes back Earthside and reports."

"I see," Rick said, uneasiness inside. "Where do I come in?"

"You hit him for us."

Rick Venner was staring again. He got out, "I'm no hit man, Moore. I've never killed anybody in my life."

"There's always a first time," the otherwise silent Mark Donald murmured.

"Shut up, Mark," his chief said. He brought his eyes back to Rick Venner. "Well, it's your ass or his."

Rick said, "Why don't you get one of your own boys to take him? Most of them look as though it wouldn't be the first time."

Moore sighed again. "Can't you see? If Rocks Weil shoots a cop trying to put the arm on him, it sounds perfectly natural. But suppose one of my Security men does it. A howl would go up. And a couple damn more IABI men would be on the scene as quick as they could be shuttled in. They'd dig up things that we simply don't want dug into. Use your head, Rocks."

"I'm trying to, while I still have it," Rick said. "Wizard. I hit Pete Kapitz and then his boss, John Wilson, has me hauled back Earthside and I wind up in one of those brand-new euthanasia suites."

Mark Donald chuckled softly, but Al Moore was shaking his head. "Don't be a cloddy, Rocks. There are no extradition laws in Lagrange Five. We're not subject to Earthside laws of any country, not even the Reunited Nations. We fake a trial for you and sentence you to twenty years hard labor on Luna. But what we actually do is stash you off in a comfortable hideaway, complete with as good food as you'd get here at the hotel, all the guzzle you want, a mopsy or two to keep your bed warm. Then, when you decide it's safe to go back, we smuggle you down to Earth again. No strain. Everybody happy."

Rick pretended to be thinking about it.

Al Moore said to his underling, "Issue Rocks a shooter, Mark."

The other stood, brought a 7.63 calibre Gyrojet pistol from an inner pocket, and presented it to Rick Venner.

Rick took it hesitantly and put it away in his inner coat pocket. They even knew his taste in hand guns though, as he had truthfully told them, he'd never used one on a job.

He said, "I'll think about it, Moore."

"Don't take too long," the Security chief said flatly. "This Kapitz is breathing down our necks. We suspect he's already reporting some of his findings. We'll keep in contact, Rocks. Hold yourself ready until we make arrangements to finger him for you."

Rick stood, looked from one of them to the other, wearily, then turned and left.

When he was gone, Mark Donald gave his superior the eye and said, "Where in the hell do you figure on stashing him while he's supposedly serving this twenty years of hard labor?"

Al Moore grunted cynically. "Don't be silly, Mark. We'll stage it this way. When Rocks gives it to Pete Kapitz, we'll be sure that this damned freelance writer, Bruce Carter, is in the vicinity to see it. One of our boys, maybe you or Nat Luke, get into the act and gun down Rocks after he's shot Kapitz. That'll give Carter the story of his life and he'll hustle back to Earth to write and peddle it. Nobody will doubt the story, if somebody as big as Bruce Carter tells it the way he saw it. So that way we kill two birds with one stone. We get rid of both this IABI snoop and the freelancer, too."

Mark Donald shook his head in admiration. "Jesus, I'm glad I'm on your side. I'd hate to be on your shit list."

Moore growled, "We've got to have at least six more months before we're ready to let anybody blow the whistle on us. Then we'll be ready and not give a damn. In fact, if nobody else blows it, we'll see to it ourselves."

His underling said, "Oh, there's just one other new development, Al. Joe Evola and Dean picked up that Alvar Saarinen guy. We twisted his arm a little and it turned out he wasn't from the KGB like we thought. He was from that top-secret outfit of theirs, the Cheka. He broke easier than we expected. It turns out that this new scientist, Suvorov, was sent up by that outfit. That defection bit was a lot of shit."

"I'll be damned," Al Moore said, truly surprised.

"Should we pick him up, too?"

The Security Commissioner thought about it. "Hell no," he said. "Leave him alone. They undoubtedly sent him to try and fuck up the closed-cycle ecology system, but it's so fucked up already there's nothing worse he could do." He thought about it some more. "Don't let Sol Ryan in on this development. It won't do him any good to know and he's running confused as it is."

"When control is necessarily extensive, power accumulates, and thus the danger of usurping this power. If scores of people have hijacked airplanes, how about hijacking a little world out there in space?"
—*Brother David Steindl-Rast, founder of* House of Prayer Movement.

Chapter Fourteen

Bruce Carter and Pete Kapitz met by chance in the lobby of the L5 Hilton. Both wore Earthside suits. They'd already found that wearing the standard space coveralls made them conspicuous in the hotel. Carl Gatena had supplied Bruce with more suitable outfits and Mark Donald had come up with the equivalent for Pete. They paused for a minute to chat.

The freelancer said, "How goes the search for Rocks Weil?"

Pete viewed him sourly. "You know damn well how much interest I really have in that."

Bruce said, "Well, maybe your excuse for being in L5 is about to go down the drain. I saw a couple of Security men with Rick Venner in tow. It looked as though they were taking him to see Al Moore."

"Damn," Pete said. "You're right. If they turn him over to me, I'll no longer have an excuse for staying. By the way, it would seem that Rocks isn't the only one on the lam up here. Not only that girl I told you about, but I spotted a Syndicate member, guy named Natale Lucchese who's holding down a job as a Security officer."

"I'll be a sonofabitch," Bruce said, interested. "But then, I guess, with ten thousand people up here, you're bound to find just about every type of person on Earth, from small-time crooks to Nobel Laureates. How's your assignment going otherwise, Pete?"

The IABI agent scowled. "Actually, more successfully then I'd expected. There's a hell of a lot brewing that the average investor in LFC stock down Earthside doesn't know about. And I suspect that if he did know, he wouldn't be so quick to tie up his money. In fact, when I get back, I'm going to sell mine. Take a loss if I have to."

Bruce contemplated him speculatively. He said, "You know, Pete, I think I'm going to stick my neck out. How'd you like to attend a secret meeting of the Central Committee of an underground outfit that wants to overthrow the present administration of the L5 Project?"

Pete Kapitz boggled. He got out, "Are you around the bend, Carter?"

"Nope. I don't think so. I ran into these people yesterday. Some of the things they told me about the workings of this project set me back plenty, in spite of the fact that I'd already heard a great deal along the same line."

"But, make sense, hombre, how in the hell could they expect to overthrow the Solomon Ryan administration? A strike or something?"

"No. And nothing violent. They think that if they can get somebody to get back Earthside and reveal all the information on Lagrange Five mismanagement, that the stink will bring about a change in the upper echelons of the Lagrange Five Corporation. What the hell they expect to happen then, I don't know. At any rate, their leader, or one of them, invited me to sit in on a meeting of their Central Committee. It seems to me this might be the chance you're looking for. If Roy Thomas wants to find out about the inner workings of the project, you couldn't do better than listen to these characters beef."

"You think they'd let me come?"

"We sure as hell can try. I'm to meet this Adam Bloch in about ten minutes."

"How do we get out of this fucking hotel without passes? They've got Security guards posted everywhere."

"Some gumshoe you are," Bruce said, smiling. "Come along."

He led the way down the hall that entered into the downstairs offices of the Security department. Garbed as they were, they drew no attention. They casually stepped through the doors that led onto the street and turned left.

"I'll be damned," Pete said. "Al Moore and his boys aren't as efficient as they think they are."

"They probably don't have much cause for tightening up. From what I've seen, the usual colonist stays as far away from Security as he can. As usual, nobody loves a cop."

"Huh," the IABI man grunted.

The park was only a few blocks down. For that matter, anything was only a few blocks away in the small, jam-packed town. All over again, Bruce Carter decided that he'd hate to spend five years of his life in the place. Not to speak of being a colonist, signed up to spend the rest of his life here.

"You'd be better at it than me," Bruce said to his companion. "Check to see if we're being followed."

"I doubt it," the other said. "Nobody followed us out of the hotel."

They remained as inconspicuous as possible among the pedestrians and bicyclists, who seemed somewhat thicker than usual. Possibly it was a shift change. They walked near the houses, rather than in the middle of the street. The freelancer had no difficulty in finding the house of Adam Bloch. As the teacher had told him, it was a small, two-storied one, constructed of gray moon brick and plastic. Bruce consulted his wrist chronometer.

It was two minutes to four. Right on the dot. He came to a halt, gave a last searching look in all directions, and then stepped quickly to the door and knocked. Even the door was constructed of aluminum, he noted. Thus far, the only wood he'd seen outside the hotel were the few straggly trees that Pal Barack said that he tended in the park. For that matter, the wood at the hotel was sparse and to be seen mostly in the desks and other furniture in the more opulent offices and living quarters.

The door was answered, not by Bloch, but by the window washer ... what was his name? ... Cris Everett.

His eyes widened and he said, looking at Pete Kapitz, "Who in the hell's this, Carter? Adam said you were coming, but he didn't mention anybody else."

"I'll explain him to Bloch," Carter said. "Suppose you let us in off the street, before somebody spots us."

"Yeah, well, okay," the small man said, though unhappily and still suspicious. He had a put-upon type face, meant to be suspicious. He stepped aside and they entered.

The whole bottom floor was devoted to the living room and in it, on the usual metallic furniture, were seated Bloch and three others, none of whom Bruce recognized. One was a plain-faced woman, her hair done up in a scarf, wearing coveralls identical to those of the men.

Adam Bloch stood, scowling, as Cris Everett had done, at the IABI agent.

Bruce nodded at the assembled Central Committee and said to Bloch, "This is Peter Kapitz. He's an IABI operative."

Several sucked in breath.

Bruce said, "He has nothing to do with L5 Project authorities. In fact, he's been sent up here secretly to nose around and find out what's wrong with the project's workings—if anything. So, I'd think he's as good a contact for you people as I am. Possibly better. He's working directly under Roy Thomas, President Corcoran's top aide. Thomas, evidently, suspects something offbeat's going on."

"How do we know we can trust him?" the woman said. She had a grating voice.

Bruce took her in, shrugging. "Yow do you know you can trust me? You're taking a chance on both of us. I vouch for him. I've known him off and on for years."

Adam Bloch nodded in resignation and extended his hand to the IABI man. "We've already stuck our necks out," he admitted. "We can't stick them out any farther. Sit down, gentlemen."

There was just enough seating capacity for the five Central Committee members and the two newcomers. Bruce and Pete sat on a small couch, side by side. Adam Bloch made no effort to introduce any of his companions by name.

Bruce let air out of his lungs and said, "All right, here we are. Why are you people interested in replacing Ryan's administration of the Lagrange Five Project?"

Bloch, evidently as chairman of the meeting, took the ball. "Let's put it this way, Carter. The basic contract issued by the Corporation is the one almost all of us have signed. Some specialists, technicians, engineers, get more, but most of us make thirty thousand a year, tax free. Of this, ten thousand is paid us on a monthly basis in the form of credit which we can spend here in Island One with the credit cards the corporation issues. It's all milked from us by our buying so-called luxuries at outrageous prices."

Pete said, "But you also accumulate a bonus of twenty thousand a year. In short, at the end of a five-year contract, you've got, tax free, a hundred thousand dollars. That's a lot of money to save in five years for the average working stiff."

"Like hell it is," Cris Everett sneered. "It's nothing at all."

Both the freelander and the IABI man looked at him, frowning their lack of understanding.

Bloch took over again. "That hundred-thousand bonus is paid in the form of LFC stock. And if the corporation went bankrupt, that stock would be worthless. It wouldn't bring a penny a share, because the so-called assets of the Lagrange Five Corporation wouldn't have any value to anybody. If the L5 Project fails, then all this hardware up in the sky isn't worth a damn to anyone, not even as junk. It'd cost more to get it back than it'd be worth Earthside. Who in the hell wants an island in the sky that doesn't work?"

Bruce said slowly, "It goes the other way, too. If the project succeeds and the L5 Corporation starts beaming power down to Earth, as planned, then that stock of yours will boom. If you hang onto it, you'll be rich."

Bloch shook his head at him. "Mr. Carter, I do not know a single colonist or contract worker who believes that Island One can be finished and succeed in beaming microwave power to Earth, in the reasonably near future. Not a single one. You two are tyros in the field. We are the people up here actually at work on the project. We are the ones who know."

Pete said, "Back there at the hotel are the men in charge. They're still optimistic. Bruce here tells me that you're just a teacher. Do you think you know more about it than Doctor Soloman Ryan, the Father of the Lagrange Five Project?"

One of the committee members who hadn't been introduced to the outsiders said heatedly, "Look, I'm one of the junior engineers working on the SPSs. Anybody can tell you that there are still a lot of kinks in the whole idea, but suppose we iron them all out, which I admit is possible, given time. Wizard. We get this first SPS operational. The power beam is formed by means of a phased-array antenna involving microwave generators, or Amplitrons, and ferrite-core phaseshifters. The beam will illuminate a target area at the Earth of some 50 square kilometers. The physical limits of the optics prevent the focusing of the beam into a smaller area. The power densities will approach a kilowatt per square meter at the center of the beam. This is somewhat less than the intensity of sunlight, so, in spite of early fears, birds and animals will in no way be fried by such beams. But consider this, now. We are spending God only knows how many billions of dollars so that, from a point in distant space, we may beam to 50 square kilometers of the Earth's surface, somewhat less energy than the unaided sun, at least on sunny days, regularly delivers to the same area. Of course, the microwave energy continues to arrive in all weather and at night. And it's far more easily converted to electric current than sunlight, since the inefficient heat-producing part of the conversion has already been done in space. And the steady supply eliminates the need for storage, which remains the major problem with solar conversion electricity on the Earth's surface."

He paused for a moment, then added simply, "Mr. Carter, Mr. Kapitz. How many such SPSs and how many such areas of 50 square kilometers will be required in order to provide electrical power to a city the size of, say, New York?"

Bruce and Pete were eyeing him emptily.

Adam Bloch took over again. "Gentlemen, what it amounts to is that Solomon Ryan and his closest associates at the first projections of the space colonization scheme were wide-eyed, enthusiastic dreamers, as impractical as the most unworldly college professors. They were physicists, mathematicians, chemists, and engineers who *taught* engineering rather than practicing it. What is the old truism? Those who can, do; and those who can't, teach. In common with almost everybody else in Lagrange Five, I like Sol Ryan as an individual, but I have also come to believe him a dreamer, not a realist."

"Those are pretty hard words to use on a man with Doctor Ryan's achievements," Bruce said. "How about giving us a good example of his being as, ah, naive as you seem to think him."

The junior engineer interrupted. "Just a minute on that achievements thing. Offhand, I can't think of any breakthroughs Sol Ryan has made in the field. For instance, the idea of the mass driver wasn't exactly first hit upon by him, you know. Arthur Clark developed the concept in a paper entitled *Electromagnetic Launching as a Major Contribution to Space Flight*, in 1950. He gave it rather wide circulation in a short story, *"Maelstrom 11,"* in 1962. And the idea of self-sufficient space colonies is almost as old as science fiction. Heinlein, among others, way back in the thirties or forties, had a story entitled *Universe*, in which he had an interstellar spaceship as large as one of Ryan's Island Fours, and with a closed-cycle ecosystem."

Bruce nodded to that, but looked back to the teacher.

Adam Bloch was thinking about the challenging question. He said, "Very well, your demand is a valid one. Let us take this example. Early in his days of promoting space colonization, Doctor Ryan seemed especially taken up with the eventual possibility of what he called homesteading in the asteroid belt. It should be called the planetoid belt, by the way, since it's composed of small planets, rather than asteroids. At any rate, in an article in, I believe, *Harper's*, he mentioned in passing that a real maverick would be free in L5 to take off with a kind of vehicle he could build himself and stock with all the basic mining and agricultural equipment he and his family would need to homestead an asteroid for possibly $50,000 to $100,000."

Pete said, "What's so unrealistic about that?"

"Everything," Bloch told him. "Later, in his best-selling book on space colonization, he went into greater detail. He gave a thorough account of just how this homesteader could do it. His homemade spaceship, built of aluminum, would be a sphere about thirty feet across. In it he stocks food for two years for himself, his wife and infant child. It also contains the propulsion engine, air recycling equipment and, I assume, water recycling equipment as well. He also carries lots of seed, fish, chickens, turkeys, and pigs, and, of course, the feed for them. He also carries spare parts and one-of-a-kind tools. He also carries all the equipment he will need for homesteading his asteroid when he gets there, including mining equipment, agricultural equipment, and a grinder to grind up chunks of the asteroid into soil for farming, as well as chemical processing equipment. Besides all this, he carries in that 30-foot sphere a large quantity of sheet aluminum for construction."

The female member of the committee laughed softly. "Sounds a little crowded."

"Yes," Bloch went on. "So they take off, with four similar craft built by friends. Twenty-three persons in all, similarly equipped, but also including two dogs which they expect to throw a litter of pups along the way. They expect to take a year to reach the asteroid belt. Now, mind you, this homesteader is, of necessity, a mechanic, a tinkerer, a jack-of-all-trades. Remember, he built his own spaceship. However, he is not, I assume, an M.D. In short, he is taking his infant child and his wife on a one-year trip in free fall, without a doctor available, not to speak of a dentist. It is to be assumed that the other twenty colonists are of similar background. However, let us stretch a point and say that one of them is a doctor and a dentist to boot. It is to be hoped that he includes all the equipment of a hospital, along with operating needs and a dentist's chair and all the devices needed by dental technicians to make bridges, caps, and so forth. Even then, a real serious illness would have him in a spot since he'd be a GP rather than a specialist. I'd hate to see the need for a kidney transplant, for instance."

Cris Everett muttered, "I'd like to see those pigs, in free fall, throwing a litter of piglets."

The woman said, "I'd like to see them cleaning up after those animals in zero gravity. Are they going to recycle all the manure, or use it for fertilizer?"

"In his description of this pioneering effort, Ryan doesn't mention hydroponic farming along the way," Bloch said. "It is to be assumed that most of the animal and human manure will be flushed overboard or used for fuel, which gives us a mild idea of the amount of water recycling stuff they would have to carry. At any rate, once in space, the five ships get together and, as they go, the men build an assembly bay, a cylinder 25 feet across and more than 200 feet long, of aluminum plate, which they've brought along."

"Jesus," the woman grated. "Those thirty-foot spheres are sounding more crowded by the minute."

"But that's not all they build on their way to the asteroid belt," Bloch said. "Once the assembly bay is completed, they construct in it a number of crop-modules, which are cylinders about 20 feet across and in lengths of nearly 200 feet. When done with these, they put in a lightweight floor and under that set up pigpens and chicken coops. All from the aluminum sheets they've brought along with them. It doesn't say where the fish are kept."

Pete had been staring at this description. Now he said in protest, "You've got to be kidding."

"No, I'm not," Bloch said. "I told you the man is not to be taken seriously. He has the homesteader mention, in a fictional message back to someone Earthside, that so far everyone's been healthy and nobody's got any tooth problems yet. And he says that if they can last to the Belt, where there are dentists, they'll have escaped the biggest problem that hits groups like theirs. Now, picture the obvious. The equivalent would be for a covered wagon to cross the United States and the homesteader driving the team saying to his associates, 'When we reach California, our troubles will be over, because there are dentists in Australia.'"

"I don't think I get that," Bruce said.

Bloch looked at him. "Ryan evidently has an uninformed idea of just what the asteroid belt is. It's not exactly as though your wife could go over to the nearest other asteroid that's been homesteaded and borrow a cup of sugar. The asteroid belt extends in thickness for millions of miles, largely between the orbits of Mars and Jupiter. For instance, the asteroid Flora is 204 million miles from the sun and the asteroid Hygeia is 292 million miles. In short, their orbits are 88 million miles from each other."

Bruce began to see what he was getting at.

Bloch continued. "There are some 2,000 asteroids large enough that we have tracked their orbits and examined them to the extent modern equipment allows. It is estimated that there might be as many as 100,000 large enough to make any difference. Then they go down in size to boulders, pebbles, and even dust."

"Now a hundred thousand asteroids sounds like a good many, but when you consider the sector of space involved, the number is tiny. Our homesteader is going to be lucky if he settles an asteroid that has a neighbor as near as, say, the Earth is to the moon. Each sizable asteroid, on an average, may be a million miles from the next. In short, our 23 colonists are probably going to be millions of miles from the nearest source of needed spare parts for their equipment and the other necessities of human existence, ranging from medicines, safety pins, and light bulbs, to lubricating oil, salt, and toilet paper. Such things, just possibly, might be available at the larger asteroids such as Ceres, which has a diameter of almost 500 miles and will most likely some day be mined by Earth entrepreneurs. If it is, the settlers would undoubtedly consist of considerably more than 23 souls, and would be supplied adequately from Earth."

"You're making quite an argument," Bruce admitted.

"Here's the biggest blooper of all," Bloch said, obviously winding it up. "What is the cash crop to be? Conceding that they are successful in building a living habitat and that after another year in free fall, eating dehydrated food and going without medical care, they are successful, rotating their habitat to produce artificial gravity, growing their own food, and mining the homestead asteroid for the raw materials they need. When their funds run out, how are they going to trade for the endless necessities that they must have? New tools, spare parts, raw materials not available on their little asteroid, medical replacements, and all the rest. Do they expect to grow bumper crops, transport them over fabulous distances to large settlements, and compete against farmers better equipped and with more land than they have? Or are they going to mine raw materials that the larger asteroids don't have? Such as what? Is their little asteroid going to be composed half of gold, or diamonds, so they could profitably ship their products back to Earth or Lagrange Five? Nonsense!"

He held up his hands as though in plea to Bruce and Pete. "I ask you, isn't that a child's fantasy? Has it anything to do with reality? Can you just see this idiotic homesteader taking off on a year-long trip in free fall with an infant child and no medical aid available? Is his wife equally mad to allow her child to be subjected to such a situation? No matter how they tried to exercise it, the kid would be plagued by a hundred different muscle, bone, and circulatory disorders. There would be inevitable calcium resorption from the bone and loss of muscle tone. The same, of course, would apply to the adults, but at least they are fully grown. It's extremely unlikely that the infant would be healthy after a year in free fall. Would the authorities at Lagrange Five, or Earth, allow them to go? No. Come, gentlemen, Solomon Ryan is not to be taken seriously."

The door opened behind them and a voice growled, "All right, everybody, the place is surrounded."

As one, the seven occupants of the small living room bobbed to their feet. It was Sergeant Joe Evola, the Security man. He wore the standard green coveralls, carried a police baton in his right hand, and had a sidearm holstered at his hip.

He said sarcastically, "Hi, Bruce; hi, Pete. Sol Ryan must have been around the corner when he allowed you two up here. It hasn't been a week and you've managed to wind up with the biggest crackpots in the island."

Pete said, "Why the shooter, Evola?"

The surly Security sergeant looked at him cynically. "For self-protection, obviously. You think I want one of these lamebrains to try and jump me?"

Bloch said, "I demand an explanation for this intrusion into my quarters."

Evola said wearily, "You'll get it, you'll get it. Come on, we're all going to the hotel." He gestured at the open door with his baton.

"And suppose we refuse?" the woman snarled.

He looked at her as though sorrowfully. "Lady, I've got twenty men outside. Why, damned if I know. I could have brought you in by myself. But Al said take a whole squad along, just so there won't be any trouble. What trouble? Did he think you'd take a runout powder? Where in the hell would you run to?"

Adam Bloch said, in resignation, "We might as well go. He's right. There's no place to hide, even if we were interested in hiding."

The freelancer and the IABI man accepted the majority will and drifted out the door along with the others onto the town's street. The day was well enough along that the technicians had already begun to warp the reflection vanes beyond the island's windows so that dark was creeping over Island One.

If Joe Evola had twenty men at his command, most of them were invisible. He led the way, followed by the group arrested—if arrested was the term—and four more Security men brought up the rear. They bore batons but Bruce didn't notice sidearms. It was as mild an arrest of supposed subversives as he had ever seen. They headed up the street on the closest route to the L5 Hilton, all keeping silence. The few pedestrians looked at them in mild interest but that was all. Sergeant Evola led them to one of the side doors, rather than into the front entry. They entered the hotel and ascended by a rear staircase to the upper floor. They ran into no other occupants of the hotel.

Pete Kapitz, swearing inwardly at the mistake of accompanying Bruce Carter, had expected to wind up in the office of Al Moore, but instead, they were taken to those of Solomon Ryan. Joe Evola's four Security men remained in the hall outside. The remaining eight of them filed through the reception room toward the door of Ryan's sanctum sanctorum.

Ruthie looked up from her desk. "Sol's expecting you, Joe," she said. "Go right on in."

"Wizard," Joe said, opening the door and standing back to let the others precede him.

Inside the office, spaced around it in comfortable chairs, drinks handy, were Solomon Ryan, Alfred Moore, Ron Rich, and Annette Casey. All of them looked up in disgust or, perhaps in Annette's case, mere amused resignation.

Sol Ryan looked at Adam Bloch, his face chiding. "I thought you were a friend of mine, Adam," he said sadly.

The teacher's voice was even. "I hope that I still am. It is nothing personal, Sol. It is just that I have come to the conclusion that under your guidance, this project is doomed to failure. Perhaps it is under anyone's guidance."

"So behind my back. . . ."

"The only reason we've continued our discussions secretly is that Mr. Moore's . . . ," Bloch took in the Security Commissioner, ". . . men go so far out of their way to suppress any free discussion at all."

"Shit," Joe Evola muttered.

"Shut up, Joe," Al Moore told him. "Take these nitwits down to the office. I've already made arrangements about them."

The sergeant herded the five Central Committee members out. They seemed resigned.

Bruce said coldly, "Where are they being sent? To some concentration camp? Or prison?"

"Oh, for *Christ's sake*, Bruce," Ron Rich moaned.

Annette Casey laughed, took a sip of her glass, and came to her feet. "You two like a drink?" she said. "You look as though you could use one. And sound even more so."

"Sit down, fellows," Sol Ryan told them gently.

Bruce and Pete took chairs.

Al Moore said, in disgust, "What's this concentration camp, prison crap? You think we have so much extra labor around here that we can spare the people to run a prison? Or, for that matter, that we can spare Bloch and his stupid friends from their own jobs?"

Bruce said, "Well, then, what are you going to do with them?" There was puzzlement in his voice.

Ron Rich said, resignation in his voice and looking put upon, "What'd you think we're going to do with them? They haven't done anything except sound off their half-assed opinions. We'll give them a tough lecture about disrupting the project by giving news people and other visitors half-baked ideas that could cause a lot of trouble back Earthside."

Al Moore said, still disgusted, "We might send a couple of them to the Luna base. Give them a taste of really uncomfortable working conditions. What did they think they were coming up to when they signed their contracts, some kind of Utopian paradise? There's still a lot to be done up here before living conditions can improve much."

Pete Kapitz said, his voice mild, "You don't seem to do so badly, Al." He looked at Annette, who had gone over to the well-stocked bar. "Make mine bourbon," he told her.

"I'd like some of that stone-age grappa," Bruce admitted.

Sol Ryan said to Bruce, "I'm surprised at you, Mr. Carter. We've given you every cooperation we could. And in no time at all, you ferret out the most vocal malcontents in the island."

Bruce took the drink Annette brought him, nodded his thanks to her, and turned back to the L5 head. "They have quite a story to tell."

Ron Rich said, "Holy Zoroaster, Bruce, with ten thousand people up here, wouldn't you expect a few soreheads?"

"Yes," the freelancer admitted. "But I wouldn't expect the overwhelming majority of the colonists and contract workers to be in that category."

"And neither would I," Sol Ryan told him with a sigh. "Have you already taken a poll, Bruce? Where do you get your figures?"

Bruce immediately felt on the defensive. He had no answer to that, really. He said, "So far as there being no prison, nor concentration camp, it looks to me like the whole project is a concentration camp, save for us here in the L5 Hilton."

Sol Ryan looked uncomprehending. Rich looked further put upon and disgusted. Annette chuckled softly.

Al Moore said, "What in the hell do you mean by that?"

Bruce said doggedly, "It's been made clear to me that

even when a contract worker's time has been served, he isn't allowed to return to Earth. If he doesn't extend his contract, he is supposedly put on standby for Earth transport, and he remains here indefinitely—on standby."

Ryan was staring at him. "Good grief, why?"

"That's what I'd like to know. Some have it that you're afraid to release anybody who might tell the true story of circumstances up here."

The Father of the L5 Project gawked at him in continued amazement. He said, "But Bruce, the policy of hiring five-year contract workers was only established about five years ago. Only a few who signed up under it have served the time. Those that have are returned home as soon as it is practical."

Al Moore said harshly, "Wizard. You've made an accusation. What's it based upon? Give us an example."

Bruce looked over at him. "Very well. Pal Barack told me all about it. When he applied to be returned to Earth, he was given the runaround."

"Pal Barack?" Ryan said. He looked at Annette.

She shook her head. "Never heard of him, Comrade."

Al Moore said to her, "Check with Captain Borgia in Personnel."

All eyes upon her, Annette put down her glass and seated herself at her desk. She flicked on a screen and murmured into it. Bruce and Pete could hear neither what she said nor what was said in return.

Finally, she looked up and said, "Pal Barack, a landscaper, kind of a gardener. Evidently, a member of the WITH-AW-DOH Club along with Adam Bloch and the others that Joe picked up earlier. His contract expired a couple of days ago. Captain Borgia reports that he was in a great hurry to return Earthside; he's now on his way."

Bruce couldn't disguise his surprise.

Pete Kapitz said softly, "I was under the impression

that there wasn't to be another passenger freighter leaving for the *Goddard* for another couple of days or so."

Annette looked at him in exasperation. "It would seem that he simply couldn't wait. The captain sent him over to the moon base by space tug. There's a passenger freighter in Luna orbit there that is scheduled to return to the *Goddard* immediately. He'll be on it."

"He's a jerk," Ron Rich said. "In the long run, he'd be back sooner if he'd waited for the next one due here. It takes a while to get to the moon base."

Annette shrugged shapely shoulders, took up her drink again and said, "Possibly he figured there wouldn't be space available on the next ship leaving here. They're usually more crowded than the ones departing Luna."

Al Moore said, "If you think we're lying, I suggest that tomorrow you go to this Barack's home and check. Call on his neighbors, or locate some of his friends. They'll tell you whether or not he's really left. Now, is there anything more you think you've discovered that's sinister about L5?" His tone dripped sarcasm.

Pete Kapitz changed the subject. He said, with the curiosity of the policeman, "What do you mean, no jail? What do you do with your criminals? Ship them back to Earth?"

Al Moore looked scornfully at him. "If we did, every contract worker and every colonist who had a peeve and wanted to go home would commit some petty crime to get the chance to return. Hell no, we make them serve out their contract time. Actually, there's practically no crime up here, unless you consider smuggling and black marketing. There's not a lot to steal, for one thing. We don't use money, we use corporation credit cards. And besides, the type of person who comes up here, on the average, isn't the criminal element."

Pete said, still curious, "Well, how about crimes of passion? Two cloddies get into a fight over some mopsy?"

"A couple of neurotics, eh?" the Security head said.

"What do you think we do? We turn them over to the Medical department for therapy and, as soon as possible, put them back to work."

Annette took orders for new drinks, mixed them, and served, while Bruce sat there stewing and feeling increasingly defensive.

A fresh grappa in hand, he said, "From what I understand, the kind of contract your people have to sign, this whole thing is like a company town of the later nineteenth, early twentieth century. The workers are so tied up that they can't leave, no matter how badly they wish to."

Sol Ryan took that, even nodding. "I see what you mean and it's largely true, Bruce, much though we dislike the situation. But, can't you see? Given the circumstances, it has to be this way. Can't you understand the expense involved in bringing a worker up here, and especially, a colonist and family? It costs roughly a hundred dollars a pound to bring bulk freight up, but a human being is another thing. They can't be trusted to mass lifters, they have to come up by shuttle. They have to be put up for sometimes lengthy periods at the *Goddard* waiting for a passenger freighter going from Earth orbit here to L5. They have to have life support systems every moment they're in space."

Ron Rich said earnestly, "Bruce, there's a billion people down on Earth who'd like to come up here, just for the ride and the experience of seeing L5 and Island One. They'd like to be tourists, spend a couple of weeks or so, and then return home. They'd just love to sign a contract so that we'd be put to the expense of bringing them up and then, after their visit, say, 'Sorry, I've changed my mind. I want to go home.' We'd go down the drain if we allowed them to do it, Bruce."

"That's why we had to do up such severe contracts," Sol Ryan said earnestly, his irrepressible charm reaching out. "They had a hard time talking me into it, for one. Frankly, I don't think the contracts would stand up in most advanced countries. But they don't have to. We're not under the jurisdiction of the United States of the Americas, Common Europe, or anyone else. But realize that no potential colonist or contract workers have to sign one of our contracts if he doesn't wish to. He can take it to his lawyer to be checked out, and if his lawyer says no, refuse to join us. Nobody is coerced."

"But once in," Al Moore wound it up, "we're tough. We make sure he or she lives up to it."

"Holy Zoroaster," Ron said in complaint. "The way everybody's talking you'd think anybody who signs with the Lagrange Five Corporation is a damn fool. But look what it means. When you get back, even after only five years, you've got a hundred thousand dollars tax clear. But you've got more than that. You've got on your work record that you've spent five years in space. Do you realize what that means? That is, if you want further jobs Earthside? It means that you're a king. Look at the early astronauts. They were paid plenty, as astronauts, but when they retired there wasn't a job in the United States that wasn't open to them. One became a Senator. One became president of a major airline. Others became high executives of any multinational corporation they chose to go into. Some former construction worker in Island One might not get that sort of treatment but, believe me, he has available almost any job in his field he's interested in. He's a goddamned hero."

Bruce sighed. "All right," he said. "I'm still learning. I'm still just looking around waiting to get convinced one way or the other about things I see. Let me think about it."

He came to his feet, as did Pete Kapitz, who had largely remained silent during the whole discussion.

Annette said brightly, "Don't forget, Bruce. We have a date tonight. I'll meet you in the bar in half an hour. We'll, ah, reverse that arrangement we started on."

"Wizard," he told her, with a slight grin to respond to her jibe. He nodded at the others and turned to go. Pete Kapitz followed him.

When they were gone, Al Moore said thoughtfully, "Did they swallow it?"

"Sure, Al," Ron said, finishing his drink and standing to go for another. "Why not? It makes sense, doesn't it? Besides, Carter might have his reputation as a freelancing muckraker, and Kapitz for a top-notch cop. But sum them up, especially out here, and they're both a couple of cloddies."

Annette said, "I wouldn't be too sure. Especially about Bruce Carter, Uncle Al."

The Security chief looked at her and snorted. "You go soft on anybody you sleep with," he said. "What do they do to you?"

"Multiple orgasms," she told him.

Sol Ryan was frowning. "What are you all talking about? We didn't say anything that wasn't true. I thought we really went out of the way to explain about the contracts to Bruce."

"Yeah," Moore said.

Out in the hall, Pete Kapitz and Bruce Carter headed back in the direction of their respective rooms.

"Too pat," Bruce muttered.

Pete squinted over at him from the side of his eyes. "You think so?"

"Yes." Something came to the freelancer. "You know, it's one thing, the President of France sending up a case of vintage champagne as a present to Sol Ryan, or Islamics sending up ten thousand bucks worth of Beluga caviar. But who in the hell would there be in Sicily that would send him a gift of fabulously aged grappa? Who in Sicily could afford it, for that matter?"

"The space colony project is offered as the solution to virtually all the problems rising from the limitations of our earthly environment. That it will solve all of these problems is a possibility that one may legitimately doubt. What cannot be doubted is that the project is an ideal solution to the moral dilemma of all those in this society who cannot face the necessities of meaningful change. It is superbly attuned to the wishes of the corporation executives, bureaucrats, militarists, political operators, and scientific experts who are the chief beneficiaries of the forces that have produced our crisis. . . . It avoids the corporate and governmental big-dealing that will be bound to accompany the expenditure of a hundred million dollars."
—*Wendell Berry*, poet, novelist.

Chapter Fifteen

The next meeting of Roy Thomas with President Paul Corcoran was a near duplicate of his last, even to the timing. He sat for only a few minutes in the outer office of Gertrude Steiner.

She had told him, her stiff mouth registering disapproval, "The President is with Admiral Stocker and General Feldmeyer. When they have gone it will be time for his half hour of meditation."

"Wizard," he said, taking a chair.

She looked at him in exasperation. "You are the only man in Washington who dares intrude on his meditation."

"Possibly that's because I'm the only one who knows what he meditates about," he told her, his smile on a bias.

"Mr. Thomas!"

"Just call me Roy," he said. He looked down at his pants leg and detected an ash burn there. The suit must be older than he thought. He hadn't smoked for years, under doctor's orders. He'd have to tell Patricia to remind him to buy another outfit or two, the first time he had an opportunity. Now that he thought of it, he seemed to be somewhat out of style. Not that he gave a damn for the vagaries of fashion.

There was a slight hum from one of the secretary's desk gadgets. She sighed, flicked a switch, and said, "Mr. President, Mr. Thomas is here." And a moment later, "Yes, I told him, but evidently he thinks the matter quite important."

She looked up at the President's right-hand man and said, "He says to come in, Mr. Thomas."

But Roy Thomas was already on his way.

He took the same chair he had occupied on his last visit and directed his eyes at the Chief Executive of the United States. Handsomest man to occupy the White House since Kennedy, he decided, all over again, and the most vapid since Harding.

Paul Corcoran, his voice brisk, said, "Roy, I've been having second thoughts about you prying into the L5 Project. You're playing with dynamite. Besides, the latest reports are that Doctor Ryan and his people are on the verge of breakthroughs that will wind up all the last bugs within a period of months."

"Prepare to have third thoughts, Paul," his top aide said grimly. "As to those reports, they remind me of the ones that used to come from Viet Nam. You know, they could see the light burning at the end of the tunnel. The war was always going to be over, victoriously, in about six months."

The President viewed him with less than enthusiasm. "You mean you've actually hit upon something?"

"Ummm," the other told him. "Actually, a fluke. Based on a report from Peter Kapitz. He's the agent John Wilson assigned to me."

Paul Corcoran took his lower lip in his teeth and pouted. "I can't believe it. In fact, I'm not sure that I want to believe it. Anything said by this administration against the L5 Project would have unforeseeable reverberations."

"Ummm," his brains behind the throne repeated. Roy Thomas sighed and said, "Paul, when I was a young fellow I spent several years as a newspaper man. One of the things it taught me was to have my ears go up every time I ran into the term non-profit organization. Whenever I came upon one, it became a challenge to find out just who was profiting. And someone invariably was."

The President said testily, "Roy, what in the name of Goshen has this got to do with the Lagrange Five Corporation? It makes no pretense of being a non-profit organization. As soon as the SPSs begin microwaving energy to Earth, it will start paying dividends."

"If it ever starts beaming energy," his top aide told him, the gaunt face registering skepticism. "But I wasn't talking about the LFC. I had in mind New Kingston University."

Paul Corcoran's face didn't have to go far to go blank. Now it made the transition.

Roy Thomas said, "The post-industrial world is now with us, in the advanced countries, Paul. In the early days of the industrial revolution, the labor of blue-collar workers was the basis of society. Almost everybody was a blue-collar worker or a farmer. Two hundred years later, they were in a minority; the majority of useful workers were white collar. They processed the products of the blue-collar workers and the farmers; they performed services ranging from distribution to teaching, to government, to medicine, to entertainment, and so on. But now we've gone a step farther. The important thing, above all, in modern society is knowledge and, ah, thinking. And our universities and colleges have come into their own. Supposedly, they're non-profit. But have you ever considered the funds that pass through, say, an Ivy League university? Big government grants, foundation grants, big donations from publicity-seeking multimillionaires who can usually write them off on their taxes. Then, there are the research projects for multinational and other corporations. Oh, never fear, fantastic sums pass through a modern university."

"I suppose you're getting to something," the other said impatiently.

"Yes. A well-organized criminal element with sizable funds on hand could do well dominating one of our larger universities, such as New Kingston. Bootlegging, prostitution, labor unions, even gambling were profitable fields of yesteryear, but almost meaningless today. Today, power and wealth pass through the universities and their think tanks."

"Come, come, Roy, out with it. What's roaching you?"

His aide began laying it on the line. "Peter Kapitz mentioned that he had spotted a Syndicate member, Natale Lucchese, now going under the name Nat Luke and working as a Security officer in Island One. Somewhat surprised, Kapitz checked up on the man and found that he had a degree in the humanities from New Kingston."

"Syndicate?" the President said, scowling. "You mean the old Mafia, or Cosa Nostra, or whatever they called it? Don't be silly, Roy, they haven't existed for decades. Next you'll be mentioning Robin Hood and his merry men."

"That was my first reaction," the other said grimly. "But it didn't check out that way. You might almost say that they went underground. They had plenty of money and plenty of brains, or, if they didn't, they could hire them. They must have seen the handwriting on the wall. Even organized crime, of the old school, was no longer proving profitable. They had to get into more legitimate efforts and, above all, they had to change their image.

The old picture of a Sicilian with a tommy gun under his arm had to go." His chuckle was as thin as his face. "To be replaced by, of all things, a college professor, complete with gray beard and the black robes of learning."

"Oh, now really, Roy. This time you've truly gone too far out. How in the world . . ."

The scrawny, ill-dressed little man shook his head. "I checked it, Paul. It wouldn't be as difficult as all that. New Kingston was chartered back in the 18th century and was originally meant as a school for Protestant ministers. It failed to flourish as did Princeton, Yale, and Harvard. In fact, it has been on the verge of folding on various occasions during the past couple of centuries. However, somehow it managed to keep its head above water. For some reason, early in the game, probably as far back as such Mafia prominents as Lucky Luciano, the crime families chose the small but dignified and honored college to send their children to. They made less of a ripple than they might have in the Ivy League institutions. New Kingston was quiet. When they decided to take over, I don't know. But it might have been as far back as half a century ago. Given their resources, it wouldn't have been difficult to infiltrate their alumni into the trustees of the corporation and into the academic senate."

Corcoran was scowling in disgust. "Confound it, Roy. This is becoming sillier by the minute. Charles Cyprus is a personal friend of mine. As president of New Kingston, he gave me every support during the campaign."

Roy nodded. "I know. A very distinguished gentleman. Government grants, since your administration has taken over, must be gratifying to him."

"Now, see here. Even from you, Roy. . . ."

Roy Thomas ignored him. "His father had the family name changed from Ciprio, which I understand is well known in the vicinity of Palermo even to this day. At any rate, to get to the point, my checking this out is thus far incomplete. I have been working with only three of my most trusted aides. However, I suspect that every official of importance in New Kingston, including the chairman of the Esopus Institute, a think tank on the level of the Hudson and Brookings, belongs to one of the old families. I mean *all* of them! The administrators of departments, the deans, the board of trustees, the vice president of academic affairs. His name was originally Biamco, by the way."

The President was flabbergasted, but he managed to get out, "What are you leading up to, Roy? Suppose that you're right. How does it involve us? As you pointed out, these people are now legitimate. Generations have passed since the days of Al Capone. I should think that their becoming valued members of society would be considered most praiseworthy. The university is a noted one and high in the ranks of our institutions of higher learning."

His top aide was shaking his head cynically, his smile inverted.

Paul Corcoran snapped, "Confound it, New Kingston is only a *school*, not a sink of perversion and criminal activity! It's a non-profit . . ."

"Yes, but the Lagrange Five Corporation isn't."

His superior gaped at him.

Roy Thomas said, "And several of the university's academicians sit on its board."

"Are you suggesting . . ."

"Doctor Solomon Ryan was only three years of age when his father legally changed the names of all family members. Salvatore Tramunti hence became Solomon Ryan." The President's assistant twisted his mouth wryly. "And eventually the Father of the Lagrange Five Project."

The country's chief executive slumped back in his chair. "You can prove this?" His voice was hoarse.

"Of course."

"But . . . but *why*, Roy? I . . . I'm confused. I. . . ."

"Mr. President, the Lagrange Five Corporation has at its disposal the spending of tens of billions of dollars, francs, marks, pounds, yen. An increasingly small fraction of this goes to such established corporations as, say, Rockwell International, Johns-Manville, McDonnell Douglas, Grumman, Chrysler, and Rocketdyne in America; or, say, Dornier, VFW-Fokker, and MBB in Germany, or equivalent corporations in France, Italy, and Great Britain. It's what originally sparked my suspicion. Who's ever heard of the overnight aerospace corporations getting the cream of the big contracts emanating from LFC?"

The President was indignant. "Why haven't our established corporations put up a howl?"

"For the same reason you dragged your feet about this investigation of mine. What did you say? Speaking up against anything the LFC does is like speaking up against mother and apple pan dowdy."

The President became decisive, as though rising to the occasion. He flicked on a desk screen and snapped, "Miss Steiner! Sell my shares in LFC!"

Roy Thomas could hear the faint gasp come over the inter-office communicator.

He said quickly, "Cancel that, Paul. It'll bring things to an immediate head, if it got out that you're dumping your LFC stock."

Paul Corcoran glared at him. "Nobody would know except Gertrude."

"Balls."

The chief executive was indignant. "I trust Gertrude implicitly. She has been my secretary since I was a State Senator."

"Ummm," Roy told him. "But before the hour is out, she sells *her* LFC shares and before the day is out, so

298

does your wife, Molly. And tomorrow, Gertrude's secretary sells hers, and so, probably, does every member of your staff. Followed, the day after, by every member of your cabinet, and their aides."

Paul Corcoran blinked, pouted, then said, "Maybe you're right."

The other said nothing.

The President flicked the desk screen back on. "Cancel that last order, Gertrude. I was jesting." He banged the communicator off.

He turned back to his top advisor and took a deep breath and a new tack. "Roy, I just can't believe that Professor Ryan is a charlatan. I've met him half a dozen times. Why, he's been to dinner twice, right here in the White House. He's absolutely charmed Molly. How could a scientist of his eminence be connected with criminal elements?"

Roy Thomas shook his head. "I've never met the man, but I was as unbelieving as you are. I had Lenny Robinson check him out thoroughly. All the evidence is that he's authentic as far as being a top physicist is concerned. He's twice been nominated for the Nobel, though he didn't make it. What we've got to realize is this: being born into the Syndicate families doesn't mean that one is stupid. Undoubtedly there are family members who are, but they couldn't be the ones pushed into prominence in New Kingston University. Their best brains would be promoted. And it's a fallacy, anyway, to think that criminal minds are necessarily second-rate. Among other things, it's according to how you define criminal. An adventurer such as Napoleon can loot half of Europe on his behalf and that of his second-rate family, and he comes down to us as a military genius and outstanding statesman. In our own field, there are uncountable politicians who came to power by fraudulent means and then milked contemporary society but who are now

299

ennobled in history books. I won't even bother to mention the founders of most of the great American fortunes. When a man steals millions, or even billions, he is not a criminal; he's a great financier, a great industrialist, an honored entrepreneur."

"You sound like a goddamned commie."

"Ummm. But the fact still remains that some decades ago, the Mafia took over New Kingston, and when one of their boys, Sol Ryan, came up with the L5 Project idea, they took it to their bosoms. They pulled all strings available, and by this time there must have been quite a few available to them, launched the Lagrange Five Corporation, and are now fucking the world flat. It's the biggest rip-off of all time. Three-quarters of the human race have been put on the sucker list."

"But Roy," Corcoran wailed. "How could so many be diddled? It's unbelievable!"

His aide shook his head and rubbed his right fist over his stomach, as though soothing an ulcer. "Evidently not. It isn't the first time human beings have been suckered into some ridiculous enthusiasm, though admittedly never on such a scale. Possibly, communications didn't allow anything of this magnitude before. But look at the Crusades, which went on for centuries. They even had a Children's Crusade.

"Or take war. Who can explain the enthusiasm in both the North and South for the Civil War, in which both sides were bled white? Take the First World War. There was no excuse for getting in, but there was scarcely a vote against it, either in Europe, on both sides, or in America. We went in supposedly to make the world safe for democracy and, when we'd won, there was less democracy than before it began. So it would seem it is with the L5 Project. People are thinking with their hearts, not their heads. They want space colonization to work, and simply won't hear anything said against it."

"But, Holy Goshen, Roy, this is the first time I've ever heard anything against it. It doesn't make sense for it to go on this long without somebody taking a closer look. Every government on Earth is backing either the West's L5 Project or the Soviet Complex's space platforms and asteroid belt project."

His aide leaned back in his chair, recrossed his thin legs, and nodded acceptance. He said ironically, "I suspect that one reason governments support it is that it keeps the minds of the people off their real troubles. Dissent has fallen off drastically. Almost everybody thinks that the space colonization project will solve all the burgeoning economic and political problems that confront us. All radical and even liberal movements have fallen off drastically. Socialists, syndicalists, libertarians, neo-anarchists, Euro-communists, all have seen their followers drop away wholesale. Every entrenched government in the West gives the L5 Project at least lip service. It's an updated version of giving the people bread and circuses. In this version, the circus is so big they can afford most of the bread."

Paul Corcoran didn't seem to know what his advisor was talking about. He said impatiently, "Roy, what do you have in mind now? This is catastrophe! Frankly, my mind's spinning. Why, this administration has thrown everything into the proposition that all our energy problems would be solved by microwaving solar power down from space. Which in turn would eliminate most pollution problems, especially when heavy industry was moved out there. And the space colonies, when they began to build islands Three, Four, and Five, would absorb the world's excess population."

"Wizard," the other told him. "That's the story everybody swallowed. But from Kapitz's preliminary report, the whole project is fucked up. The reports their publicity people are sending back here to Earth are completely exaggerated. They're spending money like madmen and not getting results."

"Well . . . confound it, Roy. What do you recommend we *do*?"

"Go into higher gear in this investigation. So far, I've just scratched the surface. Among other things that Kapitz has dug up is the fact that the Arab Union is subsidizing the L5 Project to the tune of five billion a year. Why, for Christ's sake? And what does the Syndicate have in mind eventually? They must know that sooner or later the whole mess will collapse. Then where will they be with half the human race out for their blood?"

The President's classical face registered determination. "As always, I have complete faith in you, Roy. Behind you one hundred percent. Just tell me your plans and I'll implement them."

The other twisted his thin face. "I don't have any. We can't just drop the axe on them at this stage. God only knows what would happen."

His superior ogled him in dismay. "You mean that you don't know what to do?"

Roy Thomas made an impatient negative gesture. "Not at this stage. Right now, I'm busy accumulating ulcers. We need more information. I suggest that we have John Wilson put a hundred or so of his absolutely best and most dependable men onto digging further into the Syndicate's relationship with the Lagrange Five Corporation. I suspect that they are alone in this. That they *are* the LFC, period. But we're not sure. Also, I assume that Wilson has some IABI men permanently assigned to the International Zone of Tangier. Ever since it was reconstituted, it's been the world center for espionage and counterespionage, on both a political and corporate level. He must have a few moles there. Let them go to work investigating the L5 Corporation. Hell, if he's as efficient as his department's publicity people claim, he should have a mole or two in some upper bracket position in LFC. And if he has anybody bought in the Arab Union, perhaps he can ferret out what in the hell the Arabs are doing helping finance the L5 Project."

"All right," the President sighed. "You have my go-ahead. See John and tell him the whole story." He looked at the desk chronometer and sighed again. "My whole meditation period has elapsed."

"My heart bleeds for you," his gaunt aide murmured under his breath.

"What?"

"Nothing." Roy Thomas pushed himself to his feet.

Paul Corcoran said hopefully, "Do you think it would be possible for me to deal directly with my broker? That is, to instruct him to sell my. . . ."

"No," Thomas said. "I'll keep you informed, Paul."

* * * *

If the President's chief assistant had duplicated his last call on his superior, the duplication continued in the upper floor offices of the Director of the IABI in the soaring Inter-American Bureau of Investigation Building.

The small eyes of John Edward Wilson glared at him. He said, "You've got to be off the wall, Thomas."

"I wish the hell I was," Roy said flatly. "Frankly, I haven't the vaguest idea what to do next, except dig out some more information; something we can work with. There has to be some answer, but at this stage, God only knows what it is."

"You put a couple of hundred men on this, digging into the LFC, and you'll have leaks."

Roy Thomas eyed him unblinkingly. "There'd better not be, John. This is supposedly your field. Figure out some way where security is tighter than the Manhattan Project."

John Edward Wilson closed his porcine eyes and took a deep breath.

The presidential aide had turned to leave, but now he hesitated for a moment and said, "By the way, I've had just three men working on this, José Sanchez, Tom Finklestein, and Lenny Robinson." He twisted his mouth. "In your time, you've come in contact with all three, usually when you and I haven't exactly been seeing eye to eye. Now, things are different. I'd like you to put guards on them, around the clock. At least two men on a shift."

Roy Thomas didn't know it, but he had just condemned his three closest friends. When he was gone, John Edward Wilson opened his desk drawer and brought forth his special transceiver.

Roy Thomas, despite his intellect, also didn't know that in the past two hours of conversation he had condemned himself. He rode to his Alexandria home, dismissed his chauffeur, and strode up to the porch of his home, to the expected greeting by his overly plump wife. They were cut down together by thirty rounds of Gyrojet rocket slugs fired from a silenced submachine gun from the window of a slow, cruising hovervehicle.

For himself, Thomas did not rage with his namesake against the dying of the light.

He hadn't been particularly fond of living. But just before the blackness moved in, he found time to rage for Pat. Patricia had always liked living.

At almost the same time this was happening, John Edward Wilson was in the Oval Office. He'd had as little trouble getting an immediate audience with Corcoran, supposedly the most difficult man in the world with whom to get an appointment, as had Roy Thomas earlier in the day. Gertrude, the ultimate in appointment secretaries, hustled him through, beaming. It wasn't as though the nattily attired director was the same element as sourpussed Roy Thomas. She had never figured out how the gaunt, thin, unlovable Thomas had ingratiated himself with her lifelong boss. Nor had she ever been able to figure out why Paulie Corcoran had chosen Molly in preference to her. Surely not because Molly was a reasonably close relative to the Duponts, or Dodges, or whoever her wealthy relatives were. He never even came anymore to Gertrude's apartment for their formerly refreshing debauch every Tuesday. These days he meditated instead.

Not that she had any objections to anything the great man desired.

The director was saying, "Mr. President, for a long time I've been suspecting Roy Thomas was losing his grip. This ties it. From what you say, this ridiculous investigation was his idea from the first. The way he represented it to me, it was your project. In fact, he gave me to believe that you had a bug in your bonnet, as he put it."

"Why, that's tomfoolery."

"The whole thing is, Mr. President."

"But the fact is, John, his investigations, though only preliminary, have turned up some devastating facts."

"I doubt it, sir. Can you be specific?"

"Among other things, persons high in the administration of New Kingston, including President Cyprus and Solomon Ryan, have changed their names from Italian to more, ah, American ones."

John Wilson let air out of his lungs in disgust and worked his heavyset face into a grimace. He said, "I would wager that half the Jews and Middle Europeans who have emigrated to the United States have Americanized their names. Why, most of us couldn't even pronounce the majority of Polish or Hungarian ones. The fact that an Italian has Americanized his name doesn't mean he's a member of the legendary Mafia. There are tens of thousands of Ciprios and Tramuntis in Italy, most of whom have probably never even heard of the

Mafia. I imagine that there are thousands of Capones in Italy who have never heard of the infamous Scarface Al."

Paul Corcoran said, "But the fact is that the Lagrange Five Corporation is granting its lushest contracts to obscure firms, rather than to our long-established aerospace corporations. Why should that be?"

Wilson sighed, "How should I know? I'm no engineer. But I'm sure that the LFC has some of the most competent administrators on Earth supervising its purchases. Perhaps these newer companies are underbidding the older ones. It's no secret how often in the past our industries have defrauded the government with inflated estimates and bids and even then run into monstrous overcharges."

The President took his lower lip in his mouth and pouted.

The other failed to be charmed. He said softly, "So far as that changing of names is concerned, Mr. President, my own grandfather legally changed ours shortly after the First World War."

Paul Corcoran had a stubborn streak in him, besides which, he dreaded going against the man whose wits had served him so well in the past. He said, "Well, I see no reason why we can't go along with Roy. If he's making a mistake, we'll soon find out. And, if we're very discreet, no one will ever be the wiser."

Wilson shook his head at him. "Mr. President, there are very powerful elements connected with the LFC, some of them quite ruthless. Big money is almost always ruthless. What I am especially afraid of is that if it gets out that you are investigating them, they might in turn seek revenge by investigating *you*."

"Me? Have you gone around the bend, John? My life is an open book."

The IABI head narrowed already small eyes. "Nobody's

life lacks some fine print, Mr. President. Suppose, for instance, that they tracked down that Burroughs, Ten Cyck and Burroughs real estate deal made when you were still a State Senator?"

The other's face went gray. "What ... what do you mean? I don't know what you're talking about, John Wilson."

The police official said, his voice cold, "I believe you do, Mr. President. And there are other things they might stumble upon. Take your wife's investments, through Switzerland, at the time the Nicaragua canal was being negotiated with so much support from your administration?"

Paul Corcoran's eyes bugged. "Are you ... are you threatening me?"

John Wilson was horrified, his expression aghast. He said urgently, "Certainly not, sir. I was simply pointing out your vulnerability, given a vengeful attempt to expose any innocent examples of questionable judgment you might have exercised in years now long past."

The President's shoulders slumped. "Damn it to Goshen," he complained. "I wish Roy had never got off on this bent. It's damn inconsiderate of him. And he won't even allow me to dispose of my thirty thousand worth of LFC shares."

The other's voice was smooth. "Why, I'd be glad to take them off your hands, sir. I've been planning to increase my portfolio."

"You would?" The President's eye took on a wary slyness. "As a matter of fact, I believe Molly has some as well."

His visitor puffed out already plump cheeks. "I'll be happy to take them over as well. As a matter of fact, I have recently come into a generous legacy and was expecting to invest further in LFC shares. You see, Mr. President, I have full faith in the organization."

"So I see. I hope that you are correct. But now, the question is, how are we going to put this to Roy? He doesn't take kindly to being thwarted and he's too good a man for me to risk losing." There was a touch of apology in the presidential voice.

Before the IABI man could answer, one of the President's desk screens buzzed. He answered it in irritation and the voice of Gertrude Steiner came through. Her words were indistinguishable to the President's visitor, but the shock in her tone was there. The President's face was empty after he had flicked off the box. He turned back to Wilson, his eyes unseeing.

"Roy Thomas," he got out. "He and his wife have been shot to death in front of his own house."

"How terrible," the other said, shaking his head in utter disbelief and in sympathy. "But it's like I said, Mr. President. There are some ruthless elements who have invested deeply in the Lagrange Five Corporation. Undoubtedly, they received news of his investigation and, afraid it would rock the boat, took this drastic measure. I'll put the full resources of my department into hunting down the infamous assassins." He came immediately to his feet.

After he was gone, the President's eyes were sick. "I'll bet you will," he muttered under his breath. "I wonder what *your* family's name was before your grandfather changed it. . . ."

"*In the long run, it may well be that the people working at the orbital manufacturing facilities may build very comfortable and earthlike habitats. . . . In the early days, though, it seems almost certain for economic reasons that the orbital facilities will house a selected, highly qualified, highly motivated population, nearly all of whom will be working, and working hard. They will not be in a utopian paradise or a laboratory for sociological experiments. The orbital facility will be much more like a Texas tower oil rig, or a construction camp on the Alaska pipeline, or like Virginia City, Nevada, in about the year 1875.*"
—*Gerard K. O'Neill, before the Senate Subcommittee on Aerospace Technology and National Needs, January 19, 1976.*

Chapter Sixteen

Annette Casey awoke to find Bruce Carter on the pillow beside her, on his back, his hands behind his head and staring up at the ceiling. They were in his room.

She ran her hands through her short, black curls in a wake-up gesture and said, "Top of the morning, comrade."

He looked over at her, taking in her brunette beauty. "Where'd you ever get a name like Casey?" he said. "I'd taken you for Spanish, or possibly French."

"Haven't you ever heard of the Black Irish?" she said, yawning. "After the Spanish Armada got its ass whipped by Francis Drake and the boys, it couldn't return directly home because the British fleet was between them and Spain. So they continued north, rounded the top of Scotland, and sailed down past Ireland. But some of the ships had taken a few holes in the fracas and sank, leaving their crews to make their way to land as best they could."

She yawned again and wound it up. "The Irish colleens of the time were hospitable. Ergo, the Black Irish."

"A likely story," he told her.

She took him in. "What were you looking so pensive about, just now? Figuring out something else that's wrong with the way Sol's muddling through on the L5 Project?"

He looked over at her. "As a matter of fact," he said, "it had just come to me how little there's been published, Earthside, in the way of letters from colonists and contract workers; or, say, short articles for the home-town newspaper, or whatever. I don't believe I've ever seen anything of that type, anywhere."

On Annette Casey, a frown looked good. She said, "These construction workers aren't the letter-writing kind."

"Come on, come on. With ten thousand people up here, there's going to have to be one hell of a lot of mail. If each one wrote only one letter, or even a postcard, a month, that'd be 120,000 pieces of mail a year. Surely, some of the more interesting letters, describing some extraordinary element of building Island One, or the SPSs, would wind up being published."

She snorted at him. "Holy Zoroaster, comrade, did you think we utilized old-fashioned mail, sheets of paper stuck in envelopes? If we did, the postal rates would have to be as high as the Pony Express of old. Something like five dollars an ounce. And, even then, think of the space that'd be taken up."

It was the freelancer's turn to frown. "Well, what do you do?"

"Radio and telex, going both ways. A colonist writes his letter and brings it in to Communications. They radio it down. At the New Albuquerque shuttleport it's typed out and sent on its way to the addressee. Very simple. No charge."

"Wizard," he told her, his expression letting it be known that he was less than satisfied. "But suppose somebody did want to send an ordinary letter. Possibly, he or she didn't want anybody, not even a radio engineer, to see the contents."

She shrugged shapely shoulders. "No way. Oh, I suppose what you could do would be to give your letter to somebody returning to Earth and let him mail it for you."

His eyes went up to the ceiling again, thoughtfully. "And I suppose that between the time the colonist turns over his letter and it's radioed down, each letter is thoroughly read—and censored."

"Oh, fercrissakes, darling."

"Otherwise your malcontents, such as Adam Bloch and his club, would be sending down a stream of letters and even articles, beefing about the things they see wrong about the project. The fact that I've never seen such letters or articles published is rather definite proof that efficient censorship is utilized."

She sighed in disgust. "All right! What would you expect? For the same reason we don't ordinarily welcome freelance writers such as yourself up here, we don't allow material to go out that hasn't been checked. One crackpot like Bloch writing a stream of letters to the editor could cause more stink than an epidemic of crotch rot."

"Wizard," he said in resignation. "Given your viewpoint, I suppose it makes sense. It's just that I don't like censorship in any form. I'm a devoted freedom-of-speech man."

"But there are limits," she said snappishly. "Who was it who said that you can't allow someone in a crowded theater to jump up and yell, 'FIRE!' "

"Why not?" he growled. "Freedom of speech is more important than a few theaters full of people. Particularly the type of people who are attracted by the sort of entertainment available in theaters today. Besides, the guy sitting behind him has just as much right to jump up and yell, 'HE'S CRAZY! THERE IS NO FIRE!' "

"Oh, you're impossible."

He grinned at her. "Practically nothing is impossible."

"Well, then, you're damned improbable."

He looked at his watch. "Darn it," he said. "We've really slept in this morning, after that workout last night. What are you, some kind of barracuda?"

"Look who's talking. Doesn't that thing of yours ever get soft?"

"Oh, it's like that all the time. You ought to see it when I get horny."

"Braggart."

He threw the sheet back and swung his legs out to the floor. "I wanted to see Academician Suvorov this morning. Coming up from Earth, he promised me an interview after he'd had a couple of days to get oriented."

She said, "He's right here in the hotel. We moved him into the former office of Nils Petersen, two floors up. Petersen's name is still on the door, so you can't miss it. Kind of a grumpy old duck, isn't he? The Russian, I mean."

They were both nude. He headed for his clothes which, in their mutual hurry the night before, he had thrown over a chair. He reminded himself to get fresh ones from Carl Gatena.

"You're lucky to have him with you up here," he told her. "He's probably the most celebrated ecologist alive."

"Could I come along? I'd like to see how you operate. How you go about interviewing somebody."

He was climbing into his pants. "No, you can't. You'd inhibit him. As Ryan's secretary, before you he'd pull his punches on anything that wasn't upbeat."

"You expect him to be critical?"

"Frankly, yes," he said, picking up his shirt. "Even

313

when I talked to him in *Goddard,* he had his doubts about the feasibility of a closed ecosystem."

She said, "You're the first man I've ever seen who puts his pants on before his shirt. It's impractical. How about meeting me for breakfast in about an hour, in the dining room?"

"It's because I'm shy dressing in front of a lady. I want to get covered up as soon as possible." He thought about breakfast. "See here, sweetie, I love you dearly. In fact, I've already been considering asking you to marry me. As you put it once, we could make such beautiful music raking some muck together. But aren't we overdoing this? We've never been out of sight of each other for more than minutes at a time. I thought that you were up to your ears in work as Sol Ryan's Person Friday."

She yawned, still once again, and stretched. "You're prettier than Dr. Ryan," she told him. "It's that dimple in your chin."

Finished dressing, he headed for the door. "Okay, the dining room in about an hour. I don't think the interview will take that long. For one thing, I don't know what the hell he's talking about."

He headed for the stairway, sorry now that he'd made the date for breakfast with her. He was mildly hungry and could have eaten before looking the Academician up. He had no definite appointment with Suvorov. Perhaps the other wouldn't even remember him.

He had no difficulty in finding the office formerly occupied by Nils Petersen; as Annette had said, it was two floors up. He knocked at the door and promptly received a "Come in," in Esperanto.

Leonard Suvorov was seated at his desk, stylo in hand, several books spread out before him. To his right, the screen of the data banks library booster was lit and a page of another volume was on it.

The Russian looked up at Bruce's entry, frowned only

momentarily, then said, "Ah, the writer fellow. Pull up a chair and rest it, to use the Americanism." He indicated a straight chair, right next to the desk.

Bruce took it, relaxed, and crossed his legs. "Where did you pick up that particular Americanism?" he said. They were both speaking English now, rather than the international tongue.

The heavyset biologist smiled ruefully. "Ai, Ai," he said. "Have I made a mistake again? I'm an omnivorous reader. Some years ago I went through a period of devouring American suspense novels. I picked up some of the idiom, I suppose."

As he talked, he picked up the stylo, which he had put down to shake hands. Now he pulled a paper pad between them and printed on it.

"ROOM IS ELECTRONICALLY MONITORED BY L5 SECURITY."

Bruce Carter raised his eyebrows but then nodded. The freelancer said, "Sir, you'll remember that in the *Goddard*, when I asked you for an interview, you suggested that I wait until we arrived here in Island One. That you needed some time to get even first impressions of the magnitude of your task."

"Yes, of course," the Russian said. As Bruce talked, he had printed again.

"I BELIEVE BIONOMICS ATTEMPTS HERE ARE A FARCE AND THAT MY PREDECESSOR PETERSEN WAS MURDERED TO PREVENT HIM FROM REVEALING THE FACT TO SCIENTIFIC COMMUNITY EARTHSIDE."

Bruce, even as he read, was saying, "So, I thought I'd drop by and see how you felt about it all at this stage."

"Well, frankly, young man," the other said heavily, as though thinking it out as he went along, "I'm afraid that I'm still in much the same position as before. Unhappily, my colleagues, Nils Petersen and Professor Chu Sing, aren't here to brief me on what has already been accomplished. Dr. Petersen met with an unfortunate accident here in Island One and Professor Chu returned to Earth where he was struck by an automobile."

He had been printing again as he talked.

"I SUSPECT FOUL PLAY IN HIS DEATH."

Bruce let his voice reflect disappointment. "But didn't they leave notes on their work?"

Suvorov was again writing, even as he answered.

He said, "Unfortunately, Petersen's papers have all been mislaid. I suppose that Doctor Casey, of Sol Ryan's staff, will turn them up sooner or later. Professor Chu's notes seem to be all in Chinese. I doubt if there's a person in the island who could read them."

"I READ MANDARIN AND HAVE PERUSED CHU'S PAPERS. BOTH PETERSEN AND CHU HAD CONCLUDED THAT CLOSED ECOSYSTEM WAS IMPOSSIBLE AT THIS TIME. WHEN PETERSEN WAS KILLED, CHU FEARED FOR HIS OWN LIFE AND PLANNED TO RETURN TO EARTH SURROUNDED BY SECRETARY AND AIDES."

Bruce took the stylo from the other's hand and wrote. "WHAT CAN I DO?"

Aloud he said, "Well, this is a disappointment, but I suppose the thing for me to do is to come back in a few days." He handed the writing instrument back to the other.

The Russian, even as he spoke, wrote again. He said, wryly, "I'm afraid that it will be more than a few days before I have a very clear picture. But we shall see."

"GET BACK TO EARTH SOON AS POSSIBLE. TAKE ALL MEASURES TO EXPOSE SITUATION, INCLUDING CHU'S DEATH."

Bruce Carter came to his feet. "Right," he said. "I'll look you up again before I leave. It's indefinite how long I'll be staying."

Leonard Suvorov took up the sheet of paper they had been writing on and, taking a leaf from the book of experience of his Cheka contact, Alvar Saarinen, tore it into pieces and put them into his mouth, chewed, and swallowed.

He said, "Very good, my young friend. See you around, as you Yankees put it." He didn't get up to accompany the freelancer to the door.

Bruce left and, for a moment, stood in the hall, trying to make sense of it.

Was the noted scientist out of his mind? However, on the ace of it, the story made some sense. Bruce Carter had heard of both Doctor Nils Petersen and Professor Chu Sing. They were almost as well noted in the field of bionomics as was Suvorov himself, and if they had reported to the scientific world that Sol Ryan's plans to create a closed ecosystem in Island One were impossible, it would have been disastrous to the L5 Project. All ultimately depended upon such a closed system. It didn't make sense to continue the fantastic expense of supplying the needs of ten thousand people in space from Earthside. As a temporary expedient, it was one thing, but sooner or later such a closed system simply had to be achieved.

Very well, such a report would have been a disaster. No one would have taken the word of even Solomon Ryan against that of Petersen and the Chinese. But that didn't mean that the powers of Lagrange Five were so ruthless as to have the two scientists murdered to insure their silence. Certainly, the genial Sol Ryan couldn't have been privy to such a conspiracy, not to speak of Annette. And through their hands went every thread of the complicated tapestry that was the L5 Project. They would have known of the plot. Wouldn't they?

He shook his head and decided to take it up with Pete Kapitz. This was obviously just the sort of thing Pete and his boss, Roy Thomas, were looking for. And they'd have the resources to check it out. He headed for Pete's room, two floors down and immediately next to his own.

The hall was deserted save for one man coming toward him, carrying a leather tool satchel with MAINTENANCE stenciled on its side. It wasn't until they were within a few feet of each other that Bruce saw, to his surprise, that it was Cris Everett, the sour-faced window washer and member of the Central Committee of Adam Bloch's so-called underground. Bruce came to a halt.

The other approached him, looking up and down the corridor furtively. He put his mouth to Bruce's ear and whispered, "Can they bug a hotel hall like this?"

The freelancer whispered back, "Damned if I know. Not very effectively, I imagine. And whoever was doing it would have his work cut out deciding who was talking."

Everett whispered, "Jesus, I'm glad I found you. I sneaked into the hotel as a repairman. Adam's hiding out. He wants to see you."

Bruce squinted at him. "Why?" he said. "What happened to the others?"

The window washer looked up and down the hall, nervously, and still whispered. "They were shipped out to the Luna base by Security. But Adam's a teacher and there aren't any kids over there; too rugged. He and I got a chance to slip off and we're hiding out with some Club members."

Bruce said, "Come along. I'm on my way to see the IABI man, Peter Kapitz. Something else has come up. Things are coming to a head."

Peter Kapitz had been up on the roof attempting to raise Roy Thomas again on his scrambled transceiver. It hadn't worked out that way. The voice that answered was that of John Edward Wilson, Director of the IABI and his ultimate superior.

Wilson had said flatly, "There have been some developments, Kapitz. Your orders are to return as soon as possible. Further, you are to discuss with no one at all anything concerning your assignment, or anything that you have thus far discovered in your investigation. Nobody whatsoever. Is that understood?"

Kapitz was set back. "But, sir," he said. "I have just begun to get results. To my surprise, I've got quite a bit of the very kind of evidence Mr. Thomas sent me up for."

"We'll discuss your evidence later, Kapitz. Meanwhile, make immediate arrangements to return."

Pete Kapitz didn't like it. Why, he didn't know. After all, Wilson was the Director of the Bureau. He said, hesitantly, "But, sir, Mr. Thomas has explained that I am working directly under the President. I was to report only to Thomas, take orders only from him."

"There have been some changes," the other said grimly. "Among other things, Roy Thomas is no longer with us. I have discussed this with President Corcoran. Now, no more of your confounded lip. Return to Greater Washington immediately."

"Yes, sir," Pete said unhappily, even as the lardy face of his superior faded from the tiny screen.

When he returned to his room, it was to find Rick Venner seated there in the best chair his quarters afforded.

He began to demand an explanation, but the other held up a hand for silence, pointed around the room at the TV screen, the phone screen, and other electronic features of the furnishings, and then at his ear.

Pete shook his head and scowled at his visitor. "No. It's not bugged. Not any more. I deactivated it the first day I was here. The next day, they repaired it twice, while I was out of the room. And I deactivated it twice again. Evidently, they've given up. I don't know what the hell they expected to hear, anyway. Now what in the name of Jesus do you think you have in mind breaking into my room?"

Rick Venner stood and took a chubby Gyrojet pistol from his pocket and fixed his eyes on the other thoughtfully.

Pete Kapitz stared at the gun. Like a damn fool, he told himself, he had left his own weapon in his handbag.

"Okay, Rocks," he said. "But you obviously won't get away with it."

Rick reversed the gun and handed it to the IABI man, then turned and reseated himself. He said, conversationally, "There's a contract out on you, Kapitz."

Pete gawked at him. "A contract! Are you out of your mind? What are you talking about?"

"Al Moore's given me the job of hitting you."

"Why?" the IABI man said in bewilderment.

"Because he knows that you weren't really sent up here to look for me. Somebody's sent you up to snoop. And our friend Al evidently doesn't think the L5 Project can bear any snooping, for which I don't blame him. From what I've already seen and heard, the whole thing's a shambles. Christ only knows what would happen if all those investors in the Lagrange Five Corporation found it out."

Pete slumped down to the side of the bed and tossed the gun the other had given him to the bed cover.

He said fretfully, "All right, give me the whole story."

Rick said, "I don't know the whole story, but to begin with, Al Moore and Mark Donald are both pros. I've been a grifter all my life, and it takes one to know one. For that matter, I suspect that all these Security bastards are pros. At any rate, Al Moore wants you hit. He figured out a very neat way to pull it off without anything pointing to him, or to the L5 Project administration in general. Your cover was that you were looking for me. Wizard. Moore figured on setting it up in such a way that I'd hit you while Bruce Carter, that writer guy, was on the scene. Supposedly, I had the perfect motive for plugging you. You were after me. Then, according to Moore, I'd be arrested and sentenced to twenty years or so hard labor. But they promised to put me in a hide-away where I could live it up until I thought it was safe to return to Earth."

Pete gave him the eye for a long moment. "Why didn't you do it?" he said.

"Because I'm not a killer and particularly because I'm not stupid. Dead men tell no tales. As soon as I'd hit you, they would have gunned me down. Bruce Carter would have had the action story of his life. And no fingers would be pointing at the L5 Project."

"Why'd you come to me?"

"Where else is there to go?"

Pete took him in.

Rick said, "We're in this together now, Pete. It's you and me and, frankly, we haven't got a chance in a million."

The IABI operative sighed, picked up the gun, and tossed it over to the jewel thief. He came to his feet, went over to the closet, and fished out his luggage. He came up with another gun, just slightly larger than the one he'd returned to the other. He tucked it into his belt, under his jacket.

Rick Venner put his weapon away, too. And they looked at each other for a long moment, neither of them with readable expressions on their faces.

There came a knock at the door; they both started and shot another look at each other. Pete Kapitz shrugged and walked over to the entry. He opened up carefully, his right hand under his jacket. Bruce Carter came in, followed by an apprehensive-looking Cris Everett.

The writer looked first at Rick, then Pete. "What the hell goes on?" he said.

"We're having a love fest," Rick told him, his grin on a bias. "The original plans involved you being in on it." He looked at the window washer. "Who in the hell's this?"

"Cris Everett," Bruce told him, sending his eyes to Pete.

"Sit down fercrissakes," Pete said. "I haven't even had breakfast yet, but does anybody want a drink?"

Nobody else had had breakfast yet either, but all wanted a drink. He didn't bother to ask them their preferences, but poured out four rugged charges of brandy.

Bruce looked over at Rick and said, "What spins, Rocks?"

"Jesus," the other complained. "Everybody in Island One knows who I am. You'd think I'd just been interviewed on the local Tri-Di news show."

Pete handed the drinks around and told the newcomers the story he'd just had from Rick.

Bruce said glumly, after assimilating it, "You haven't heard anything yet." He described his interview with the Russian scientist.

The IABI man stared when the writer was through. He said, "Did you believe him?"

"Not then, but I think I do now, after what you've said."

Pete finished his drink, stiff-wristed, and whacked the glass down on the desk. He muttered, "There's over two hundred men in Security." He looked at Cris Everett. "How're they armed?"

The window washer scowled. "Sometimes they carry guns. You saw that sergeant who arrested us. But usually they only have billy clubs."

Rick said, "Don't be fooled. They've got guns, all right. A type like Al Moore would feel naked without a small arsenal near at hand." He looked at Everett and repeated, "Who in the hell's this?"

Bruce said, "Cris Everett. He's a member of the Central Committee of the WITH-AW-DOH Club. It's an underground outfit that wants to change the ways the Lagrange Five Corporation is doing things." He added, with a touch of bitterness, "They thought they were secret, but it turns out Al Moore knows all about them." His eyes widened suddenly and he snapped his fingers and turned to Everett. "Listen, how many members altogether do you have in the Club?"

"Why, about a thousand."

"No more than that? I thought you people said that practically all the colonists and contract workers feel the same as you do."

The smaller man was disgusted. "They do, but they don't want to stick their necks out. They're afraid they'll wind up on Security's malcontents list and their return Earthside might be held up. If things came to a head, at least nine out of ten would line up with us. Everybody but those finks who work in the hotel."

Bruce said, an edge of excitement creeping into his voice, "Listen, do you Club members have any guns?"

Everett's look was blank. "Guns?"

"Well . . . or any other kind of weapons."

"Holy smog, Carter, what would we be doing with weapons up here?"

The other three were also staring at Bruce now, obviously wondering what he was driving at.

He said urgently, "Couldn't you people improvise some in your workshops?"

"Sure, given time. Given time, the boys in the manufacturing facility could whomp you up a tank, complete with cannon."

"We don't have time," Rick said sarcastically. "I've got a sneaky suspicion that this is all going to be over in an hour or so, one way or the other." He eyed Bruce. "What did you have in mind, Carter?"

Pete Kapitz had been frowning at the freelancer as well. "Yeah," he said. He went over to the bar and got the bottle and poured them all another jolt.

Bruce shook his head. "We need manpower, but most of all we need weapons. If we could just seize the broadcasting station here in the hotel for as little as fifteen minutes, we could sound the alarm and broadcast both throughout Lagrange Five and the moon base and to Earth. The stink that'd raise might stop them from more bloodshed. Christ only knows what this conspiracy is all about, but once questions begin being asked, we'd soon find out."

Rick said mildly, "Pete and I are heeled. Gyrojets, the most efficient handgun thus far developed."

Bruce bug-eyed him. "You are?"

"Yeah," Pete said.

The freelancer spun on Cris Everett. "You said that Adam Bloch wanted to see me. Let's go. We can't run the risk of just the four of us taking over that broadcasting station. We need more men."

"Here we go again," Rick said mildly, coming to his feet. He finished off his brandy and nonchalantly threw the glass into a corner.

"There are some pretty interesting engineering questions that have to be answered before you are going to be able to really design things in detail like (the) space colonies."
—Russell Schweickart, Astronaut

Chapter Seventeen

Under Rick's guidance, they left the hotel in the manner he had worked out, through the kitchens and to the alley behind the Hilton. The three newcomers to the island, all dressed in Earthside garments, went on ahead through the building, chatting away animatedly, while Cris Everett, in his role as a repairmen, followed about twenty feet behind, as though having no connection with the others. Their passage through the kitchen solicited only mild irritation from those working at breakfast.

In the alley, Everett caught up with them. He took in their clothes without enthusiasm. "You're going to stick out like sore thumbs in those outfits," he said sourly. "I hope to hell some Security man doesn't spot us and tag along after, just for the hell of it."

"We'll have to take the risk," Pete said. "Besides, if anybody tries to stop us, there'd better be at least four of them and they'd better be armed. Gentlemen, the chips are now down."

Once again, the window washer, carrying his maintenance satchel of tools, pretended to be no part of their group. He walked along twenty or thirty feet before them, seemingly minding his own business. They continued after him, supposedly still absorbed in their discussion.

Bruce had expected to be taken somewhere out of the town limits of Lagrange City, to one of the more isolated buildings spotted throughout the Island One cylinder. Such buildings could be seen from the window of his room, some of them located on the same strip of livable surface as the town itself, some on the alternating strips above. They were, he assumed, individual homes of those who preferred to live outside the town, agricultural buildings and other structures devoted to building or maintaining the island.

But evidently, Adam Bloch and his friends preferred the anonymity of the larger settlement. It was easier to stay hidden. The building in which the underground head was sequestered was only three short blocks from the hotel itself. However, the four were not fated to reach their destination without interruption.

As the three supposedly arguing, Earthside-garbed pedestrians strode along the narrow street, a voice called out to them.

"Rick. Hey, Rick!"

They came to an unhappy halt. Tony Black, Rick Venner's housemate, came up. He had been heading in the opposite direction. The furtive black marketeer eyed the three questioningly.

"Where you going?" Black said. His eyes went up and down Pete Kapitz and Bruce Carter.

Rick said, "Oh, just taking a stroll with these gentlemen."

"Well, Fred Davis, your supervisor, is looking for you. He wants you to take another crack at going out into space today."

Rick's mind raced. He said, "Look, Tony. I'm, ah, busy. Tell him I'll see him later."

Tony Black blinked at him. He said, with a touch of indignation, "You can't do that. He's your supervisor. You're still on the payroll as an electrical engineer. Until he decides you're simply not suited for working outside, he's boss and what he says goes."

Cris Everett returned. He said, "What in the hell's going on?"

Tony Black's eyes narrowed. He took them all in, all over again.

Everett said quickly, "This funker is bad news. Supposedly, he's a black marketeer, but most of us suspect he's a Security plant. He gets away with too much, too easily."

"Holy smog, Rick. What's the matter with these guys?" Black blurted.

"Things begin to add up," Rick said, his voice less than friendly. "The Penman never told me I was to have a contact up here. You turned up too fast and got me under your wing where you could keep an eye on me." He looked at Pete and Bruce. "We'd better bring him along."

"I'm not going anywhere," Black blurted.

Pete Kapitz pushed back the flap of his jacket just enough so that the other could see the pistol in his belt. "Come along," he said coldly. "We'll decide what to do with you later."

The other's lips went white. Obviously, courage wasn't a forte of Tony Black's. "Come along where?" he got out, tremor in his voice.

"Just come along, and you'll see, won't you?" Bruce said with pseudo-pleasantness.

The black marketeer's eyes darted up and down the street, but he seemed to find nothing reassuring. What was he hoping for, a Security officer?

Rick took him by the arm. "Let's go," he said to Everett.

The window washer resumed his status as guide and within minutes they had reached a larger and taller building than was usual in Lagrange City, other than public ones. It was five stories in height and covered an area greater than most of its neighboring structures.

Cris explained, even as they went through the common entry. "Some of the contract workers teamed together and got their land allotment in one piece. Each floor is a separate flat. And each flat has four people, usually all men, but sometimes a man and wife, or a man and a mopsy shacked up. Sometimes a couple of guys and a girl. There's not enough women up here to go around. Not by a damned sight."

The flat they were heading for was on the second floor. They trooped up the stairs and Cris did a fancy knock at the door, obviously a planned signal.

Adam Bloch himself answered and was surprised by seeing five persons, rather than two. He took in Rick suspiciously and stared at Tony Black.

Cris said quickly, "Let us in. We'll tell you all about it."

Almost reluctantly, the older man stepped back and the newcomers filed into the living room. Rick noted that it was at least double the size of that in the house he'd been invited to share with Black. Larger, but just as barren of color and comfort. As usual, the furniture was all metallic and unpainted. There were no rugs or carpeting on the floor, no art on the walls or elsewhere.

Bruce, Pete, and Rick all looked about warily.

Adam Bloch said, "There's no one else here. They're all at work this time of day. Now, what's this all about?"

Pete Kapitz pointed to the corner of the room farthest from either door to the hall or the large windows that extended from floor to ceiling in lieu of one wall. He said to Tony Black, "You sit down over there and don't bother to make a move or utter a peep."

"What're you going to do 'with me?" the frightened man said.

"That's one of the things you never know," the IABI man told him. "Now shut up."

Adam Bloch said, in resignation, "I suppose that we should all sit down." He looked at Cris. "I've just heard bad news."

"That's the only kind of news there is lately," the window washer told him, taking a seat as had the others.

The teacher said, his voice low, "There was an accident in the space tug taking Helene, Fred, and Manuel to the Luna base. According to the news reports, three of the passengers were killed. It didn't report the names of the three."

"It didn't have to," Cris muttered.

"This is really piling up," Bruce said. "There's no doubt about it now. Like Pete said, "The bets are all down. We've got to have a showdown with Moore and the others."

"Wait a minute," Pete said. He indicated Tony Black with a tilt of his head. "How about lover boy, here? Do we want him sitting in on the conference?"

Bruce looked at the black-market man doubtfully. "What can we do with him? We can't let him loose, that's for sure. He'd blab to the first Security man he could reach."

"Knock him over the head," Rick said cheerfully. "We can't afford the manpower to guard him and the way these buildings are constructed without locks and keys, there's no way to confine him."

Their prisoner's eyes bulged and his face went gray. Tony Black was far from a hero.

He got out, "Look ... look ... you don't have to worry about me."

330

"We're not worrying about you, Tony," Rick said cheerfully. "We're just wondering whether or not to knock you over the head. And it occurs to me that now's as good a time as any for you to do some talking. You just might know something of interest."

"What's going on here?" Adam Bloch said. He looked at Rick. "Who're you? And what's this sneak doing here? It's almost certain that he's connected with Security."

"We can get to me a little later," Rick said. "What's that about you doing chores for Al Moore, Tony?"

"Yeah, sure, sure, I'll talk," Black babbled. "You don't have to worry about me. Sure, I work for Moroni. He's got men infiltrated everywhere. Knows everything's going on."

"Who's this Moroni?" Bruce Carter said.

"Alfredo Moroni. Al Moore. He's top man in the island for the Corporation, the Syndicate. They run everything from down below. But here at Lagrange Five, he's the capo."

"I'll be damned," Pete Kapitz said. "Some things are beginning to clear up. What's Mark Donald's real name?"

"Marco Donnello. His old man's Alphonse Donnello. You're a cop. You've heard of him."

"The New Orleans family, eh? I thought he was long dead and the family dissolved."

Bruce said suddenly, "Look, what's Dr. Ryan's real name?"

"I don't know, but that mopsy secretary of his, Doc Casey, is a Costello."

Bruce muttered bitterly. "Black Irish! Shit!"

Pete Kapitz said to the frightened Security informer, "What kind of weapons does Al Moore, uh, Moroni, have at his disposal?"

"Oh, you know how it is. Just about everything. Rifles, riot guns, tommy guns, grenades, smoke bombs, gas bombs." The other was cooperating wholeheartedly.

Adam Bloch gaped at him. "But why?" he said, bewildered. "What would he need with such equipment in a place like Island One? What's going on here?"

Bruce said, looking at Pete and Rick, "Suppose I tell it."

They both nodded, and for the next ten minutes, the freelancer brought Adam Bloch up to date. At the end of that period, the teacher was aghast.

"I had no idea," he got out.

"Neither did we," Pete said in disgust.

Bruce got in plaintively, "The thing is, I still can't figure out why. I've been all steamed up about space colonization for years. It's in the cards. What in the hell's gone wrong? Why isn't it working?"

The teacher said, his forehead wrinkled, "I'm beginning to suspect deliberate sabotage. Though, actually, even that isn't necessary to have brought us to our present position; the whole damn project has been handled as though by amateurs. It's unworkable as now presented. Each month that goes by, Ron Rich . . ."

"Richetti," Tony Black offered hopefully.

". . . reports to Earth new successes, but the fact of the matter is, it's unlikely that the L5 Project will ever get further along than it is now. In fact, unless new floods of funds continue to be raised on Earth, I suspect it will begin to regress."

"But why?" Bruce said, exasperated.

The older man sighed and said, "I've been trying to get it over to you, the last two times we met. The original theory was that 98 percent of the raw materials needed to build Island One, and the larger islands to follow, would come from the moon. Even that isn't realistic. The moon lacks some of the raw materials needed for such a project. It's not just a matter of aluminum, titanium, iron, and the few others, including copper, lead, zinc, not to speak of carbon, hydrogen, and nitrogen. But aside from the raw materials, practically everything has to be brought up from Earth. Ryan, in his book, seemed to think that we would manufacture our needs up here. But have you ever considered the needs of modern man? Do you realize that in every man's home there are literally thousands of products of modern manufacture?"

"Thousands?" Rick said, doubt in his voice.

Adam turned his eyes to him. "Yes. Consider just a few. Toothpicks, toothbrushes, toothpaste, salt-and-pepper shakers, salt, pepper, toilet paper—did you think we were going to recycle our toilet paper?—Kleenex, medical supplies—from aspirin on up—flashlights, spare flashlight bulbs, batteries, ball-bearing pens, pencils, erasers, electric razors, shoes, hairpins, eye glasses, contact lenses. . . ."

"Oh, no, come on," Bruce protested. "There's no reason why some, probably most of those, can't be made up here."

"Sure," Adam nodded. "For instance, any competent mechanic, given a sliver of steel, could hand-make a sewing needle. But when you consider manufacturing sewing needles for ten thousand people in all their different sizes, including sewing machine needles, knitting needles, darning needles, and what not, it makes more sense to bring them up. Do you realize what would be involved in tooling up to make needles here in Island One?"

"But that's just the beginning of what we have to bring up from Earth. The light bulbs. Not heavy, but bulky, so they use up one helluva lot of room in transport. Consider the number of different sizes of light bulbs and different types. They run from different-sized flashlights to the bulbs in refrigerators, to those for illumination about your home, to larger ones in industry or streetlights, to searchlights to . . . oh, hell, just consider the variety of light bulbs. Do you want to tool up for all of these out here in space for only ten thousand people?"

He cut it off in disgust. "What you've got to remember is that modern manufacturing is mass production. Nothing else makes sense. Suppose, for instance, that we decided to build our own computer printers here in space. The thousand or so that we need. Down Earthside, it might cost twenty-five dollars to manufacture one. But. . . ."

"Hey, wait a minute," Bruce said. "I've bought a few in my time, but never for twenty-five dollars."

"I didn't say that was what they retailed for. I said it cost that to manufacture them. And when they come off the computerized, automated assembly lines, by the hundreds of thousands, I doubt if the cost is much more than that. Between production and consumer are one hell of a lot of distributors, retailers, salesmen, advertising people, and government taxes to take a rake-off. At any rate, suppose we built them ourselves out here. I doubt if a team of competent mechanics and technicians, working by hand and making each piece required, could put together a reliable printer for less than a hundred thousand dollars. Consider for a moment, just how many individual parts would be involved, each one that they'd have to tool. Oh, the hell with it. I won't go into it any further. Suffice it to say that mass production of modern, manufactured needs doesn't make sense. Ergo, practically everything comes up from Earth. Not only our food and clothing, our air and water, largely, but everything for all practical purposes that we use."

"Well, what are you building up to?" Rick said, scowling at the teacher.

Bloch threw up his hands in a gesture of disgust. "It's a vicious circle. To ever finish this island, to get the mass driver working and the catcher in space catching the raw materials it shoots up, to get the closed ecosystem going, to get the space smelter operating—if any of these things are ultimately possible—we need more highly trained workers. But if we bring them up, we then have to supply them. Which means that more and more of our transports have to be utilized for that purpose instead of bringing up the materials we need to continue the work. They've gotten as far as they have so far only by spending countless tens of billions. How much longer the suckers Earthside are going to pony up such amounts is debatable."

Pete said, "Whether or not it'll ever be possible to complete the L5 Project, the fact remains that the immediate thing is to bust Al Moore and his gang."

"That'll be a neat trick," Rick muttered.

Pete sent his eyes over to him. "Not as tough as all that. For one thing, we've got the element of surprise. Obviously, if Moroni was surrounded with his whole two hundred Security men, all armed, we wouldn't have a chance. But he's not. We've got two guns. They'll have to do. We'll get together our force and, in a surprise raid, capture the broadcasting station and hold it long enough to get our message over to both the L5 workers and to Earth. By the time our Syndicate friends can get organized to overwhelm us, it'll be too late."

Rick said, "Not too late for Al to finish us off, though."

The IABI man shook his head. "If we get our message out, he wouldn't dare."

Adam Bloch said, "What force were you talking about?"

Pete turned to him. "You'll have to supply it. Say about twenty men. Not only should they be good, strong physical specimens, not afraid of a fight if it comes to that, but they should be in electronics. We can't be sure that the technicians at the broadcasting station will come over to us when we break in, although some of them might. We'll have to operate it ourselves."

"Twenty men," Bloch said, looking at Cris Everett.

Cris said thoughtfully, "That shouldn't be too difficult. We don't dare use our pocket communicators. Transceivers might be tapped. But I can go out and contact a couple personally and have each of them go out and contact two more apiece and those four will go find others. We can all rendezvous back here."

Pete said, "Right. And have them arm themselves as best they can. Pieces of steel bars, baseball bats, or whatever, just so they're small enough to hide in their coveralls until we break into the hotel."

Bruce Carter said, "Well, if that's the plan, you'd better get to it, Cris, before somebody smells trouble."

Everybody nodded acceptance and the window washer left in a hurry.

Rick looked over at Tony Black. "We still have the problem of dream boy," he said.

But Pete Kapitz was negative. "No. He's no problem. I brought these up from Earthside." He brought forth a pair of handcuffs. "They were supposed to be part of my cover. To be used when I'd caught the elusive Rocks Weil."

"That's going to be a question we'll have to solve later," Rick said wryly. "Even if this unlikely romp is a success."

Pete said nothing to that. He looked over at Bloch. "Is there a strong pipe or something in the house that I can cuff him to? These shackles come from our Department of Dirty Tricks. They're tuned to me so that nobody else can open them without a laser or some such."

Before the teacher could reply, the door crashed inward. In it stood Sergeant Evola, a small submachine gun in his hands. He brought down the heavy boot with which he had forced entrance and for a moment stood there, legs spread, alert for reaction. Behind him crowded more Security men. His gun was centered on Pete Kapitz, but he took them all in one at a time and seemingly found no immediate cause for calling upon his firepower, or the support of his men.

He said dourly, "You cloddies are like in a revolving door. It's getting monotonous rounding you up. Don't any of you ever get smart?"

He swept the gun around the room, as though inviting response. There was none. For a moment, he eyed Tony Black and Rick, as though surprised at their presence. Then he shook his head, as though it didn't make any difference. He walked a few steps into the room and swung the gun again. Four of his men entered behind him, all Gyrojet armed. They were typical heavies, burly of build, expressionless. There were still more of them out in the hall.

"Jesus, Joe," Tony Black blurted, hustling to his feet. "You came just in time."

"Shut your mouth, stupid," Evola growled. "It took us two years to build your cover and now you do your best to bust it."

Tony said hurriedly, "Listen, Joe, that Cris Everett just left. He's going to round up about twenty of the WITH-AW-DOH Club funkers. The idea was to raid the hotel and take over the radio. . . ."

"We've already got him," Evola said. "Shake them down." This last was to his security men.

As they were being frisked, Pete Kapitz said in disgust, "How in the hell did you find us?"

"Don't be stupid, Fuzzy," Evola told him. "We've been tailing you, one way or the other, ever since you got out of the passenger freighter. Hell, since before that. That's why I was sent down Earthside. Just to ride up with you." He looked at Bruce Carter stolidly. "And you. You're a laugh. That Russian scientist pal of yours knew his office was bugged, but he didn't know there was a lens up in the ceiling. It could pick up everything you both wrote on that notepad."

Bruce sighed, but kept his peace. What was there to say?

The security men who frisked them came up with the pistols Pete and Rick had carried.

"These two were heeled, Joe," one said, seeming surprised.

"I know," his superior told him. "Turn the guns in to the armory."

Tony Black said ingratiatingly. "You want me to give you the whole story, Joe? I been listening to them for...."

"No, stupid. Take off. What Al doesn't already know about the whole story, he'll find out. Report to Donnello tomorrow. He'll probably be too busy to see you the rest of the day."

The black marketeer hurried out, glowering at Rick, in particular, as he went.

Joe Evola looked his prisoners over. "We might as well get going," he said. "The boss is waiting. He's real fed up with you types."

"The capo, don't you mean?" Bruce muttered.

"Button it up," the other told him. "Let's get going." He handed his submachine gun over to one of his men, who folded the collapsible stock and tucked it into his overalls so that it was inconspicuous.

They filed out into the street, the security men holstering their weapons before they emerged from the building. A disgusted Cris Everett was there in the custody of two more of the goons. He was added to their number.

Bruce wondered fleetingly what would happen if he made a sudden dash for it. But dash to where? Even Adam Bloch, who probably knew the island as well as anybody, hadn't been able to hide out successfully. Even had the freelancer known someone to appeal to, it wouldn't take much time for him to be found. A simple house-to-house search would take care of it. And from what little he had seen of the landscaping of the interior of Island One, there'd be precious little in the way of places to hide in the supposed countryside. No, there was nothing for it.

They roused only passing interest among the other pedestrians and cyclists as they returned to the hotel. Evidently, Joe Evola and the rest of the security men held little respect for their prisoners' abilities to cope with the situation. Several of the raid party dropped away and there remained only four, including the sergeant, to escort them to their confrontation with Al Moore.

They entered the L5 Hilton by the same door they had the last time Bruce, Adam Bloch, and Cris Everett had been apprehended, and retraced the route up to the offices of the Security Commissioner. There was no one in the reception room and Joe Evola impatiently ushered his captives toward the inner office.

"Stay out here," he clipped to his remaining three men.

The door to Moore's opulent sanctum opened before them and they marched through. Bruce Carter wasn't particularly surprised to be confronted by not only the Security Commissioner and his ever-present aide, Mark Donald, but Ron Rich as well. For once, the public relations head had no air of hail-fellow-well-met. But, for that matter, the other two didn't look particularly hospitable either. In fact, Moore's expression bore ample indication of inner rage.

Bruce Carter summoned his coldest front. "You've torn it now, Moore," he said flatly. "Or should I say, Moroni?"

The Security Commissioner glowered at him.

"Balls," Joe Evola grunted. He'd closed the door behind him and now leaned against it.

"Quiet," Moore snarled at him. He turned his glare

back to the freelancer. "You're the one who's torn it, you stupid funker. Sol was out of his mind, inviting you up here at this stage of the game. A year or two ago, yeah. But not at this crucial point." His infuriated eyes went to Pete Kapitz. "And the same damned thing applies to you. Wilson was drivel-happy sending you here."

Pete said, "He couldn't stop it. I was sent by Roy Thomas, working with the okay of the President. You've had it, Moore. I've found out exactly what Thomas was looking for. And don't think I'm ignorant of the fact that John Wilson was in with you. He's the only one that could have broken my cover. You Syndicate people have infiltrated to some pretty high levels, these days. But this'll be the end of Wilson."

"You're digging your own grave by the minute, Fuzzy," Mark Donald murmured.

Moore said, "Sit down, for Christ's sake. I don't want to have to look up at you. You think this operation is such small apples we have to put up with bullshit from half-assed dizzards like you two?"

Adam Bloch, Cris Everett, and Bruce Carter took places on a comfortable couch facing the desk. Pete Kapitz lowered himself into an easy chair and Rick Venner, looking more possessed than the others, took a straight chair. Across from them were Moore, behind his desk, and Ron Rich and Mark Donald flanking it.

Adam Bloch said evenly, "You've gone too far, Mr. Moore. Sufficient evidence has been accumulated to prove that the space colonization plan has been deliberately sabotaged by the present administrators appointed by the Lagrange Five Corporation."

The Commissioner turned his eyes to that source. "To the contrary, *Mister* Bloch. Everything is going on schedule. You see, it depends on which plan you're talking about."

"... many years ago I stated that in the long run *there will be more people living off the Earth than ever lived on it*. But that is looking a century or so ahead, and I don't believe that we should concern ourselves with vast space cities this side of 2001. The technical problems are so enormous—there are so many possibilities for disaster owing to some trivial oversight or violation of ecological principles—that we must prove we can make cities work down here before we design Astropolis ... What we should *start thinking about now are space villages, not space cities*. We will need them in the quite near future for the industries and services that will undoubtedly be established in Earth orbit."

—Arthur C. Clarke

Chapter Eighteen

"Hey, take it easy, Al," Ron Rich muttered less than happily.

Mark Donald looked over at the flack. "Why?" he said. "What difference does it make?"

The publicity man's eyes were uneasy, but he said in surrender, "Yeah, I suppose so." He fumbled for cigarettes, giving the impression of having washed his hands of it all.

Al Moore was obviously in a high fury, not far this side of control. It came to Bruce Carter that there had been recent developments beyond any that involved himself and his associates present. On the face of it, matters were coming to a head. It became increasingly obvious that Al Moore held a higher position in the affairs of the Lagrange Five Project than was ordinarily realized; and that he was in a state of upset.

Bruce said carefully, "Then there's more than one plan involving Island One? More than the basic plan revealed to the man in the street, Earthside?"

Al Moore snorted disgust. "I'd think that by this time even a half-baked professional snoop would have figured that out. Get me a drink, goddammit, Ron."

The publicity man sighed, got up from his chair, and went over to the bar. He obviously knew the Commissioner's preferences and took up a highball glass and a square bottle with a black label. "Ice?" he said.

"No."

Rich brought the bottle of bourbon and the glass to the desk, poured a sizable slug, and began to return to the bar.

"Leave it," Moore said tightly, knocking back half of the whiskey.

The flack shrugged and left the bottle, looked at Mark Donald and raised his eyebrows. The security lieutenant shook his head. He seemingly wasn't much happier about all this than was the publicity man, but he didn't want a drink.

Al Moore eyed Bruce in contempt and said sarcastically, "Yeah, there's more than one plan. There's almost always more than one plan when it comes to an operation as big as this, muckraker." He leaned back in his chair and breathed deeply for a few moments, but failed to regain much of his disrupted control. He said, "Let me give you a few lessons in economics. You won't ever be able to profit by them, but a snoop undoubtedly remains a snoop right up until the last and it'll be good for your curiosity. Remember the cat in the rhyme who was curious right up to the end?"

The eyes of the prisoners were on him, registering variously, but none of them said anything. Bruce remembered the old saying, right enough. *Curiosity killed the cat.* And then the corollary, which Moore hadn't mentioned. *Satisfaction brought it back.* However, Bruce Carter had few illusions. He doubted his future, no matter the extent to which his curiosity was satisfied.

Moore had another pull at his drink, took another breath, and said, "Yeah, it's the biggest operation of all time. And let me tell you something, Carter, and you, Bloch, and the rest of you. In these big operations, somebody always makes it rich." He snorted a wry laugh. "Did you think that the contractors involved in building those Egyptian piles of rocks didn't rake off plenty? Or take something bigger, much bigger: those Crusades back in the Middle Ages. Besides the ordinary slobs who were conned into them, Europe was bled white of both aristocrats and their wealth over a period of a couple of centuries or so. And when the dust settled, guess who wound up with the gravy? Mostly it went to those Italian free cities like Venice and Genoa that supplied the ships and supplies to the suckers. It was the beginning of the end of feudalism, by the way. Those so-called free cities represented creeping capitalism getting its foot in the door. But even the Crusades were peanuts compared to some of the real operations to come. Take the big wars—the Napoleonic wars, World Wars One and Two, among others. The organizations that got those under way didn't exactly starve to death during and afterwards. Do you think General Motors, IBM, Dupont, the oil corporations, and the rest went broke as a result of the Second World War?"

Bloch said dryly, "The outfits on the other side didn't do so well."

Moore poured some more spirits and sneered at him. "Bullshit. Were you laboring under the illusion that Krupp and Thyssen and such outfits as Bayer were bankrupt as a result of Hitler? Sure, they had some factories and mills leveled, but it wasn't a drop in the bucket to all the billions they'd sifted out to Switzerland, Sweden, Argentina, and the other neutrals. Ten years after the war was over they were as powerful as they'd ever been. Same thing applied to Japan. The big operators didn't suffer. A few of the big names that had hit the news were brought to trial and sent over for war crimes, such as using slave labor, but not a single one of them served their time. They were all, including Krupp, possibly Hitler's biggest backer, released and their property restored."

"All right, all right," Bruce said. "You've made your point, I suppose. What in the devil has it got to do with the Lagrange Five Project?"

Moore laughed cynically. "Like I said, Carter. It's the biggest operation of all time and like all the rest, somebody winds up with the gravy." His voice took on a still nastier tone. "Can you imagine controlling several hundred billion dollars, francs, marks, pesos, and every other fucking exchange in the world? Suppose you were only able to rip off three percent? It'd make General Motors, Krupp, Mitsubishi, and all the rest look like a bunch of pikers, wouldn't it? Not that the limit was three percent. And all legal, by the way, or damned near, and when you get to legality, that's near enough."

Pete Kapitz pretended to yawn and said, "You haven't told us anything yet, Moore. We're up on the fact that the Syndicate was throwing a lot of weight in the Lagrange Five Corporation, probably the controlling interest. It's obvious they've been milking it in the way they've distributed contracts. But it looks as though the boom is lowering. Roy Thomas is onto you and he's big enough to do the job."

"Thomas is dead," Moore said flatly.

Pete stared at the security head. It never occurred to him to doubt the other. It made sense and fitted in with John Wilson ordering him back to Earth. Wilson had said something about Thomas no longer being with them, but Pete had thought he had simply meant that the President's aide was out of favor with the White House. Without doubt, the Director of the IABI had brought

President Corcoran around to his way of thinking, as well. Pete Kapitz had no illusions about the present President of the United States.

Adam Bloch seemed never to have heard of Roy Thomas. He said now, "But it's over, Mr. Moore. Whether you were able to, ah, rip off, as you put it, three percent or more of the multi-billions that have gone through the hands of the Lagrange Five Corporation, it's over now. And when the full stink of it all hits, you people will have to answer. Frankly, I'd hate to be in your shoes."

Moore's smile was inverted and mean. "Don't be too happy about that aspect, *Mister* Bloch. We've been working on this operation for a long time. Whose names do you think head the original sponsors of the LFC? The biggest scientists, the outstanding statesmen, the most noted humanitarians, the ranking religious leaders, the bleeding hearts of every non-communist nation in the world, that's who. They all bought the space colonization dream. Who the hell do you think sits on the Board of Directors? People like me? Shit we do. Not even old chucklehead Sol Ryan has any official position. Our work is done behind the scenes."

Pete Kapitz put in softly, "You people never did figure it would work, did you, Moore? Since Sol Ryan and his dreamers first came up with the idea there in New Kingston."

"Isn't that a little obvious?" Ron Rich murmured grudgingly. In disgust, went over to the bar and poured himself a drink, seeming not to care from what bottle it came.

Al Moore pretended surprise. "What do you mean, it didn't work? Of course it worked. It *is* working. All according to the real plan I've been telling you about. All we need is about six more months, then we go into Part Two."

"And pick up your marbles and disappear while the L5 Project disintegrates, eh?" Bruce Carter said emptily.

Moore looked at him in continued, pretended surprise. "Why, what a thing to say, my muckraking friend. You don't think we'd allow all this just to go to rust, do you?"

"Take it easy, Al," Ron Rich muttered again.

"Oh, be quiet," Mark Donald growled at him. He repeated from earlier, "What difference does it make?" He looked at his chief. "But let's wind it up, Al. We've got things to do."

"What's your hurry, Mark?" Moore said, a slight slur in his voice. "These gentlemen have been prying around ever since they got here. Hell, *Mister* Bloch has been at it for over a year. Give 'em a break."

"You don't make much sense, Moore," Bruce told him. "Obviously Island One, and everything else that's been put together out here in space, isn't going to rust. Not in a vacuum. But the moment the L5 Corporation collapses, it all becomes some of the most worthless junk ever known. As somebody pointed out the other day, it'd cost more to haul it back to Earth than the scrap would bring."

The Security Commissioner was still in his insulting, expansive mood. He poured more from the square bottle, without taking his eyes from the freelancer. "Who's talking about scrap?" he said reasonably. "In six months, we'll have several more luxury hotels up here, and most of the landscaping will be in a reasonable condition. *Then* let the whole thing bust."

His listeners were staring at him as though he was considerably drunker than he had as yet managed.

The office door burst open, almost sending Joe Evola, who'd been lounging against it, sprawling. His Gyrojet was half from his coveralls, his body half into a gunman's crouch, when Sol Ryan came storming through. Annette Casey, considerably more possessed, followed after.

The Father of the Lagrange Five Project stood there,

momentarily speechless in consuming anger, breathing deeply, his eyes glaring at the Security Commissioner behind the desk. It evidently was a morning for men in a rage.

Annette ran her eyes over the assemblage. "Hi, comrades," she said. She took in Bruce Carter, her mouth askew. "My breakfast date," she murmured.

"My Black Irish colleen," he returned.

Still breathing deeply, Sol Ryan said, "I've just had an interview with Academician Suvorov and Rudi Koplin." There was ultimate indignation in his voice. He seemed to notice no one present save Al Moore, at whom he was glowering.

The head of security of Lagrange Five, looking dangerous, took a pull at his glass. "Yeah, I know," he said flatly. "You should have kept your charming nose where it belongs, Sol. You should have minded your own business."

"What *is* my business?"

"Cooling off the Winchells, Sol. And that's all your business. That should have been clear to you from the first."

Sol Ryan, absent his charisma, strode in fury to the other's desk and pounded the flat of his right palm on it. "Damn you, Moore," he shrilled. "I'm not a child. I knew the families would take their cut from the contracts, as a result of their investments. It didn't seem overly important. If they didn't, the older, established aerospace corporations would have. It's all part of contracting, or so I told myself. And the families are in legitimate enterprise now. But this! The whole project, the whole dream, has been subverted, betrayed!"

The other said disgustedly, "You never knew what the whole dream was, Sol. You got to believing your own bullshit."

The glare intensified. "I'll expose the whole, perverted story!"

Moore shook his head. "Forget about it, Sol. Don't worry. You'll be taken care of. But meanwhile. . . ." He looked at Joe Evola, who had recovered from the cavalier manner in which the indignant figurehead of the L5 Project had sent him staggering. The gun had disappeared back into his clothing. "Joe," Moore said, "have one of the boys take Doctor Ryan back to his living quarters. Have two or three men put in with him. Sol is, from now on, incommunicado. He's devoting himself to some special research or something. Ron can figure the press releases out. Nobody sees him without my okay. Nobody but me. Got it?"

"Sure, Al," Joe said, advancing toward the shocked scientist. "Come on, Sol." He took the other by the arm.

Ryan flung him off. "Are you mad?" he demanded of Moore, his breath coming so hard he was panting.

Bruce Carter said ironically, "Nice to see you, Dr. Ryan. It brings to mind something you told me the first time we met. Which in turn brings to mind a short verse I remember from school days. It involves three unanswerable questions. The title was, *Quis custodiet ipsos custodes?*"

Ryan, looking as though he was in half-shock, stared at him. "That's from the Roman poet Juvenal," he got out, as though not quite able to comprehend what was going on, certainly not this meaningless diversion. "It means, *Who's to Watch Over the Watchers?*"

"That's right," Carter said, his voice still ironic. "You told me that you of New Kingston University were watching over the L5 Project, whips in hand, to prevent hanky-panky. The verse goes.

"Who's to watch over the watchers,
Those who would carry the lashes?
What was the tune that Joshua played?
Who hauls the janitor's ashes?"

349

Annette chuckled softly, "Comrade, comrade," she murmured. "Touché." She sank into a chair on the other side of Rick Venner.

Bruce said musingly, now looking at Moore, "So far as the second question is concerned, it's hard to say just who is going to be given the credit for wearing Joshua's robes and calling the tune that crumbles the walls of the L5 Corporation. But crumble they will. This particular Jericho is past due for a fall."

Al Moore ignored him and said to Joe Evola, "Get Sol out of here; he looks sick."

Indeed he did. The eyes of Sol Ryan were not a well man's now. He had seemed to collapse inwardly. He said, in a queer, detached voice, "Yes, yes. I've got to think about this. Have got to. . . ." His sentence dribbled away, as though he wasn't quite sure what it was he had to do.

Joe took him firmly by the arm and led him through the door into the outer office. In moments, the sergeant had returned and assumed his former stance. He'd obviously turned the task over to a subordinate.

Al Moore had his eyes fixed on the relaxed Annette Casey, as though not quite sure what to make of her.

She said easily, "Drinking this early in the day? How about one for me, Ron?" She brought her easygoing attention to Al Moore. "Somebody's got to keep up the front, Uncle Al. Run interference between Sol and the hundred and one jokers who are always trying to get to him."

He still scrutinized her.

She sighed and said, "You should've let me further into this sooner. Ryan was obviously a puppet, behind that boyish enthusiasm, charming everybody and his cousin. But there has to be somebody pulling the strings. And whoever's doing it ought to know what's going on on the stage."

"Bitch," Pete Kapitz muttered.

Al Moore nodded finally. "Wizard," he said. "You continue on the job. You're still Doctor Solomon Ryan's secretary."

Ron Rich brought her a tall glass. "Scotch and water?" he said.

"Thanks, Ron." She took it and settled back into her chair, her eyes going from one to the other of the room's occupants. "What in the hell's going on?" she said.

Al Moore, thrown off by the scene with Ryan, scowled and took another pull at his own drink. His eyes, now alcohol-dull, narrowed and he brought himself back to his earlier nasty frame of mind. He said, "Our chumpals here were trying to throw some monkey wrenches in the works. I was putting them straight on a few things."

"Such as the real plan behind the space colonization plan," Bruce Carter said. In actuality, he was surprised at his own coolness. He had few illusions about his chances in the immediate future. But somehow he was finding himself able to continue his role as freelance writer as though expecting nothing untoward was going to happen, or could happen.

Moore surveyed him contemptuously. "Yeah, and you might as well sit in on this, *tesora mio*," he said to Annette. "Some of it's probably new to you, as well. I was about to point out to Carter and friends that there's as much to be made in the collapse of an empire as there is in the building."

"I think that Rhett Butler made the point in *Gone With the Wind*," Adam Bloch said. "But he was talking about the American South and the carpetbaggers who savaged it. What are *you* talking about, Mr. Moore?"

Al Moore's grin was slack now as he said, glass in hand, "I'm talking about sin cities. You know what a sin city is, *Mister* Bloch? Or a sin country, for that matter?"

Bruce said, "Panama City, Tangier, Macao, Hong Kong,

351

Singapore, Istanbul, Port Said. When the old freelancer travel writers couldn't come up with anything else to write about for the men's magazines, they'd dream up a sin city. In a sin city, anything goes. Wide-open gambling, prostitution, narcotics, pornographic shows, black market, smuggling, homosexuality, every sin you can afford. Mostly, it was a lot of crud. I suppose that Tangier was the nearest thing to a real sin city that ever came along, shortly after the Second World War."

"Give the snoop a prize," Moore chuckled. He let his eyes go from Bloch to Carter to Kapitz. "But that's the final plan. Island One becomes the biggest sin city of all time. It'll make Babylon look like Boys Town."

Even Rick Venner, who to this point had kept his quiet peace, stared at him now.

"Use your heads," Moore said contemptuously. "It's a natural. After we've spent a few more billions of the sucker money the Corporation's been hauling in, the interior of Island One'll be all prettied up. More hotels, a lot of swank, private homes and condominiums, even some small resort towns. And then, say in about six months, we deliberately bust the bubble. We dump our holdings in the Lagrange Five Corporation and, at the same time, we leak some of the true facts about the Project, that it's come a cropper. Overnight, the whole thing falls apart; everybody probably blaming every-body else. Chaos. The L5 Corporation goes bankrupt. And with nobody to foreclose. Nobody wants the pieces. The whole project isn't working and it's not going to work. It's worthless."

All except Mark Donald, Ron Rich, and Joe Evola were staring in fascination at him.

"So from nowhere," he grinned sarcastically, "comes up another, newly organized corporation. They say they'll buy it lock, stock, and all the barrels. They plan to abandon the Luna base, the attempt to build SPSs, the manufacturing facilities, the ore smelters, and the rest of the dream that turned into a nightmare, and make Island One into a space resort. Everybody thinks they're crazy. So they pick up the whole thing for peanuts."

"That would be drivel-happy," Pete Kapitz snorted. "What in God's name would you do with a resort a quarter-million miles from the nearest tourist?"

Moore turned his nasty grin to the IABI man. "We'd turn it into the sin city to end all sin cities. Everything goes. Everything ever dreamed up before for far-out, freewheeling towns, and a lot more not conceived of previously. No place on Earth ever had it so good. Switzerland had some far-out banking, but nothing like Island One. Switzerland was surrounded by Germany, Italy, France; if she'd gone too far she was always faced with the possibility of invasion. Macao and Hong Kong were right in the laps of the Chinese and always threatened with takeover. Tangier belonged to Morocco, and when it looked as though it was too good a thing, financially, the Sultan stepped in and took over. Of course, he soon saw he'd killed the goose that laid the golden eggs and let the International Zone be revived, but it was never quite the same. Oh, believe me, Earthside sin cities had handicaps we won't have here in space."

Adam Bloch said in disgust, "Don't be ridiculous. If Island One has proved a failure under the Lagrange Five Corporation, with all the billions plowed into it, how can you possibly make it a financial success?"

The other said evenly, "Because we're going to dump all the things that fouled it up. No more moon base, no more ten thousand colonists and workers having to be fed, housed, and clothed. No more multi-billion-dollar freighters bringing up heavy machinery and raw materials. We'll keep on just enough workers to run Island One and we won't be working on a lot of expensive experiments. We'll just be maintaining this space colony as nicely as we can for those who can afford it, and fuck everything else. All the basic expense has already been met. The island is here. We have the space shuttles and passenger freighters necessary to bring up our paying customers and the supplies we'll need."

Adam Bloch said, "The problem of the closed ecosystem still hasn't been solved, Moore."

The other looked scornfully at him, taking another pull at the whiskey. "It won't have to be. Oh, we'll continue some hydroponics growing of fruits and vegetables, and breed chickens, turkeys, rabbits, and pigs, but largely we'll bring everything up from Earthside. It'll be expensive, but the expensive sins we have in mind will pay for it."

Bruce Carter said, shaking his head impatiently, "You're completely around the corner, Moore. Suppose that it did go through, the way you have in mind, and you got your hands on the whole project practically for free. Having some no-restriction banking, all-out gambling, sexual perversions, and narcotics aren't going to begin to pay your overhead."

Moore grinned. "There's a lot more to it than that, snooper. For instance, there'll be no extradition from Island One. No Earthside laws will apply. Anybody who wants to, uh, retire here and has the funds, has a perfectly safe refuge. South American politicians escaping with their country's treasury, or small-time crooks like Rocks, here, who've taken a big score." He nodded in the direction of Rick Venner.

"But that's just the beginning. We'll have a course, a stock market to end them all, where everything'll go. There'll be no taxes—income taxes, corporation taxes, *any* taxes. And there'll be other items. In this super-resort, we'll have a space hospital for those ultra-rich with heart troubles, or whatever, where low gravity, or even free fall, makes the difference between living and dying. And there won't be any medical restrictions. If you want to clone yourself, or transplant chimpanzee balls into your scrotum, great. And we'll probably lease out the Construction Shack for scientific research; any kind of research, just so they pay the bills. We'll milk it all ways from Tuesday and, most of all, the families—the Syndicate, as you call it—will have a perfectly safe base of operations for all our Earthside interests. They ran us out of Sicily in the old days, they lowered the boom on us in the States, Castro ran us out of Cuba, and when we settled some of our operations in the Bahamas, both the British and the States put pressure on us there. But not here in Island One. This'll be the ultimate refuge. We'll be under nobody's jurisdiction but our own."

Annette said admiringly, "It's a pretty picture, Uncle Al. What happens to the colonists and contract workers who have all those stock bonuses coming to them? Won't they put up a howl?"

"Indeed," Adam Bloch muttered.

Moore laughed. "Let 'em howl. We'll send all but the best of them back to Earth. That stock is LFC stock and, like I said, the LFC will be bankrupt."

Bruce Carter nodded his head. "It's a story worth writing up," he said.

Rick Venner laughed softly. "I'm afraid you'll never get around to it, chum-pal."

Al Moore looked at him as though fully realizing for the first time that the other was present. He scowled and said, "What the hell are you doing here?"

Joe Evola said, "We picked him up with Bloch and the others, Al. He and Kapitz were heeled."

Rick said mildly to the security head, "You gave me the shooter to carry out the contract on Kapitz."

The other was still scowling at him. "Sure, but what were you doing with Kapitz and Carter?"

Rick shrugged. "I met them on the way up from Earth. In view of the job you had set up, I thought it'd be a good idea to get them used to the idea of me being around."

"Why, you funker," Cris Everett snarled.

"Quiet," Joe Evola growled at him.

Rick said easily, "You mentioned that under ordinary circumstances you might be able to use a man like me, Al. Used to thinking on my feet, and so forth. Wizard. The way things seem to be trending, it looks as though you'll be able to." He twisted his mouth. "I'm available."

Pete Kapitz grunted contempt, but looked as though he wasn't overly surprised.

Moore took the jewel thief in thoughtfully. "You might be right at that."

Rick said reasonably, "Why don't we handle it more or less the way you originally had in mind? We'll take Kapitz and Carter out in front of the hotel. I'll let both of them have it. Great. You stage a dramatic arrest and I'm hauled off and supposedly thrown in the banger. The news is released to Earth. It makes a super headline story. The notorious Rocks Weil shoots a top IABI man *and* the famous writer, Bruce Carter, and the intrepid L5 security puts the arm on him. You want another six-month leeway to finish construction of the island here? Okay, that'll raise some of the dust needed to hide what's going on."

Moore thought about it. "Makes a lot of sense," he slurred. "Whaddaya think, Mark?"

All the others in the room were staring at Rick Venner, most of them in shocked horror. Bruce had his eyes closed, as though in resignation.

Moore's lieutenant said hesitantly, "I don't know. We could handle it ourselves, Al."

Joe Evola said, "I can do the job, Al. I never did like this Kapitz bastard."

Rick laughed and said, "Tell you what I'll do, Joe. I'll match you for it." He dug a hand into his trousers pocket.

"What the hell are you talking about?" the dour security sergeant said to him.

Rick came to his feet and brought forth a coin. "You call it, I'll flip it. Call it right and the job's yours. Otherwise, lend me your shooter."

Moore laughed tolerantly and poured another shot of whiskey. His eyes were dull.

Joe Evola grunted, "Heads!"

Rick flipped and let the coin fall to the floor. "Tails," he said and held out his hand.

Frowning unhappily, Joe Evola brought forth his stubby Gyrojet and grudgingly handed it over. Rick checked it automatically as he stepped back toward the center of the room. He deliberately flicked off the safety, brought the gun up to chest level, even as he turned, and fired point blank at Al Moore.

The rest all came in split seconds. Rick Venner had been correct when he said he was no killer. He was also less than an adequate marksman. Even at this distance, he missed his aim, whatever portion of the anatomy of the security head he was firing at. The rocket slug, making its characteristic whip-snap sound as it broke the sound barrier, a few feet from the muzzle, slammed into Moore's right shoulder, sending him spinning backward and out of his chair.

A less than adequate shot Rick Venner might have been, but he was cool. He fired again and this time full into the falling man's belly.

Mark Donald had not achieved his position as bodyguard by accident. He blurred into action. His left hand flicked back his jacket, his right drew his weapon with a speed that Wyatt Earp would have envied. Venner's need for a second round to finish his victim gave the Syndicate gunman the time to snap off his own shot unimpeded. And even as he fired, he was out of his chair and lurching toward his foe.

Rick collapsed, the gun flying away from his hand and out across the floor. Mark Donald, cursing wildly, stood above the fallen Venner and fired twice more at almost point-blank range into Rick's flailing body as Pete Kapitz and Joe Evola scrambled for the Gyrojet on the floor.

Adam Bloch, Cris Everett and Ron Rich, no men of action, sat rooted to their seats; nor did Bruce Carter do any better. Annette Casey, however, stuck out a fashionably shod foot and neatly tripped the oncoming Joe. He slammed forward, his face smashing into the floor.

Pete Kapitz, already lunging on all fours, swept up the gun, continued his momentum, and rolled. His fingers expertly fitted to the gun's grip and trigger guard. Mark Donald, still raging above the fallen, shattered Rick Venner, spun, his gun seeking the new target.

Cris Everett didn't look like a hero, but proved to be one. His small body was out of its seat as he flung his arms around the security man, the firearm between them. The gun blasted twice and agony took over the little man's face. But he hung on. Donald swore viciously and tried to wrestle out of the dying man's desperate grasp to get his weapon back into play.

Pete Kapitz shot him neatly in the head, the high velocity rocket slug tearing the top of it away.

Annette Casey was the first to find words. Her eyes went around the shambles. "Holy Mary," she said. "I'm afraid Venner and Everett have had it."

Bruce Carter, Ron Rich, and Adam Bloch still sat rooted to their places. Only seconds had transpired since Rick Venner had taken possession of the sergeant's gun and made his play. Joe Evola was sprawled unconscious on the unkind floor upon which he had shattered his jaw. Pete Kapitz stood shakily, his gun still held as though he was expecting new targets. And then he heard the pounding feet outside and spun in the direction of the door.

Two of the security police Evola had originally left in the reception room came charging in, guns half drawn, their faces incredulous. Pete nailed them both, expertly, without hesitation. Despite his appearance, in action Pete Kapitz proved he had been there before—and survived it. Still aiming his pistol at the doorway, Pete dropped to one knee and checked the unmoving Cris Everett. "Damn! Everett's dead. How about Venner?"

Annette, uncharacteristically shaken, knelt beside the body of Rick Venner. Hands crimson with Rick's blood, Annette shook her head. "Losing too much blood to live, I'm afraid. There's barely a pulse here." With a flash of anger: "But he might die under a medic's care if one of you big strong men can carry him."

Adam Bloch picked up the all-but-lifeless body and staggered toward the doorway. "Clinic's not far," he grunted, "unless I get stopped on the way." Annette and Pete traded headshakes, knowing that Bloch's bravery had probably come too late.

Then Annette stooped to retrieve two objects that had fallen from Rick Venner's left hand. She held them toward the others as evidence. "Two coins," she mused. "One with heads on both sides, the other with tails on both sides."

Bruce Carter sighed. "Once a scammer, always a scammer to the end. He palmed the one he didn't want to flip."

Ignoring her uncle's body, Annette opened a desk drawer and brought forth a twin to the Gyrojet which had finished the Security Commissioner. "Look, we must rescue Sol *now*, before this anthill of goons is stirred up! If we can get Sol to the broadcast center, he can crack this thing wide open; his voice means more than anybody's. If he winds up a casualty, we could have a civil war on our hands."

Bruce stooped to pick up Mark Donald's handgun. "I'm no Michener, but I'm with you."

Pete frowned. "What's a michener?"

"*The* Michener. A writer who walked into a no-man's-land to help refugees."

"I hope he didn't shoot himself in the foot as you're about to do," Annette said wryly.

Bruce raised the gun barrel and by chance aimed it toward the one person who was still motionless in a chair. Ron Rich saw the barrel sweep toward him and moaned.

Deadpan, Bruce snarled, "I've always wanted to shoot a PR flack. Anybody have a better idea?"

"No, no, nonono," Ron crooned in terror.

"Tear Evola's clothing into strips and tie Rich up," said Pete. "Don't worry, Rich, we aren't like your pals."

Moments later Kapitz, Annette, and Bruce Carter hurried out the door. An ashen-faced Ron Rich lay bound and gagged on the floor and considered the carnage he had helped create with his years of expert flummery.

"The Earth is the cradle of mankind, but one cannot live in the cradle forever."
—*Konstantin Tsiolkovsky*

Aftermath

The security goon who kept Sol Ryan isolated in his quarters found himself even more isolated when he opened the door for Annette and found himself staring into several gun barrels. He put up no resistance. Neither did the guard at the broadcast center. After all, it was Doctor Solomon Ryan himself who strode into the broadcast booth surrounded by armed assistants.

Ryan spared himself nothing in the broadcast. Distraught, he laid his mistakes on the line. The LFC had degenerated into the biggest racket ever conceived. Ryan could offer no answers to the problems that lay exposed, and he said so. He admitted abject failure, calling himself a cat's-paw and a deluded fool. He asked no mercy. He could, he said, only leave the project in the hands of more competent people.

Bruce Carter, who'd jotted notes to bring coherence to what he had to impart, spoke next. Bruce gave devastating and checkable proofs. He suggested an immediate meeting of heads of state in the Americas, Common

Europe, and the Reunited Nations to face this emergency. He suggested immediate, worldwide prosecution of the Syndicate families on charges ranging from mail fraud to murder. It was with a supreme effort that he finished the broadcast with a lie, but Pete Kapitz had insisted.

"We do not need immediate assistance because the Syndicate leaders here were casualties," he said. "But our own casualties included men we will sorely miss: Cris Everett; the jewel thief, Rocks Weil, who gave his life in our behalf; and finally, IABI agent Peter Kapitz, who is not expected to survive."

Sol Ryan then ended the broadcast by promising further bulletins. If neither he nor Carter were party to those bulletins, he said, the world should expect more foul play.

Later they sat in Ryan's office to review the situation and, if possible, to piece some of their mutual dream back together. It was into one of their dejected silences that Adam Bloch entered.

"Join the wake," said Bruce, with a wave toward the liquor.

"Not for Venner, I hope," said the teacher.

"And why not? He earned it," said Annette with heat.

"Because," said Bloch, pouring a drink with jauntiness, "it looks like he'll pull through." He answered several exclamations with, "One slug missed his heart by an inch. Another was deflected by a rib, and a third shattered both bones in his forearm. He won't be tossing coins for a while. It might've been better for him if he *had* died, once he goes Earthside again."

"Who says he has to?" Pete shot back. "You could hide him up here. Hell, you could hide *me*. It's been a long time since I saw much future in the policies of John Wilson," he added in an aside to Bruce Carter.

"That's why you wanted on the casualty list," Bruce nodded. "Gave you time to make your choice, eh?"

"Right. Speaking of choices, why did the Arab Union choose to keep ponying up five billion a year to the LFC?"

Annette said, tiredness in her voice, "It didn't go to the corporation, Pete. It went directly to Syndicate families, with no intermediaries."

Sol Ryan, seemingly aged a full ten years, stared at her in total dejection. "I had no idea. I suppose I should've guessed."

Adam Bloch found a chair—and a lecture topic. "It makes sense. It was to the Arab Union's advantage to see the whole world enthusiastically plowing much of its resources into solar power stations. They'd probably been tipped off by consultants at New Kingston that effective solar power was not in the cards—not immediately, anyhow. Meanwhile, petroleum is still the mainstay and nobody kicks because it's only "temporarily" expensive. No *wonder* the Arabs subsidized the LFC. To them, five billion is only a medium-sized kickback!"

Bruce nursed his drink and scowled. "I'm not sure that's valid."

"Sure it is," Bloch said. "Look: where are all the appropriations for Earth-based alternative power schemes? I'll give you a hundred dollars, Carter, if you can name one major country that's still seriously engaged in hydroelectrics, harnessing wind and tide, alcohol fuels, or any other major competitor to oil. The SPS funding has taken the lifeblood out of research in further developments of fission and fusion reactors, too. Everyone thought the SPSs would be beaming cheap power down soon. It was in the Arab Union's interest to perpetuate that myth while selling their oil."

To this, Bruce Carter could only shrug. He was spared further argument by the arrival of the two savants, Koplin and Suvorov. Within minutes, the hardened construction spacer, Freddy Davis, arrived as well. From his exchanges with Bloch, it was clear that Freddy Davis was an active member of the WITH-AW-DOH club. Surprisingly, Davis seemed willing to help continue with the island's work.

Davis was gleeful about Venner's luck and toasted him. But Bruce Carter had trouble understanding the thief. "I wonder what motivated Rick Venner. He's really Rocks Weil, of course. A lifelong criminal. His lining up with Moore made sense."

Pete shook his head. "No, it didn't. We weren't a very good bet, but we were the best he had. It wasn't enough that he's an old pro thief. He's not a member of the families. No matter how much he might have tried to ingratiate himself, sooner or later he would have become superfluous to them. Besides, from what little I've learned about Rocks Weil, over some years of trying to catch up with him, and the little I've seen of him since we came up here, he's a pro of the old school, sometimes known as a gentleman thief. He's not the sort to approve the deliberate killing of poor old Pavel Meer, nor anyone else for that matter. He's no gunman; he proved that when he only nicked Al Moore with his first shot. He had to follow it up with another, and that gave Mark Donald his chance. And I rather doubt that Rocks Weil is the type of criminal who would willingly milk the poor by selling them shares in a dream he knows is false. His code might involve stealing a ten-carat diamond from some multi-millionaire, but not a hundred dollars from some schoolkid who'd saved his lunch money for a year to participate in the colonization of space."

Annette said softly, "Well put, comrade."

Pete's eyes went to her. "Which brings you up, Sweetie. What was this *Uncle Al* stuff? I didn't exactly expect you to swing into action on the side of the angels."

"Moore was a distant relative. We're highly interrelated in the families. For instance, Sol is a second cousin."

She managed to dredge up a touch of self-deprecating humor. "Possibly I saw which side of my bread the butter was really on."

"That wasn't it," Bruce Carter said softly, without looking at her.

"Maybe not," she said, taking in the demolished Father of the Lagrange Five Project, Sol Ryan. "Possibly I started off with the dream myself and in my enthusiasm was willing to follow Sol to the ends of . . . space. And possibly it came to me, bit by bit, that he was being screwed flat." She snorted cynically. "It's one of the mistakes the families made when they started to expose their young to a different culture—to education, to selfless ideas. They came up, at least occasionally, with people like Sol Ryan."

"And Annette Casey," Bruce said softly.

"Thanks, comrade," she told him, and didn't go on with it.

It was then that the door banged open—it seemed a day for precipitate entry—and an indignant Mary Beth Houston barged in, eyes flashing, her fists going in a stereotype adolescent stance to her hips.

She glared at Sol Ryan, who couldn't bring himself to even register her arrival.

"Right from the first I began to suspect somebody was pulling my leg," she said with the indignation of the overly put-upon. "I knew I wasn't being shown the real Island One. And now . . . now, that broadcast. Why . . . it's all been a big joke."

"Yeah," Freddy Davis said, speaking for the first time since he had toasted Rick. "And very funny."

"Well," she flared. "It isn't a joke and I'm not going to stand for it."

In his time, Bruce Carter had often read of someone's eyes flashing. As a writer himself, he had refrained from using the term. He had never seen eyes flash. Now he reversed himself on the point. He was witnessing flashing eyes.

Leonard Suvorov said, his Slavic voice heavily skeptical, "What are you going to do about it, my dear?"

"I'm going to take it up with the Friends of Lagrange Five! There're millions of us and not only us, the Spacists, too. We're not going to let a lot of crooks stop space colonization! You'll see!"

"There are going to be a lot of people feeling that way," Adam Bloch said, shaking his head.

Bruce looked at the indignant secretary of the Friends of Lagrange Five thoughtfully, then turned his eyes to Annette Casey, bypassing Sol Ryan who didn't look as though he heard or cared what was going on.

The freelancer said, "What shape's the Project in, right now?"

Annette scowled at him. "You mean financially? About the same as it's always been, maybe a little worse. From the beginning, it's been a hand-to-mouth affair. It's always been a matter of issuing new blocks of stock, encouraging investment, getting donations, getting foundation awards. It was a matter of keeping the public enthusiastic, keeping them keyed up, keeping the dream alive. That's why Ron Rich had to continually escalate the publicity. Success always had to seem right around the corner. Everything was going fine. Now was the time to invest."

Mary Beth, who had finally sunk into a chair through sheer emotional exhaustion, snapped, "Don't we know it? Why, down Earthside, we're shown Tri-Di shows of beaches and lakes and boats having races and all. And orchards of trees all heavy with fruit and...." She temporarily ran out of indignant breath.

Bruce said, "That should have been a clue for me. Those ultra-pro publicity shots were taken in Saudi Arabia in a mock-up of what Island One was supposed to look like. I should have known then that the Arab Union was a partner in the scam." He turned his eyes to Rudi Koplin. "In what shape is the Project—given your viewpoint?"

The chubby scientist shrugged hugely. "Time, time. It is a matter of time. All this rush, rush, is impossible. Now we are destroyed. But if we had time . . . one by one, we solve the problems, eh?"

All present, save Sol Ryan, were now watching Bruce Carter, wondering what he was driving at.

He turned his attention to Freddy Davis, the veteran construction engineer. "If you were in control, what would you do?"

The old-timer snorted at the idea of him being in control, but said, "Most of the basic work's been done. At fantastic expense, of course, but it's done. A lot of things, such as the smelting facility and the mass driver on Luna, and the Catcher out in Luna orbit, aren't working yet, but the plant is largely finished. If it was up to me, I'd send back to Earth at least half of the jokers up here. All the so-called colonists who aren't actually needed on the job, most of the wives, all the old folks, all the kids. And everybody else who isn't *directly* involved in the building of Island One itself." He shot a look over at Adam Bloch. "Such as teachers."

"Go on," Bruce said, as Bloch's face reddened.

"I'd cut out all the classy horse shit," said Davis. "Things like this Vegas-type hotel. I'd stop the junkets of VIPs. I'd eliminate such parasites as security goons. I'd stop shipping up fancy grub, guzzle, and clothes for the big shots. Particularly, I'd immediately let everybody who wanted to, go back. If you've lost the dream, you're a lousy worker anyway."

Pete Kapitz said, "You'd shortly wind up with nobody up here at all."

The aging construction worker received that negatively.

"The hell we would; I'd stay, for instance. It's a challenge. I think we had more morale, more enthusiasm among the actual workers, including technicians and engineers, back when it was really tough, when we were working out of the Construction Shack, or out of bubble shelters on Luna. Just so you don't give us this Ron Rich bullshit that Island One is an almost-completed paradise. We'll eat dehydrated food if we have to, but just don't give us that crud about fruit dropping off the trees. And don't feed us any lies about twenty thousand dollars a year bonus. It didn't take most of us very long to figure out we weren't ever going to get that bonus. Give us a clear-cut contract and pay us off monthly; the whole amount. If we want to blow the whole thing on guzzle and other luxuries, wizard. We know luxuries are going to be expensive up here, but don't put us in a position like we've had where we watch you big-shots living like gods while we're brewing jungle juice."

"Wizard," Bruce said. "You think that by shipping about half of the present population back and clearing up some of the mess, you'd still have a valid, working personnel and could continue?"

Davis said sourly, "I'd think so. And at this stage in the game of trial-and-error experimentation, I'd think a couple thousand really dedicated workers would be all we needed."

They sat and thought for long moments, probably in as many different directions as there were persons present.

Bruce said finally, "Okay. Mary Beth seems to be of the opinion that L5 supporters Earthside can still be rallied around. Possibly she's right. Al Moore pointed out earlier that the Crusades were one of the biggest operations the world ever embarked upon. They took place over at least two centuries and, in spite of failure after failure, the believers kept coming back. It would seem that man has both resiliency and stubbornness. And Mr. Davis tells us that the basic work has already been done. Given a more realistic approach, the job could go on, at considerably less expense than before."

The freelancer turned his attention to Koplin, the Polish scientist. "And Professor Koplin thinks that given time, the problems confronting the Project could be solved."

Koplin grunted agreement.

Bruce now took in Leonard Suvorov. "However, the very basic brick wall still confronts us. Space colonization is simply not practical unless we can achieve a closed ecosystem. Space platforms, such as the *Goddard*, Earth-supplied and with up to a hundred personnel, yes, but not space cities. And, from what I understand, the science of ecology has not yet reached the point where a closed ecosystem is possible. We simply don't know enough about bionomics to create one. So the Lagrange Five Project might as well be allowed to go down the drain, without further blood, sweat, and tears, not to speak of wealth."

The Russian stirred and, as though almost regretfully, demurred. He said slowly, feeling his way along, "I have not said that obtaining a self-sustaining biosphere was impossible. However, along with my colleague, Rudi, I demand time. Given time, yes, such a system will eventually be achieved. It has been pointed out by various biologists that at the present we do not entirely understand the self-sustaining biosphere on Earth, not to speak of creating one in a space colony. However, possibly we do not need *complete* understanding to achieve one. Down through the ages, man has utilized elements in nature which he did not completely understand. The first telegraphs were in wide use before we had scratched the surface of our understanding of electricity."

He had all of their closest attention now, even that of

the benumbed Sol Ryan. He took a deep breath, ran his plump hand back through his thinning red hair, and said, "For instance, this morning I revived an interesting idea. Suppose that we brought up from Earth a few hundred tons of the best Earth soil, complete with its microorganisms, bugs and earthworms, and complete with its decayed vegetation. And suppose that we spread this out over several acres of our Luna soil and put in a crop of, let us say, alfalfa. When it has grown, suppose we plowed back the alfalfa. And the next crop, and the next, perhaps each year spreading this new soil, part Earth, part Luna, over a wider area." He stroked his chin and laughed in deprecation. "Perhaps, to use the Americanism, we would find we had it made. At least, I would like to try it—and various other things that have come to mind. If the LFC people had really cared, this would have been done long ago. Island One has been milked, not nurtured."

"I'll be damned," Pete Kapitz said.

"Ummm," Adam Bloch agreed.

Annette Casey, uncharacteristically quiet for so long, looked at the Russian and said, "It has been brought to our attention that your defection from the Soviet Complex was a sham. That you were sent here by the Cheka."

The Academician chuckled with heavy humor. "But my orders were unique, Doctor Casey. The politicians in the Kremlin were of similar opinion to that of the Arab Union; they did not think that the L5 Project could succeed and wished to prolong its agony while their own Asteroid Belt Project was developed. They sent me to assist in keeping it barely alive. My sole contact with them was broken by Mr. Moore's security people and now there is no possible way for the Cheka to reach me to retract my orders."

Adam Bloch said, "You mean you really want to help?"

"Of course. I shall continue my work here—if other

371

developments permit. It may take many years. But I suspect that my Soviet Complex colleagues will need similar years to begin exploitation of the asteroid belt. Perhaps when we have both succeeded, it will become obvious to all concerned that the only thing that makes sense is for the two projects to be amalgamated and for space colonization to become a world endeavor."

Sol Ryan said, his voice a low whisper, "I suppose that there could not possibly be a place for me in. . . ."

Bruce looked over at him in compassion. "I'm afraid not, Doctor. Nor anyone else connected with New Kingston and the families. The best you can do to serve is continue what you began with your broadcast. Throw your full weight and what remains of your prestige into exposing the Syndicate's position in the Lagrange Five Corporation. The stink is going to be high, and we can only guess at the final working out of the whole mess, but you should be able to help."

Annette looked at him, eyebrows up quizzically. "And me?" she said.

Bruce frowned. "Possibly a place for you could be found . . . in the background. After all these years on the scene, your know-how about the Project must be as great as anybody's."

Her mouth was slightly lopsided. "And where do you work in, comrade? You seem to have taken quite an interest."

Bruce Carter eyed the drink in his hand with dry amusement. "Now that Ron Rich has lost all credibility, I suspect that Island One could use an honest flack—if those two words aren't mutually exclusive. I'd like to give it a try. Besides," he added, with a sidelong glance, "I have a breakfast date to keep. Maybe a series of them."

"Here's to honest reporting," said Pete Kapitz, with hidden meaning for Bruce, and sipped his guzzle. "Too bad *I* haven't got a job here that's made to order."

"Of course you have," said Suvorov.

"Nope; Island One has had enough security crap here to last for the life of the project."

"Security *crap*? Quite right," said the Russian. "But I am not entirely, ah, unversed in these matters. Among the workers and even among ourselves, there will always be temptations to bring to Island One things that it should not have."

Annette gave a vigorous nod. "Amen! Hard drugs, for example. Or saboteurs."

Pete tossed her a glance that was almost hopeful. "Saboteurs?"

Adam Bloch clinched the argument with, "You think the Arab Union would let us get on with a *real* SPS and not fight it?"

"My God," said the agent, his fertile mind leaping ahead. "I think I've just, um, succumbed to my injuries. "And you need more than a few guys doing the overt security checks. You—that is, *we*, will need at least one Mister Inside."

"A new Americanism?" This from Suvorov.

"An old truth," said Pete. "Someone in supply, for example, who knows every possible way for a scam to be run on any operation. Someone on the covert side. Who can get on the inside of almost any illegal operation—because he has a first-rate criminal mind. But he's *our* criminal, luckily." Now Pete was grinning openly.

From Annette, Bloch, and Bruce came the chorus: "Venner!"

"Mister Inside," said Suvorov musingly, rolling the phrase on his tongue. "A useful phrase. I also think it should work. What say you, Koplin?"

The Polish scientist nodded vigorously. "I say we must raise a toast to Misters Outside and Inside," he said, moving toward the ranks of expensive hooch, "and to the sad departure of Kapitz and Venner."

Most of the others chuckled, but Freddy Davis held up one restraining hand. He belched, having had three drinks already. "Can't do that," he warned, slurring it slightly.

Annette paused with her drink aloft. "Why not?"

" 'Cause I can get at least four toasts outta that," he explained, beaming. "And I intend to use 'em all, if somebody'll just pass me that bottle of Centenario tequila!"

The Newest Adventure of
the Galaxy's Only
Two-Fisted Diplomat!

THE
RETURN
OF
RETIEF

KEITH
LAUMER

When the belligerent Ree decided
they needed human space for their
ever-increasing population, only
Retief could cope.

$2.95

**BAEN
BOOKS**

See next page for order information.